A Vengeful Realm

Book One: The Scales of Balance

Tim Facciola

Cover Design by Lunaris Falcon Studios

Publishing Services provided by Paper Raven Books LLC

Printed in the United States of America

First Printing, 2023

Paperback ISBN: 979-8-9862855-2-8

Hardback ISBN: 979-8-9862855-3-5

"How many times do I have to tell you?" a father asked his son.
The boy shrugged. "Twice?"

This is for the stubborn dreamers,
the inquisitive souls,
everyone who dared ask for a second chance,
and those patient enough to grant it.

Thanks, Dad.

SILVER SUMMITS
STONESIDE
THE ISTHMUS
SENTIGARD
MARSTEAD
SALMANTICA
SOUTHGROVE
STORMBU
GEYSER
BRUSOS
AR
HYLAN MOUNTAINS
STOCKHEL
SINION
CASSIUS
NEW RHEYNIA
THARSEO'S BASTION

VALTARCIA
THE VALE
NORTHRIDGE
HARBOR
BAY OF
BASTARDS
VALENFORTH
THE SUN SEA
KLAYTOS

Prologue

He shook his head, steadying his swimming vision. Swirls of gold fended off an unrelenting blood-red sea until the shape of a balanced scale emerged, woven stark and clear against the crimson backdrop of the tapestry on the wall.

Foreign yet familiar, the scale insignia remained a mystery to him. If he had seen it before or knew its meaning, nothing came to him. Not just the forgetful nothingness of being unable to remember a symbol, but the oppressive void of a blank mind.

Sitting upon a wooden bench, he turned from the puzzling tapestry. A bandage encased his left palm but failed to stifle the flow of blood dripping onto the ground and pooling between his feet. His head throbbed with each plop from the saturated swathe as he tried recalling how he sustained the wound in the first place.

Surrounded by a dozen others in a stone, rectangular room—the air stained by the coppery scent of blood—he reached for the hilt of his short sword. But the others in the room bore similar dressings. The passive and amiable conversations did not resemble the sound of those trapped or abducted. No one was bound, yet he still felt imprisoned.

"You don't look well." A woman beside him rested her javelin against the wall to place her bandaged hand on his right arm. Her brow pinched atop sapphire eyes, a tight braid of silver-blonde hair draped over her cloaked shoulder.

A rush of blurry recollections flooded his mind, as if he should remember her, but like sand between the cracks of his fingers, the moments fled before memories could be grasped.

"Zephyrus?" she asked, readjusting a dagger on her hip to slide closer to him.

Zephyrus? Is that my name? It's bad enough not knowing where I am, how I got here, or why my hand is bleeding, but not even my own name? He considered it, mouthing the word. *Zephyrus…* it felt familiar, but not quite right.

"Burn me, Zeph," said the man sitting beside him. "Ya look worse than I feel." His teasing tone contradicted what Zephyrus might have expected of someone with two curved sicas holstered across his back. His creased forehead, the crow's feet at the corners of his eyes, and the letter "A" branded into his forearm foretold a difficult life.

Examining the stranger's face, Zephyrus hoped for some glimmer of recognition, and although he felt like they had a rich past together, he could recall none of it.

Zephyrus shook free from the woman's touch, looking between her and the man on his other side. "I don't remember. Anything."

Saying it aloud made the truth hurt more. He grimaced as his two companions exchanged glances of pursed lips and raised brows.

"You don't remember us?" the woman asked.

"You remember me, though, right?" The man's jovial eyes darkened as wrinkles furrowed his scarred mug.

Something in his face made Zephyrus want to tell him the right answers… to make him proud. He wanted to say, *"Yes, of course,"* but it wasn't true. Whoever this man was to him in the past, each memory and every moment was scrubbed from his mind and scoured until not a trace remained.

"No."

The man rubbed his face with his hand.

"Gory ghosts, Patrus, I knew we shouldn't have come here," the woman said.

"Probably just a bad reaction to the ritual," Patrus said. "Just the tea they made us drink. We'll be fine. Everything'll be fine." He put his unscathed hand on Zephyrus's shoulder and glanced around. "It's gonna be alright, kid. We're at Tharseo's Bastion. You, me, and Threyna." He pointed at the woman with the silver-blonde braid. "We came… tip the scales…"

He blew out his cheeks and scratched at the scruff of his neck. "Come to think of it, I don't remember anything since leaving the Templar. But we're supposed to be here. Part of the Nine Acts or something." He raised his own bandaged hand and gestured to it. "We'll get our prophecies, see for sure if you're the Wielder, and be on our way."

Tharseo's Bastion? Nine Acts? Wielder? Questions with answers he should have known landed like gut punches. A growing dread climbed from the pit of his stomach, tightening in his throat. Not nausea, not fear, but something far more sinister.

"No." Zephyrus rose to his feet, drawing the attention of others in the room. "There's something else. Something important." It was there, on the tip of his mind. He reached for it.

Threyna pulled him back to his seat. "Easy now."

Patrus raised his hand to calm the onlookers disturbed by Zephyrus's behavior.

Whatever Zephyrus was reaching for in his mind fell away, dropped into the void. Lost to the abyss that his mind had become.

Threyna sighed, her gentle touch suddenly firm. "You are where you need to be, exactly when you must. We'll figure this out. Together."

Zephyrus's nostrils flared, but he eased onto the bench.

"Check your pockets," Threyna said. "Maybe we have a written order from the Templar somewhere." She inspected her cloak and britches for any sign of their purpose.

"I got nothing," Patrus said.

"Me neither," Threyna said. "Zephyrus?"

Shaking himself from his maddening thoughts, he dug into his pocket with his unbandaged hand. His fingers closed around a slender cylinder.

Hope filled his lungs. Yanking it from his pocket, he found a tightly rolled scroll. Unrolling it, he quietly read aloud.

King Varros Helixus,

The time has come for peace to reign. Your policies have pleased us and given us hope under the Six of New Rheynia. No longer shall we pursue vengeance or the Judges' Treasures. Take this emissary of peace into your service as our sincerest gift.

AVR

Zephyrus shook his head. Not one bit of this meant anything to him. Not the names, places, or initials at the bottom. Nothing.

Who is AVR? Who are the Judges, and what are these Treasures?

"Burn me!" Patrus bolted upright. The others in the antechamber startled at the sudden outburst. Patrus winced and sat back down, allowing them to return to their conversations. He leaned closer to Zephyrus and Threyna to whisper, "This can't be right."

Patrus's reaction only made the sinking stone in Zephyrus's stomach grow heavier.

Threyna shook her head at Patrus. "The Templar wanted us to make peace with King Varros, to warn him about the—"

"Peace?" Patrus hissed. He stood up, jabbing his finger in Threyna's nose. "Don't you dare, Warlock. This is your doing, isn't it?"

Threyna bolted upright with equal fervor and slapped Patrus's hand from her face. "You think I'm responsible for why we can't remember? And blood and bone, I was hardly with the Warlocks."

Zephyrus's confusion and frustration swirled into a tempest. Before he knew it, he was on his feet, separating Threyna and Patrus. He didn't know who had the right of the matter, but the public argument they were about to have wouldn't solve anything.

"Keep calm," Zephyrus said. "We can figure this out together."

Patrus reclaimed his seat first, elbows resting on his knees, fingers interlocked behind his head. Eventually, the ice in Threyna's eyes settled, and she sat, arms crossed.

Zephyrus took a deep breath, sitting between them. "What do we know?"

"I know the Elders wouldn't have sent us to give up," Patrus said. "Not while our people are enslaved to build castles for King Varros Helixus, construct shrines to his Valencian Gods, and die in the fighting arenas. I'm tellin' ya, this is a test. Or a trick. Or—"

Threyna inhaled through her teeth. "A trick? Do you hear yourself, Patrus? There is a threat greater than Drakes and Helixuses. If the Elders want peace, even a temporary one, we must obey."

"No," Patrus said. "You been with us all of a fortnight. Don't claim to know what the Elders want. Zeph and I been with the Templar over ten years. This don't make any sense."

None of it made sense to Zephyrus. Ten years he'd known Patrus, yet he couldn't remember anything before the balanced scale tapestry. He scratched his head, pulling strands of auburn from the knot on the back of his head.

The heavy wooden door at the opposite end of the room swung open.

Clad in a gray cloak, a portly gatekeeper with a hooked nose stood in the doorway. "The Seers will see you now. Line up according to your number and follow me."

Excited chatter broke out amongst the other dozen people. They each held up their bandages, comparing the red numbers on the back of their hands. Zephyrus flipped his hand over, and on the back of his wrist, disguised in the scarlet blood, was the number thirteen. Patrus's and Threyna's bandages were scrawled with eleven and twelve respectively. When they got into line, Zephyrus followed, but tightness gripped his chest.

Threyna seized his trembling hand and squeezed. "We're right where we're supposed to be," she said through a tight-lipped smile. "We'll figure this out."

He released a trepidatious breath. He was happy to be in the company of others who cared about him—even if he couldn't remember why they did—but he couldn't shake the unease that burrowed into his gut. Like leeches on his soul, the absence of his memory sucked the comfort from Threyna's words. He could feel it in his bones; something was wrong.

The procession trailed from the antechamber and down the hall. The sullen temple corridors smelled of mildew. Dilapidated not only by time and neglect, Tharseo's Bastion bore battle scars. Deep slashes traversed the walls where deflected swords and missed strikes left a token of their presence. Scorch stains sullied the exposed wooden beams overhead. Fine moldings and elegant stonework told of the temple's former majesty, but now they remained a testament of man's destructive nature.

Patrus stepped out of line, allowing Threyna to pass. The two exchanged a disdainful glance but said nothing. He put his hand on Zephyrus's chest, stopping him from following Threyna. As the space grew between them and the rest of the procession, Patrus whispered.

"Have faith. The Judges will guide us. I don't know if this is one of the Acts, but we'll get to the bottom of this, Zeph. But whatever happens, we are *not* following that letter." He nodded at Threyna ahead of them. "Regardless of what that Warlock says."

He patted Zephyrus on the arm. "I know you're the Wielder. And once the Seers of Celestia prove it, we'll get the Treasures together and see our people to freedom." Patrus smiled. "I believe in you, Zeph. You were meant to turn the tides of this war. Not serve the other side." He scoffed, grinning. "If you're an emissary of peace, I must be Tharseo himself."

Zephyrus returned Patrus's grin, but the sentiment Patrus expressed in words stopped at Zephyrus's mind, never reaching his heart. Patrus knew who he was, where he'd been—he had people he loved and principles he believed in. Zephyrus didn't know his own name. The Acts, the Wielder, the Treasures—they meant nothing to him. All he wanted from the Judges were his memories back.

As the two quickened their stride to rejoin the line, the gatekeeper shepherded the others through an archway and into a long, narrow room with a vaulted ceiling. Patrus caught up and took his place in front of Threyna before entering.

Zephyrus followed behind, ushered in by acolytes in white robes with three black, vertical lines upon their chests. The stone hallway was traded for wooden floorboards, warped by time and rotted by infestation. A threadbare runner stretched across the floor before equally worn and mismatched tables with unbalanced scales atop them. Despite the different tables and scales, the balances all tilted at an identical angle, one side weighed down by an offering of blood.

They filed in, stopping before the table marked with the corresponding number on their bandages.

Patrus rubbed his hands together. "Time to embrace fate."

Zephyrus thumbed the scroll in his pocket. The sinkhole in his stomach threatened to cave in. *"You are where you need to be, exactly when you must,"* Threyna had said, but if Zephyrus was meant to be here, he wasn't supposed to be doing *this.*

Two impossibly tall figures clad in black robes entered the narrow room. The Brothers, the Seers of Celestia, assessed the first scale.

Looking down the line of eager participants, Zephyrus's skin crawled. Clammy sweat clung to his brow. *I don't belong here… but if not here, where?*

A thin man standing behind the first scale presented his unbandaged palm to the Seers. They dragged a white blade across his flesh, but not a single drop of blood fell onto the scale. After uttering a few words for the acolytes in white to record on parchment, they moved on to the next hand, the next scale, the next fate.

Something didn't feel right about the ritual. *Why aren't they bleeding? The blood should have flowed to balance the scale.*

Zephyrus's stomach protested the closer the cloaked figures drew to him, but his feet might as well have melted into the floor.

Patrus was next. He thrust his hand at the dagger-wielding Seer. The blade bit into Patrus's palm without ceremony, but his passion yielded the same result as every other—a bloodless wound. With the acolytes gathered around, quills at the ready, one of the Seers spoke.

"There is but one way to defy death," the Seer said. "Live."

Zephyrus had to bite back a scoff that tore from his lips. *That's their sage wisdom—live?*

While Patrus bowed, thanking the Seers, Threyna hummed with a self-satisfied grin.

"I reckon that wasn't the prophecy of the Wielder?"

Patrus grunted, glaring at her. He whispered something under his breath as the Seers moved on to Threyna.

Despite her mocking, the moment the Seers' shadows loomed over her, her demeanor changed. Her fingers rubbed together at her side. She averted her gaze from the Seers as if they were distracting her from something else more important in the present moment.

"Your hand." The Seer held out his long, dark, spindly fingers. Threyna took a deep breath, reaching for the Seers with the hesitance of touching a hot kettle.

Zephyrus's stomach twisted in knots as the Seer sliced the dagger across Threyna's palm.

She flinched as the flesh split before the blade, but no blood flowed. Instead, black vines spread from her wound, slithering outward. But when Zephyrus blinked, they vanished. Zephyrus pinched the bridge of his nose with his thumb and forefinger before tracing the scruff of beard down his cheeks and chin. No black vines, just a bloodless wound.

Did I imagine it?

Neither Patrus, the Brothers, nor the gathered acolytes seemed to take notice of the slithering black tendrils that momentarily erupted from Threyna's wound, but she continued to stare at the gash in her palm.

The Seer with the dagger said, "You shall find that which you seek, but you possess all you need."

Patrus hmphed. "Suppose you're not the Wielder either, Warlock."

Threyna lifted her gaze from her bloodless palm to the Seers of Celestia, but they had already moved on, leaving an acolyte to tend to her fresh wound.

As the Seers stood opposite Zephyrus, with only an unbalanced scale between them, Zephyrus felt a chill run down his spine. Dressed in black, they loomed like shadows stretched long by the setting sun. Even their faces were concealed in the depth of their cloaks.

Beneath the hoods veiling the Seers' faces, their voices came in perfect synchronicity—low in both tone and volume, but abundantly clear. "Step forward."

Patrus, holding his freshly bandaged hand, nodded in encouragement, but the strangling sensation from deep within Zephyrus's soul wanted none of it.

"You are where you need to be, exactly when you must."

Zephyrus inched closer to the two Seers, hoping Threyna's words held truth. Thumbing the scroll in his pocket, his trust teetered.

"Your hand," one Seer said, gesturing toward the scale. The other held a tremendous tome bound in dusty leather. Zephyrus reluctantly released the scroll in his pocket and extended his right palm. The Seer took him by the wrist. His touch, as cold as death itself, sent gooseflesh rippling up Zephyrus's arm.

"Your other one," the second Brother said, taking Zephyrus's bandaged left hand in an equally chilling grip.

Zephyrus's eyes locked onto the curved blade grasped in the Seer's hand. Sharpened to a gleaming white, the dagger drank the room's darkness and reflected the dancing torchlight. He closed his eyes and inhaled sharply. To whatever god would listen, he prayed. *Please give me answers... a sign, a clue, a memory—anything!*

Steel bit into his right palm. Searing pain coursed, not just through his hand, but his entire body. His knees buckled, and his jaw clamped tight. He wanted to scream, but as sudden as lightning, the pain vanished.

Blood flowed into the scale.

Excited murmurs filled the room as the weight of Zephyrus's blood leveled the scale.

"What does that mean?" Zephyrus looked from the Brothers to Patrus. Patrus's eyes were wide enough to stretch the wrinkles of his crow's feet.

The Seers' black eyes flashed bright white, and their hands flared with the warmth of life. Thunderous voices erupted from beneath their cloaks, reverberating off the stone walls.

"The son of the Fallen will rise to prey upon the unworthy. Under cloaks and shadows he hides to bring light to those hoping. When the rivers and streams run dry, he will summon the unworldly to sever the chains that bind the realm to the holy."

Zephyrus balked. He didn't know what he was expecting after the cryptic responses Patrus and Threyna received, but he wasn't expecting this. He only had more questions. And another bloody hand.

The acolytes, wide-eyed and slack-jawed, frantically wrote each word as it was stated. Another acolyte wrapped Zephyrus's newly bloodied hand in a fresh bandage.

"Zeph!" Patrus's bandaged hands held his own temples. "I always knew it, but burn me!"

The other ritualists cheered. Acolytes opened the door beneath the red tapestry of the balanced scale and led Zephyrus into a sanctuary with three immaculate statues upon an altar.

"Behold, Judges!" one of the acolytes said to the statues, hoisting Zephyrus's bloody palm in the air. "Your chosen Prophet!"

Cast in bronze, the statue on the left depicted an old man with a long beard clad in an elegant cloak, a large book cradled to his chest. A woman in elaborate scale armor held a short sword in one hand and a scepter in the other. The Judge in the center—taller and broader than the other two—reached his sword for the sanctuary ceiling.

Smiling faces surrounded Zephyrus, but their excitement didn't stop the cold sweat from clinging his tunic to his back. His mind worked to grasp something forgotten, something important, but his memories failed him. The more he tried to remember, the faster the thought slipped through his fingers.

There's something here. Something I'm supposed to do...

"Tip the scales and burn me!" Patrus said, parting through the flock of people still chattering like squawking birds. "I knew it. From when you were a boy, I knew."

Zephyrus wrenched free of the acolyte's grip and seized Patrus, smearing blood down his arm. "Patrus, there's a reason we're here. Something else. Something important. Why else—besides the prophecy—would we come here—"

A shrill horn echoed through the chamber.

Silence fell. Again, the horn trumpeted.

"Slavers," one of the ritualists said, his face drawn.

Acolytes in white scrambled to the Seers in black, spiriting them toward the statues. The gatekeeper ran back the way they'd come from. But the rest were paralyzed.

An acolyte urged Zephyrus toward the statues, but when some of the ritualists went to follow, the acolyte stopped them. "There's no room for you to hide with us."

The ritualists protested, red-faced with fists shaking.

"Wait, what?" Zephyrus asked.

"There's not enough room for everyone," the acolyte said, taking Zephyrus by the wrist. "The Harbinger comes with us."

Patrus seized Zephyrus's other wrist. "He's not the Harbinger. You heard his prophecy. He's the Wielder."

The acolyte didn't back down. "Not one moment after his prophecy is spoken, the slavers come to Tharseo's Bastion. And you think he's the Wielder? No. He's the Harbinger. The *Age of the End* must come."

Murmurs carried the words *harbinger* and *wielder*, but they didn't mean anything to Zephyrus.

The gatekeeper returned, pushing open the sanctuary door. Panting, he lifted a finger. "One ship. At least thirty slavers." He weaseled through the crowd, heading toward the statues where the acolytes and the Brothers sought refuge.

"What about us?" a ritualist asked. "What are we supposed to do?"

"Run. Hide," the acolyte said. "But you can't come with us." He tugged on Zephyrus's wrist, dragging him toward the statues and away from Patrus.

Heat rose to Zephyrus's neck, blood coursing through his veins. Prophecies and memories aside, he knew in his bones he couldn't abandon these people. He couldn't leave Patrus and Threyna.

Zephyrus set his feet and wrenched free of the acolyte's grip. His lips curled into a snarl. "You want me to hide? Thirty slavers come to your door, and you forsake the people you prophesy over?"

The horns continued sounding, louder with a shorter time between each—more and more urgency behind every blare.

The acolyte exhaled, dark skin contrasted by his white cloak. "Your fate is sealed. The Judges' plans for you will come to pass. Exiled or enslaved, the Three Prophets will usher in the Return. So hide." His eyes fell to Zephyrus's sword. "Or fight. And may the Judges preserve the rest of us." The two swiveled and ran across the sanctuary, following the Seers of Celestia and the other acolytes behind the statues.

Patrus addressed the ritualists. "He is the Wielder. We can fight."

"Thirty men," Threyna said, drawing her javelin from the holster on her back. "We can take them."

All eyes fixed on Zephyrus. With the Seers and acolytes only focused on saving themselves, and no one searching for guidance from Patrus or Threyna, it fell upon Zephyrus to lead. Grinding his teeth, he glanced at the warrior statue with the sword, its stony gaze staring straight at him. If he wanted to escape this place, it would not be by running. It would not be by hiding while others were left to fend for themselves. The king's jester or the Judges' prophet, Zephyrus would not forsake others in need.

He seized the hilt of his short sword. Despite the sting of his slashed palms, its heft and grip felt familiar in his hand. It rang as he drew it from its sheath to the cheers of the ritualists.

They exited the sanctuary and returned to the main foyer. Beyond the weakened temple walls, men called out orders. Thunder struck against the barred wooden door, threatening to cave it in. Each blow from the battering ram rattled the iron chandeliers suspended from the ceiling, raining dust upon the ritualists. Some had weapons of their own—swords or daggers—but others had to settle for whatever they could find—candlesticks or broom handles.

Boom!

"We make our stand here," Zephyrus said, before the fracturing door. Beside him, Threyna dropped her stance low, gripping her javelin with both hands.

Patrus drew his twin sicas on Zephyrus's right. "They want to sell us."

Boom!

Patrus leaned closer. "They won't make much if we're dead, so they'll attempt to surround us—take us alive. But whatever happens, don't do *that* thing." He extended his fingers from the grip of his curved sica, wiggling them. "They'll take us alive if they don't know what you can do."

Zephyrus shook his head and wrinkled his nose. "What does tha—"

Patrus leaned close, finger raised. "Worst comes to worst, we surrender."

Boom!

The walls of Tharseo's Bastion quaked as the battering ram splintered the front doors. The reverberations rattled Zephyrus's teeth, but Patrus's words shook his resolve.

"We'll live," Patrus said. "Just like the Seers prophesied. We'll defy death. We'll get our memories back, find the Treasures, free our people—whatever the Acts require. The Judges have determined your path, as long as you live to walk upon it."

Boom! The bar holding the door snapped. Slavers clad in black, boiled leather charged in with sword and shield. They splayed out, forming a line.

A slaver with a scar across his upper lip stepped ahead of the rest, lowering his steel. Condescension dripped from his presence even before he opened his mouth. "Drop your weapons. Only tellin' ya once."

Ritualists loosened their grip on their weapons, glancing between one another. Moxie wavered with each passing moment; hope quivered in time with fluttering knees.

No future—no life—awaited beyond those doors if they surrendered. Only chains. Death.

"What's it going to be?" the slaver asked. "Haven't got all d—"

A javelin flew through the air and speared the slaver through the chest.

Sound ceased. Vision tunneled. Time slowed, and all choices evaporated. Zephyrus charged as the slaver fell to Threyna's javelin. Two shields stepped forward, covering their fallen leader with swords raised in defense.

Zephyrus jumped, thrusting his steel into the first shield. Despite the pain in his palms, he shoved the shield backwards. Patrus swept in beside him, his sica hooking around the top of the other shield. With a yank, he lowered the shield. Zephyrus stabbed at the opening. Steel met flesh, piercing the slaver's neck.

He dropped, sputtering blood.

As the slaver fell, clasping his hand over the gash in his neck, a numbness washed over Zephyrus. A cold, cruel emptiness invaded the space where the loss of innocence should have been, had he not killed before.

No time for sentiment, Zephyrus blocked an incoming slash and ducked another. Threyna rushed in beside him, punching his attacker in the ribs with a silver dagger.

Another fell. Another died. But Zephyrus felt *alive.*

He slipped between two slavers, blocking one hack and redirecting another. He shoved into a shield, sending its carrier stumbling. Patrus intercepted the stumbling slaver and drove his sica in the space between his neck and shoulder. Another stabbed at Zephyrus. He dodged and bashed against the shield. Once. Twice. His backslash carried the shield's momentum out of the way, exposing his belly. Zephyrus rammed his sword, hilt deep, into the slaver's gut.

Patrus carved into a slaver with several short swipes of his sicas. Threyna moved through them like a wraith of death, untouchable to their steel.

From over the line of slavers, beyond the broken door, a projectile blacked out the sky. Opening mid-flight, a weighted net descended, ensnaring Threyna.

Zephyrus rushed to her aid, but the slavers cut him off. He stabbed and hacked at their shields, but more nets flew through the air, raining down on the ritualists. Threyna fought with her bindings, but the net contained her long enough for swords to swarm around her.

Half a dozen ritualists struggled to free themselves, but with Threyna unable to hold the left side of the room, the slavers flanked Zephyrus, Patrus, and the unbound ritualists.

"Drop your weapons and yield!" said the slaver standing over Threyna, his blade under her chin. Blond hair hung to his shoulders, framing his thin face and crooked nose. "Do it, or they die!"

Threyna growled at the slaver. She lifted one hand in surrender, but the other still clutched the silver dagger.

"You're bluffing," Zephyrus said, adjusting his stance so he stood back-to-back with Patrus. The stalking slavers stood over the ensnared ritualists. Those still on their feet watched Zephyrus, unsure if they should fight or lay down their arms. "A slave trader with no slaves makes for a poor man."

The slaver laughed. His sword pressed against Threyna's throat, drawing a trickle of blood. "The three of you are fighters. Lanistas will pay decent silver for gladiatorial recruits, but we'll get gold for the three of you. This lot won't fetch more than a couple coppers. Still think I'm bluffing?"

"Live, Zeph," Patrus said.

Zephyrus grit his teeth. *There has to be another way. A better way.*

But how many could he and Patrus slay before they were overtaken? Even if they somehow managed to fight their way free, how many others would die for them to live?

He couldn't do it.

Zephyrus growled but lowered his sword. "Don't hurt anyone. We surrender."

"What?" Threyna spat. "Zephyrus, no. We can't—"

"We must!" Zephyrus's voice reverberated off the foyer ceiling. He set his blade down. Steel clanged to the ground as Patrus and the others did the same.

"Kick it over here," the slaver said, beckoning toward Zephyrus's sword. The grotesque grin beneath the slaver's crooked nose fanned the flame of Zephyrus's fury.

He wanted to fight. He wanted to remember. But Patrus said it might come to this. He had to trust Patrus, or he'd be lost.

"Zephyrus, don't do this," Threyna said.

He couldn't look at her. *Do you know what will happen to you if I don't?* To spare their lives, he kicked the blade to the slaver's feet.

The slaver stepped on the sword's hilt to stop its skid. "Good, now—"

Threyna tore the net with her dagger, bursting free from its bindings.

She swiped at one slaver, deflected the strike of another, and stabbed a third in the neck. It all happened so fast. Before Zephyrus could react, the blond slaver slashed diagonally across Threyna's back.

A red tear streaked from her right shoulder down to her left hip. Her light gray cloak drank the blossoming blood, staining it scarlet. She dropped to her knees. Her dagger clanged against the stone floor.

"No!" Zephyrus strode towards her, but the slaver directed his sword to the apple of Zephyrus's throat.

"Two Rheynians at a Celestic temple." The slaver shook his head. "You're gonna get it worse than she does." He grabbed Threyna by the braid and slid his steel across her throat.

A scarlet crescent stretched. She clasped her neck, but blood spewed between her fingers from the fatal wound. Zephyrus dove and caught her in his arms before she hit the floor.

Anguish flooded her sapphire eyes. Her lips quivered as blood bubbled down her chin and choked the oxygen from her lungs. Life fled her, leaving a pale shell in its wake.

She coughed and choked until her final gasps. Despite Zephyrus's pleading, or the pressure he placed on her wound, death claimed her.

A knot formed in Zephyrus's chest, stealing breath from his lungs. He didn't know what he lost in her, but a gaping hole opened within his stomach, and the stone of dread that had been growing there plummeted.

Patrus knelt before the slavers, his face long with accepted defeat. Zephyrus fixated on Threyna's corpse. She stared to the heavens beyond, black lightning coursing through the whites of her eyes. He pulled her lids down, unable to look at her.

Dead…

Zephyrus lay Threyna down. His bandaged hands, soaked in her blood and his, trembled. The blond slaver loomed over Zephyrus, blotting out the sun through the entryway like a dark cloud. Blood dripped from his blade to plop to the ground. Threyna's blood.

Dead…

Kneeling on the ground beside Threyna, Zephyrus couldn't move. He couldn't breathe.

The slaver grabbed Zephyrus's collar and pulled him close until they were nose to nose. He pressed the bloody tip of his blade against Zephyrus's chest. He nodded in Threyna's direction. "You're a slave of New Rheynia, property of the Six of Valencia. You'll die in the arena to the roar of the crowd." He shoved Zephyrus away. "But we'll be rich!"

The other slavers cheered, but Zephyrus felt sick.

Blood for gold. What scale could ever balance the two? What Gods would condone this?

Zephyrus ground his teeth, but he could do nothing to stop the slavers from binding him and the others in manacles. Nothing as they were dragged out the doors. Nothing as Threyna's silver-blonde braid drowned in a sea of blood. Nothing but think about Threyna's comforting words from earlier.

"You are where you need to be, exactly when you must."

CHAPTER 1

THE SNAKE AND THE MONGOOSE

Danella

Stockhelm

Danella didn't want to kill her husband, but he wasn't leaving her any other choice. If she didn't act soon, everything would fall to pieces. But the thought of him dead and cold ruined her. Every time he spoke her name or touched her cheek, she imagined him splayed out before her, and her heart grieved.

Can I go on without him, the love of my life?

But the choice was his.

Danella's lectica traveled the dirt road through the villages of Stockhelm toward the town square and the epicenter of the festival. She tore back the red curtain of her canopied sedan. Ahead, beyond the porters carrying her lectica, vibrant pavilions, colored to suit the emblems of their benefactors, lined the pathways where merchants, for both the plebeians and the patricians, sold their wares. Filled to capacity, not an empty lot from the Crystal River to the pulvinus of the makeshift tourney grounds remained.

People bowed in deference or waved as her caravan passed. She needed to remember the serenity of moments like these. The dancers' beauty, the musicians' talent. The intelligence of the plays and puppet shows. The gladiators' determination and the knights' strength.

This is what it's all for—to preserve this.

The cheers surrounding Danella's lectica swelled as horse hooves pounded the pathway, approaching quickly. Danella glanced out the window just as her husband, Varros—King of New Rheynia—rode past on his white mare. He reined in the blustering beast, rearing it back and circling around to the awe of the surrounding plebeians.

He looked as any king should. His graying blond hair hung wavy below his ears. The crown atop his head appeared placed by the Gods themselves. His blue velvet doublet with golden finery was draped underneath a majestic cloak, divided down the middle—white on the left with a blue pegasus of House Helixus, blue on the right with a white Drake chimera.

How many husbands honor the sigil of their wives' house?

After Varros's marriage was annulled so he could marry Danella, seal the Treaty of 940 with matrimony, and end the war that divided New Rheynia, she feared he would never love her. She pleaded with her father not to give her to a man twice her age, with a ten-year-old son. But despite it all, she grew to love him, and she'd never forget the day she realized it.

Following her father's death, her brother's time as king was cut short by the traitorous Hechts. While Danella wept, Varros's first act as king was nailing every male Hecht to the Six Arrowed Star, proving he wasn't like his weak and blaspheming forefathers.

Now their own son, Damascus, represented the unity of New Rheynian society and the everlasting harmony between Salmantica and Valtarcia. Damascus was nearly twenty now, and for the past two decades, peace reigned. But a new war loomed, and if Varros was no longer the man she believed him to be, he needed to be replaced. Even if that meant deposing him herself.

The porters carried her lectica past the statues of the Six Gods of Valencia as they neared the town square. It was the only redeeming quality about Stockhelm, but that was why they were here—why they needed a chancellor, and why Danella was prepared to give the order to assassinate her husband, should he not do as asked.

Varros swung his mare around, trotting alongside the lectica, beaming ear to ear in the glow of plebeian approval.

Danella's stomach fluttered. *This is my chance. Make him see reason.* "Are you ready for your speech, my dear?"

Varros's curls bounced with the rise and fall of his mount. He grinned with one side of his lip and jabbed his thumb in the direction of the tourney grounds. "Do you feel their excitement? They will cheer for anything I say if it brings them closer to seeing Aelon Ironpine in the melee."

"So you'll address it—what we talked about last night?" *And every night since you exiled that mage a year ago.*

"When the time is right, my love." Varros took a deep breath as if he hadn't a care in the world. "I love the fresh air of Stockhelm. Don't you?"

Fear sat beside her, holding her in a cruel embrace. *What does that mean, you confounding Helixus! When will the time be right?*

Danella maintained her façade, aside from her twitching eye. She'd tried everything with this man—said everything a wife could say to her husband. Tear-streaked cheeks, red-faced anger, and composed dialogue were all dismissed, but today was his last chance. The Gods were clear, their will declared. The snake had won.

"It has the potential to be a beautiful day," Danella said, *but it could also be the worst day of my life.*

The sun glimmered off Varros's obsidian crown, his chin lifted to the clouds. "No castles, no slums, no filth staining the streets."

No comforts, no temples, and these 'streets' are trails of dirt.

"It's a refreshing change of scenery," Danella said, longing to be back home in Salmantica.

"It's a pity your father didn't settle here instead," Varros said.

Danella didn't want to imagine how different life would have been if, after her father led the Great Migration from Rheynia's disaster-ridden shores, he had built Castle Sentigard here in Stockhelm. Rheynian culture would have disappeared long ago.

The plebs enjoying the festival were proof that assimilation had already occurred. Rheynians garbed in flowing linens with leather sandals exposed their flesh to the Gods as if they didn't know what lay beneath.

Father would roll in the crypt if he witnessed this. But if Father were still here, this would not be the case.

What began with accepting innocuous cultural elements such as clothing, music, and customs inevitably ended with religion. And that was dangerous.

How quickly people forget why we fled Rheynia in the first place.

The Celestic prophecies meant nothing to Varros—like most Rheynians—but Danella did not dismiss blasphemy's validity. The unnatural Celestic magic was very much real, and she had no doubt if they allowed this *Return of the Judges* to happen, this kingdom would be doomed, just as Rheynia before. That's why the Facets of Perfection were provided by the Six, to guide humanity in the way everlasting. Not to be forgotten so they could fall into the Judges' hollow embrace and awaken the Six's wrath.

The Age of the End… it will not come to pass. Not while I am queen.

Varros droned on, but Danella couldn't allow him to ignore her. Not anymore.

"Varros," she said, cutting off his societal ruminations. He woke from his daydreams to meet her gaze. "The mage." The words were barely louder than her breath, but the way Varros swallowed, she knew he understood. "Timing aside, will you say something?"

He averted his gaze, just for a moment, but it was enough for the seeds of doubt to grow roots within her churning stomach.

"Aren't you the one always telling me to have faith?" Varros said. With a bow of his head and that stubborn Helixus smirk, he clicked his teeth, urging his mare to canter.

Danella slumped into her seat. *Have faith? After a year of asking—no, pleading—for you to admit exiling the mage was wrong only for you to deny me at every turn, faith is the only thing keeping me going.*

Not leaving anything up to chance, she closed her eyes and prayed once more. *Please, Gods of my father, show Varros the needs of the many. Let him see the error of his ways. The life of one mage is not worth starting another war. Please, Gods. I call upon you to provide him the intelligence to do what is right, the strength to do what is difficult, the determination to do what is best, and the faith to believe in the beauty and serenity of Valencia.*

Her litter stopped. It was time. Moisture dampened her palms. She nearly stepped on her dress as she exited her lectica but managed to maintain her façade. She smiled and waved to the cheering crowd as her personal guard approached her side.

"Your grace," Ser Daenus said, leading her to the pulvinus that overlooked the tourney grounds. Daenus's graying, stubbled cheeks betrayed how lethal he still was with a sword, but that wasn't why she chose him as her Queen's Guard. She selected him because of his faith.

Daenus leaned in. "Are you unwell?"

Knots tangled her stomach. *I may have the man I love assassinated; why wouldn't I be unwell?* She swallowed, composing herself. "If Varros does as I've implored, I'm calling it off."

"As you wish, your grace." His jaw tightened, but Danella knew what he was thinking—the snake won. The Gods had spoken.

Daenus escorted her to the base of the pulvinus where Varros waited. Varros took her hand, and together they ascended the stairs to the dais overlooking the tourney grounds where they sat upon their thrones. Atop the pulvinus, she couldn't tell if she heard cheering or protests coming from the crowd at her feet.

Varros lifted his hands to silence the crowd.

Please, you stupid, affable fool, do as I have asked.

"Good people of Stockhelm. Citizens, who have traveled from Salmantica and Valtarcia to aid us in this glorious celebration, I thank you. This day marks the beginning of a new Stockhelm."

Her hands trembled. *A new Stockhelm? What does he mean by that?* Her fidgeting fingers formed into fists. *Patience, he will get there.*

"Soon, we shall provide the Six with a display of our faith by offering blood and skill in the Valencian Arena." Varros swept his arm in the direction of the newly constructed gladiatorial arena to the roar of the plebs.

The festival drew people of every background New Rheynia had to offer. The earls, counts, and barons would be fools not to be present for anything the royal family attended, not to mention they all had vested interests with the tourney knights they sponsored or the merchant tents they owned. As much as this festival had to offer the patricians, it might have had even more for the plebeians. The plebs hadn't had this much excitement since the New Rheynian games ended four moons past. They would flock for any street brawl or display of barbarism.

Danella never favored the gladiators' brutality, but the common people craved it. The tournaments testing the knights' skills were much more impressive to her… but they would be called to arms if war erupted.

That won't happen. Varros will do what is right.

"Since the Treaty of 940…"

This is it! Say it, Varros: mages will not be exiled, but executed.

"…we have had twenty years of peace and prosperity. Salmantica and Valtarcia have come together, united under the Gods of Valencia."

Danella stiffened, chewing the inside of her cheek. *Six save me, that was a perfect opportunity. Varros, what are you waiting for?*

"Now it is time for a Stockhelm great house to better serve the people of this land and give the plebeians a voice in the senate."

Danella's feet tapped beneath the cover of her dress. *Don't change the subject. The Treaty, bring it back to the Treaty.*

"Today the two men—you, the people have chosen to contend for the right to be the Chancellor of Stockhelm—are here to present the titans their houses were founded upon." The king referenced each side of the square as the gladiators entered.

Beasts of men, layered in muscle and painted with scars, bore the colors of their owners. In black-and-white armaments, the gladiators of Baron Ebron Brusos entered from the east end of the tourney grounds. To the west, Earl Lentulis Cassius's men took position, clad in purple and gold.

"People of New Rheynia, join me in prayer as we praise the divine with a moment of silence." The king's words evoked a stillness that enraptured the entire world. Even the winds died, contributing in prayer.

Danella's hands quavered. *Please, for the love you bear me, please, Varros. Say it.*

The silence stretched on until once again Varros broke it. "Gratitude. Now onto the festivities. To peace and prosperity."

The crowd roared, drowning Danella's hopes.

Fear's cold, callused grip seized her heart. Then rage roiled in her stomach. *That's it? He didn't say anything about the mage, about the exile being a kindness that would not be offered again. He didn't say it!*

She feared this, but now it was reality.

Varros sat on the throne beside her, and her façade returned.

"Not the right time," Varros whispered, failing to meet her eyes.

It will never be the right time. Forgive me, my love, but you leave me no other choice. Danella brushed the crushed velvet of his sleeve, willing herself not to crack under the moment's pressure. "Wonderful speech, my love." She nearly choked on the words.

"Don't patronize me." Varros's voice was as unyielding as a storm, but he refused to look her way. "It will never be enough, you know. Nothing I say can stop what's been set in motion. Peace bought by blood seldom lasts, for vengeance knows no end."

Danella coughed. A thousand questions flooded her mind, but one rose to the surface. "You won't even try?"

His slate-blue eyes fell upon her like the nightly rains—restrained wrath behind a veil of secrets. She fell in love with those eyes, but now she couldn't bring herself to look at him.

What are you not telling me, my love? How many secrets do we hold between us?

He was so close she could reach out and touch him, but she'd never felt so far away.

"What do you think I've been doing?" Varros slumped to the other side of his throne, pulling his arm away from her touch.

Her hopes crumbled to ash. *So this is how it ends—how we end?* She swallowed the grief of what she was about to do. The time for idle chat was over. Action needed to be taken. She couldn't let him welcome the Return of the Judges.

Every person's life was about to be torn apart. Death and destruction were inevitable. She set her jaw, preparing for the pain she was about to unleash.

Yet it will be the death and destruction I cause, not the Gods' wrath. I will do what must be done to uphold the realm Father built. I'm sorry, but you've left me no choice.

Ser Daenus waited for her command, but once she gave it, the chain reaction that followed couldn't be undone.

She recalled the omenators' ritual. A snake and a mongoose fought to the death. The snake represented the Revivalists' mission to restore the ways of Valencianism—the mongoose, Varros's leniency. The Gods chose the winner, and the future of New Rheynia. She had hoped the mongoose would win, as it had time and time again, but even the Gods had lost faith in Varros. The mongoose succumbed to the snake's poison. The Revivalists would win, and Varros, her husband, the man she loved, would die.

Her face flushed warm, and pressure built behind her eyes. She squeezed the arm of her throne, grounding herself. She was stone. No. Stronger than stone. Steel.

Family, faith, future.

She met Ser Daenus's eyes and nodded. He returned the gesture and raised the standard of Varros's sigil—the blue pegasus and the white chimera—the signal to cue the assassin.

No turning back now.

CHAPTER 2

THE REVIVALISTS

Laeden
Stockhelm

Iylea warded Laeden away with a gentle touch on his chest, separating his lips from hers. "I must be going. The queen will have noticed my absence."

Laeden tugged her back into his arms. "The queen will forgive you." He kissed the crook of her neck, glancing out to the path from their sequestered position between two pavilions.

Iylea stifled a giggle and squirmed away. "Why don't you come with me? Shouldn't the prince be with his family, viewing the Festival of Stockhelm from the pulvinus?"

Laeden shrugged, avoiding her gaze. "Damascus *is* with his family. They would never admit it, but it's easier for them when I'm not seen."

Iylea's focus fell to her red-and-black maid's dress, and Laeden lifted her chin to look into her yellow-green eyes. He caressed her heart-shaped cheek with his knuckle, brushing a dirty-blonde strand behind her ear.

He'd turned down a dozen patricians' proposals to wed their second or third daughters. He wouldn't be locked into a loveless political marriage or strong-armed into caring for senate squabbles and court drama. Those women were all the same, but Iylea was different. He didn't care if she was a handmaiden—to him, she was the only one in the world.

"What will you do, then," Iylea asked, "if you won't join me on the pulvinus?"

"There is a friend I would have words with."

Iylea waited, as if expecting him to continue, but Laeden didn't want to divulge more. She wouldn't ignore him as everyone else had whenever he mentioned the Revivalists, but it would make her worry.

She placed her hand on his bearded cheek. "Be careful, would you? This business with the Revivalists…"

Six, save me. Nothing gets past her. Laeden stroked the curve of her jaw with his index finger and kissed her forehead. "I can hide nothing from you, can I?"

Iylea blushed. "No, I suppose not. But perhaps it's worth speaking with your father. One more time."

Laeden bristled. *A lot of good that's done so far.*

"Groups like the Revivalists rise and fall like the tide," his father had said. *"They get together, voice their frustrations, but then they go home. They go to work. Life goes on."*

That wasn't a good reason to disregard them. Unlike the Salmantic patricians, Laeden listened to the disgruntled and fear-mongering plebs. They spoke of a holy war, reclaiming New Rheynia from the "Celestic King" who spat on the Treaty. Laeden didn't agree with his father's decision to exile the mage, but did that make his father Celestic? No.

"It's idle talk, Laeden," his half-brother, Damascus, had said. *"Relax."*

Laeden wasn't convinced. Crown prince he might be, but Damascus's patrician-bred, castle-lifestyle didn't send him to the bowels of the city to hear the *idle talk* for himself. Laeden heard the whispers, and though the Revivalists had yet to act, that didn't mean they wouldn't.

Circumventing his family, Laeden sought Ser Daenus's aid, the queen's bodyguard and Captain of the King's Guard Knights. When asked, Ser Daenus said, *"Should we arrest them? Bring them up on treason charges?"* Then he broke out in laughter, calling Laeden paranoid.

Laeden ran his hands through his hair, pushing it behind his shoulder. "No one believes me, Iylea. Every time I voice my concerns, they treat me like a court jester."

Iylea traced a Six Arrowed Star on the breast of his blue-and-gray tunic. "I believe you, Laeden, more than you know. Be safe." Standing on her tiptoes, she pressed her lips against his. "May the Six watch over you."

They parted ways; Iylea returned to serve Laeden's stepmother, the queen, while Laeden pulled his tattered traveling cloak tight to conceal his fine clothes beneath. Where he was going, it wouldn't serve him to draw attention to himself.

These festivals were odd events—a combination of two worlds that didn't belong together. The plebeians and patricians, the tourney knights and gladiators, the Salmantics and Valtarcians—they mixed like water and oil… or like Laeden and the patricians.

The vast fairgrounds housed tents displaying merchants' wares—stages for dancers, jesters, and actors to perform—and the arena where the melee would happen that afternoon. An air of excitement swirled through the atmosphere, yet Laeden couldn't help but sense sinister intentions. Large gatherings, such as these, were opportunities to make statements.

What kind of statement might the Revivalists try to make today?

Laeden scanned the armorer's pavilion. His informant should have been waiting, but he was nowhere in sight. Laeden examined the sun's position and drummed his fingers on his arm.

He stopped himself from running his fingers through his hair like his mother used to do when he was a nervous boy. Securing the hood of his disheveled cloak, he strode over to the armorer's pavilion.

The black-and-gold lion insignia, signifying the patronage of Atonus Allos, the Royal Master at Arms, marked the pavilion as a patrician's armorer. No pleb could afford any of this, but that didn't stop Laeden from looking around while he waited. Fine swords and elegant armors were emblazoned with gemstones or engraved with sigils of New Rheynia's great houses.

"Have anything with the falcon of House Faire?" Laeden asked, keeping his hood low, and the falcon tattooed on his forearm well covered. Having something with his mother's sigil would grant him comfort, or at the very least distraction.

"Faire?" The merchant's bald scalp wrinkled. "On the wrong side of the festival, pleb."

Laeden ignored the barb and picked up a small throwing knife with the Six Arrowed Star of Valencianism embossed into its hilt.

Is there anything yet untouched by the Gods these days?

The hilt was heavy and solid, the blade four inches of obsidian death.

The merchant stalked over. "Put that down. You have no business touching anything you can't afford."

Laeden bit back a retort. Coin was the least of his worries—one of the few benefits that came with his father's marriage to Danella Drake—but now wasn't the time to brandish gold.

"Apologies." Laeden put the blade back where he found it and retreated from the merchant, only to bump into the person he was waiting for.

Aelon Ironpine. That wasn't the name he had growing up in Valtarcia's lower city, but no longer was he the bright-eyed, mud-wrestling champion of the Vale. He was Salmantica's most renowned tourney knight.

Aelon's blue eyes twinkled with mischief as he sauntered past Laeden with the type of arrogance only a lauded tourney knight could possess. Wearing a fine red-and-black doublet embroidered with the chimera of House Drake, he appeared as if he ruled New Rheynia.

Aelon picked up the throwing knife Laeden had set down and examined it.

"Ah, Ser Aelon," the merchant said. "It would be my honor if you were to wield any of my wares in the melee this afternoon. Is there anything you would like to see?"

"This blade," Aelon said. "I'll take it. Your finest sheath as well."

"Of course, Ser Aelon. Right away."

As the merchant hurried to find the appropriate sheath, Aelon scoffed at Laeden. "Imagine how quickly he'd move if he knew you were a Prince of New Rheynia?"

Laeden sank deeper into his hooded cloak. *So much for being inconspicuous.*

The merchant returned with the sheath, beaming. Aelon flipped the merchant a gold coin.

"Gratitude," the merchant said, but frowned once Aelon handed Laeden the throwing knife.

"Let's go," Laeden said, dragging Aelon from the pavilion. "We have matters to discuss."

Once they were far enough away from the pavilion, Laeden nudged Aelon in the ribs. "Was that necessary?"

"What good is celebrity if you can't use it to dissatisfy people?" Aelon asked, brushing back his honey-colored hair. "If you wanted the knife, you could have just announced yourself, and he would have given you half his wares for the honor of looking at it."

Laeden laughed it off, as he always did whenever his place in court was mentioned. He knew what they called him behind his back: a pseudo-prince. He wasn't accepted by the patricians because of who his mother was—wherever she was now—but Laeden was proud of his heritage and didn't envy his half-brother Damascus one bit.

"Perhaps, if I were Damascus," Laeden said. "Besides, I don't want anyone knowing about our conversation."

Aelon lowered his brow. "Is that why you're wearing such a soiled cloak? It's certainly off-putting enough."

The two walked through the excitement and glee of the fairgrounds. While it was good to see Aelon, the reason for their conversation was anything but joyous. Aelon joined the Revivalists when they first formed—the haphazard fool. Once he realized they weren't just some social group, he was in too deep, but that made him Laeden's ideal ally.

"Make way for Earl Lentulis Cassius!" a voice said from across the path. The people applauded as a dozen gladiators in purple-and-gold linens waved to the onlookers. The men were bestial giants, corded with muscle and covered in scars borne from hard training and the punishing lessons of the arena.

"Absolute carnage," Aelon said, as they stood off to the side to let the procession of gladiators pass. "The old way has got to die at some point."

"Tournaments have their place for the patricians, but the plebs will always idolize the gladiators," Laeden said. "Can you blame them? We once watched the games together as boys."

Gladiatorum was still a way of life for the plebs that kept the kingdom running. The plebs had free entertainment to divert their minds from the trivialities of their daily lives—a gift from the middle-class lanistas, who were honored to display barbaric shows to mingle with the patricians. In turn, the lords used the lanistas' patronage to gain political influence within the senate to make appeals to the king. It was a broken system, but it worked as it was intended to.

"I suppose," Aelon said. "Albeit a lifetime ago."

"A lifetime, indeed," Laeden said. "But without the ludi to keep the plebs happy, the great houses wouldn't receive the coin that goes to paying the pampered tourney knights to ride around on horses and poke one another with wood."

"Harsh." Aelon paused, then snorted. "But if it keeps me getting paid, I'll take it."

They secreted themselves between two canopied pavilions—out of sight and beyond earshot, if they remained discreet.

Laeden wiped sweaty palms on his britches. "What can you tell me of the Revivalists?"

Aelon took a deep breath. "Laeden, don't get involved. It's dangerous enou—"

Laeden gave him a leveling stare. "You said you'd help. Why else are we here?"

Aelon scuffed the ground with his finely cobbled boots. "Hoped you'd recall what friendship was."

Laeden exhaled. "Come on, Aelon. Tell me."

"Are you certain you want to do this?" Aelon asked, but Laeden's tapping foot was his only answer. "Fine then," Aelon said. "You were right. The Revivalists are planning an attack. Today—during the melee."

A rush of exhilaration filled him. *The naysayers were wrong.* "Chimera's breath, I knew it." His father didn't listen. None of the senators would hear him absent a marriage to their daughters. Damascus would hear none of it. Even the guards were ignorant. But Laeden was right.

"This is serious," Aelon said, putting his hand on Laeden's shoulder. He seldom inflected sternness in his tone, but there was no denying it.

"What can you tell me?" Laeden asked, settling his fraying nerves. "What kind of attack? A specific target, general chaos?"

"You don't understand." The apple in Aelon's throat bobbed as he swallowed, his eyes darting back and forth before whispering, "They're going to assassinate your father."

Laeden's jaw fell agape, and his stomach seized. *No...* He furrowed his brow. *They would be so bold as to attack the king in broad daylight? And you weren't going to tell me?* There would be time for that later, but not now. The Revivalists needed to be stopped.

Laeden stepped closer. "How?"

"I don't know."

Laeden growled. "Tell me what you *do* know."

The audacity... Kill the king? Laeden understood the Revivalists' frustrations after his father had disregarded the mandates of the Treaty of 940, *but to assassinate him?*

"There will be some sort of diversion, but the strike will come from one of the handmaidens."

The apprehension coiling within his gut struck like a serpent. As if venom flooded his bloodstream, Laeden remained transfixed—paralyzed. *Iylea...* Laeden fought through his shock and whipped around, making his way to the pulvinus with Aelon on his heels.

"Which handmaiden?" Laeden asked.

It couldn't be Iylea, but that didn't mean she wasn't in danger. As if that wasn't bad enough, his father was the target. He needed to stop the Revivalists.

"I don't know," Aelon said. "But slow down." He grabbed Laeden by the wrist and yanked him off the path. "You can't take on the Revivalists by yourself. This is madness, even for me. Six, when did I become the voice of reason? Just warn the guards to be on the lookout."

"Don't you think I've tried? They won't listen to me. Only I can stop this now."

"Why do you think I didn't want to tell you? You're going to get yourself killed, or worse—me!"

Laeden put his hands on his hips and pursed his lips. Aelon was right, but Laeden needed help. Allies, trustworthy ones, were difficult to find. The only ray of light was that the melee wouldn't begin until later in the day.

"What can I do to help?" Aelon asked.

Laeden appreciated Aelon's concern, but he'd already helped enough. Without this information, Laeden's father was as good as dead. "Last I checked, you're still Aelon Ironpine. You'll be in this melee, no?"

"Winning it, but yes, I—"

"Gratitude, but I need to find more inconspicuous aid." Laeden surveyed the fairgrounds, searching for any semblance of help. Priests enrobed in fanciful vestments knelt before the statues of the Six. *No chance.* Squires buffed their knights' armor to a radiant shine. *Too busy.*

"What will you do?" Aelon asked.

In the distance, on the outskirts of the festival, a row of wagons pulled to a halt. Not just any wagons—slavers' wagons. Laeden slid his coin purse from his belt. "I'm going to buy the most desperate man I can find and make good use of him."

CHAPTER 3

A Note, a Prophecy, and So Much Death

Zephyrus II

Stockhelm

Shackled. Prodded. Beaten. Zephyrus, Patrus, and the rest of those discovered at Tharseo's Bastion were transported—first by boat, then by wagon—to be delivered to the flesh dealers. They weren't the only ones. Zephyrus sat in a cramped wagon amidst a line of others, each filled to capacity, with the long faces of soon-to-be slaves as they bumped along the rocky road.

Patrus hummed a tune, deep and slow. His eyes closed, face a veil of utter calm.

Zephyrus tried to yank his manacled hands apart, but the chain would not give. He maintained a stoic expression, but on the inside, a tempest roared. Swirling questions encircled him. The Templar, the Warlocks, the letter to the king. And that was just the beginning. The prophecy—the Wielder, the Harbinger. But most oppressive was the emptiness beside him.

Threyna is dead.

"Patrus," Zephyrus said. "She's gone." He clenched his hands into fists, despite the pain inflicted by the Seers' blood sacrifice. His bandaged hands were stained crimson, both with his and Threyna's blood. "Why did she do that?"

Patrus returned from his reverie. "It's okay, Zeph. *We're* okay. We'll get out of this."

He wanted to believe him. But he didn't. He couldn't.

"That slaver," Zephyrus said. "The one who..." His voice faltered. No sound came forth. He swallowed the knot in his throat. "He said I was going to get it worse than her... *'Two Rheynians at a Celestic Temple.'* What's that mean?"

Patrus took a deep breath. "You were born Rheynian, but you're not a Valencian. You took to the Judges, and they have chosen you. But don't worry about that. You're not gonna end up like her. We're getting out of this."

"How?" Zephyrus asked, his voice a low growl amongst the whimpering captives.

"Your prophecy," Patrus said.

Heat rose to Zephyrus's ears. He wished he could remember something about the Judges, their treasures, the Return, or any of what was going on. "What does it mean? The Wielder? The Harbinger?"

"And the Herald," Patrus said. "Burn me, that tea messed you up, eh?" He huffed. "The Three Prophets of the Return. We of the Arcane Templar have protected the Treasures, makin' sure they don't fall into the wrong hands, waitin' for the one to be named the Wielder and gather the treasures of Stockhelm, free the people, and save us from the Rheynians. The Herald will commune with the Gods and weaken our enemies. And the Harbinger—the Judges' wrath incarnate will usher in The Age of the End."

Zephyrus's head fell into his hands. The chain of his manacles clinked together as the wagon bounced over the bumpy road. His mind wanted to piece the overload of information into digestible quantities, but it was too abstract, intangible. Familiar, but distant in the faraway reaches of his shattered mind.

"You said I was to turn the tides of this war," Zephyrus said. "Why? You said I could *'do'* things prior to the slavers bursting through the door. What did you mean?"

Patrus shook his head, short and fast. His eyes darted side to side before leaning close, his voice no louder than a breath. "Can't talk about that here."

Of course. Zephyrus pulled the letter from his pocket, his patience waning thin. "What about this? Can you talk about this?"

"I told ya to get rid of that," Patrus said, reaching to snatch it away.

Zephyrus pulled it back. It was the *one* piece of tangible evidence that suggested who Zephyrus was. He wasn't going to *get rid of it.* "This says the exact opposite of the prophecies. You called me the Wielder—to find the Treasures and free the people. But this says I'm an emissary of peace. That we won't seek the Treasures or vengeance, let alone bring about '*the Age of the End.*'"

The wrinkles framing Patrus's face hardened, and his dark eyes burned like coals, but he moved his hand with tender care, cupping the back of Zephyrus's neck. The heavy chain binding his hands hung between them. He pulled Zephyrus close until the crowns of their heads were resting against one another. "I'm sorry, kid. I'm sorry this is happenin' to ya, but I'm on your side. Ya gotta trust me."

The anger and frustration within him broke like a dam. Embraced in Patrus's protection, Zephyrus blew out a trembling breath. His face flushed warm; his eyes and nose began to water.

Patrus gave his neck a squeeze. "Fate ain't always fair. Burn it—rarely is it ever. I wish it weren't the case, but this is no time for peace. We're at war." He pressed his index finger into Zephyrus's chest. "You—a Rheynian boy, but a man of Celestia. You are our hope. When that scale filled..." He shook his head. "I knew they'd choose you. But seein' it with my own eyes, proudest moment of my life. We're in this together. You and me. And we're gonna get out of this, ya hear me?"

Patrus's speech layered more pressure upon Zephyrus's shoulders, but at the same time, it gave him the support to bear it. *I'm not alone.* Zephyrus nodded, their heads still joined together. Patrus gave Zephyrus a pat on the back of the neck and let go to meet his eyes.

"So what's the plan?" Zephyrus asked.

Patrus squinted his eyes and bit his lower lip. "I know I called ya the Wielder, but truth is... I don't know which of the Three you are.

Your prophecy shared words or even lines from each of the prophecies of the Three." He shrugged. "I'm no scholar, but I know what these people *believe* you could be. The Wielder is a symbol to rally behind, but you gotta lean into it. Help fate along. If you take that step, these folk will follow you anywhere."

Zephyrus blew his lips out and rested the back of his head against the jarring wall of the wagon. Patrus was right; it wasn't fair, but he didn't want to be enslaved or end up like Threyna.

"I'll be your Wielder," Zephyrus said. "Tell me what I need to do."

"That's the first step of faith," Patrus said, half a smile cracking across his face. "For now, just listen." He cleared his throat and began to sing in a deep voice. As he sang, his voice grew louder, and the groans of the other captives ceased. After a few lines, many joined in to add their voices to the choir.

Oh Judge, hear me. I am the seed, give me your love to grow like the trees.

Oh Judge, believe. I will redeem all of those who gave up on thee.

Back in the lands we once called home,
where balance ruled and mothers would sow.

We will return, we will return.

Oh Judge, see me, I am in need. Give me the strength to help the weak.

Oh Judge, believe. I will succeed, lifting up those on fallen knees.

Back in the lands we once called home,
where balance ruled and fathers came home.

We will return, we will return.

Oh Judge, tell me, where I find the Three,
to take back what's ours!

Oh Judge, believe, I will defeat those who sought to make us bleed.

We will return. The Judges return.

The melancholic rise and fall of the tune matched the lyrics in a wonderfully tragic story of faith, redemption, and inspiration. A swell of camaraderie overwhelmed him, joining him with those he suffered alongside. Whether he was the Wielder or not, he could help these people.

"Do you really think we can escape?" a man asked Patrus. He wasn't one of the ritualists from Tharseo's Bastion, but the same chains bound him.

"Of course we can," Patrus said. "All is possible with the Judges." He put a hand on Zephyrus's shoulder. "We have the Wielder."

"That didn't help us when the slavers came," said a woman from the Celestic temple.

"We were outnumbered then," Patrus said. "He surrendered to save our lives. Isn't that right, Wielder?"

Zephyrus's mouth dried up like a desert.

Give them something to believe in.

He didn't believe it himself, but if it meant freedom and answers, he would play the part Patrus presented him with.

Zephyrus forced himself to swallow. "There are more of us now, and many more in the wagons ahead and behind. We will escape." He looked at the letter *A* branded into Patrus's forearm. "You were once a slave, Patrus. How did you escape?"

"Burn me," Patrus said, massaging his temples.

"That's the mark of Invinius Auros." A man pointed at Patrus's brand. "He freed his slaves. You didn't escape."

The rest of the people in their wagon deflated. Hope was a fickle thing. Patrus nodded at Zephyrus and gestured to the rest of the wagon's occupants, as if willing him to do something—anything to regain the crowd.

To make them believe, I must first. Zephyrus hammered the wooden seat with his joined fists. "Patrus might not have escaped slavery, but he found freedom, and so will we."

His outburst jarred the captives from their self-pity. Sullen gazes rose to meet his eyes. *Now I've got their attention, but I must stoke this flame.*

"Freedom is only found by those who seek," Zephyrus said. "Will you seek?" The long faces on the group of bound men and women tightened into stern looks of determination. "Freedom only answers the door for those who knock. Will you knock?" Heads nodded, and mouths lifted words of praise to the Judges. "I will not go passively into slavery. I will fight. But what will you do? Will you wait for the chains of servitude to destroy you? Or will you join us? Who is with me?"

"To freedom!" Patrus said.

Trembling hands tightened to fists. Quivering lips became shouts of resolve. More and more, the cowed men and women rose from despair and set their purpose on the horizon.

"We fight," Patrus said. "But we're not an army. First chance you get, you run. Help each other, and by the grace of the Judges, we will make it out of this."

"For the Judges!" Zephyrus said, and the others joined in the call.

Patrus clapped Zephyrus on the shoulder. "If this ain't the Act of the Shepherd, I'm not sure what is." His crow's feet spread as his grin widened.

Zephyrus returned the sentiment, but the smile never reached his heart. Although Patrus was right that the people would draw strength from him leaning into his prophecy, that didn't ease his vacillations or assuage his doubts. Nor did it help him recall these Acts Patrus kept referring to.

One thing at a time. For now, we fight. And that I can do.

The wagon rolled to a halt. Beyond the wooden doors, a calamity of voices, the groaning and snorting of horses, and the clash of steel overwhelmed him. When the wagon doors swung open, Zephyrus stepped into a whole new world. The sun loomed overhead, illuminating a circus of pandemonium. Wagons filled with soon-to-be slaves unloaded before a stage where onlookers bid on people, shaking fists of coins at the auctioneer. Past the stage, pastel-colored pavilions housed exquisite linens, metal suits of arms, and weapons of every style. Dancers twirled ribbons through the alleys between pavilions, filing onto a stage of actors and singers.

Is this some kind of celebration?

Bile climbed to his throat. He expected this slave trade to be some seedy underground business, not an attraction at the local fairgrounds. He was certain, even before losing his memories, he never saw anything like this before—at least he hoped not.

Men and women, in whatever mismatched clothing they wore during their abduction, cowered on the stage before the bidding slave owners. One by one, they were escorted to their new masters like sheep toward a lifelong slaughter. The slaves outnumbered the slavers three to one in this area of the fair. If they all fought together their chances would be significantly greater, but too many faces were long with accepted defeat. One after the other, they were sold off for just a few coins. They needed something to believe in.

I'm not alone, Zephyrus reminded himself. He took solace in Patrus's composure. *We're gonna get out of this.*

"Next up, martial men!" the auctioneer said, gesturing to two broad-backed men. One with a square jaw and thick, angled brows, the other as slender as a sword with piercings through his ears. "Carsos and Ixion—sound additions to any ludus. These future gladiators might be the next champions of New Rheynia! See the bloodlust in their eyes? How many will fall beneath their blades? You could be the owner of one of these titans."

Gladiators. The slaver who robbed Threyna of life said this would be his fate. *A fate worse than hers.* He shook his head. *No. I will escape this fate or die trying.* Sweat beaded on his brow and down his back, but he was determined.

"We make for the pavilions," Patrus said. "Once you see an opening, you run, ya hear? You run, and you don't look back 'til you're clear."

Zephyrus bit his lip and nodded.

"Fifty silver for Ixion," a slaver said.

But as Zephyrus examined the crowd, the slaver who spoke was a native of Stockhelm.

"Fifty to the bodyslave of House Brusos," the auctioneer said. "Do I hear sixty?"

Zephyrus bristled. *Even the slaves are buying slaves?* Anger bubbled from his belly to his brow. *How is this possible?*

Another man bid, then another, each raising the cost of the fighting slaves until a hunched man with thin gray hair and a crooked smile stepped forward. "200 for both slaves."

Gasps filled the crowd at the amount he was willing to pay, but the casual callousness with which he spoke made Zephyrus grind his teeth. He so flippantly bought *people* like they were clay pots. Zephyrus would not be a clay pot or any tool that served these vile people.

"Sold to Liario of House Cassius!" the auctioneer declared. "The Head Lanista only grows stronger, leaving Brusos empty-handed… again!"

The crowd sniggered.

Patrus leaned in. "We're next."

The slavers pushed them onto the platform. Men pointed and jeered, bidding on them by shaking coin purses in their direction.

Threyna's blood on Zephyrus's hands made him wonder if she knew something he didn't.

She fought to the end to escape this.

"Next, we have several slaves who were found at the heretic island temple," the auctioneer said. He gestured at Zephyrus and Patrus. "Two of which slew nearly a dozen men between them. We will start the bidding at 200. Each."

Patrus and Zephyrus exchanged a glance. Anxiety bubbled in his stomach. Sweat clung to his tunic. He closed his eyes, only to see the slaver's blade carve across Threyna's throat. If he fought, he was far more likely to receive a spear in the guts than reach the pavilions. But if he stayed, he and Patrus would be enslaved—a fate worse than death.

No turning back.

Zephyrus began to sing. The other slaves from their wagon joined him. "Oh Judge, believe, I will defeat those who sought to make us bleed."

The jeering crowd fell silent. The auctioneer's eyes widened. "Guards, silence them!"

Zephyrus stepped to the edge of the dais. "I am the Wielder. Follow me to freedom!"

He leapt from the stage and charged at the nearest slaver. The others from his wagon followed, shouting in unified chaos as the slavers scrambled to stop them. Zephyrus surveyed the other wagons. Their success was contingent on more than just their number to join the fray.

A moment passed. Then another. With a roar, another wagon of manacled men and women began to rebel. One after the other, more lifted fists in defiance, and order devolved into mayhem.

Zephyrus's momentary relief ended as a slaver stepped in front of him. Instincts took over, and he bowled into the slaver, shoving him onto his back. Bidders stepped out of the way, afraid of what he was capable of.

Zephyrus rounded the stage and looked to the pavilions. *If we get to the fairgrounds, we can hide. Make our escape.* Zephyrus sprinted, his worn leather soles pounding the dirt path to his chance at freedom.

A slaver armed with a short sword jumped in front of him, cutting off his escape. "Halt!"

Zephyrus didn't stop. He charged at the slaver rearing back his sword. The slaver's steel swept horizontally, attempting to cleave him in two. Zephyrus slid underneath it on his knees, then popped to his feet.

He was the wind. The wind could not be cut. He clenched both fists. He was stone. Within his shackles, he swung both hands into the slaver's cheek like a hammer. The slaver fell to the ground, sputtering and unable to breathe. Zephyrus resumed his flight to the pavilions, but Patrus wasn't behind him.

Zephyrus skidded to a stop and wheeled around. Chained men and women ran amok. Slavers gave chase to corral them, but Patrus was nowhere to be seen. Zephyrus scanned the tumultuous scene until he found Patrus behind an unopened wagon.

Patrus pulled the lever and swung the doors wide, waving for the imprisoned to flee to safety. *That damned fool…*

Zephyrus turned to the pavilions in the distance leading to freedom and the uncertain future. He whipped back to find Patrus again. Not only did Patrus hold the key to unlocking Zephyrus's amnesia, he meant something to him. He didn't need his memories to know that Patrus was more than just his friend—a brother in arms, a mentor, a father-figure.

I can't leave Patrus.

Patrus unhitched a horse from its bridle and slapped its rump. The horse reared and charged into a group of armed reinforcements. The guards scattered, but their leader directed them right at Patrus.

Burn me!

Zephyrus charged back into the center of the slavers' auction as guards reformed around Patrus. At full speed, Zephyrus sidestepped another slave fleeing in the opposite direction, jumped over a downed guard, and closed in on Patrus. Patrus opened another locked wagon and ushered the prisoners into the madness.

Before Zephyrus could reach Patrus, a guard with an iron half-helm and black leather armor leveled a spear at Zephyrus's belly. "Don't move!"

"Patrus!" Zephyrus shouted.

"On your knees!"

Patrus spun to lock eyes with Zephyrus, but he was too far away. Upheaval, everywhere. Fighting, fleeing, chaos—chaos he caused. Zephyrus knelt down and put his hands up. His fear vanished. His resolve was all that remained, but the guard didn't know that.

The guard raised his spear point. "Hands on your hea—"

Zephyrus lurched to his feet and lunged at the approaching guard. The guard's eyes widened as he repositioned his spear to thrust. Too late. Zephyrus wrapped the spear shaft in his manacles. With a pivot, he wrenched the spear from the unsuspecting guard, casting it to the ground, but another advanced. Zephyrus raised his manacled chains to catch a vertical slash of the approaching guard's short sword. Out of the corner of his eye, a third stabbed at him with his sword. Zephyrus lurched out of the way, diving to the ground outside of their reach.

Where did they come from?

The newest swordsman leered at him. Blond hair framed his thin face and crooked nose. *The slaver who murdered Threyna.* "You just don't know when to quit."

Distracted by the slaver, he barely sidestepped a stabbing spear. Reeling, Zephyrus ducked and stepped over the advances of the two guards and the slaver. He kicked the slaver away and rolled inside the spearman's reach to work his way around the spearman's backside. Wrapping the chain of his manacles around the guard's throat, Zephyrus forced the guard to drop his spear. Zephyrus torqued at the last moment to use the guard as a human shield, blocking the slaver's incoming stab. The disarmed spearman screamed as the slaver's short sword pierced his belly. Zephyrus dropped the screaming spearman and picked up his fallen weapon.

With the advantage of reach, Zephyrus pressed the guard back, jabbing, slashing, and thrusting with fury. The spear felt like an extension of his arm, a part of him he couldn't imagine ever being without. The guard fell, leaving only Threyna's murderer to stand between Zephyrus and Patrus.

"You'll never win," the slaver said. "Even if you defeat me, you'll nev—"

Zephyrus hurled the spear at the slaver's leg. He attempted to swat it aside, but the spear pierced his thigh, protruding out the back of his leg. He howled in pain, but Zephyrus was already on him. He tore the sword that slew Threyna from the slaver's hands and spun, building momentum. The sword slashed across the slaver's neck. Through flesh and bone, the steel sang, sending the slaver's head rolling to the ground in a spray of gore.

"That was for Threyna."

Zephyrus dropped the sword and retrieved his spear, but Patrus had already moved on, deeper into the slavers' auction. He helped two young children out of yet another wagon. Zephyrus turned to the pavilions in the distance.

"First chance, run…" Why didn't Patrus take his own advice?

With freedom so close, it felt foolish to go back. But with Patrus nowhere near safety, Zephyrus couldn't leave.

Most of the freed people were running for the fairgrounds or the shoreline, but some had seized weapons. Their plan had worked, but none of it mattered if he and Patrus couldn't escape. Zephyrus ground his teeth and pushed onward, cutting down every slaver on his way to Patrus. Patrus helped a little girl over a wooden fence about twenty paces away. Already, a number of those still chained had made it beyond the fence to descend the dunes to the coast below.

He's going to get us killed…

A guard clad in purple and gold swung his short sword at Zephyrus's midsection. Zephyrus lifted his spear to block, but the shaft cracked in two under the stress of the blow. He kicked the guard away and countered with two jabs. The guard chopped down, blocking Zephyrus's thrust, but when his steel met the shaft, the spear shattered.

"Kneel!" the guard said, poised to strike. Just then, Patrus charged into the guard's back, catapulting him, face first, to the ground. The sword flew from the guard's grasp. Zephyrus seized the sword and buried it into the prone guard's back.

"You were supposed to make for the pavilions," Patrus said over the dying guard's wails. A wall of pikemen, clad in black scale armor, closed in, blocking off the road to the pavilions. "Too late now."

Those Patrus helped escape ran down the beach, and while some guards gave chase, others remained to make sure no one else had the opportunity to run. They were trapped.

"Fate has led us here," Patrus said, taking a deep breath. "Drop your sword, Zeph. We surrender."

"Surrender?" Zephyrus didn't let go of the sword. He scoured the landscape, searching for a way out, but there were none. Guards, some in black scale, others in purple and gold, closed in on all sides. Other slaves, who had yet to flee, were cowed, forced to their bellies, and hogtied. Nearly a dozen guards surrounded the two of them.

No. This can't be happening.

Patrus knelt down and put his hands up. "Put it down, Zeph. It's over."

"Drop the blade!" a guard in black scale said. "Down on your knees."

"Six hells, enough!"

The soft sound of steel biting into flesh was accompanied by a forced breath of air. Zephyrus whirled in horror to find a guard in a purple-and-gold surcoat standing over Patrus's kneeling form.

On his knees with his hands up, Patrus's eyes widened. His jaw fell open. Blood spilled down the front of his tunic. The guard's blade was buried to the hilt in Patrus's shoulder, its point protruding out of his belly.

"No!" A wave of incomprehensible emotions flooded Zephyrus. Memories rich with love, respect, and admiration entered into his mind, overwhelmed his heart, and dissolved in his hands like ash, leaving nothing to take hold of. Beyond the man himself, the vault of truth and memories that he represented swayed in the throes of death.

Patrus mouthed something to him, but Zephyrus couldn't make out the words. A whirlwind of fear, guilt, and fury replaced the emotions he couldn't process.

Rage exploded in his chest with each beat of his heart. The soldiers shouted, but he didn't care. He dodged a thrust, blocked a hack, and countered with a flurry of jabs and slashes, landing one in his nearest adversary's neck; he fell to Zephyrus's feet, screaming as he died.

The swordsman who butchered Patrus removed his blade, letting Patrus fall prone.

Zephyrus erupted in a blood-curdling cry and charged the swordsman, stabbing with reckless abandon. The swordsman deflected, but now, the surrounding soldiers were just toying with him. One spear sliced across Zephyrus's back. Pain raced through the flesh between his shoulder blades. Zephyrus roared, turning to meet them. He blocked another thrust, swiping the tip aside and down, plunging it into the earth. He jumped on the downed spear, fracturing the shaft. Spinning, he slashed at the other pikeman's face, catching him in the chin and sending him sprawling to the ground. But the swordsman struck.

Fire slashed diagonally along Zephyrus's chest as the blade blazed a red comet across his tunic. He blocked another thrust, another slash, and made space for himself. But more soldiers closed in, replacing the fallen.

Patrus lay prone on the ground. Zephyrus begged to see signs of life, but his motionless dead eyes stared through him. The blood in Zephyrus's veins became viscous.

He lost.

It was over. The swords closed in. Zephyrus dropped to his knees at Patrus's side. He reached for Patrus's still body. With Threyna's blood on Zephryus's hands, the puddle pooling beneath Patrus's body was even more painful. Zephyrus touched his fallen friend's shoulder, not knowing the full extent of what he lost.

The swordsman who murdered Patrus sauntered over to Zephyrus, his bloodied blade leading the way. He had a squashed nose and black hair peppered gray at his temples. A smug smile stretched across his face.

"Any last words?"

Zephyrus closed his eyes trying to see in his mind's eye what Patrus tried to say to him. With Patrus's last breath, he mouthed the word *"live."*

Zephyrus didn't want to. He'd rather die a free man with a quick death than suffer a lifetime in slavery.

"You can't die," a voice whispered. *"You will be my chosen Prophet, but first, you must be an Emissary of Peace."*

Zephyrus swallowed. Pain lanced through his stomach. No one around him spoke these words, but they echoed in his mind.

"Who are you?" Zephyrus channeled back.

"I am Vykannis the Brave," the voice said. *"The last Judge of Celestia."*

His stomach twisted at the words, nearly doubling him over.

"Pull the scroll from your pocket. Live. And together, we will remake the world."

Zephyrus didn't understand. He couldn't. But at the behest of one of the Judges, he reached into his pocket and pulled the scroll addressed to the King of New Rheynia.

"I am a gift to King Varros Helixus," Zephyrus said, holding up the scroll, his stomach still roiling. His fingers, sticky with his, Threyna's, and Patrus's blood, stained the parchment.

The guards didn't seem to care. Their blades closed in.

This was the end. He had failed. Fate had failed. Even Vykannis, a Judge of Celestia, was not enough to help Zephyrus fulfill Patrus's dying plea. He closed his eyes, ready to die, fate and purpose left unfulfilled.

"Stop!" A man stepped forward, clad in a travel-worn cloak with the hood covering his face. He pulled back the cloak to reveal an elegant blue-and-gray doublet.

"Prince Laeden?" The auctioneer pushed through the guards to follow.

The prince had shoulder-length brown hair and a close-shaven beard. He held his hands out to stay the steel directed at Zephyrus, but the guards and slavers kept their weapons level.

"What did you say?" Prince Laeden asked Zephyrus.

Zephyrus eyed the prince.

"Repeat after me," Vykannis said, *"I am a gift."*

"I'm a gift," Zephyrus said. The knots in his stomach constricted.

"For King Varros Helixus."

Repeating Vykannis's words, Zephyrus extended the scroll to Laeden. The prince plucked the bloody scroll from Zephyrus's fingers and read it, his eyes darting left and right over the bloodied parchment.

Laeden turned to the auctioneer. "Name your price, but he will not be harmed. He's leaving with me."

"Prince Laeden," the auctioneer said, "I know it's not customary for a distinguished patrician such as yourself to frequent the trade, but this is… unprecedented. This slave incited a riot. Men are dead and slaves escaped because of him. He should be stoned on the Six Arrowed Star for his crimes against the Six."

"Chimera's breath," Laeden said. "Precedence be damned. I said lower. Your. Weapons."

One by one, the surrounding swords thirsting for his blood slunk back to their scabbards.

"Another chance at life, Zephyrus," Vykannis said. Each word echoed in Zephyrus's mind, sending a sharp pang through his gut. *"Do you still deny your fate?"*

A note, a prophecy, and so much death, but still alive. He should have been grateful. But the Judges chose the wrong man. Patrus lay dead, Zephyrus kneeling in his blood.

"Live," Patrus had said, but Zephyrus wished he were dead too.

CHAPTER 4

HANDMAIDENS

Laeden II

Stockhelm

"You've certainly made a mess of things," Laeden said to the most expensive slave ever purchased in the history of New Rheynia. He handed him his travel-worn cloak. They stood between the temples on the far side of the fairgrounds, as far away from the commotion as possible. The only passersby were the Faceless—the black-clad, masked servants who dedicated their lives to the Six.

The slave didn't say a word. His fiery eyes were cloaked in smoke after the ordeal, smoldering as he eyed the statues of the Gods. Besides his eyes, his face was just as expressive as the Faceless's masks.

This was the largest mass escape of slaves since the Treaty. The auctioneer said nearly fifty escaped, half as many were retained, and the remainder were killed. Laeden had to pay for the whole lot of them to walk away with the man's life, but the Gods were at work. Laeden was never particularly devout in his faith in the Six, but he wasn't foolish enough to ignore when they made their presence known. Coin would come and go, but fate—that was something he couldn't afford to waste.

"What is your name?" Laeden asked.

The slave stared at his boots, covering himself in Laeden's tattered cloak. "Zephyrus."

Laeden held the bloody note up to him. "Who gave you this, Zephyrus?"

Zephyrus didn't meet his gaze. Didn't speak.

Laeden drummed his fingers against his thigh and pursed his lips. "My father's name is on this letter. The Gods sent me to the slavers' market, and there I find you—the ringleader of the largest slave outbreak in history, with a note declaring you an emissary of peace."

Nothing. The slave might as well have been listening to the wind.

Fate can be downright insufferable at times…

"I'll ask you again," Laeden said, his patience and his time waning. "Who gave you this? Who is AVR?"

Still nothing…

"If you'd rather, I can deliver you back to the slavers. I'm sure they'd be happy to hold an execution to—"

"I don't know," Zephyrus said, his voice as cold and flat as a block of ice cut from the Silver Summits. "I don't remember anything before waking up at Tharseo's Bastion."

"Chimera's breath…" Laeden considered this. The man could fight, that much was clear, but the letter spoke of the Judges' vengeance and the Treasures of Stockhelm. With fair skin and red hair, Zephyrus looked more Rheynian than the Six Arrowed Star.

"I will deliver you to my father," Laeden said, "but for now, you work for me."

"And why would I do that?" Zephyrus asked.

Laeden hmphed. "Because you need protection from the slavers. I separate you from the slavers' justice—and they will be seeking it, I promise you that. They won't challenge you if you are in service to me, *but,* in exchange, you will help me defend my father."

Zephyrus ran his bandaged palm over his red hair tied back in a shaggy knot. Caked with blood, he looked like he'd been through all Six Hells and back.

Zephyrus rubbed his scruffy beard with the back of his hand. "What's to stop me from running?"

Laeden snorted. He reached past Zephyrus, pointing with his index finger. "See those two, there, in the yellow cloaks? They're Jackals, a branch of the King's Vigiles who hunt down escaped slaves. You've given them quite a bit of work to do. They'll be howling for the rest of the week with all the bounties they'll collect. You can run, but escaped slaves tend not to remain as such for very long."

The two Jackals dragged the body of a dead man toward the slavers' market. Alive or dead, it made no matter—Laeden's point was made.

Zephyrus bit his lip, watching the dragged slave. "If I work for you and fail?"

"You won't," Laeden said, patting Zephyrus's shoulder. "For if you fail, and my father should fall, he won't need you as a gift. And I will have no more use for you."

⚖

"The strike will come from one of the handmaidens," Aelon had said. Laeden couldn't let that happen. He lost his mother as a boy. He wouldn't lose his father too.

Examining the pulvinus, everything appeared as it should. Iylea attempted to conceal her grin as she spotted him, pouring a goblet of wine for the king and queen. The King's Guard Knights stood close, everyone on edge since the slave outbreak. But other than that, no one—handmaidens included—gave reason to rouse suspicion.

Someone will look conspicuous. Someone must. But no one did. He tried to think which of the queen's attendants might have a motive, but nothing came to him. The least he could do was talk to his father again. He wished to ask of this AVR person, but that would have to wait until the Revivalists' plots were foiled. If fate brought Zephyrus to him, fate would keep his father alive.

Laeden waited to speak with his father while Pelitus, commander of the Jackals, clad in black-and-gold armor, addressed the king.

"Many got away, your grace, but we will scour the countryside and recapture every last one. Captain Heclan Allos has assured me that we will have the Vigiles and the Lions' support in making certain all slaves are brought to justice."

"Six save us," Queen Danella said, putting a hand to her chest. "That's what all that noise was—a rebellion?"

"Not a rebellion," King Varros said, "just a few people seeking freedom."

"That's how all rebellions start," Danella said, in a quieter tone, speaking more to herself.

"They rallied behind someone who claimed to be *the Wielder,*" Pelitus said, his beady eyes darting back and forth between the king and queen.

Danella leaned forward in her throne. "A Prophet of Celestia?"

"A man," Laeden said, stepping forward. "Just like any other." Almost imperceptibly, his stepmother's eyebrows narrowed. "Many escaped to the beaches, heading to the southern jungles. They will be caught, and the *rebellion* will be over; however, there is something I would like to discuss of a more urgent nature. Father, a word, before the festivities commence?"

King Varros nodded to Pelitus in dismissal, then raised his goblet to the parade of gladiators entering the temporary arena. "My son, the festivities have already begun."

"Just a moment of your time, your grace." Laeden never called his father by his title. He hoped it would be a subtle enough cue that this wasn't a laughing matter.

His father smiled and motioned Laeden to come closer.

"A private moment," Laeden said. He whispered so not even the queen beside him could hear, "It pertains to the Revivalists."

His father sat back and fixed Laeden with a reproachful glare. "I believe nothing more needs to be said on the matter."

Laeden pursed his lips and exhaled through his nostrils. *Of course. Why would you ever listen to me? If Damascus brought this to your attention, would you dismiss him too?*

Laeden stood up, straightening his doublet. King Varros was many things—charismatic, competent, honorable, and always fair—but he was also ignorant and mercilessly stubborn. This was not the time for those qualities to present themselves. Being dismissed was nothing new to Laeden, but that didn't mean he liked it. This would have to be done the hard way.

"Your grace," Laeden said with a bow.

What good is being a prince without the power to protect anyone? He scoffed at himself. *Pseudo-prince.*

As Laeden turned from his father, he saw Markus Cassius waving from the other end of the pulvinus. He gestured to an open seat beside him.

Seeing that his father wouldn't listen, Laeden hoped Markus might be more accommodating. Making his way past Damascus and his guests, Laeden approached Markus. He took his seat and turned to see Zephyrus, still at his post.

When Laeden had filled Zephyrus in on the Revivalists' plot, he realized Zephyrus was telling the truth about his lack of memory. From social hierarchy and etiquette to common history and current events, Zephyrus was either an utter fool, or exactly what he appeared to be. The auctioneer warned him that Zephyrus declared himself the Wielder, but Laeden didn't place stock in the Celestic prophecies. There were already six Valencian Gods to worry about; he wasn't going to concern himself with three more Judges.

Zephyrus only wanted his freedom. He was a soldier of some kind, so if Laeden gave him the proper combination of freedom and direction, Zephyrus would be as obedient as any within the king's barracks.

"Is everything all right?" Markus asked, noticing Laeden's distraction.

"Fine," Laeden said, forcing a smile.

Markus's sister Nallia leaned over from beside Damascus. "You missed Baron Brusos's gladiators, pitiful showing as it was. Where have you been?"

"The question of the decade," Damascus chided, sun glinting off his golden Drake eyes.

Just trying to stave off a slave rebellion and regicide. Laeden smiled but failed to offer an explanation. Within a moment, the interest shifted as the herald introduced each of the Cassius gladiators. Onlookers cheered with pride and waved the purple-and-gold banner with the scorpion of House Cassius as Stegavax, the Champion of the house, was announced.

"I expect this year will be his last as Champion," Nallia said. She pointed to another gladiator a few men down the line from Stegavax. "That's Fenyx."

Fenyx had the prototypical physique of a gladiator, but that's not what caught the eye. The entirety of his left side was burned and scarred like something out of a nightmare.

"Our doctore has been working with him since his procurement at the age of ten," Nallia continued. "After a decade of study, he will be the finest gladiator to step onto the sands."

"You certainly know your gladiators," Damascus said. "And your dueling, if the rumors are true."

Nallia's cheeks blushed against the amethyst jewels adorning her ears and neck.

Markus guffawed. "If you speak of Aemos Horne's attempt to court my sister, then yes, the rumors are true; he dueled her from sunrise to the nightly rains and still could not make her yield. Not once."

The pulvinus broke out in laughter, but a shrill cry erupted from somewhere in the crowd. Laeden stood, scanning for any sign of distress. His hands gripped the banister of the pulvinus. *The distraction!* He spun toward the king.

Nothing.

He wheeled to locate Zephyrus.

Nothing.

He looked back to the crowd to find a boy had picked up a girl and whirled her around.

Laeden settled back. He turned to check Zephyrus again, but he was no longer there.

Six curses. Laeden stood to get a better look, but a loud crash redirected his attention. His heart exploded in his chest. He whipped around, reaching for his sword.

A spilled goblet.

"A bit jumpy, are we?" Markus asked.

"Apologies, your grace," the handmaiden said, attempting to clean her mess.

Laeden took a deep breath. Looking back to the base of the pulvinus, Zephyrus returned to his post. Laeden exhaled, reclaiming his seat.

"Cantella," Danella said to the jittery handmaiden, "take a moment to settle yourself. All is well, dear. No sense fussing over spilled wine."

"Speak for yourself," Damascus said, evoking a laugh from his retinue.

Cantella removed herself, allowing other handmaidens to finish cleaning.

Laeden pulled Markus close. "The Revivalists. They're planning something."

Markus nodded. "They are a threat not to be ignored. Soon, after my father wins the omenation against Brusos and becomes chancellor, he will rally the plebs together. The Revivalists will dissolve before they do anything reckless."

"They plan to attack the king—today," Laeden said. "During the melee."

Markus's jaw hung slack. "Six save us." He ran his hand through his black hair, pushing it behind his ear, inspecting the sun's position. "That doesn't leave much time. What's the plan?"

"Do you have any men from the academy with you?" Laeden asked.

"I'm the *apprentice* Master at Arms," Markus said. "I don't have a retainer of Lions."

"Iylea?" Danella said. "Where has that girl gone?"

Laeden whipped around. *Where did she go?* She was here a moment ago. He was so consumed with the threat of the Revivalists he hadn't noticed her absence. *Is she in danger?*

He turned back to Markus. "Stay here and watch my father. Remain as close to him as you can without drawing notice. Keep an eye on the handmaidens." Without further explanation, Laeden descended the stairs of the pulvinus.

"Where are you going?" Markus asked.

"I'll be right back!"

Laeden's feet raced to keep pace with his hammering heart. He made his way to Zephyrus, hoping that if Iylea ran from the pulvinus, he would have spotted her. Praying she wasn't in danger, his mind churned in search of another explanation as to why she'd left the viewing dais. Before he could arrive at one, he was struck by the thought of having left his father. In the game of Reign, pawns were traded all over the board for the king's sake. Handmaidens didn't even warrant a tile, but Laeden couldn't just leave her.

Laeden approached Zephyrus, looking around for any sign of Iylea. "See anything?"

"Armed men to the east," Zephyrus said, "suspicious-looking, but that's all."

"Have you seen a young woman, a handmaiden wearing a black-and-red dress?"

Zephyrus nodded at the chancellor's tower to the east. "One went in there."

"Alone?"

Zephyrus shrugged.

Laeden's feet were already moving. The sandstone tower climbed to the sky in the distance, but the melee would begin any moment. Time mocked him with each grain of sand through the hourglass.

Find Iylea. Father next.

He rushed into the chancellor's tower. Still under construction, the windows were covered, leaving Laeden in darkness. The hard-packed earth, from the entrance, turned into marble flooring; a flickering light illuminated the corridor ahead.

Why would she come in here?

Laeden leaned forward, listening for any sign of Iylea, but his foot slipped on the wet marble. He barely caught himself. Though it was too dark to see, he put his finger into the puddle and brought it to his nose.

Sticky to the touch and tinged with the unmistakable scent of copper—blood. A trail of it, leading to the lit corridor as if a body had been dragged.

Laeden quickened his step, drawing his sword.

A loud horn blared in the distance. Laeden wheeled.

The melee. The Revivalists could strike at any moment, but he'd come too far to leave without Iylea. Hoping Markus and Zephyrus would be enough in his absence, he returned to the trail of blood and rounded the corner, sword at the ready.

Sprawled on the ground—naked, with appendages bent at odd angles, a woman's body lay still. Matted, blood-soaked hair covered her face.

Nausea climbed Laeden's throat. "No, no, no!" He knelt and brushed back her hair.

Cantella…

Laeden hung his head. He felt guilty for his relief that it wasn't Iylea, but Cantella, a girl who had served in Sentigard for years, was dead. Deep purple bruises encircled her neck from strangulation. The killer took her clothes, then slit her throat and ditched the body.

The assassin isn't a handmaiden—she's disguised as one!

Laeden ran for the pulvinus.

CHAPTER 5

The Right Thing

Zephyrus III

Stockhelm

"L*ive.*"

Patrus's plea clung to his mind like a curse. First Threyna, then Patrus, now even Vykannis had seen fit to abandon him with his ceaseless questions. Since telling Zephyrus to present the scroll, the Judge had gone silent. Without his memory or Vykannis's aid, Zephyrus couldn't absorb the gravity of Patrus and Threyna's deaths, nor could he discern the scroll's true meaning. Laeden seemed equally confused about its contents, which didn't inspire confidence that any direction would be coming from him. On every front, Zephyrus felt hopeless.

Live… but how long can one live without hope?

Yet attempting to run now and risking the slavers' retribution or the Jackals' wrath was a slight to Vykannis's protection and Patrus's last wish.

Why didn't the old man just run for the pavilions like he told me to do?

No amount of fist clenching or teeth grinding was going to bring him back, and with Laeden's father as the only source of potential answers, Zephyrus had no choice but to sit and wait for the Revivalists to make their move.

An armed group of men by an armorer's pavilion grew from four to six. With each passing moment, they appeared more and more like the distraction Laeden feared would expose the king to the true assassin. Zephyrus gripped the pommel of the sword Laeden procured for him.

Zephyrus's job was to disrupt the distraction, to allow the guards to protect their king. He thought it strange for Laeden to run off in search of a girl, but he didn't attempt to understand a prince's priorities.

Zephyrus didn't want to risk his life to save a king who allowed people to be bought and sold as pets, used as tools, and discarded when they lost their purpose.

Perhaps I should be helping the assassins instead of stopping them.

Patrus had spoken of war against New Rheynia, and Vykannis had said together they would remake the world, but first, he had to play the part of an emissary of peace. For now, he was Laeden's slave, at least until he made it far enough away from the slavers and Jackals to attempt another escape.

The horn blared signaling the start of the melee. Knights in fine armor charged one another before a crowd of onlookers. Zephyrus eyed the six armed men by the pavilion, but they didn't move.

A morning star crashed against a horned-bull helm, sending a combatant to the mud. Another horn sounded as attendants dragged the woozy bull-helmed knight from the arena grounds. A second trumpet followed for a different knight's departure. Again. Again.

The horns! The armed men shifted their weight, ready and waiting for the signal.

Zephyrus's neck prickled at the anticipation of another battle. He didn't need his memories to know how to wield a sword. Within Tharseo's Bastion and at the slavers' auction, Zephyrus had cut down dozens while protecting others or manacled. Now, untethered and angry, he could take his rage out on these Revivalists. He *wanted* to fight.

Zephyrus swallowed. *Does that make me the Wielder? Or the Harbinger?*

A blur of motion darted by. Laeden bolted from the chancellor's tower towards the west side of the pulvinus.

The horn blasted for the sixth time, and the armed men drew their swords and charged.

Zephyrus pulled his steel from its scabbard and stepped into the path of the charging men. They didn't slow, but he would not step aside.

Zephyrus let out a cry, born of frustration and imbued with fury. Their footsteps closed the distance, stampeding toward him.

Zephyrus took a deep breath and gripped the hilt of his sword with his ritual-ruined palms. In another few strides, the charging men were upon him.

He knocked the first swordsman's blade aside and, with an outstretched arm, caught the saboteur across the chest. The swordsman's momentum sent his legs up to the air and his back to the ground with a thud. Zephyrus sliced at the back of another attempting to run by and slammed his hilt into a third. While the armor absorbed most of Zephyrus's strike, the force sent the man sprawling.

One got by him, but he hacked his ankles, grounding the swordsman. Four more continued in pursuit. Zephyrus backpedaled to the pulvinus to keep the saboteurs in front of him. He stood before the stairway and called for aid.

The four swordsmen advanced as one. Help wasn't coming.

Zephyrus dodged a stab, sidestepped a thrust, and ducked a swinging blade. He countered. His edge caught the nearest swordsman right under the elbow, dropping the appendage to the ground. He kicked the screaming one-armed man away and squared off against the remaining three. The one who Zephyrus had sliced the ankles of crawled to his feet.

"Outta the way!"

Zephyrus took the offensive, spinning and slashing between two of his opponents. He sliced one across the leg and the other along the arm, but the third got by him to climb the stairs.

"Laeden!" Zephyrus shouted.

Zephyrus kicked one of the men's knees out and chopped into his neck. The body fell from his sword. A panicked thrust reached for him, but he avoided it and plunged his blade through the swordsman's stomach. He retracted to slash at the wounded man whom Zephyrus had taken down earlier. Both fell to the earth.

He took in the carnage, as men died before him. Whoever he was before, he wasn't just some emissary. *A messenger couldn't do this.* Without any time to ponder, Zephyrus climbed the stairs of the pulvinus as fast as he could. If the king died, Zephyrus's answers died with him.

CHAPTER 6

THE ASSASSIN

Laeden III

Stockhelm

Laeden climbed the stairs two at a time, praying he wasn't too late.

"What is it, Prince Laeden?" a guard asked.

Laeden pushed past him. The melee was in full swing, several people already eliminated.

Any moment now…

"All handmaidens, report!" Laeden said.

The queen sat upright. "What's the matter?"

"Don't cause a scene," his father said.

But Laeden intended to. He flipped a tray holding carafes of wine. "Now!"

Markus came to Laeden's side. "What can I do?"

"The east staircase—guard it."

Markus moved to purpose, but too late. Zephyrus shouted Laeden's name in warning.

The distraction!

One of the men made it by Zephyrus. Blood-stained and weakened, but armed and angry, the swordsman advanced, poised to strike. Earl Cassius stood closest to the stairs. Cassius's wife shrieked as the attacker closed in. Cassius yanked his bodyslave in front of the assailant. The blade erupted through the slave's back and out his belly in a spray of blood and gore.

Panic.

Markus confronted the man, his weapon level, but Laeden was watching the wrong thing. *The distraction.* Even knowing what to expect, he fell into the trap. Heart thumping in his ears, he spun to face his father.

Behind him.

Wearing Cantella's dress. The assassin's black hair framed stone-gray eyes intent on murder. The red-and-black dress hung off her, too big for her slight frame, but with all eyes on the melee, and swordsmen swarming the pulvinus, she might as well have been a ghost. The king didn't see her. The King's Guard Knights focused on the distraction. Laeden's breath caught in his throat. The assassin drew a short stiletto from her hairpiece, a mere stride behind the king.

Laeden pulled his new throwing knife from his belt and reared back. The assassin stepped closer, readying her stiletto to deliver a killing blow.

Six save me.

Laeden flung his knife. The obsidian blade flew through the air, toppling end over end. His father's eyes widened as the blade flew at him. He turned away from the incoming blow.

The knife flew past and bit into the assassin's shoulder just as she was about to strike. She stumbled backwards, her face a mask of bewilderment.

"Protect the king!" Laeden shouted.

The King's Guard Knights toppled the would-be assassin, pinning her to the ground. Markus disarmed the attacker who killed Cassius's bodyslave and forced him to yield.

"Another one!" Damascus shouted, leveling his sword at Zephyrus.

"Stop!" Laeden said. "He's with me."

Damascus lowered his blade, but Zephyrus did not.

The melee continued, though the crowd was more concerned with the events on the pulvinus. The king put his hands up to the crowd and cheered on the knights. Onlookers roared with approval, and all interest returned to the melee.

With attention off of him, the king said to his guards, "See them gagged and bound, then escort them to…"

"Your grace." Earl Cassius came to the king's side. "My ludus is only a short way past the Crystal River. The dead and detained can be put to cart and held within my barracks, where you may question those still drawing breath."

"How very kind," the king said. He turned to the guards securing the assassin and the swordsman. "See them delivered to Earl Cassius's ludus."

"Varros?" The queen wrinkled her brow and shook her head. "You can't mean to stay here *and* send our guards away. We're in danger! First a slave outbreak and now this?"

Laeden couldn't believe his ears either.

"Settle down, my love. You know what they say of lightning. The danger has passed. Now set your mind to clearer skies." He sat and resumed watching the melee. When no one else sat, the king addressed everyone on the pulvinus. "Sit, lest we draw attention away from the melee."

Laeden didn't move, but watched as the two subdued were carried off.

"Everyone sit," the king said in his king's voice. This time, everyone obeyed, spare Laeden and Zephyrus.

Laeden strode over to Markus. "I need those captives to talk."

Markus stood after barely touching his seat. "I shall accompany the wagons. Nothing will happen on my watch."

Laeden let out an uneasy breath and nodded his appreciation.

Markus, Ser Daenus of the King's Guard Knights, and a few of Cassius's men left to escort the Revivalists to Cassius's ludus.

A hand on Laeden's shoulder forced him to whip around and reach for his dagger. Zephyrus forced the dagger back into its sheath before it could be fully drawn.

"It's just me," he whispered. "The handmaiden who ran past earlier…" Zephyrus pointed to Iylea, standing on the other side of the pulvinus, her arms wrapped about her waist as if trying to console herself.

Relief washed over Laeden like the ocean's spray on a hot day. He wanted to wrap her in his arms and praise the Six for her safety, to tell her how he loved her and assure her that he would never let anything happen to her. But he was a prince, and she a handmaid. Though she stood mere strides from him, she may as well have been a realm away.

He tried to catch her eye, but she was lost in thought. *Later*, he promised.

"She's safe," Zephyrus said. "Your king is safe."

Laeden released his breath and stepped back. "Gratitude, Zephyrus." He gestured to Markus's empty seat beside him. Hesitantly, Zephyrus sat, covered in the blood of the slain. Damascus, Nallia, and a number of other guests atop the pulvinus eyed him, shifting their weight in the opposite direction, but none gave voice to their inward thoughts.

Laeden took his seat, scouring the buzzing fairgrounds for signs of danger. The onlookers of the melee cheered as Aelon swept Haedron Allos's leg out from under him and met Aemos Horne's hack. Even as the final three contestants traded blows, they failed to offer Laeden a temporary distraction. Every lingering eye in the crowd was a cutthroat, plotting another assassination attempt, every shout a siren alerting of the next attack.

Between Aelon's information, Zephyrus's aid, and Laeden's refusal to listen to the naysayers, they narrowly avoided a tragedy. Laeden was unsure who to thank—the Gods, the Judges, or whoever AVR might be. Either way, they intervened to make this outcome possible, and Laeden was grateful. However, the path forward was shrouded in mystery. *What now?* The Revivalists were no longer something to be taken lightly. They would strike again.

But when they do, I will stop them. Whatever it takes.

CHAPTER 7

THE REVIVALISTS

Laeden IV

Stockhelm

"I underestimated the Revivalists," King Varros said from atop his white mare. They rode side by side as they crossed the wooden bridge, fording the Crystal River. His father attempted to gain eye contact, but Laeden kept his gaze on the horizon. The *clip-clap* of the horses' hooves and the creaking wagon wheels carried them closer to the haven of the Cassius ludus.

"If it weren't for you and your man—" His father nodded to Zephyrus walking beside Laeden's horse. "—I don't know what would have happened."

Zephyrus kept darting nervous glances at the king. Laeden thumbed Zephyrus's scroll in his pocket. His father was the only one capable of providing Zephyrus with answers, but Laeden wanted answers himself—who this AVR was, and what in Six Hells the scroll was talking about. Regardless, Laeden couldn't help but commiserate with Zephyrus. He didn't want to imagine not being able to remember Iylea.

He returned his attention to his father. "You live to make amends." Laeden wanted to point out this *was* his father's fault. If he had listened to him to begin with, or just killed the mage instead of exiling him to Klaytos, the Revivalists may never have formed in the first place.

The king was the law, and this precedence threatened the fabric of society. The Treaty of 940 was clear: Celestics were enslaved, mages were executed. The Salmantic Senate helped write the treaty, and the Vigiles and Jackals were charged with enforcing it. His father's decision, absent the Inner Council or the senate's approval, was a kick in the shin to everyone.

And for what?

His father left his mother in order to marry Danella and bind the Treaty in matrimony. He hated his father for it, but he also understood. For peace and prosperity, for honor and justice. What was love in the face of duty to the realm?

But if that was the case, why violate it? Doesn't he realize his hypocrisy?

"I know what you're thinking, Laeden."

"That I wish you'd say what you mean and mean what you say?" Laeden asked, attempting but failing to keep the heat from his voice.

He met his father's eyes. For a moment, he looked tired, haggard in a way he'd never seen before, but beneath Laeden's stare, his weariness solidified into the king's steely gaze.

"You're a Helixus and a Faire," his father said. "You're more like your mother than you'll ever know. Your heart is true for all to see. You fight to 'defend the weak,' as the Faire words say. But no, I do not regret my past decisions."

How dare he speak of Mother. Laeden had already pressed past prudence with his last comment and wasn't prepared to jab at the wounded Chimera, but *how can he be so blind? How many will die in Revivalist plots?*

Seven had already fallen: five mercenaries attempting to distract the guards, Danella's servant Cantella, and Cassius's bodyslave. Seven.

How can the life of one mage be worth seven already dead? Laeden considered his own hesitation in choosing between his father, the king, and his lover, the handmaiden. *Is there something personal—something more that I'm missing?* His father was always reserved, never sharing more than needed. *Does he have something to hide?* The scroll in his pocket certainly suggested so. When the time presented itself, Laeden would show him the scroll, and he expected answers, but now was not the time.

His father's head drooped until his obsidian crown fell to his brow. Repositioning the crown, he sat up tall. "One day, perhaps, you'll understand, but there's been too much bloodshed. If I killed the mage out of fear of groups like the Revivalists, then they've already won."

Laeden began to protest, but his father raised his voice to cut him off.

"At this point," his father said with a sigh, "all we can do is start a coalition charged with keeping the peace."

"A task force?" Laeden asked. "Like the Jackals, but targeted toward the Revivalists?"

"Aye, you have made your case. How do you measure Ser Daenus?"

Laeden shrugged. Ser Daenus served as Danella's bodyguard, her stern and stoic shadow—skilled with a blade and as honorable as they come, but he ignored Laeden when he warned of the Revivalists.

Attempting to keep the bitterness from his voice, Laeden asked, "What about him?"

"I am of a mind to name him leader of this task force," the king said.

Laeden's grip on his reins tightened. His eye twitched as he swallowed the words he wanted to say. *If it were up to Ser Daenus, you'd already be dead. I positioned Zephyrus, I discovered the assassin would be disguised as a handmaiden, and I stopped her from burying a stiletto in your neck. You would be dead if not for me.*

"The Sentinels, charged with the protection of the royal family and uprooting the Revivalists' threat," Father mused. "The honorable Sentinels and the Revivalists' syndicate, that could be a song for the ages, don't you think?"

Laeden pulled on his reins. A signal coursed through the ranks beyond them until the entire caravan stopped. The king turned his horse to face Laeden. He eyed Zephyrus, who had been silent this entire time, and coughed.

Zephyrus took the hint and backed away, giving them privacy.

With the composure of having spent most of his adult life within castle politics, Laeden held the king's steely gaze. "I should be the leader of this coalition."

"You're *in* the royal family," his father said.

It took all of Laeden's might not to scoff. *Another battle for another time.*

"All the more reason why I can't fail," Laeden said. "Father, I've been the only one to see the Revivalists for the threat they are. They aren't just some gaggle of perturbed idealists thinking they could do better if they were in power. They tried to assassinate you, and they would have succeeded had it not been for *me*. Not Ser Daenus. *Me.*"

His father tossed his head like a braying horse. "Laeden, this is above you."

As soon as the words passed his lips, the king grit his teeth and raised his fist to his mouth. "My words do not match my meaning. My concern rests in your safety."

Laeden's ears grew hot. The collar of his doublet felt like it tightened around his neck, but it was only the angry words he chose to swallow. He knew what his father meant—*he doesn't believe in me.* Nothing new. But Laeden couldn't trust this task to anyone else.

"I can do this, Father. I will not fail you."

"What is the meaning of this?" Danella asked as she and Ser Daenus approached from the wagon. "Why have we stopped?"

King Varros repositioned the crown atop his graying waves. "We are discussing a task force concerning these Revivalists."

"Surely that can be done once we are out of harm's way," Danella said.

"Laeden wishes to lead this task force himself."

Danella balked before fixating on Laeden. She wrapped her arms around herself. "Laeden, it's too dangerous."

"If my father, my king, and the future of our country is in danger, I am the only one I trust to see him protected," Laeden said. "If it weren't for my *paranoia*, this conversation would have been very different. But fortunately, I stopped them."

"But Laeden," Danella said, inflecting her words with a mother's pleading.

But she's not my mother.

Danella put her hand on Laeden's arm. "What if they aren't just after your father? What if they're after all of us? Six save us, but think of the pandemonium if both you and Damascus were ensnared in the Revivalists' schemes. I was thinking perhaps it would be best if you two were separated.

Gods forbid you both be taken and New Rheynia is left without an heir. You could stay with your grandfather Hallon, in Valtarcia."

Laeden jerked his head back, scoffing. *Heir?* "Are you serious?"

"I will name you second behind Damascus's claim," Danella said.

Laeden couldn't believe his ears. *A true prince? But at what cost?* He saw through Danella's plot. *She's patronizing me. As long as someone else leads the Sentinels.* He turned from his stepmother to his father.

"I will not be sent into exile out of fear. If you are afraid the entire royal family may be targeted, then the best place for me is here, leading the Sentinels."

"Laeden, darling, think about the well-being of the realm. Anyone can lead soldiers, but not everyone can lead the country. Why not leave such work for… I don't know—someone like Ser Daenus?"

Laeden bit his lip, heat rising up his neck to his ears. "With all due respect," he said to Ser Daenus, "the king would have been slain today, had the task for his safety been left in Ser Daenus's hands."

Ser Daenus glowered at Laeden, but Laeden didn't care. It was true.

"Why don't we wait until we get home to discuss this?" Danella asked. "We can—"

His father cut Danella off. "Laeden will be named captain of the Sentinels."

Warmth blossomed in Laeden's chest. His shoulder blades fell away from his ears to settle back down his rib cage. "I will not let you down," Laeden said before Danella could retort.

The king nodded. "It's settled then."

"That Helixus pride." Shaking her head, Danella picked up her skirts and swept off without another word, Ser Daenus brooding in her shadow.

The king sagged beneath the weight of his crown, but this was how it needed to be. After today's events, Laeden was convinced he was the only one capable of protecting his father. He could handle himself just fine, and he wouldn't be bribed into hiding in exile.

"Let us continue to the Cassius villa before we get caught in the nightly rains," the king said, looking to the darkening sky.

The road west to the Cassius ludus continued to snake through the Stockhelm countryside, gradually gaining in elevation. The sun colored the skies an ominous orange as it descended to cast long shadows over their caravan. They rode in silence as they approached the Cassius ludus embedded in the Hylan mountain range, but the silence gave Laeden a moment with his thoughts.

A swell of satisfaction filled him, but the weight of responsibility hung overhead. He would need aid in many different forms, but no one would have a stronger resolve than he. However, never again could he put Iylea's safety before the king's. The thought ate at him until they arrived at the mountain villa.

As they approached the sandstone fortress's outer gate, Markus, two of Cassius's men, and a few of the Drake household guards waited to greet them. Like the shadows cast by the setting sun, their faces stretched long in dismay.

A stone sank in Laeden's stomach as Markus stepped forth.

"We have a problem."

CHAPTER 8

TRUST

Zephyrus IV
Stockhelm

"What do you mean, dead?" Laeden asked, veins bulging from his neck as he examined Cassius's men.

"What happened?" asked an older man styled in elegant purple-and-gold robes. Earl Cassius, the slave owner, lifted his chin to the darkening sky. "Liario, explain."

Liario stepped forward, hunched and weathered—the slaver who outbid all the others at the auction. The guard beside Liario wore the same purple-and-gold surcoat as the man who murdered Patrus.

The thought of his bloodied blade ripping from Patrus's shoulder set Zephyrus's knees quivering. The man's face burned into his empty well of memories: a squashed nose, black hair—peppered gray at the temples—and a smug smile.

He's here.

Zephyrus no longer cared about the scroll in Laeden's pocket or what the king had to say about it. It didn't matter if he was the Wielder, the Harbinger, the Herald, an emissary, or nothing at all. Patrus, at the very least, was his friend—maybe his only remaining friend—and Patrus's murderer was here. Somewhere.

While Laeden and the king argued with Earl Cassius and Liario, Zephyrus hid beneath his hood to conceal his face. It would not do well for him to be recognized here. Within the gates, the yellow sandstone walls of the mountain the ludus was carved from enclosed a courtyard. Erected wooden stables extended off to the right side of the gate, where the back end of a wagon was just visible.

Zephyrus snuck past the arguing men, inspecting every guard in purple and gold.

I will find you. And I will kill you.

Slinking away, he clung to the long shadows of twilight, relying on their aid to cloak him. Approaching the corner of the stables, incomprehensible whispers hid behind the argument in the distance.

Closer he crept, entwined in the encroaching nightfall. He peeked around the corner. Two more wagons lay ahead. Zephyrus snuck behind the last wagon, the voices growing louder. He stalked up to the middle wagon until he could hear.

"The omenations were wrong," a man whispered, "but we will not fail. We cannot. If one stands in the way of the Gods' will, that one must die… even a king."

A second voice gurgled an incoherent response from the back of a wagon, the scent of death thick in the air.

I thought all the captives were dead. Apparently not all—not yet at least.

"The Six will watch over you. Your assignment has ended, but you will be rewarded for your faith. For the Six."

Zephyrus prowled closer like a predator in the wild. The soft sound of blood gushing from a mortal wound hung in the air. He leaned around the wagon to glimpse the back of a man in a purple surcoat, his dagger embedded in the assassin's chest.

The Cassius guard set the body down and wiped the blood off his dagger. He turned, resheathing his blade to face Zephyrus.

Him. Black hair, graying at the temples. A squashed nose. *Patrus's murderer.*

Zephyrus's teeth ground together, and heat rose to his cheeks. Thunder rumbled in the distance, and forks of lightning stretched across the eastern sky. Yet Zephyrus's anger bellowed louder and struck harder than any storm.

Recognition washed across the murderer's eyes. He ripped his gladius from its scabbard.

Zephyrus drew his steel, slow and purposeful, ready and waiting for vengeance.

"Guards!"

Zephyrus charged before any could try to stop him. A tempest of steel. A storm of hacks and slashes. He thrust at the golden scorpion sigil over the guard's breast, but the murderer blocked. He chopped, only for his attack to be deflected. Zephyrus slashed again, but the guard met his force. He shoved the Cassius guard away and struck again.

The clang of steel rang shrill against the thunderous resonance off the mountain, but after another short exchange of blows, their swords collided. Deadlocked, the two measured their strength against one another.

Earl Cassius and several of his men ran to their position. "Cease!"

Laeden followed close behind. "Zephyrus, stand down!"

Close enough to feel the warmth of the guard's breath, Zephyrus glared. *Patrus surrendered. And you killed him.*

Neither released the deadlock. Zephyrus's muscles tensed against the sustained output.

"This slave started the riot at the slavers' market," the murderer said. "Called himself the Wielder!"

"Him?" the queen asked, pointing at Zephyrus. "The Wielder started the riots..."

"He serves Prince Laeden," Markus said. "Father, tell your man to stand down."

Earl Cassius did not acquiesce, despite his son's insistence.

Through bared teeth, Zephyrus hissed. "He spoke with one of the *dead* captives before stabbing her in the heart, silencing her forever."

"Your slave is mistaken," Earl Cassius said. "Lenox's loyalty is beyond reproach."

With the tension too thick to cut with a sword, the king stepped into view. "Set your blades down. Now."

Lenox's black eyes flared with an all-consuming rage across from Zephyrus's gladius. Not for a second did Zephyrus trust him. If he lowered his defenses, he would die. Lenox would kill him. *Just like Patrus.*

"Enough." Laeden stepped between Zephyrus and Lenox, forcing them apart. "Sheathe your blades." Laeden nodded to Markus. "Inspect the assassin for wounds you didn't see earlier."

"A stab wound to the chest," Zephyrus said. "Identical to Lenox's dagger."

"The slave doesn't know what he saw," Lenox spat. "Yes, I finished her, but she spoke nothing but nonsense in the last gasps of life."

Laeden snarled. "We needed her *alive*."

"There's a stab wound to the heart," Markus said.

Laeden's grave glare settled upon Lenox before he addressed Cassius and the guards. "Everyone, away from the bodies. No one goes near them without my leave. And you..." He stabbed his index finger at Lenox. "You will submit to questioning."

"Him?" the queen asked. "This *Wielder* leads a revolt, and you trust his word over Earl Cassius's loyal man?" She lifted her palms skyward in the king's direction, as if hoping he would intervene, but the king's focus remained on Laeden.

"I don't trust anyone," Laeden said. "But we will get to the bottom of this. Earl Cassius, if you please, allow me to examine the bodies. Alone. Take your men inside before the nightly rains arrive, but leave Lenox with me."

"On whose authority?" Lenox asked.

"The captain of the Sentinels," the king said. "Prince Laeden speaks with my authority on all matters pertaining to the Revivalists."

"My king," Lenox said, "I am no Revivalist."

"Then you should not fear my questions," Laeden said.

Lenox growled, but backed down, sheathing his steel.

Cassius furrowed his brow as if he were about to protest but thought better of it. "Very well. We will await you inside."

The queen whispered something to the king. His nose wrinkled, but he beckoned Laeden aside for a private word, drawing a scowl from Laeden.

After the tense exchanges, Cassius and the rest of his men escorted the king and queen indoors. The grounds outside the stables emptied, leaving Zephyrus, Laeden, Markus, and Lenox alone with the bodies.

Lenox cast a leveling stare at Zephyrus, promising death. Zephyrus clenched his jaw until his teeth hurt. The setting sun fell beyond the horizon, and a light rain began to descend, but nothing could defuse Zephyrus's rage.

"Markus," Laeden said, "question Zephyrus on his account of these events. I will speak with Lenox."

Markus placed a firm hand on Zephyrus's shoulder. "Consider it done, Captain." Markus steered Zephyrus away from Lenox and Laeden, escorting him to a vacant stable out of the rain.

"We can trust no one," Markus said, crossing his arms before Zephyrus.

Markus was tall and broad of shoulder. His narrow face looked too small for his body. Shoulder-length dark hair hung straight and neat behind him. Clad in a black-and-gold doublet with a roaring lion embroidered into the breast, he didn't share the same colors or sigil of his father's purple and gold.

Markus pointed to the wagon of the dead. "If not for you, Zephyrus, those six men would have killed more than one slave. For that, I will hear you out, but you must know… the two captives were dead upon arrival. I'm certain. Checked them myself."

Zephyrus didn't balk. He had nothing to hide. "I know what I saw. I know what I heard."

Markus pursed his lips. "Very well. You saw Lenox kill the captive—stab wound to the heart. I believe you. That puncture wasn't there upon my initial inspection. But my question is why were you by the wagons in the first place?"

Zephyrus's composure cracked. First a twitch of his eye, then a wordless gaping.

"You serve Prince Laeden, correct?"

"For the time," Zephyrus said.

"What were you doing so far from his side?" Markus stepped closer to Zephyrus. Zephyrus opened his mouth, but again, no words came to mind. The truth wouldn't do in this case. *I was looking for Lenox. Vengeance. Blood.*

"The way I see it," Markus said, "you and Lenox met once already today."

The sight of Lenox's blade buried to the hilt in Patrus's torso flashed in Zephyrus's mind.

"You knew he would be here," Markus said.

"He wore the same colors as the guards out front," Zephyrus said. "I thought I would find him here, somewhere."

Markus advanced closer, his arms still crossed before his barrel of a chest. "And what did you hope to do once you found him?"

Zephyrus blew out his cheeks. "I hoped to kill the bastard." His fingers curled into his palms, digging into the raw wounds from the blood sacrifice the Seers took to reveal his inconclusive prophecy.

Markus stepped back but reset his jaw. "Why?"

"He murdered my only friend," Zephyrus said through his teeth. His mind might not have been able to process the loss, but his body certainly did. His chest hurt. His face flushed hot, and tears welled in his eyes. "He surrendered… he rescued people. He never lifted a sword…"

Markus put his hand on Zephyrus's shoulder. "What happened between the wagons? You said you heard Lenox speaking with the assassin. What did you hear?"

Zephyrus took a moment to recall. He was so fixated on avenging Patrus he hadn't been paying attention and struggled to remember the words. Steadying his breath, he gathered his recollections. "He spoke about killing the king… in service to the Six."

Markus blanched, his bewilderment palpable even in the dim light of the torches. Zephyrus didn't know anything about the Six, but men who killed in the name of the Gods were the most dangerous type. Either they were fanatical extremists, or their Gods were worse than their believers.

"You're sure that's what he said?" Markus asked.

Zephyrus nodded. "Told her she would be rewarded for her faith. Then stabbed her through the heart."

Markus rubbed his narrow chin, then ran his fingers through his hair, stretching the skin of his forehead. "Apologies for your loss, Zephyrus, but take peace knowing that if what you say is true, the murderer of your friend will be brought to justice. If Lenox is found guilty of treason, he will be nailed to a Six Arrowed Star."

Markus's words should have pleased him, but only a callused numbness remained. *Justice? A murderer's life for Patrus's? This very day Patrus saved fifty from enslavement. How could the weight of their lives balance any scale?*

"Markus," Laeden called over the rain pattering down on the roof of the stables.

Before Zephyrus could retort, Markus held up a finger, instructing Zephyrus to wait while Markus and Laeden spoke. The two stood close, whispering to one another under the awning of the stables. The rain continued to fall, heavier with each passing moment, pelting the wooden roof. Thunder roared, and lightning cracked in the distance, leaving little chance for Zephyrus to make out the words between them.

Zephyrus ground his teeth as he and Lenox exchanged glares across the stables. Being nailed to a symbol of the Gods he served was a kindness Lenox didn't deserve.

Eventually, Laeden and Markus broke apart. Laeden waved at Lenox. Expecting Laeden to wave Lenox toward them, he waved Lenox away. Zephyrus didn't believe his eyes.

They're letting him go.

Lenox grinned as he tossed his purple cape over his shoulder, turning his back on Zephyrus. Zephyrus swallowed as Markus and Laeden turned toward him—their faces long, eyes cold. An uneasy pressure built in Zephyrus's chest as the two stalked toward him.

Zephyrus could barely contain himself as he bore into Markus. "You said—"

Laeden held up his hand as the two stopped before Zephyrus. "Lenox is lying. Markus is convinced you're telling the truth, so I have little doubt Lenox is in the Revivalists." Laeden paused long enough for Zephyrus to fear the coming of the word *but.*

"You let him go." Zephyrus could barely speak the words, the injustice salting his wound.

"Let me explain," Laeden said. "Considering your absence of memory, I'll spare you the finer details, but Earl Cassius is vying for the chancellorship—a political office in Stockhelm that would make a favorable ally in bringing the Revivalists to their knees. If Lenox is involved—as we believe he is—he's likely not the only one beneath Cassius's roof. I can't trust Cassius if I can't trust his men," Laeden bit his lip. "Unfortunately, this is where things become complicated."

Zephyrus's toes curled, gripping the soles of his leather boots. *Complicated?*

Laeden shuffled his feet but lost none of the sternness in his voice. "Because you led the outbreak at the slavers' auction and declared yourself the Wielder, my father has forbidden you from my service… but you've proven too dangerous a threat to be allowed to go free."

The tension Zephyrus held in his feet climbed his bones to the base of his neck. Anger thickened his blood until his veins bulged like a dam threatening to burst. *You wish to deliver me to the Jackals, then? I'd like to see you try.*

"However," Laeden said, "you're far too valuable an asset to remain unutilized."

Bile climbed Zephyrus's throat. *Utilized. Like a tool.* He kept his face placid, steadying the thunderous beating of his heart to a rhythmic drum. He swallowed, afraid to ask, but needing to know. "What do you plan to do with me?"

Laeden exchanged a glance with Markus before meeting Zephyrus's eyes. "You will serve as a gladiator."

From deep within him, fury gathered, collecting pressure that threatened to explode.

"*You'll die in the gladiatorial arenas,*" said the slaver who slew Threyna.

Tremors overtook the muscles of Zephyrus's face. *No.* His eyes darted between Laeden and Markus. *I'll take my chances with the Jackals if I can get past these two. Just need to wait for the right moment to make my move.*

"We need to know which of the guards we can trust," Laeden said. "From the barracks, you'll be able to spy on the guards, and with your information, we can purge House Cassius of the undesirables and ensure the Sentinels have a trustworthy ally as chancellor."

"Observe and report," Markus said. "Once we know who we're dealing with, we'll strike them from this world."

They stand too close together for me to push past, but within the stall of the stables, perhaps I can use that to my advantage. If I fight first, then flee—

Laeden and Markus stared at Zephyrus, waiting for a response.

"A gladiator? A spy?" Zephyrus asked. "For honesty and loyal service, you enslave me. What of Lenox?"

Laeden and Markus exchanged a look before Markus stared at his boots.

"He will remain in House Cassius," Laeden said. "If we're right, and he is the Revivalist we believe he is, he'll lead you to the other traitors."

Zephyrus fixed Markus with a smoldering stare, but Markus wouldn't meet his gaze.

"Treason is rewarded with patience. I see."

There is no justice in this world—only fate.

Zephyrus's taut muscles relaxed as Threyna's words from Tharseo's Bastion revisited him. *"You are where you need to be, exactly when you must."*

"Is this where I must be?" Zephyrus channeled to Vykannis. *"Is this what you want?"*

No answer.

Laeden stepped forward, holding out a pacifying hand. *Now. This is my chance.* But Zephyrus didn't move. Couldn't move.

Perhaps it's right—I'm meant to be here.

As a gladiatorial spy, Zephyrus would get another chance at Lenox. Another opportunity to avenge Patrus.

Laeden placed his hand on Zephyrus's shoulder. "Lenox will meet his end. As will all the Revivalists. But your service will not go without reward. I will speak to my father about the scroll and report my findings to you, as you will to me." Laeden pulled the scroll from his pocket and placed it against Zephyrus's chest.

Zephyrus accepted the scroll, Patrus and Threyna's blood forever stained to the parchment. *Patrus wanted me to get rid of this, but it keeps finding its way back to me.* He cradled it within his bandaged palm.

Laeden patted Zephyrus's shoulder. "I owe you a debt, Zephyrus. One that will not be forgotten. But now, I need your trust."

Trust?

Markus stepped forward, the clinking chains of manacles held before him.

"You're not my slave," Laeden said. "You're my ally. I wouldn't ask this of you if I didn't have to—if I didn't think you were capable."

Zephyrus grit his teeth as Markus offered the chains of his enslavement. He didn't trust Laeden, but Lenox was here. If he served Laeden well, answers would come—but whether he was the Wielder, Harbinger, or Herald, Zephyrus was something to be feared, and Lenox would learn the full extent of the beast he'd awoken.

"Very well," Zephyrus said, embracing his fate. He extended his wrists toward Markus. "Send me in."

CHAPTER 9

HOPE

Zephyrus V

Stockhelm

"I trust you found what you were looking for, my prince?" Cassius asked upon their entrance.

Thunder roared, resonating through the vestibule of the Cassius villa. Windswept rain careened down the angled roof into the bath underneath the sky window of the atrium. White marble traced with gold fineries made the entranceway to the villa appear larger than it actually was, but it still amazed Zephyrus. He couldn't help but compare the threadbare rugs and tapestries at Tharseo's Bastion to the fine purple cloth his wet boots now sullied.

"Earl Cassius," Laeden said over the noise of the storm's wrath. "These present circumstances place us at an interesting crossroad. Might we speak in a more secluded setting?"

Cassius nodded, beckoning them deeper into the villa, speaking trivialities for the sake of hearing his own voice. Laeden, Zephyrus, and Markus accompanied the Earl of Stockhelm through the atrium and around the bath. Paintings of gladiators, golden-tipped weapons, and busts of past champions littered the walls.

"How long since you were last home, Markus?" Cassius asked.

"Too long, Father. Before my apprenticeship with the Lions."

"Ah, but soon you shall no longer be the apprentice." Cassius waved them inside a room opposite the atrium. "Let us convene in my tablinum."

Liario, the hunched man who bid on Cassius's behalf at the slave auction, waited outside the office. He opened the door, escorting them inside with an obsequious grin.

The floor of the room had a tile mosaic depicting a golden scorpion. Cassius took a seat behind an intricately carved mahogany desk; his pet, Liario, took his place behind him, like a scowling crow perched on his shoulder. Cassius gestured to two cushioned chairs before him, instructing Laeden and Markus to sit.

Zephyrus stood between the two chairs, biting his lip and testing the strength of the manacles about his wrists. He supposed he'd better get accustomed to being treated as a hound.

If it gives me the opportunity to avenge Patrus, I will suffer the indignity.

"Earl Cassius," Laeden said, sitting forward in his chair.

"Please call me Lentulis," Cassius said. "No need for titles, my prince."

Zephyrus stifled a scoff at the hypocrisy, but that was what this society was founded upon. The king spoke of peace and prosperity, but for whom?

Slaves toil for the masters. Masters toil for the royals. Who must the royals bow to?

"Lentulis," Laeden said, directing his glare at Zephyrus. "Unfortunately, my *slave* lied, slandering the good name of your guard, Lenox. I offer my sincerest apologies if my diligence offered any insult, but please understand that was not my intent. I favor you to win the chancellorship, and once you take office, I hope to have your support in bringing the Revivalists to justice. For tonight's misunderstanding, I offer you this slave as recompense."

Zephyrus dropped his gaze to the tiled floor, his fists curled, straining against the iron links of his bindings. Laeden had instructed him how this would go. This was just posturing—a way to convince Cassius to welcome a spy under his roof. Didn't mean Zephyrus liked it.

"He's a capable fighter," Liario said from behind Cassius. "A promising gladiator, no doubt, but he led the outbreak, the largest in our nation's history. Is it wise to accept such a *gift*?"

Cassius raised his wispy white brows. "It seems more like you are passing your burdens off to me. Why should I accept your headaches and make them my own?"

Markus leaned forward in his seat. "Father, you are the only lanista capable of forging him into something of worth—perhaps the next Champion of Stockhelm, if not all of New Rheynia. With a little discipline and the proper motivation, there's no telling what could become of him under the finest lanista in the land."

Cassius's grimace softened.

Flattery is the fastest way to any inflated man's heart.

Cassius licked his thin lips. "I will not suffer insubordination or blasphemy. If even the word *freedom* passes his lips..." Cassius slid his finger across his throat. "He will be executed—gift of the prince or not."

"He's your slave," Laeden said with a shrug. "Hopefully, he serves you better than he served me. And once again, my sincerest apologies for doubting the trust of your guards."

Zephyrus ground his teeth until his head hurt. The muscles between his shoulder blades wrenched into knots. Even though this was all a farce, it didn't change the truth. Lenox was a liar and a murderer. All Zephyrus did was wake up in the wrong temple and receive a prophecy from the wrong Gods.

"Live..." Patrus's curse upon him. *What is life without freedom?* The wounds on his palms ached with the injustice of it all, the rolled scroll still clutched within.

Cassius's face twisted into a self-satisfied grin. "Very well, I accept."

Liario's eyes twitched. His crooked smile melted, but he remained silent.

Cassius turned his flinty gray eyes on Zephyrus. "Renounce the Judges and accept the true Gods of Valencia. Submit to the Facets of Perfection and yield to my authority."

Laeden's knee began to bounce beside him. Markus tensed, gripping the arm of his chair.

Zephyrus held Cassius's gaze. He didn't yet know what he believed, but he was not about to be forced into choosing. He'd heard the voice of Vykannis the Brave, a Judge of Celestia. He wasn't sure if that made him the Herald, but he wouldn't forsake the Judge, despite his absence since saving his life at the slavers' auction. Zephyrus's flesh was already bound and chained as a slave. He would not so easily give up his convictions as well.

When Zephyrus didn't respond, Cassius shrugged. "Nothing a night out in the rain can't fix. Fear not, my prince. I've broken many resistant slaves. He will be no different. Guards!"

A handful of Cassius's guards manhandled Zephyrus out of the tablinum and down a flight of stairs into the barracks of the gladiatorial ludus. Voices echoed off the stone walls, and cell bars rattled as they passed men stuffed into cells barely large enough to lie down in. The inhabitants pressed their faces through the bars as the guards shoved Zephyrus past.

"On you go!" a guard said, shoving Zephyrus down the hall of barred cells to a wooden door. Another guard unlocked the door and swung it open. A rush of windswept rain buffeted against him. Lightning cracked the sky. Thunder roared overhead.

"Move it!"

With Zephyrus's hands bound, the scroll from AVR still clenched in his palm, the guards shoved him beyond the cover of the door. The rains cascaded upon him, soaking him within moments. Lightning streaked across the sky, illuminating what appeared to be a large rectangular training area. A row of wooden crosses thatched with hay and cloth stood before him—some sort of training dummy.

"Secure him to the palus!" the guard shouted over the rain.

Zephyrus's feet squished into the wet sand with each resisted step. One of the guards undid his manacles, but the other four shoved his back against the wooden cross. Zephyrus struggled hopelessly against them. His hands were once again secured behind his back, binding him to the palus.

"Hold him still." One guard pulled a dagger from his belt. Zephyrus's eyes widened as distant lightning reflected off the blade's edge. He struggled against his bindings and the men securing him, but to no avail. The dagger drew closer. The guard with the knife grabbed Zephyrus by the collar of his wet tunic and pulled it towards him, the blade aimed at his throat.

He wished he died fighting. He wished he died beside Patrus. He'd come this far, *and for what?*

The guard slashed through the tunic, cutting it from the collar down to the sleeve. The wet tunic hung in tatters from Zephyrus's other shoulder before the other guard tore it free. Next, his britches were slashed and stripped from his body, leaving him nude in the downfall of rain.

"Dogs don't wear clothes." The guard spat in his face. "Neither will you." He sheathed his dagger, and the other guards relinquished him from their grasp, leaving him to slide down the palus. The five guards clad in purple and gold strode from the training square, retreating inside.

Zephyrus released a breath he didn't realize he was holding. Gasping for air to pay back the deficit, Zephyrus was content to still be breathing.

Still alive…

Zephyrus looked to the angry sky as the rain poured down. *Is this my fate? A Prophet of Celestia, drowned by the rain.*

Threyna's words returned. *"You are where you need to be, exactly when you must."*

"Is this what you want?" Zephyrus shouted against the storm.

No response.

Did I only imagine hearing Vykannis? Did I agree to Laeden's plans on a falsehood?

Perhaps the scroll of parchment crushed within his fist had the truth of it. *I am just a gift to the high and mighty—a tool to be used, abused, and discarded.* The rains persisted, the unrelenting storms raged, and no answers, no memories, and no hope came to him.

CHAPTER 10

VISIONS

Iylea

Stockhelm

New Rheynia was not a safe place for people like Iylea. If anyone—even Laeden—were to discover her curse, she could be nailed to the Six Arrowed Star.

Iylea was a dreamer. She thought everyone dreamt the way she did, but she couldn't believe that lie anymore—not considering how frequent, accurate, or debilitating they'd become.

Last night, before the Festival of Stockhelm, she dreamt of a sword piercing meat, a snake eating its tail, and Laeden holding his father's crown. She ignored them, as always, but today's events were too real to deny.

Cassius's bodyslave—the piece of meat—pierced by the Revivalists' sword. The Revivalists' assassins—captured and sent ahead to Cassius's ludus—were murdered, perhaps by the Revivalists' own men, just like the snake eating its own tail. And if not for Laeden's efforts, the king would have lost his crown.

These weren't just dreams. They were prophecies.

Iylea thought after the king exiled the healing mage, perhaps times were changing, and people like her might be safe. The formation of the Revivalists set everything back.

While Earl Cassius's slaves prepared the showroom for the royal family's retinue, Iylea distracted herself in the high arched ceilings painted with a mural of the New Rheynian houses. In the center of the dome, the red-and-black chimera of House Drake reigned with the crown atop the lion's head and the words *Family, Faith, and Future* over the ram's horns.

Amidst the many sigils, Iylea focused on those of Laeden's heritage. The blue-and-gold winged horse of House Helixus flew underneath the chimera, their words *Honor and Justice* written in flowing cursive in the majestic creature's wake. Below, the white falcon of Laeden's mother's house flew across a blue backdrop with open wings and outstretched talons, carrying the banner of House Faire's words, *Defend the Weak*.

Once, the Falcons of Faire were among Valtarcia's elite, but after Geraldus Faire denounced the practice of bestowing the bastard name on those born out of wedlock, he had cast down the entire Faire name. To protect the few, he had jeopardized the many. Now, noble or base-born, all Faires were labeled plebeians. Such was the cost of lending aid to the downtrodden.

Laeden embodied the words of his parents' houses so well.

That's what made her nervous. She told him to be careful. The only problem was that he believed volunteering himself to lead the Sentinels against the Revivalists was the *careful* thing to do. He could handle himself, but what worried her was he would not hesitate to sacrifice himself to save his father, his half-brother, or even his stepmother in the line of duty.

Queen Danella strode into the showroom, Ser Daenus on her heels. Try as she might to hide it, the day's events even wore on someone as strong-willed as the queen. Be that as it may, Iylea needed to remain composed, lest she end up on a Six Arrowed Star.

The queen summoned Iylea with a wave. "You're shaking, Iylea. Are you well?"

Iylea clenched her trembling fingers, not realizing they were moving on their own accord. "Yes, your grace. Apologies."

The queen gave her arm a gentle squeeze, lifting Iylea's eyes from the floor. "Apologize for nothing, dear. This day has tested us all, but the Six will prevail, and peace will reign. You have nothing to fear."

Iylea swallowed, wishing it were so. She bobbed her head, thanking the queen for her encouragement. The queen smiled and took her seat upon the dais overlooking the showroom's center stage.

Iylea always held a prejudice against the people of Salmantica. Her father was slain in the New Rheynian War, and her mother was murdered by Salmantic soldiers during the occupation that followed. Their country of zealots placed the Gods so far above people that they lost sight of what the Gods truly wanted for their people in the first place, but Queen Danella was different. If she and King Varros were the first rulers of New Rheynia instead of her father, Damascus Drake, perhaps things would be different. Perhaps she would have been safe. But with the rise of the Revivalists, no one was.

It wouldn't be long before this conflict turned into a full-fledged war. She had seen it. *He* had shown her. She shuddered at the thought of the pale man with the red eyes from her recurring visions. It wasn't his appearance, or even his demeanor, that frightened her when he visited her dreams. No matter how kind a God was while showing her dreams of the future, it didn't change the danger it put her in.

"Soon," he would say, his red eyes burning like the sun. *"Soon, Iylea."*

She was not eager to learn what that meant.

Earl Cassius led Laeden and Markus into the showroom. The change in Laeden from this morning was already drastic. He could no longer linger amongst the plebs if he were to fulfill his role as captain of the Sentinels. He stood proud, shoulders back, brown hair flowing in his wake as he climbed the dais reserved for the most honored guests beside his family.

"Let us provide a spectacle while we feast," Cassius said, plucking a goblet of wine from a serving tray. "But first, a toast. Everyone raise your cup to the King and Queen of New Rheynia. Long may they reign!"

The guests raised their cups. "Long may they reign!"

Cassius ordered his men to prepare gladiators for entertainment. Iylea didn't want to see more fighting. There wouldn't be blood in this exhibition, but the risk of such, which made the contests so entertaining for others, made her want to vomit. She had attended numerous games in her time as a handmaiden, but of late, she had seen too much bloodshed.

She curtsied before Queen Danella. "My queen, I am feeling unwell. May I—"

"Go rest, my dear," the queen said. "It has been a difficult day. Earl Cassius's slaves will have us well attended."

Lady Cassius beckoned over a slave girl. "Odetta will lead you to the house-slave quarters." Iylea bowed her head. Odetta approached, her bronze skin glowing. Something in her pale, mint-green eyes unnerved her. Stifling a shiver, Iylea met Laeden's gaze as Odetta led her past his seat to exit the showroom.

They returned to the atrium before a broad marble staircase. Odetta stretched her arm across the stairwell, barring Iylea's path, a peculiar look in her eyes.

"Soon," Odetta said.

Iylea contorted her brow and leaned closer. "Soon what?"

Odetta shrugged. "That is all he told me to tell you… Soon."

A cold sweat trickled down Iylea's spine, and every hair on her neck stood erect. She opened her mouth to speak, but the words were choked off. She wiped the moisture of her palms on her dress and clenched her fists. "Who told you that?"

Odetta blinked, as if she didn't understand the question.

"Iylea?" Laeden's footsteps clamored off the Cassius atrium until he stopped before the staircase. "Is everything well?"

She stifled a shiver that threatened to shake her entire body. *Laeden can't know…* Iylea couldn't look at Odetta. Keeping her composure, she said, "Everything is fine."

Laeden addressed Odetta. "I would speak with Iylea, alone."

Odetta bowed. "The chambers are up the stairs, to the right, third door on the right."

Iylea nodded, refusing to lift her eyes until Odetta took her leave.

Once they were alone, Laeden wrapped his arms around her. "Everything will be okay."

She let him hold her, knowing he was wrong, but unable to tell him otherwise. She didn't want to believe it herself, but that didn't change the truth. *War. Terrible war. Soon.*

A sudden dizziness struck her.

It's happening again. No. Not here. Not now!

"I know," Iylea said, pulling away from him and turning toward the stairs. She grabbed the railing to steady herself, but it seemed to move with her. "I'm just tired. Overwhelmed by the day's events." She gave him a shy smile, her vision becoming fuzzy around her periphery.

I need to get away from him. He can't know…

Laeden stepped closer and cupped her cheek in his hand. She closed her eyes, sinking into his embrace, praying to the Gods he wouldn't notice what she felt inside.

"Goodnight." He kissed her forehead.

"Goodnight." She spun, and the stairs swayed beneath her. Keeping her feet, she ascended, never looking back at Laeden. She couldn't.

To the right… Her heart exploded within her ribs as if it were too large for her chest. Pressure grew behind her eyes, making her lids feel heavy. She needed to get to her room. Then she'd be safe. Her secret wouldn't be discovered.

Down the corridor… She staggered down the hallway, using the walls to pull herself forward. She was afraid to look through the veil of her mind into the window of the Gods. The pressure behind her eyes grew as if they were being pressed out of her skull from within. *Almost there. Third door on the—*

Iylea caved. Her eyelids snapped shut, unable to open them. It was only when her eyes were closed that she saw what the Gods wanted her to see.

With the hallway of the Cassius villa still visible, black wisps of screaming souls floated like ghosts through the walls to swirl around her like a tempest. A pale man with a crown on his head stepped through the wall—his face gaunt, eyes dead. Black veins slithered down his forehead like rotten vines. Gooseflesh pimpled Iylea's arms as his dreadful gaze and haunting grin fell upon her.

Iylea's scream caught in her throat. She tried to open her eyes but couldn't. She wanted to run, but knew he wasn't there. *He can't hurt me.* Even still, she wanted to run as fast as she could. *I just have to get to my chambers...*

Only two doors away from the haven of her room, she fell to all fours. She struggled to her feet, but cloaked in black, a figure leaned against her door, waiting—always waiting. His red eyes peered at her from under his hood.

"You?" Iylea's voice trembled.

"Your abilities have progressed beyond my expectations."

Iylea swallowed hard enough to choke on her tongue. She wanted to run, but the storm of souls and the haunting man with the crown surrounded her. She fought to lift her eyelids, to look away from the red-eyed man, but it was impossible.

His bony finger stroked down her cheek. A tear streaked from the corner of her eye, following his touch.

"Don't be afraid, my child," the God said. "Together we will make right all that is wrong in this world. The Creator's Reckoning comes. Soon. We will meet again. Face-to-face."

With a flash, they were all gone—the red-eyed God, the skeletal king, and his ghastly army. Her eyes opened, and she saw clearly again. Iylea whipped her head back and forth, scouring the corridor for any witnesses to her ordeal.

She was alone.

The pain behind her eyes persisted, but she forced herself to her feet and entered the slave quarters. Limping inside, she closed the door behind her and collapsed onto the bed.

Safe...

She yearned for Laeden, but he couldn't help her. No one could. No one could know. Her sight was her curse. Her burden to bear.

No one can know, she reminded herself. *No one.*

CHAPTER 11

OMENATION

Zephyrus VI

Stockhelm

The rain slowed as the storm traveled past. Soaked to the bone, Zephyrus shivered, his teeth chattering uncontrollably. As warmth fled his body, so too did his desire to fight. Exhausted but unable to sleep, his eyes closed, but all he saw was Patrus's fallen form. He shook the thought away, only for it to be replaced by the gash in Threyna's throat.

How long before I suffer the same fate?

The door to the barracks swung open, the light from within illuminating part of the training square. One guard strode out, a different one than those that strung him up. He looked around conspiratorially before pulling a curved metal tool from his cloak. He crept close.

"I'm Saulus," the guard whispered. "I'm getting you out."

"Getting me out?" Zephyrus couldn't believe it. With large eyes, high cheekbones, and a pointed chin, Saulus didn't look like a god, but he must have been sent by one. Zephyrus forced himself to his feet while Saulus made his way around him to break the chains of the manacles securing him to the palus.

"Gratitude," Zephyrus said while Saulus wedged the metal tool between one of the links of the chain binding him.

"This is gonna hurt, but it'll be over soon," Saulus said. He torqued the metal tool, tightening the chain of the manacles. Zephyrus grunted as iron bit into his wrists and yanked his back into the palus. With a snap, the chain broke, and the tension holding him captive released. Saulus's eyes darted side to side as if to make certain no one saw, but no alarms were raised.

Zephyrus sighed in relief. "What now?" He scoured the training square, searching for an avenue of escape. The moon's persistence outlasted the dark clouds, shining light through the thinning shrouds, but Zephyrus didn't see any way out.

Saulus reached back and cast the metal tool over the cliff. The tool of his freedom disappeared into the night.

"Time to set you free," Saulus said.

Zephyrus turned to thank him when the edge of a dagger caught the gleam of the moon. Zephyrus attempted to secure Saulus's wrist, but too late. The dagger sliced across his bare chest, crossing another slash he suffered earlier that day. Zephyrus stumbled back, but Saulus advanced. "Guards, help! He's trying to escape!"

"Bastard!"

Saulus thrust again, but this time, Zephyrus seized hold of Saulus's wrist. The doors to the barracks burst open, and half a dozen guards advanced with swords drawn. Saulus wrenched his wrist free and reared back to stab again, but Zephyrus punched Saulus across his pointed chin. The thin man teetered. Zephyrus launched himself at Saulus. He seized the blade and tore the hilt from Saulus's grasp. Zephyrus stabbed him in the stomach. Again and again, Zephyrus reared back with short, sharp punches into Saulus's midsection. Blood spouted from his mouth as the would-be assassin fell limp. Still. Cold.

Dead.

The other guards pointed their blades, demanding Zephyrus to drop his. He let the bloody dagger fall from his red hands. The pouring rain couldn't wash away the death staining his bare flesh fast enough.

One guard, the size of a house, stepped forward; his face hid behind a thick brown beard that concealed all but his beady eyes and bulbous nose. "By the Gods. Send for Earl Cassius."

Zephyrus allowed himself to breathe… *Still alive. But for how much longer?*

Zephyrus was bound again, for perhaps the fifth time that day. Given a loincloth, he was escorted through the now-empty barracks, up the stairs, through the villa, and into a large showroom. He stood beneath high, arched ceilings covered in a mural from end to end. The cavernous room was elevated on the outskirts, with steps descending to the floor where a giant pool with a granite slab at its center sat beneath a sky window. Cassius, his family, the king, queen, princes, guards, and knights sat on the elevated outskirts of the room, while the gladiators stood at its center. All around the circular room, jaws stretched to the floor.

Cassius wheeled on Laeden. "This is your idea of a gift? A fighter who can't be controlled is no gladiator."

Laeden was speechless, but the gladiators, standing in a line at the center of the showroom, muttered amongst themselves.

Liario emerged from behind Cassius. "Perhaps a quick death is the only fitting solution."

"What's happened?" Cassius's daughter asked, examining Zephyrus, covered in blood.

"This slave killed one of my guards after trying to escape," Cassius said for all to hear. "And an example will be made of him."

"An example, indeed," his daughter said. Her full lips parted in a smile of straight white teeth. She tossed her waves of chestnut hair over her shoulder as she twisted an amethyst ring about her finger with her thumb.

She inspected him how a craftsman might admire a useful tool, or how a dog might a piece of meat. "He escaped his bindings and killed a trained, armed man. And you would execute him? Father, this is what we do. We are lanistas! I would make an example of him, yes, but one to follow. Doctore…"

A dark-skinned man standing straight and tall, a leather whip in hand behind his back, approached the dais, head bowed. "Yes, Domina?"

"Could we not make use of a man with such skills?"

"Discipline can be taught," the doctore said. "Obedience can be trained. I can forge him into something of worth if you command."

Zephyrus inhaled sharply. *Something of worth? Something of worth! Even their slaves are brainwashed.*

"He led the slave outbreak," Liario said. "There's no disciplining this dog. He called himself a Prophet of Celestia! You said, 'If he mutters a word of freedom, he will be executed.' Kill him, my earl, and be done with it."

Zephyrus's muscles tensed. Laeden's lips drew to a hard line, but he gave no objection.

"Enough!" Cassius barked. He turned to the king and queen. "I apologize for such ill diversions."

"No apology necessary," the queen said. "He should be executed. Not for who or what he is, but his actions."

Laeden's nostrils flared. He bit his lip, rising to his feet. "Might I suggest an alternative, Lentulis? We are all followers of the Six, but we have yet to ask them for their counsel. Ignoring blasphemous prophecies and heresy, why not let the Gods decide his fate?"

Zephyrus glared at Laeden, disbelieving that this was his form of aid in the matter.

"An omenation," the king said. "The only appropriate recourse. But what question do we pose the Gods, and how shall we see it measured?"

"I would like to measure his skill with a blade," Cassius's daughter said.

"Very well, Nallia," Cassius said. "If he wins, he is worthy of training. If he dies, then..." He shrugged. "All in favor?" The cavernous room echoed with cheers.

Zephyrus swallowed the growl forming in his throat. Laeden had given him an opportunity to prove to these people that he was *worth* more to them alive than dead. It wasn't fair. It wasn't right. Yet it was the best he was likely to receive. Again, his life hung on the whims of Gods and the balance of fate, but if he had steel in hand, he had a chance.

Laeden gave Zephyrus the slightest of nods. Another chance to stay alive.

Fate… what a cruel jape.

"Who will stand against him?" Cassius's daughter, Nallia, asked.

"I will." Lenox stepped from his position along the wall and descended the stairs to stand before the Cassiuses and the royal family. "Let the Gods guide my blade."

Zephyrus's apprehension dissolved, replaced by a wave of determination.

"How fitting," the queen said. "Let us pray."

The queen droned on, calling for the Gods of Valencia to guide the true path of the impending match. An omenation they called it, to discern the will of the Gods. But Zephyrus saw it as fate. He was still alive for this purpose: to see Patrus's murderer put to ground. Wielder, Harbinger, or Herald, he would kill Lenox and avenge his fallen friend.

The queen finished her prayer. The guards undid Zephyrus's manacles while Lenox drew his sword.

Let us see whose Gods are stronger.

Zephyrus—wet, bloody, clad only in a loincloth—stood across from Lenox in his purple-and-gold armor. Eyeing the finely forged steel in Lenox's hand, Zephyrus didn't suppose this was going to be a fair fight.

Laeden drew his blade and descended the stairs. "He may wield my sword."

Cassius stopped him with a raised hand. "He can use mine." Cassius pulled a cheese knife from a nearby servant's platter and tossed it into the air.

The tranquility of the moment shattered as the cheese knife bounced down the steps with the clank of metal on marble. It toppled and spun before coming to a stop at Zephyrus's feet.

Zephyrus eyed the rounded edge. Even the cheese was safe from such a blade.

Cassius lifted his hand. "Begin."

Before Zephyrus could seize the dulled knife, Lenox charged. Lenox hacked down with a savage cut intending to cleave him in two. Zephyrus fell back, creating separation. He scuttled across the floor, pulling himself backwards with his hands to regain his footing. His heart throbbed in his ears. A chorus of disgruntled shouts filled the vaulted room, but Zephyrus was only focused on Lenox's blade, chopping down at him. Sparks flew as steel met marble, narrowly missing Zephyrus's thigh. He managed to his feet, just in time to avoid Lenox's second attack. The blade passed mere hairs away from where Zephyrus was.

"The perfect dodge is just beyond your opponent's reach," reminded a familiar voice.

Lenox continued to press, but Zephyrus's instincts took over. He was no longer the hunted. He was the hunter.

Zephyrus stepped back, allowing the blade to cut the air before him. He moved just enough to dodge, never overextending himself or misjudging the reach of the attack. He continued to back away as Lenox pressed.

Slash, hack, thrust!

Zephyrus evaded each but let Lenox believe he was getting closer to finishing the fight. Lenox was not without skill. His footwork precise, his cuts intentional, he struck in an unpredictable pattern, but Zephyrus was better. Zephyrus backed away, retreating up the stairs toward the Cassiuses to keep space between Lenox and himself.

He will tire. He will make a mistake, and when he does, I will kill him for it.

Lenox lashed out with more frustration behind each swing. Fighting against an unarmed man, Lenox would want to end the fight quickly, but his haste would be his undoing. Stab, slice, slash, chop! Each cut had more fury behind it. Lenox's breathing became short, ragged grunts.

He's losing patience. Wait for him to rush. Wait… Wait…

Lenox charged.

Wait…

Zephyrus rolled beneath an overzealous lunge and claimed the cheese knife. Lenox launched, but Zephyrus side-stepped, slashing across Lenox's cheek. Blood sprayed, causing a red tear to trickle down Lenox's face. Lenox let out a cry and thrashed with his sword. Again, Zephyrus dodged, slipping his heel just behind Lenox's. With a slight shove, the armored guard went down with a thud.

"You will die!" Lenox barked, getting to his feet. He slashed low to high, but Zephyrus pivoted out of the way and countered, nicking Lenox's sword arm in the gap of his leather armor. Lenox followed up with a horizontal slash, attempting to part Zephyrus's head from his shoulders. Zephyrus ducked under the blow and sliced across the inside of Lenox's thigh, dropping him to a knee. Grabbing Lenox's sword arm at the wrist, Zephyrus twisted, forcing the blade from his grasp. He kicked the sword aside and stood over his now-unarmed opponent.

Blood trickled from Lenox's wounds, but his pride suffered the greater defeat.

"You killed Patrus," Zephyrus whispered. "And now you'll die for it." He reached the cheese knife back to deliver the final blow. *Vengeance is mine. Patrus can rest eas—*

His arm froze, suspended in mid-air. He pulled, but he couldn't move. With all his strength, he tried to slam the cheese knife into Lenox's neck, but to no avail. A powerful force jerked his arm backwards, spilling him onto the granite slab.

"I said enough!" The doctore unwound his whip from around Zephyrus's wrist. Zephyrus tried to locate the cheese knife, but he lost it in his fall. Lenox stood, reclaiming his sword, face red with fury.

"Stand down, Lenox," Cassius said. Lenox glared at Zephyrus, shoulders heaving with labored breaths. Zephyrus wasn't ready for the fight to be over yet. He didn't need a dull cheese knife to kill. *For Patrus!* He charged at Lenox.

Not two steps into his attack, the doctore's whip snagged him around the throat with a *snap*. Zephyrus gagged. He coughed, but the tension around his neck didn't relent. He grasped at his throat, but the whip was too tight for his fingers to pry it away. Pressure bulged behind his eyes. His vision faded at the edges. His heartbeat echoed in his ears like a war drum.

"You shoulda quit while you were ahead, Zeph," said a familiar voice. But it wasn't just a voice. He was a person. Patrus stood over him, holding out a hand to help him up. He was younger and more muscled, but

had the same kind eyes. *"Don't worry, kid. I'll teach you everything I know. Everything your old man showed me."*

Zephyrus reached his hand out for Patrus's, but Patrus wasn't there. His peripheral vision blinked out, and everything faded to black.

CHAPTER 12

THE THREE

Nallia

Stockhelm

After the day's excitement, Nallia couldn't sleep. With a cheese knife, Zephyrus not only survived, but would have killed Lenox had he not been restrained by Doctore Auron. Zephyrus had survived countless scenarios that should have killed him. In one day. Regardless of what her father believed, he was a Prophet of Celestia. Never had she seen a fighter with more raw talent than he. The Gods had spoken.

He will be a gladiator of House Cassius.

After the guards dragged Zephyrus to the medicus's chambers, the festivities were brought to an abrupt end. The royal retinue stayed the night, but departed at dawn, leaving Zephyrus to her. Not Lenox, nor her father, not even the queen could overrule the Gods' will.

Zephyrus will be mine.

"You are incorrigible," Father said. "Why can't you let Doctore deal with the slave? Why must you speak with him yourself?"

"He needs to know who he's fighting for," Nallia said. "Didn't you teach me that?" she mocked in a playful tone—enough to disarm, but not so much that she forfeited her upper hand.

"You're more manipulative than the senators," he said, a hint of a smile upon his lips.

"I have to be if I'm to lead the ludus once you become chancellor," Nallia said, knowing how to appease her father.

"I suppose so. If he gives you trouble, see his insufferable nature beaten from him."

Nallia nodded, but doling out beatings was not her way. She left her father's tablinum and traversed the villa to the medicus's chambers.

After her father spent months on tedious campaigning for the chancellorship and equal time neglecting his ludus, Nallia took it upon herself to uphold her forefather's legacy. Their rival lanista, Ebron Brusos, had been jostling for her father's title of Earl and Head Lanista of Stockhelm for the last dozen years. Now he attempted to vault over her father by vying for the chancellorship, but to do so, Brusos's champion would have to beat the Cassius champion in the omenation at the Games of Stockhelm.

Luckily for her father, Nallia did not sit idly by. While he busied himself with speeches, bribes, and concessions, she took a more hands-on approach to the role of lanista.

Regardless of the omenation, Nallia didn't want her family's trade to be lost. With the increased popularity of the tournaments, many amongst the patricians were less inclined to pay for private gladiatorial entertainment. While it had never been more popular amongst the plebs, the patricians possessed the coin needed to remain profitable. Nallia took it upon herself to make sure her gladiators were not just the highest stock, but the most motivated. Her father oversaw them with the whip of discipline, but Nallia realized that men could achieve greater things if prodded by more personal incentives.

For many it was coin; they were the easy ones. A purse to be spent on women, wine, or other desires of baser nature was enough to keep them content. Others, especially those condemned to slavery because their fathers fought on the wrong side of the New Rheynian War, sent that coin to their families. Some wanted to be remembered, and having an artisan carve their likeness into tile after a victory was enough to motivate them to achieve another.

Every man wanted *something,* and Nallia made it her job to discover it and leverage the most out of every man. *Other than Stegavax, that lost cause.* Despite being the Champion of their House, he was uncontrollable, irrational, and lacked an honorable bone in his body. Perhaps that's why Zephyrus interested her so much. The Gods delivered him to her for a reason. But putting a sword in a slave's hand didn't make him a gladiator. Lighting a fire in his heart would.

She walked past the door descending to the barracks and towards the medicus's quarters, where a guard bowed as she entered. The medicus popped his head up from his vials of herbs at her intrusion. His sniveling nose and weary eyes made him appear like a timid mouse. Scanning the room, she found what she was looking for. In the back corner of the medicus's dingy chambers, Zephyrus was chained to a wooden cot.

"Unchain him and leave us," Nallia said, sending the guard into a wide-eyed stammer. "It's okay. He won't harm me. You too," she said to the medicus. Both hesitated but did as ordered.

"I'll be right outside," the guard said, letting himself out.

The door closed behind him, leaving her alone with Zephyrus. His red hair, tied back in a loose bun, contrasted with his fair complexion. Glowing torchlight flickered across his muscled physique and the host of fresh lacerations and old scars that painted his body.

He's no stranger to combat.

Zephyrus stood, rubbing his wrists where the manacles chafed him raw.

"Good morning, Zephyrus."

He examined her but said nothing. He didn't avert his gaze as she expected. *Proud.* His eyes followed her as she sauntered around his wooden cot. *Bold.*

"How are you feeling now that the medicus has tended your wounds?" she asked.

He didn't answer. He barely breathed. He stared at her like a gargoyle forged from stone.

Just get him talking. Men of talent only need to be reminded of their triumphs; that's all it takes to break their dam of silence.

"I hope you have recovered from last night's omenation. Quite the spectacle. A cheese knife versus a gladius." Nallia chuckled. "I doubt Lenox will eat a slice of cheese again."

The gargoyle didn't move.

"You are special," Nallia said, unperturbed by his silence. "The Judges of Celestia know it, the Gods of Valencia know it, and I am not so blind as to stifle that which can burn so brightly. You fascinate me—a Rheynian plucked from Tharseo's Bastion, a Prophet of Celestia. Tell me, how did that come to be?"

He didn't blink. A flush rose to her cheeks. *Gods, how frustrating.*

He hung his head. "I don't know." His voice was soft, like a secret to the wind.

"Care to elaborate further?"

"I don't know," he said louder. "I don't remember anything before the temple."

The enigma continued. "You remember nothing? Surely, there must be—"

"No. Nothing." Zephyrus failed to meet her eyes.

No amount of gold, drink, or pleasures of the flesh would satisfy one who only knew his name. A healer in the northern village of Nesonia used herbs to unlock the secrets of a lost mind. Perhaps she can help? If Nallia could give him back his memory, he would be hers to wield—a true Champion.

"But you received a prophecy?" Nallia asked, stepping around the table, within arm's reach of him. She held out her hand and pointed at her own palm. "Did it hurt?"

Zephyrus held up his bandaged left hand. "I don't remember this one, but this one…" He elevated his right, equally dressed. "Pain lanced through my entire being. But my blood ran, balanced the scale."

"Then you received your prophecy?"

Zephyrus raised an eyebrow. "You're interested in *blasphemous* Celestic rituals?"

"I've always had an interest in the Judges," Nallia said. "Don't tell my father."

Zephyrus snorted but didn't divulge more.

Nallia bit her lip. *If I'm going to connect with him now, without the help of a healer, the Judges are my path.* She tried to remember the prophecies her mother had taught her when she was a girl, but then it came to her. "Out of the darkness, born into the light, to balance the scales of Perillian's plight, a wielder of the lost to summon the three back to the land of the Judges, home to the free."

As proud as she was for remembering the prophecy, Zephyrus gave no reaction.

"That wasn't my prophecy," Zephyrus said.

Nallia's face fell. "That's the prophecy of the Wielder. I'm sure of it."

Zephyrus's eyes lit up like seeing the sun for the first time. "What are the others?"

Nallia pursed her lips to hold back her smile. She twisted the amethyst ring about her finger, trying to recall. Once upon a time, she knew the prophetic poems like the Facets of Perfection, but she was out of practice.

"Hmm, 'through whispers and visions, the Herald will rise. Communing with Gods to the Judges' delight, a beast will feed upon the unworthy to usher in the age of uncertainty.' That's the Herald. And the Harbinger…" She trailed off when she noticed the consternation on Zephyrus's face. "What's wrong?"

He shook his head. "Nothing… the Harbinger?"

She narrowed her eyes but didn't press him. "The Harbinger… 'From the depths of hell to glory on high, the chain that connects will no longer bind. When rain does not fall and crops do not rise, the harbinger has come. The Age of the End is nigh.'"

Zephyrus's face paled beneath his red beard. Waking up to a prophecy, being swept into slavery, and remembering nothing that came before… Nallia pitied him.

Sullen as he was, Nallia feared she'd said something wrong. "Are you okay?"

"Fine," he said, but his eyes remained downcast. "It's just…" He took a deep breath. "Patrus said my prophecy contained words and phrases from each of the Three. I suppose I hoped for answers instead of more questions."

Each of the Three? She hadn't thought it possible, but this made him *more* interesting.

"Fate can be cruel," she said. "But it's not absolute. You have more control over your fate than you might think. These prophecies, they're just holes in the future, waiting to be filled. If your prophecy contains elements of each of the Three, it sounds like you are destined for greatness, regardless. But what you do with that greatness is up to you."

Zephyrus frowned. "Patrus said something similar."

"Sounds like a smart man," Nallia said with a smile. "Where is he now?"

The defeated look in his eyes told her all she needed to know. *He's dead.*

She grit her teeth. "I'm sorry, Zephyrus."

Silence.

Idiot. Keep him talking. "Patrus—who was he?"

Zephyrus snorted again. "That's the worst part… I don't remember. And the only thing I have left of him is…" His eyes went wide again. "Burn me, I must have dropped it when the guard attacked me."

"When you tried to escape?" Nallia asked.

"I didn't try to escape!" Zephyrus's soft voice became as cold and cruel as iron. "Saulus broke my manacles, shouted that I was trying to escape, then tried to kill me."

Nallia bit her tongue in thought. *Saulus… but why?* "Because you're one of the Three?"

Zephyrus shrugged.

"What did you drop?" Nallia asked.

"It's gone," Zephyrus said. "Probably for the best…"

Nallia nodded, not wanting to pry any further. She'd gathered what she came for and learned a few interesting tidbits along the way. She placed her hand on his shoulder and looked him in the eye.

"Zephyrus, I will find you a healer who can help with your memories. And from now on, one of the guards I trust will keep an eye on you just in case someone else attempts the same thing as Saulus."

Zephyrus's brow narrowed. "Why? Why are you helping me?"

Nallia smiled. "Because everyone deserves to know who they are."

"But—"

"But nothing," Nallia said, seeing the stone shell fall from the gargoyle. "I will be back, and I'll bring answers."

CHAPTER 13

THE DOCKS

Laeden V

Salmantica

Laeden didn't feel good about leaving Zephyrus without speaking again, especially considering how his night ended, but his new duties could not wait. There was no time to waste when it came to securing his father's kingdom. He named Markus his lieutenant, and the two began discussing strategy the moment they left Cassius's ludus.

In the first few days, they set to work on garnering support and rallying troops to join the Sentinels' cause. The Revivalists had the upper hand in terms of time, numbers, organization, and ruthlessness. Laeden needed to be resourceful if he were to have any chance of stopping them.

"More potential threats." Markus filtered through parchments delivered by their scouts.

"Credible?" Laeden asked, jotting in his notebook. They had been following up on threats all morning, but only one of the four stops seemed to be an act of the Revivalists. Citizens attempting to help protect their king were becoming difficult to distinguish from those wishing to turn the hysteria into personal mage-hunts.

Markus shrugged. "They all seem credible on paper: an explosive fire in Marstead, stolen crops in Southgrove, a dead body upon the docks."

"Only one," Laeden said. "I suppose that's an improvement."

After a few misleading tips to start the day, they investigated Count Elrod Horne's petition: six dead slaves in his apothecary. Laeden expected to find bodies, but he didn't anticipate five of them being children.

"Anything would be better than that," Markus said, looking up from his scroll.

"I don't know," Laeden said, thinking of what would have become of his father had Aelon not given him the information to stop the Revivalists' plot. Laeden kept Aelon's name secret, even from Markus. Until he was certain Cassius's ludus was secure, he didn't want Markus's knowledge to jeopardize Aelon. Laeden was to meet Aelon under the docks at low tide, around noon, but he would have to go alone.

Laeden observed the sun's position in the sky. *Almost noon.* "Where to now?"

Markus scanned the scroll of petitions. "Closest to the docks."

Now is as good a time as any. "Why don't we split up?" Laeden said. "We'll cover more ground. I'll take the docks. You investigate the explosion in Marstead. We'll reconvene at Sentigard before the nightly rains."

With a salute, Markus made his way east towards the outskirts of the city to the borough of Marstead. Laeden pulled up the hood of his travel-worn cloak to cover more of his face. His beard had grown thick in the past week, further disguising his visage, but he was involved in a dangerous game, and it was best to play it safe. Beneath his cloak, he wore boiled leather armor, a short sword, and a dagger. Now that his title of captain of the Sentinels was public knowledge, any Revivalist grunt aiming to climb the ranks could target him, so every possible precaution needed to be taken.

Laeden strode along the Street of Silk, home to the finest textile shops of Salmantica, but the well-swept cobblestone streets and the fanciful storefronts did little to comfort him. Safety no longer existed. The Revivalists' ranks would be swollen with the rich and poor alike.

The Street of Silk emptied into the Gilded Gauntlet, the statue of the first king, Damascus Drake, erected at its center. But the circular road of commerce was better known as the Haunted Hollow. Before the end of the war, hundreds of mages were nailed to Six Arrowed Stars on these very stones. He'd been spared the sight, but he heard the screams all the way from Sentigard. The memory reminded him of the children's bodies strewn about the apothecary floor. Their young faces marred with terror as life fled from them. Another six dead.

All for one mage to be exiled.

If Laeden didn't succeed, the Haunted Hollow would scream again.

"You have to stop them," Iylea had said, her eyes wet with fear.

He would protect her, defend his father, and uproot the Revivalists. *I must. At any cost.*

He arrived at the docks to discover what he could about the body that had washed ashore. The docks, as always, were busy. Imports, exports, ferries to and from, and always a toll to be collected. The docks were home to the greatest swindlers in New Rheynia.

The Vigiles of the city watch who first arrived at the scene were joined by their commander, Heclan Allos.

"My prince." Heclan removed his helm and bowed to greet Laeden. Despite the smoky gray of his temples, he bowed deep and long—a sentiment often abbreviated when honoring Laeden. As he inclined his head, the crow's feet framing his deep-set dark green eyes creased deeper.

"Good day, Commander," Laeden said.

"I wish it were so," Heclan said. He gestured for Laeden to follow him and led him past the fisheries to the lighthouse where the body was kept. "We cannot ascertain if the murder is linked to the Revivalists, but there is something you should see. The fisherman that found the body cooperated, answering all our questions. We did not hold him, but he can be found for further questioning if you believe the Revivalists may be behind the murder."

Laeden nodded. "Anyone know who he is?"

"We wheeled the body around on a cart," Heclan said. "Asked any who passed if they recognized the man, but no one had seen him before."

"You and your men have done fine work," Laeden said. As they approached the lighthouse door, a Vigile of Heclan's Cohort Prefectus hurried to open the door for Laeden.

Walking inside, it took a moment for Laeden's vision to adjust to the change in lighting. Blinking away sunspots, his vision refocused as Heclan led Laeden to a storeroom off the staircase that led up to the top of the lighthouse.

Heclan opened the door to the storeroom. "Prepare yourself, my prince. Something about the body isn't quite right."

"What do you mean?" Laeden asked as he entered.

The body, wrinkled and pruned, was slumped in a one-wheeled cart with two rear legs. Laeden approached, standing over the desiccated body, a deep slit carved into its forehead.

"He didn't receive that from Aquarius's wrath," Laeden said, lifting his index finger to his own forehead as he examined the man.

"Indeed," Heclan said. "Drowned men usually bloat in their time at sea. It's as if all his blood was drained from him."

Laeden screwed up his lip. "Some sort of ritualistic sacrifice?"

Heclan shrugged. "That's not all." He nodded at the Vigiles.

The two city watchmen lifted the Helm's sleeves, turned his arms over, and put them down. Next, they pulled back his ripped cloak to reveal his bare chest, but aside from wrinkled skin not brought on by old age, Laeden didn't notice what Heclan was alluding to.

"No brands," Heclan said. "None."

The Treaty of 940 branded every Helm on every isle of New Rheynia. Salmantica, Valtarcia, or Stockhelm—all were branded. But this man's lack of a mark meant only one thing.

"How did a Klaytonian end up here?" Laeden thumbed the scruff of his beard.

Klaytos was a span south of Stockhelm's most southern border. If a body had washed up on Stockhelm's shores, he wouldn't have thought much of it. But for the body to drift all the way to the Salmantic harbor was beyond unlikely. Considering the condition of the body and the lack of bloating, Laeden searched for possibilities in which the Klaytonian man's murder didn't pertain to the Revivalists.

"You have to stop them." Iylea's voice resounded in his ear.

Six save me, I'm falling into the same trap as everyone else. I can't blame every cloud in the sky on the Revivalists' plots.

Laeden shuffled his feet. "Coincidence, or do you suspect the Revivalists' involvement?"

Heclan heaved a deep sigh. "In my line of work, nothing is a coincidence, but Six save us all—Revivalist or not, whoever did this is dangerous."

Laeden nodded. "Have a medicus do a full examination. Perhaps we can derive how this was done. But, if the Revivalists are behind this, I have little doubt they will do so again."

"Very well, my prince. Any specific medicus?" Heclan asked.

It was a sound question. If Laeden gave this body to a medicus in league with the Revivalist movement, he would learn no more from it than if he sent it back to sea, but he didn't know who he could trust. He would start where he was most vulnerable—the Prefectus Medicus of the royal family.

"Bring him to Sentigard," Laeden said. "Be on the lookout for any unmarked Klaytonians, anyone with stab wounds to the forehead, or people drained of blood."

Heclan bowed, and Laeden took his leave.

With his mind racing, he set off to meet Aelon. He exited the lighthouse, navigated the busy docks, and descended onto the beach, where Aelon waited beneath the docks in the wake of the receding tide. Aelon's back was to him, his hooded cloak covering him.

As Laeden approached, Aelon turned to meet him, but the figure was not Aelon. Laeden seized the pommel of his short sword and jabbed his finger at the man. "Who are you?"

The man held his hands up to reveal empty palms, startled by Laeden's outburst. Surveying the rest of the docks to make sure no one else waited to take him unaware, Laeden drew his short sword.

The man dropped to his knees and pulled back his hood. "No, please! Chimera's breath, he said you could help me. Please?" Gray hair hung in a tangled web past his ears, his eyes wide with terror.

"Who said?"

"I don't know his name," the man pleaded. "He just said you'd protect me if I gave you information."

Aelon...

Although Laeden didn't appreciate Aelon making promises on his behalf, perhaps this would be safer. He sheathed his sword and advanced to yank the man to his feet.

"That depends on the information." The man nodded, blinking, trying to gather the words to speak. "Let's start with your name."

"Gareth." His voice trembled.

"And why, Gareth, should I protect you?"

Gareth swallowed, looking down at his feet as the waves rolled in. "I was with the Revivalists..." He backed away, flinching as if Laeden had reared to strike. When he didn't, Gareth continued. "We didn't think they'd be like this. Didn't think they'd kill people. Just thought they wanted change, ya know?" Gareth put his face in his hands. "We were against the mage getting exiled, but we never signed up for... this."

How many idealists were roped into the Revivalists' cause? How many remained out of fear of reprisal?

If Aelon could help Laeden find those who might turn against the Revivalists, perhaps the Sentinels could discover who was behind their schemes. This war would not be fought with swords and shields but words and promises. It wasn't Gareth's fault he got ensnared in the Revivalists' ideals. Laeden imagined there would be many more like him who deserved a second chance. Punishment wouldn't be justice. Getting them to fight on the right side, the honest side—*that is justice.*

"I will protect you," Laeden said, "but you will tell me everything you know about the Revivalists. Everything."

CHAPTER 14

THE FERRYMAN

Threyna
Salmantica

Threyna's gloved fingers traced the scar across her throat as her other hand loosened the purse from her belt. With its heft in her palm, she wondered how little it would have cost to make the ferryman betray his own people. As he held out his greedy palms, she doubted he felt any guilt over the lives he'd condemned to slavery.

Part of her longed for the freedom of that selfishness. It would have made things easier. But the other part of her knew—that selfishness, that ease with which treachery came—that was a fate worse than death. If all she wanted was numbness, she might as well have let the slaver slit her throat, or just waited in Klaytos for the Skeleton King to consume her. But she wouldn't lay down and die or become a heartless brigand living only for herself. She would fight.

Standing on the shore beside the quiet docks in the pre-dawn light, she tossed her purse to the ferryman. He caught it, testing its weight by shifting it from hand to hand. The precious stones within rattled against one another.

"This isn't gold," the ferryman said. He opened the purse to find the bright green gemstones. "What is this?"

"Viridite from the limestone Gullies of Rheynia," Threyna said. "It absorbs and retains light. Far more valuable than gold. You'll be the only one on this side of the world with it."

She hoped that was true. If it wasn't, that meant she had even less time than she thought.

The ferryman plucked one stone from the others and held it before his eye. His smile shone brighter than the moonlight that guided their evening excursion through the low-tide tunnel in the Hylan Mountains.

Placing it back into the pouch, he bowed his head at Threyna. "Pleasure doing business."

Threyna ground her boot into the sand. Blood—her blood—stained the leather. Zephyrus held her as she died. The horror painted on his face haunted her. It needed to be worth it. *She* needed to be worth it.

"You did what had to be done, Threyna," Paxoran, the God of Peace, said in her mind. *"Claim the Treasures. Together, we will stop the Skeleton King."*

Threyna gulped. He had not led her wrong in the time since he began speaking to her. If not for him, Threyna never would have survived the Skeleton King's attack on the Warlocks of Sage. Tyrus, Erowen, and everyone else were likely dead, joined to the One True God in eternal undeath. Paxoran had spared her that and led her to the Arcane Templar to learn where the Treasures she needed to defeat the Skeleton King were hidden. Paxoran gave her a way, a hope at defeating the Skeleton King—for good this time.

The Elders of the Templar didn't understand. Neither did Patrus or Zephyrus. They rejected her. They *made* her choose this way. They didn't see, didn't comprehend. What good was reclaiming their motherland from the Rheynians if every soul was under the Skeleton King's control? She needed the Treasures more than Zephyrus, more than the Warlocks, or the Templar. There were monsters worse than Drakes and Helixuses, and it was up to Threyna to kill him.

Again.

She just wished she didn't have to do it alone.

The ferryman whistled a tune while preparing his boat to sail back to Klaytos, bearing none of the guilt that burdened her shoulders.

"Why did you condemn your own people?" Threyna asked.

She couldn't let it go. She needed her heart, mind, and Inner Throne right if she were going to stop the Skeleton King. Any affirmation that the collateral damage she'd caused was somehow deserved would give her some semblance of peace.

The ferryman cocked an eyebrow. "My people? Burn me, you think all Helms share the same beliefs?" He spat into the foaming waves. "Do all Rheynians get along?"

She closed her eyes and traced the scar along her throat. The weight stooping her shoulders and drawing the corners of her lips downward grew heavier.

"All sacrifices will be redeemed," Paxoran said. *"For now, do as you must."*

She wanted to believe she didn't have a choice, but part of her wondered—did she have to separate herself from the Templar? Was telling the ferryman to warn the slavers about the ritual at Tharseo's Bastion her only option? What about poisoning Zephyrus's and Patrus's tea? Or forging a note to misdirect them toward King Varros if the ferryman failed to bring the slavers?

"You cannot let him leave," Paxoran said. *"A loose end. Besides, you must consume."*

Threyna lifted the sleeves of her cloak to examine her left arm. Between her sleeve and her leather gloves, black veins slithered down her arm like corrupted snakes—the byproduct of using the cursed blood magic. She needed to feed, or it would devour her.

"He doesn't know anything," Threyna channeled to Paxoran. *"He won't stop us."*

"Consume him."

"I can just siphon a little," Threyna said. *"I don't need a whole soul—"*

"Threyna… All of him." Paxoran's tone inflected the last of his patience.

Threyna sighed, tugging the gloves from her fingers one by one. As the ferryman prepared to shove his rowboat past the break, Threyna called out. "One more thing."

The ferryman inclined his head, and before his eyes could focus on her, her dagger toppled end over end through the air and thudded into his forehead. He staggered in the surf, reached for the side of his rowboat, and fell face first into the sea.

Threyna dragged her feet as she strolled to the ferryman's corpse in the shallows. The cold water numbed her toes but did little to assuage her grief. Despite all the death she'd doled out, the calluses surrounding her heart never thickened. Tapping into her Inner Throne, she sat herself at the center of her power. Within the temple of her mind, she was a queen of cataclysm, a goddess of destruction; a body's blood, bone, and soul were hers to command.

She lifted the ferryman from the sea and drew in breath. Her Inner Throne opened its doors to his departing soul, but instead of escaping to the afterlife, his soul—his essence—became the sustenance of her survival. Blood fled his body through the wound in his forehead, evaporating into a mist that Threyna inhaled. The ferryman's blood healed the poorly closed wounds she'd sustained at Tharseo's Bastion. As his body desiccated before her, she yanked her dagger free from his forehead, reclaimed her Viridite glowstones, and released him to the ocean's rising tides.

"Now we can be on our way," Paxoran said.

Threyna resheathed her dagger, tied her pouch of gemstones, and admired her hand. The black vines that had slithered down her forearm abated to her elbow. The cuts on her palms from the Seers' sacrifices sealed shut, leaving only a callused line. She prodded the scar where the slaver had slit her throat. Only dense tissue remained.

It wasn't the first time she had died and defied death—only the latest. By using the Skeleton King's blood magic to siphon the vitality of the other patrons and slavers at Tharseo's Bastion, she had restitched her open throat and saved her life. But every time she went to such extremes, she felt like a part of her died and never came back.

Perhaps that's why the Skeleton King is the way he is.

Her sister, Laela, had left her with the Warlocks and set off to find a cure for the curse coursing through their veins. Threyna had wanted Laela to stay, to buy into the Warlocks' war against the Valencians who stole their home and enslaved their people, but Laela, for all her martial prowess, never wanted to fight. She did what she had to in order to escape Rheynia, but she never *wanted* to fight. She had no use for the Skeleton King's cursed blood magic and sought a cure.

While Threyna doubted a cure existed, she was glad her sister left when she did. There was still a chance she was alive out there, somewhere. If she had stayed, if she had been at the City of the Judges when the Skeleton King attacked, Laela's soul might have been taken by the Skeleton King too.

Threyna's fingers fell from her throat as the ferryman's boat drifted out to sea, and his body sank into the undercurrent. The rowboat shrank into the horizon, and so too did Threyna's assurance that her ends justified the means. She hoped Zephyrus would be able to forgive her, but if the Skeleton King wasn't stopped, none of it mattered.

I did what I had to. Zephyrus and Patrus will have to fend for themselves.

The sun crested the horizon. Orange rays bled across the placid sea to point at her, as if raising an alarm of her endless crimes. She needed to leave. She needed to claim the Vykane Blade before anyone from the Templar learned of her treachery.

She pulled her hood up, turning away from the rising tide, the waking harbor, and her mounting guilt. She set off toward the tolling bell tower of Salmantica's Temple District, hoping that in the end, when all this was over, she could watch the sun rise without death on her mind, rot in her veins, or guilt in her heart.

CHAPTER 15

What Would a Champion Do?

Fenyx
Stockhelm

The ceaseless prickling woke Fenyx. Again. He rose from his cot, scratching at the burned skin along his left arm in a fruitless effort to end the tingling that greeted him every morning.

To the chain with these straw cots.

He paced within his cell, flexing his burned hand to pump life into the stiffened joints. The other gladiators were sleeping, but dawn approached, and with it his morning delivery.

Fenyx leaned against his cell door, grasping his hands around the bars. Today was a new day, another opportunity to prove his valor. The Games of Stockhelm would soon be upon them, and he would be damned if they passed absent his victory. Every day of training was a gift of the Judges, an opportunity that would not be squandered.

Footsteps approached signaling the start of his day. Auron's shadow graced his door, and with his presence, the delivery of relief. A hand shorter and two stone lighter than Fenyx, Auron drew a pouch from his pocket and passed it between the cell bars.

"Dreams still elude you?" the former gladiator asked.

Fenyx dug into the parcel, tore a strip of whiteroot from the stalk, and shoved it into his mouth. *At last.* Relief would soon be delivered.

"Dreams are for those too lazy to seek glory." Fenyx chewed the thick root. "How do the recruits fare—any future Champions who would stand in my way?"

"They will be what they will be," Auron said. "Focus on yourself and your future glory."

Fenyx grunted. "What about this Zephyrus—the Prophet of the Return?"

"Lower your voice," Auron said through bared teeth. "Better yet, speak not of the Judges or the Return. Zephyrus is a man like any other, regardless of prophecy. Now, set mind to purpose. I will greet the rising sun with prayers."

"And who shall hear them?"

Auron gave him the same reproachful glance he always did whenever Fenyx asked. It was an honest question. Did he really pray to the Six of Valencia? Or did he still cling to the Judges in secret?

Fenyx hadn't uttered a prayer since the day he was captured. Some fools believed the Six killed the Judges, and the only way for Celestics to bring them back was to overthrow their Rheynian captors. This nonsense that began at Tharseo's Bastion kept Celestics grasping at false hopes. The Wielder, the Harbinger, the Herald—all of it was complete rubbish.

The truth: the Judges delivered them into the hands of the Valencians to serve penance for their sins. Once they earned the Judges' forgiveness, their enslavement would end. Some lit candles in silent prayer for the Judges' mercy, but Fenyx did not. He kept his idols—the last possession of his childhood—hidden away, but Fenyx didn't seek forgiveness. He would prove his worth in the blood of the slain.

Fenyx gnawed on the whiteroot as he moved around his cell, rolling his head to loosen his neck, and reaching his arms up to open his back and shoulders. Shagren stirred in the cell across from him. He ran his meaty fingers through his tangled reddish-brown hair and matching barbaric beard.

Shagren was Rheynian but enslaved all the same. The bastard sons of those who fought on the losing side of the war were given an opportunity to redeem the sins of their fathers as gladiators of the arena. Fenyx didn't pity men like Shagren; he was second only to Stegavax in terms of victories in the arena. Here, bastards could rise higher than anywhere else in the world.

Give me a life of glory as a slave to a bottom-feeding pleb any day.

Shagren leaned on the bars, waiting for Auron's call as well. He spat in Fenyx's direction. "Watchya lookin' at?"

Fenyx continued to stare him down, chewing on the whiteroot with one side of his mouth. "I'm looking upon your face… I want to remember how it looks before we meet on the sands. Before your eyes bruise and your nose breaks—while you still have teeth between your mats of fur."

Shagren shook the bars of his cell, cursing and spitting.

"Silence!" Auron's voice bellowed through the barracks. "Cease babbling tongues and set minds to purpose. Rise from sleep and see dreams of glory become reality."

Auron released them from their cages to assume formation in the training square. Once released from his cell, Fenyx strode past the cells of the barracks. All empty, except one.

He stopped at the last door on the right—the Champion's cell. Home to Stegavax, it was twice the size of the other cells with a door for privacy instead of open cell bars, a double-wide feather bed, and a small, barred window allowing fresh air into the room.

Fenyx peeked inside. Stegavax lay in bed, one arm behind his head, feet elevated.

Fenyx shook his head. *When I become Champion, I won't rest on past laurels. I will train harder than ever—perfection knows no bounds.*

He left Stegavax and exited the barracks.

The training square welcomed him. He imagined the roar of the crowd every time he graced the sands. The purple of twilight gave way to burnt oranges as the sun crested the eastern horizon, cutting like a spear through the sky to light his path to glory. The rest of the men stood in formation, awaiting Auron's direction.

Auron paired off each of the proven gladiators to spar against one another while he trained the recruits on the basics of footwork and swordsmanship. As Fenyx had hoped, Auron paired him with Shagren. Once armed with their wooden weapons, training began.

Fenyx smiled, lifting the two-handed great sword in his burned hand. He swept it around in giant arcs before leveling the blade at Shagren's face, holding the sword in one hand as proof of his strength.

Doctore's whip cracked, and the world went silent and still. Everything happened in slow motion as the Burning—the unquenchable thirst for blood and the insatiable drive for victory—took control.

Shagren charged like a crazed bull, swinging his dual axes with fury. Fenyx sidestepped the first and ducked under the second. The wood whisked through the air but found no connection. Shagren kicked up a cloud of sand and chopped upward with one axe, then downward with the other. Fenyx raised his arm to shield his eyes from the sand and reared back to avoid the axes.

Fenyx swung the two-handed great sword in a wide arc, forcing Shagren to retreat. With the advantage of reach, Fenyx's blade cleaved through the air again. Shagren raised his axes to block, but the momentum of Fenyx's strike shoved Shagren off balance. Fenyx closed the distance and struck with the pommel of his sword. The hilt crashed into Shagren's cheek.

Stunned and unable to defend himself, Shagren stumbled backwards. With a grunt, Fenyx seized Shagren by his belted pauldron and dropped the crown of his head into Shagren's nose.

Cartilage crunched.

Shagren recoiled, but Fenyx sliced horizontally across Shagren's chin. Blood spurted from his mouth like water from the Stormburn Geyser. The axes fell from Shagren's hands as he crumpled to the sand.

Fenyx placed the blade over his shoulder and looked at Shagren's cronies—Wardon and Aelixo. They stared as their woozy leader spat blood.

"Medicus!" Auron called for Shagren's aid.

Fenyx lifted his burned hand up to the sky as if celebrating victory in the arena. "Is there another who would stand against me?" This caught Domina's attention. She and a guest stared down at him from their place upon the balcony. *Yes, take notice of your future Champion.* Fenyx had more to prove—the Burning wasn't sated by the quick victory.

"I will stand against you." Stegavax emerged from the barracks, growling. "Bring me swords." Long braids of hair hung behind his massive frame. Black eyes glowered atop a bestial smile of pointed teeth. Once, his ferocity intimidated Fenyx, but no longer. Stegavax would be the Burning's next victim.

"Doctore!" Domina called from the balcony. "Send Fenyx to the villa."

Auron nodded and gestured to the guards.

Fenyx set his feet. *No... Why now?*

Stegavax laughed as Nortus, the burly guard, hauled Fenyx away from glory. He wanted to fight. If he defeated Stegavax, everyone would see he was ready to assume the mantle of Champion.

Why am I being summoned now?

He released his great sword and curled his burned fingers into a fist.

Act like a Champion, he reminded himself.

Nortus returned him to the barracks and escorted him up the stairs to the villa. Retracing their footsteps to the showroom the gladiators had fought in the night before in honor of the royal family, Fenyx released his slave's anger and assumed his Champion's stoicism.

As they entered, Domina, her bodyslave, and the other woman from the balcony waited on the dais.

"You may leave us, Nortus," Domina said, plucking a grape from the bodyslave's tray. Nortus bowed and left.

"Cerberynn, this is Fenyx," Domina said. "He's been training in this ludus since the age of ten."

Fenyx bowed his head, tucking his chin to the left to hide his burns.

Cerberynn sauntered over to him, gliding down the stairs with aethereal grace. As beautiful a woman as he'd ever seen, a shade between the light-skinned Rheynians and the darker complexions of the native Stockhelm people, she approached Fenyx. She reached her hand for his shoulder, caressing his skin as she walked around his good side.

He flinched at her touch but caught himself.

A Champion would not recoil.

He stood tall and stared straight ahead, allowing her to examine him, but something about the way she prowled set him on edge worse than Stegavax's twin gladii ever had.

"He is quite the man now," Cerberynn said in a singsong voice. "I imagine he's worth a hundred times the initial investment. How did these wounds come about?" She gestured to the burns along the left side of his body.

Fenyx's lip twitched, and he shifted his weight from left to right, glancing to Domina for guidance. *Should I respond? What do I say?* He felt more vulnerable than he had wielding a dagger against a Poker's spear.

Domina nodded.

Fenyx swallowed. "My village burned…"

What would a Champion say?

"A boy was burned before he became a man and a gladiator under the roof of House Cassius," Fenyx said, holding his head high.

Cerberynn smiled. "Cleotra, you have him so well trained. I see how he fares in the art of swordsmanship… How well trained is he in the art of women?"

Domina sputtered on a half-chewed grape. "What do you speak of?"

"I love my husband, but sometimes a woman has needs that can't be met by a mere man," Cerberynn said, looking at Fenyx in a way no woman had ever looked at him before.

A bead of sweat formed on his brow. *Be a Champion. Show no fear.*

Cerberynn continued to pace about him until she stood toe to toe with him, gazing up with aquamarine eyes. He felt naked, vulnerable—clad in only his sublingaria and sandals, he wilted beneath her stare.

"Sometimes, a goddess needs a god inside of her," Cerberynn said.

Fenyx tensed. *Is this what it means to be Champion?* Fenyx reviewed every lecture Auron had ever given him on the conduct of a Champion, but came away as empty as a poor Trapper's net.

Domina guffawed in bewilderment. "You can't be serious."

Fenyx wiped the moisture of his palms on his thighs.

Cerberynn turned to her hostess. "Have you never?"

"Have I ever… what?" Domina asked.

"Shared a bed with one of your titans?"

Fenyx choked back a cough. Staring straight ahead, he counted down the moments until he could return to the training square, where he belonged.

"I would never!" Domina spat.

Cerberynn shrugged, sauntering back to Domina.

Fenyx's tension released. *Thank the Judges for Domina…*

"Do with him what you will—or won't," Cerberynn said with a wink. "I had best return to my husband before my lust consumes me." She turned to Fenyx. "I hope we meet again."

Fenyx stood motionless, unsure of what to do or say. So he did nothing, said nothing as the ladies bid their farewells. In all his bouts in Teluvar's fighting pits, with life hanging in the balance, he never felt more uncomfortable than he did in this moment.

Once Cerberynn left, Domina marched down the stairs to stand before Fenyx just as Cerberynn had before. Fenyx stiffened. For a moment, he thought she might hit him. She put her hand on his burned cheek and inspected him with discerning eyes.

What would a Champion do?

Before he could do anything, she shoved his face away, forcing Fenyx to step back.

"Remove him to the barracks."

Fenyx released a full exhale for the first time since arriving in the showroom. Nortus collected Fenyx and returned him to the training square. As his feet graced the sands once again, he was glad to be back where he belonged—where he could trade sweat and blood for glory—where things made sense.

CHAPTER 16

ALLY

Zephyrus VII

Stockhelm

"You don't owe the Arcane Templar anything." Threyna placed Zephyrus's hand over her heart. It raced like horses from an all-consuming fire. "You might not believe in him, but this is real, and *he* is coming. I *have* to stop him… no one else will. Not the Warlocks, not the Templar. Me. And I don't know if I can do it on my own. So please, Zephyrus—will you join me?"

The door crashed into its jamb, startling Zephyrus from his dreams. He whipped around to see the door, but his shackles bound him to his cot in the medicus's chambers. His reality returned to him like a kick to the chest.

No, no, no.

He tried to commit his dreams to memory, but like sand through his fingers, they slipped into obscurity. He closed his eyes and ground his teeth.

What did Threyna say?

"Good afternoon," Nallia said from behind him. "I hope you're resting well despite the accommodations."

"You mean these?" Zephyrus asked, lifting the manacles binding him to the cot. "I hadn't noticed." With his wrists chafed raw and an itch on his nose that even sleep couldn't ignore, he most certainly noticed.

"I trust no one's tried to kill you since my last visit?" Nallia asked.

"Besides the medicus?" Zephyrus asked.

"No one's killin' no one." The medicus shuffled past. "But ya need new bandages or else ya risk infection."

"I'll change his bandages," Nallia said. The medicus opened his mouth to object. "I have watched you do more difficult things a thousand times before. I'll summon you if needed."

The medicus bowed and left the room, muttering to himself along the way.

Nallia grabbed fresh bandages and set them down on the edge of the cot. "You've kept me quite busy today." She slipped something between his fingers. "Found this out by the palus."

The scroll addressed to the king.

The parchment was weathered but still intact. Zephyrus didn't know what to say. After Vykannis's absence and surviving—and nearly killing—Lenox with only a cheese knife, he thought perhaps his prophecy was real. Not just a trick, or a myth to inspire hope. When he realized the scroll was lost, it almost provided him with a sense of comfort. His past didn't matter if he trusted where he was going. Twice now, it'd been removed from him, once by Laeden, and once on his own accord, yet somehow, it found its way back to him.

"Any idea what it means?" Zephyrus asked.

"I didn't read it," Nallia said. "But I don't think anyone else lost a parchment covered in blood exactly where you said you lost something."

"Gratitude," Zephyrus said, unsure if he could trust her. For all he knew, she was one of the Revivalists Laeden asked him to uproot. *She could be just as bad as Lenox, for all I know.* Then again, in a way she was worse; Lenox worked for the slavers. Nallia was one.

"Of course," Nallia said. Beginning with his right palm, she removed the old bandage, washed the wound with wine, and applied a new dressing. "I have a healer coming this afternoon who I hope will be able to help reclaim your memories."

Zephyrus scoffed. She didn't make sense to him—a Valencian who recited Celestic prophecies. A slaver who served him. "What do you want? This isn't charity or goodwill; this is transactional. You want something."

"Don't we all?" Nallia asked with an unnerving smile. She walked around to his opposite hand. "What do you want? Besides your memories." She repeated the same process on his left.

There were many things he wanted. Of course he wanted his memories back. Then he could make sense of these prophecies and his fate. With his memories, he could understand this scroll without having to rely on Laeden or the King. He wished Patrus and Threyna were still alive. He wished Vykannis answered his prayers. And above all, he wished he had killed Lenox when he had the chance.

"Don't dodge the question," Zephyrus said. "What do you want from me?"

She finished wrapping his left palm. "Consider it a gift."

Zephyrus snorted, yanking his hand away from her. "I don't want your *gifts* without knowing the price of them." She put down the bandages and moved close until their noses nearly touched. Her emerald eyes gleamed at his defiance as if she welcomed the challenge.

She hasn't seen anything yet. I will—

"I'm a lanista, Zephyrus. We train men to fight for the honor and glory of the Gods. The price of my gift—I want you to fight for me. Not just because you're without another choice, but because you *want* to."

His nostrils flared. *Because I want to?* "I'm a slave. What I *want* is irrelevant. Bandaging my hands and summoning a healer won't make me *want* to bow and scrape beneath you."

"Yet here you are, beneath my roof," Nallia said, reclaiming the bandages and addressing his chest wound. "I don't know where you come from, but around here, I have a duty to the people of my house. The Facets of Perfection demand…" She stopped her work and cocked her head. "You don't know what the Facets of Perfection are, do you?"

She listed off a series of societal values that were, at best, idealistic fantasies propagating acceptable justifications to drag people from temples, throw them in a wagon, and sell them at auction—as long as they were made to feel like they were contributing to the welfare of society.

"You see, the gladiators demonstrate their strength and determination, but they also contribute to the household, the local establishment, and the pride of the country. The laurels of victory inspire works of beauty—songs, art, and stories that will last for generations. So by me providing you a healer, it's a gift borne of my civic responsibility to bring out the best in you."

"So it's your *civic responsibility* to uphold a society that condemns people to slavery because they worship different Gods?"

A smile broke out across Nallia's face.

Zephyrus growled. "What?"

"You've finally answered my question," Nallia said. "What do you want? Freedom. You're not the first to want that. But equality? That is a first." She placed the bandages down to meet his gaze. "I'll admit, the anti-Celestic movements go too far, and progress is slow. Even with a king as tolerant and accepting as Varros, it's difficult to change people's minds, let alone their hearts. Many fear the Judges that sent you here because of the Disasters that befell Rheynia. The Valencian Gods are jealous, and their wrath swift. The Return… Valencians who believe in it fear it. If Aeryss the Affectionate, Orsius the Wise, and Vykannis the Brave were to return… the Age of The end doesn't exactly sound welcoming."

Zephyrus set his jaw. He didn't like being played for a fool. He didn't appreciate how she prodded him for information. "The Age of The End. If you believe in the Return, why keep me here?"

She pushed a strand of wavy chestnut hair behind her ear. "You are destined for greatness. If you believe in fate and prophecies, then there's nothing I can do to stop you from becoming whatever you will be. If you believe in free will, then I'd hope you'd look upon me with the same kindness I showed you."

Zephyrus licked his lips, wanting to retort, but finding he had none. *Is she being genuine?* He bit his lip. *She's trying to charm me, but I won't fall for it.* "Leaving a lot to chance."

She finished the last of the bandages and walked around the table to admire her work. "There. 'Now ya won't risk infection, eh?'" She impersonated the medicus with a laugh.

Zephyrus didn't join in her laughter.

Nallia cleared her throat. "Some things you can't know. Some may call it 'Leaving it up to chance,' but I think you just have to have faith." She twisted the amethyst ring on her finger. "The healer will be here soon. I hope you remember everything that makes you who you are."

She smiled again. The kind of smile he wished wasn't held up by the backs of slaves. If she was with the Revivalists, or with Saulus, she would have killed him by now. He didn't trust her. How could he? But that didn't mean she couldn't be his ally. At least for now.

CHAPTER 17

THREE NOTES

Danella II

Salmantica

The mongoose won. The latest omenation's result made her wonder if she needed to kill Varros. The Six knew she didn't want to. If she could secure her father's kingdom without having to lose her love, there was little she wouldn't do. But the Gods had spoken, and Varros would live.

For now.

Even without having to orchestrate another assassination attempt, there was much to be done now that Laeden had inserted himself into the mix. She attempted to send Laeden away to live with his grandfather in Northridge. He would have been safe in Valtarcia, far from where he could stick his nose into matters that would only get him into trouble. But now, Varros foolishly named him captain of the Sentinels. And to make matters worse, he was working with a Prophet of Celestia.

She wanted him dead—this one they called the Wielder—but he skirted death, not once but twice. First she sent Saulus, then Lenox—both failed.

Lost to a cheese knife.

Lenox assured her the Prophet wouldn't survive the week, but he failed her again. After leaving Cassius's ludus in Stockhelm, Varros detoured their retinue to Valtarcia, where he rallied the people of his homeland to join

Laeden's Sentinels. The world was conspiring against her, creating more trouble for her while stealing the time necessary to carry out her plans.

After returning to Salmantica, much of her time was spent organizing Count Elrod Horne's black powder operation. A brilliant chemist he might have been, but his organizational skills left much to be desired. Meanwhile, moles within her ranks needed to be dealt with, and the only way to catch a mole was to tell it a lie and wait.

Whoever told Laeden about the assassination attempt on Varros was one of three primary messengers. Despite her careful planning and considerable precautions, a leak posed serious danger. If the Sentinels discovered her involvement, everything would come crashing down. Danella shuddered to think of the look on her husband's face if Laeden exposed her betrayal.

There were a thousand reasons not to get involved with the protestors and lead the Revivalists. Only one reason compelled her, serving the Six—and they would not tolerate the Celestics much longer.

I must exterminate the pests before the Prophets bring about the Return and doom us all.

Danella sat upon the balcony with Varros, admiring all of Salmantica below as the sun set on another day. Varros held his chin between his thumb and forefinger.

What thoughts occupy your mind, my love?

He turned to her with his steely-blue eyes. She took his hand and smiled. The omenation granted him more time in this world, and for that, she was grateful.

A knock at the door.

"Your Grace," Iylea said. "Lady Cerberynn Brusos is here to see you."

"Set her up in the study, and I will join her momentarily. We will watch the nightly rains roll in. Fetch wine instead of tea."

Iylea nodded and took her leave. Danella sighed and gave Varros a kiss on the cheek.

"She knows the omenation will choose the chancellor, right?" Varros asked. "Regardless of how many times she comes by, if her husband loses—"

"It's just a social visit." Danella waved a dismissive hand. "Cerberynn and I are friends."

"Friends who have become much more social now that her husband wishes for office."

Danella gave him another kiss. "She knows."

Her bodyguard, Ser Daenus, escorted her to the study. The study was the highest room on the eastern side of Sentigard's tower with the best panorama of the incoming easterly storm each night. She found the rain soothing, the lightning beautiful, and most importantly—the study was always empty.

They entered to find Iylea setting wine before Cerberynn.

"You may take the rest of the night off," Danella said to Iylea.

Iylea bowed and took her leave, and they got to work.

The glow of the hearth set shadows dancing around them as they sat at a long table facing the impending storm. Danella found the room fitting to their mission. It was their light which would beat back the encroaching darkness, their illumination on which the hopes of the entire kingdom hinged.

"The moles are our biggest problem," Daenus said. "If they are not dealt with, everything could be undone."

"Leave the moles to me," Danella said. "Whoever gave Laeden information will do so again. And when they do, we will strike. A healthy dose of fear in our messengers will straighten the rest out. What else?"

Cerberynn smiled. "As for the Games of Stockhelm, my husband is pleased with Tursos."

"As he should be," Daenus said. "Targarus practically wanted his own kingdom in return for that slave."

Danella cast him a sharp look. "And a kingdom we all shall have once Ebron Brusos is declared chancellor and we restore strong Valencian values to this country."

Cerberynn ignored Daenus as she drank her wine. "I have no doubt Tursos can beat Stegavax. He has become arrogant and slothful in his time as Champion."

"He is still the best in Cassius's ludus," Daenus said.

"If all goes as planned," Danella said, "Stegavax will no longer be breathing at the time of the Games of Stockhelm."

Cerberynn laughed. "I would love to see the look on Cleotra's face when my husband eclipses hers. Tell me, how will you do it?"

Danella pursed her lips. The joy Cerberynn took in this was unbecoming. This wasn't a game. This was life and death. Salvation and damnation.

Daenus spoke in Danella's silence. "Our agents within House Cassius will prod preexisting relational tensions between old rivals. Savages being savages. No foul play or suspicion. Then Tursos just needs to finish whoever Cassius chooses as his second."

"Fenyx," Cerberynn said, "I took measure of him just the other day. Just a hunch, but I believe he has a fear of fire."

Cerberynn laughed as if they'd already won. She didn't see the Wielder fight. She didn't watch him disarm and nearly kill a trained soldier, guided by the Six, before her eyes… but Danella had.

"Unless that new gladiator surpasses him," Daenus said, as if reading her very thoughts.

Cerberynn's smile melted. "New gladiator? Who? From where?"

Danella forced a smile. "He will be tended to."

At least I hope so.

Lenox was a spirited fighter and a passionate ally, but he was outmatched. It would take more than a knife in the night to stop the Wielder's terrible fate. She needed a plan, and the sooner the better, but Laeden's informant was a more immediate threat to her.

They continued down the list of what needed to be done, but already, the company had grown tiresome. She knew this noble mission could not be accomplished by her alone. She endured more of Cerberynn's idle chat until she had nearly drunk herself into a coma. Daenus escorted Cerberynn to a guest room, allowing Danella to get back to work.

She walked down the rows of shelves covered with books from floor to ceiling. At the sixth row, she stopped, walked down six dividing shelves, counted up from the floor to the sixth line of books, and felt for the release button. With a satisfying click, the false drawer built into the shelf opened.

Inside were dossiers of every contact the Revivalists had. Each plan she hatched was borne from this secret shelf. She grabbed her black leather-bound journal. The pages were filled with well-documented instructions telling who to do what, when, where, and how so her underlings could do her bidding while giving her plausible deniability, and limiting those who knew of her involvement.

She sat down with her journal.

Time to trap a mole.

Her three prime messengers were well-placed men. Banis was a baseborn child orphaned by the war and taken in by the Harbormaster. As the apprentice, Banis had access to ledgers with records of every man who stepped foot on the docks. With Banis on her side, her borders were protected by sea. She hoped he hadn't betrayed her.

Danella wrote a note for Banis, instructing him to reduce the tariffs on the newest Revivalist member, Count Elrod Horne. Elrod was in fact already a supporter, although his identity remained anonymous to most. Yet the volatility of his business with the black powder suffocated her faith in him. Not to mention Horne's pride over his lands and income relative to his contributions had become grating. So if Banis were the mole, Horne would take the fall.

Addition by subtraction.

Laegus was another messenger. Dutiful, but that didn't mean loyal. Laegus played a significant role in connecting the Revivalists to the lower merchant class. What they lacked in power and resources they more than made up for in numbers. Having the plebs accept the wave of changes Danella had in place was paramount for the Revivalists' success. If he was the leak, he had the power to rally many and more to the Sentinels' cause.

In her letter to Laegus, she instructed him to provide more resources to the Master at Arms, Atonus Allos, for joining the Revivalists. Atonus had no role in the Revivalists, although she wished he did.

If Laegus had been bought, Atonus would be seized by the Sentinels, letting his tasks fall to his apprentice, Markus Cassius—Laeden's second in command. With his hands filled with added responsibilities, he would be more likely to make mistakes. Atonus would have to plead his case, but that didn't concern Danella. Another win-win scenario.

Her last messenger was the most concerning: Aelon Ironpine—her connection to the knights of Salmantica and the aristocratic merchants. She needed them to create a smooth transition of power to Damascus if Varros needed to be… dealt with.

Aelon's skill and celebrity were invaluable. When he revealed his identity at one of the protests, his passion for Valencianism was so palpable, it encouraged others to do the same. Aelon was the type of leader who inspired followers, but whether he led them to or away from Valencianism remained to be seen.

In her letter to Aelon, she told him to deliver a message to High Priest Vellarin—one of the more troubling and lenient ministers within the Salmantic clergy. Although he had done her no wrong, if he fell ill to the collateral damage of her scheme, it would not be the end of the nightly rains.

Laeden could have known any or all of her vessels. As a rebellious boy, Laeden kept questionable company outside of the castle. He could have forged strong relationships with men across all different walks of life. *Six Hells, if Laeden bought a rebel slave claiming to be the Wielder to aid him in stopping us, is there any low he wouldn't stoop to?*

She sealed the envelopes and put them back in the secret drawer, where they would wait to be taken down the chain of command to the messengers who worked outside the castle.

"All I do, I do for the glory of the Six. Let these three notes deliver the righteous and condemn the corrupt."

CHAPTER 18

THE GUARDIANS

Threyna II
Salmantica

Threyna's new gray cloak swished behind her as she strode along the Street of Silk toward the Gilded Gauntlet. After pilfering a few purses from passerby between the harbors and the Temple District, Threyna had acquired enough coin to purchase a new wardrobe. She settled instead for fresh white linens, a hooded cloak, and boots that no longer held the soot of Rheynia, Klaytos, or anywhere else she'd set foot before.

Though the light color palette reminded her of simpler times when she wore the Premius's uniform in the Underground's legions, the complexion wouldn't age well on Salmantica's dirty streets. Luckily, Threyna didn't plan on staying long. If all went to plan, she would be receiving a new sword, cloak, and armor in short order.

With her hood pulled low and her silver-blonde braid concealed within, Threyna's gaze wandered up and down the street, searching for any sign of someone watching or following her. She'd taken the long way to the Gilded Gauntlet, which wasn't an easy task, being that all roads in the city inevitably led to the statue of Damascus Drake. By the time she reached the golden statue, Threyna decided that either no one was tailing her, or they had earned the right to follow.

"No one is following," Paxoran said. *"The Treasures await."*

Threyna grunted, eyeing the statue of the man who led the Great Migration. *If he hadn't left, could he have challenged King Bohen? Could he have stopped him from becoming the Skeleton King and condemning two generations to survive in a wasteland?*

They were questions without answers. But the undead bodies wandering Rheynia were reason enough for her grandfather Bohen, the Skeleton King, to be stopped.

The first Treasure, the Vykane Blade of Vykannis the Brave, rested beneath the cobblestone circle surrounding the statue. In the catacombs of what became known as the Haunted Hollow rested the remains of the mages nailed to the Six Arrowed Star following the Treaty of 940. Though Warlocks and Templars seldom agreed on anything, this one bit of history they both believed, and while Damascus Drake might not have been as dangerous as the Skeleton King, he was his own brand of monster.

Threyna's gaze traveled from the statue's face to his golden boots where the entrance to the catacombs waited. For whatever reason, she assumed the three Templar Guardians assigned to protect the Vykane Blade—from people like her—would be standing out front like proper sentries. But no. They would be underground, guarding the Treasure with their lives. No distraction would serve her. If she wanted to leave with the Vykane Blade, she would have to kill. Use her blood magic. Consume their souls. And this was only the first of three Treasures.

As the sun began to set over the Hylan mountains, the Gilded Gauntlet emptied. Patrons funneled out. Merchants closed their shops. Before the orange glow could disappear behind peaks, the circle emptied, aside from a pair of patrolling white-cloaked Vigiles.

As the Vigiles headed south toward the Temple District, Threyna skulked to the north side of the circle. By the time the Gilded Gauntlet was clear, the first drops of the nightly rains pattered against the shingled rooftops.

Threyna scaled the stone base of the statue to stand over the entrance to the catacombs that the New Rheynians thought they had sealed away forever. The way was paved shut for most, but to Threyna, it served only as a momentary inconvenience. She tapped on the base, searching for a weakness between the stones they mortared over to cover the descent to the catacombs.

Sensing a fault line in the structure, Threyna conjured a hooked blade and drove the point into the concrete. With a rip and a drag along the outskirts of the square stone covering, she carved the stone from her path.

Letting her hooked blade dissipate to ash, Threyna conjured a web of grasping, fingerlike projections. Her blood spawn seized the stone and lifted it from the statue's base to set it beside Damascus Drake's foot.

As the rolling thunder of the nightly rains echoed throughout the Gilded Gauntlet, Threyna descended the ladder to the catacombs beneath the Haunted Hollow. Halfway down, Threyna dragged the stone covering over the entryway, leaving it slightly ajar.

Surrounded in darkness, confined in close quarters, and breathing the dank air of the hollow shaft into the catacombs, the weight of the moment settled upon Threyna's shoulders. Three of the Templar's best mages were the only remaining obstacle between her and the Vykane Blade. Her slick palms clung to the metal rungs, but down she went, grateful she didn't have to look at the black rot slithering along her forearm from her use of blood magic.

About ten rungs down, Threyna placed her foot on solid ground. The hard-packed and unyielding earth smelled of death and decay. Two sconces glowed with the dim light of the smokeless Celestic magic fire to illuminate the dingy corridor.

Bare except for wood beams and iron supports, the hall was an unceremonious mass grave. The Valencians had dumped bodies into the ground to rot, but it was the Arcane Templar who burned the bodies and sent their souls to the afterlife.

Threyna flared her sense within her Inner Throne to seek the Templar's Guardians. As expected, three heartbeats awaited her. Sinking deeper into her seat of power, Threyna differentiated the three: one with warm blood, the byproduct of using water magic; one with cold blood, a fire mage; and another one who Threyna supposed had other abilities beyond her discernment.

Likely a force, manipulation, or healing mage.

Her time with the Warlocks taught her that the Templar's Guardians had complementary skill sets. She would need to take them out, and quickly.

Creeping along the corridor towards their beating hearts, Threyna held her breath. When she rounded the corner, the hallway opened into another, with branching paths on either side. The catacombs were larger than she had expected, considering she had thought it was just a hole in the ground with a chest for the Vykane Blade.

She passed a room with two makeshift beds, another with a door that Threyna assumed from the stench must be a privy, and a third with salted meat and wilting vegetables that smelled almost as bad as the privy.

And this was the life Zephyrus refused to give up to aid me…

Threyna was used to being alone, but she wasn't meant to be. She'd spent most of her life alone after her father was caught and detained by the Skeleton King to serve as his regenerating blood bag. Her mother and Laela had fled the Underground for the Wraith, no longer hoping to defeat the Skeleton King, but to flee Rheynia. Fate had brought her and Laela back together; they defeated the Skeleton King and ferried hundreds to safety beyond the cursed, undying island. Together, they found the Warlocks, but while Threyna was happy to find a mission to live for, Laela refused to endure the Skeleton King's curse without seeking a cure.

It's better this way.

Threyna approached the last room on the right. Three heartbeats—slow, calm, and strong—resounded beyond the entryway. Either they didn't speak, or a manipulator was bending the sound waves of their voices.

Threyna swallowed the knot in her throat and wiped her palms on her britches.

"The Vykane Blade waits within," Paxoran said.

If there was any other way, she would have taken it. She tried to play the Templar's game. She went to Tharseo's Bastion, but her prophecy didn't name her the Wielder. It didn't say anything.

"You shall find that which you seek, but you possess all you need."

The Seers were blind if they thought her blood magic would be enough to defeat the Skeleton King. In Rheynia, with infinite hollowed, shades, and darklings at her disposal to consume whenever she needed, she barely managed to kill him.

Or at least she thought she did.

Since leaving the cursed island and arriving in a land where souls died true deaths and didn't linger in the mortal realm, Threyna had to consume more and more to abate the rot.

I need the Treasures to stop him. And if I don't, he'll consume far more than these three.

She didn't want to think about what families, lives, or dreams they had. It only made what she needed to do harder. It was easier if they were nameless, faceless obstacles in her way that she could dispatch without a second thought, but if that were the case, she'd be no different than the Skeleton King.

Sinking deeper into her Inner Throne, she conjured a double-bladed blood glaive, and rounded the corner. The Guardians sat at a table, one with his back towards Threyna—the non-elemental mage, if her assumptions were correct. A woman, the water mage—if her warm blood was any indicator—looked up from whatever she was doing on the opposite side of the table. Her eyes fixated on Threyna, but the men beside her and across from her didn't stir.

The woman stood, but before she could open her mouth, Threyna hurled the double-bladed glaive at her. The point dove into her chest and pinned her to the back wall of the room. The other Guardians gained their feet and crouched into combat stances.

Threyna drew the bloodspear back towards her, ripping it from the wall and the woman pinned against it. Before the Guardians could attack, defend, or speak, the double-sided glaive rammed into the closer man's back. The tip exploded through his back and out his chest, dropping him to his knees. Eyes wide and heart racing, he wrapped his hands around the blood-borne spear in his chest cavity.

As Threyna reared back her dagger to fling it at the third Guardian, he disappeared.

A light bender.

His manipulation magic wouldn't save him. Threyna listened for his heartbeat and hurled her dagger straight at it. Before she could follow the dagger's trajectory, a tremendous force hit her square in the gut, lifting her off her feet.

The room fell away as the force launched her backwards into the opposite wall. The mage with her glaive protruding through his torso bared his teeth in a gory smile. With his force magic, he drove her back into the wall, splaying her limbs. Her rib cage compressed; her shoulders and hips felt like they were being ripped from their sockets. Threyna fought against his pressure, but couldn't move against the invisible bindings.

Blood dripped from his lips, draining into his thick black beard. His eyes glared with hatred as if her attack was personal.

"I will break your bones," the force Guardian said through his teeth. The exertion against her body flared. Invisible punches thudded into her stomach, against her ribs, and across her face. Bile climbed her throat, her body breaking beneath the will of the force mage's power.

Threyna retreated into her Inner Throne. Her body's pain became her mind's driving force. From her seat of power, she commanded the bloodspear to twist in the Guardian's chest. She wrenched the angled blade, severing the force mage's spine.

The pressure against Threyna evaporated. She crashed to the floor, limbs aching, chest heaving. Her ribs protested each inhale, but before she could catch her breath, the water mage she'd struck first doused her in a torrent of water.

Again, Threyna flew into the back wall of the corridor outside the room. Water crashed against her already-bruised body and into her mouth and nose, invading her lungs. She conjured a curved blood wall before her. Threyna fell to the floor, no longer held against the wall by the water mage's stream. With Threyna's curved wall flooding the Guardians' room, the water mage ceased her spray.

Threyna sank deeper into her Inner Throne. From where the cursed blood artifact once took the shape of a bangle, rot spread up toward her shoulder, and down toward her wrist. She needed to put an end to this. Focusing on the beating of their hearts, she conjured an arrow.

In one fell swoop, she'd kill the remaining two.

She dropped the curved blood wall, letting it dissipate to ash. Before she could fire her arrow at her invisible opponents, electricity surged through her entire body.

Threyna seized, dropping to the ground in a fit. Like a fish out of water, she flopped. Lightning surged through every fiber of her being. When it should have ended, it didn't. The current continued. Her bruised and beaten bones convulsed into the muddy floor of the catacombs.

"Do something!" Paxoran said.

The black rot encroached on her heart. If it reached her heart, she was as good as dead, but if she did nothing, the Guardians would kill her anyway.

Threyna dove into her Inner Throne, deeper than she dared. She found the water and lightning mages' beating hearts, thundering with triumph. But blood, bone, and soul were hers to command.

In the physical plane, Threyna, floundering on the ground, could not reach the Guardians. But within her Inner Throne, their hearts were just beyond her seat of power. She blocked out her imminent defeat in the physical world and strained, reaching for the source of the Guardians' lives in the immaterial plane.

The walls of her Inner Throne quaked, threatening to crumble. The stained-glass windows shattered, allowing the black rot to flood into her throne room. The sludge slithered like a sentient beast, dividing and converging, coiling, and extending. With each motion, it reached to claim her.

Rain, thunder, and lightning raged outside her walls, but she could end them all.

The black rot slithered up the dais of her throne, wrapping its tendrils around her legs, her torso. She stretched, straining to grasp the Guardians' hearts just beyond her reach.

"Do it for the Vykane Blade," Paxoran said.

Threyna extended. Not for the Vykane Blade. Not for Paxoran. But for her father, her mother, Laela, and everyone else who suffered under the Skeleton King's reign.

The black rot climbed her neck, cinching like a noose.

She seized the Guardians' hearts and squeezed.

The rain and lightning outside her throne room subsided, but the rot devoured her.

Threyna returned to the physical plane, still twitching in the mud. But in the room beyond, three bodies littered the ground around her. Blood spattered the walls, dripped from the table, and puddled on the sodden floor.

Threyna drew in a shallow breath, but ejected from her Inner Throne, she could not consume the Guardians' blood to restore herself or their souls to dispel the rot. Still twitching from the aftershocks of the electric current, her consciousness waned. As close as she was to the first Treasure of Stockhelm, her eyes closed, and sleep took her.

CHAPTER 19

THE UPRISING

Laeden VI
Salmantica

"Silence!" Laeden raised his voice to regain control of the throne room. It was the end of a painfully long day. King Varros usually held court at the beginning of each new moon, yet with the demand so high, this was the second time this week. The royal court generally heard violent acts like murder or significant theft, allowing the local courts and their senators to deal with less malicious disputes, but everything related to the Revivalists came straight to the royal court.

Some cases were from paranoid farmers every time their animals were spooked. Others were shopkeepers who suspected secret plots against them. Most were nonsense. This one, however, resulted in the deaths of six Celestics.

Six bodies littered the inside of Elrod Horne's Stockhelm Inn. They found a scroll with a poem called "The Rebels' Rhyme" on the floor between the deceased. The killer or killers even took the time to write on the walls in the blood of the slain, *"Join the Six, or die."*

"Count Elrod Horne," Laeden said, "I permit you the floor, but if anyone else speaks out of turn, they shall be removed from this courtroom."

Once the room quieted, Elrod Horne took position, his son, Aemos, by his side. "Blood is bad for an inn's business. What are the Sentinels doing to protect our investments?"

Laeden stilled his breath before answering. "My lord count, the Sentinels were established to protect the royal family and root out Revivalists. We cannot guard every inn and tavern in New Rheynia. Investigations will continue to take place to learn more of the attack, but in the meantime, I would encourage you to hire men you trust to guard your own well-being and vested establishments to prevent future acts of violence."

The crowd groaned at Laeden's verdict.

"Is this your answer for everything?" Aemos asked.

How quickly they turned into helpless, sniveling children, pointing the finger to hide from their own responsibilities. Laeden held his tongue.

The king raised his arms. "My lords." An uneasy silence hung over the room. "Investigations are taking place. Honor is our guide, justice our goal. The swiftness of which hinges on your cooperation. Our nation depends on each and every one of you. Help your neighbor and look out for one another. Do what you can to assist the Vigiles, Sentinels, and Jackals working to keep you safe. Soon, a chancellor will be appointed to defend your interests in Stockhelm. Yet we must remain vigilant. This opponent will not be an easy foe. We must be as one, for peace and prosperity."

The speech quelled their grumblings, but that was enough for one day. The king dismissed the court, and the throne room emptied, leaving Laeden, Markus and the king.

The king took off his garnet-studded obsidian circlet and set it on his lap. "Markus, would you excuse us?" Markus bowed and took his leave.

Varros Helixus's gray hair appeared thinner than usual, the creases in his face more pronounced. Sitting in the elegant throne that matched his crown, he looked small.

The burdens of responsibility.

With the crown off, his father, no longer a king, closed his eyes, grabbing the bridge of his nose with his thumb and forefinger. "Laeden, is this too much for you?"

Laeden huffed. "What? No." *Why does he never believe in me?* "We have several leads, and we're optimistic they will result in significant finds."

He looked around to make certain no one lurked in the shadows of the throne room.

The sunlight filtering through the stained-glass windows cast eerie shadows around the obsidian columns. No one was there, but these past weeks had made Laeden paranoid that someone was watching him, following him, or eavesdropping on his conversations.

He continued in a low voice. "We've found traces of black powder in Marstead, a Revivalist defector here in Salmantica, and we placed a man inside Cassius's ludus."

"And this desiccated unbranded corpse in the Prefectus Medicus's chambers?"

Laeden shrugged. "Another angle should other wells run dry."

He took a deep breath. "Look at me, son. I show you how I truly feel. I show them—" he waved his hand at where the patricians stood moments ago, "—what they need to see. Give me an honest telling of what's going on."

Laeden pursed his lips. "They're well-organized, meticulous, and calculative. But so am I. Father, I will not let you down."

His father nodded. He put his crown back on his head and stood with a groan. After a deep breath, his back straightened, his shoulders broadened, and his father transformed back into the king. "Let us hope so, Captain. I will let you get back to work."

Laeden cleared his throat. "There's one thing I wished to inquire about that may aid my investigations." He'd shirked this off for too long. "Who is AVR?"

The king's steely eyes examined him. "I haven't the slightest clue."

Laeden had learned not to trust his father's brand of truth at a young age. When he was seven, he was told his father died in the Sun Sea off the southern coast of Stockhelm. Oh how he wept. His mother could do nothing to console him. Yet, three years later, at the conclusion of the war, his father returned… without a scratch on him, and no explanation.

Biting his lip, Laeden pushed through his father's lie. "Allow me to recite a note addressed to you from a certain AVR. Perhaps you can help me make sense of it. 'The time has come for peace to reign. Your policies have pleased us and given us hope under the Six of New Rheynia. No longer shall we pursue vengeance nor the Judges' treasures.' Signed, AVR."

Color drained from the king's cheeks. "Where did you hear this?"

"What does it mean?" Laeden asked. "Did this AVR coerce you into exiling the mage instead of executing him?"

"Laeden, these are dangerous people," his father said. "How did you come by this letter?"

"Answer the question."

"Don't be a fool, Laeden. Who gave you this message?"

Heat swelled within Laeden's collar. *Me the fool? You exiled the mage. You denied the Revivalists as a threat, but me—I'm the fool.* Laeden swallowed the words he wanted to say. "I only wish to protect you, my king."

The king fixed him with an icy stare, his jaw working behind his closed lips. "Who. Gave you. That message."

The clench of his jaw, the cut of his brow—on any other man, Laeden would not have looked past the anger, but on his father, he saw it for what it was… Fear.

"Zephyrus," Laeden said. "At the slavers' auction at the Festival of Stockhelm, he declared himself a gift to you. An emissary of peace."

The king blinked, his steely eyes softening. "The Wielder?" A father's concern broke through the kingly façade. "Laeden, you stay away from him. Forget you ever heard this message. He is dangerous. The men he serves are dangerous."

"More dangerous than the Revivalists' assassins? The letter spoke of peace."

His father shook his head. "The only peace they'll accept is the destruction of everything Rheynian. If there is anything you love in this realm, you'll trust me. Stay away from Zephyrus."

Laeden blew out his cheeks. He was glad he didn't say Zephyrus was his man inside Cassius's ludus. *How could any threat be more dangerous than the Revivalists?*

Laeden bristled. "You expect me to quell the anarchy you started, yet you refuse to tell me—your son—who or what we're up against. I don't even understand why you exiled the mage in the first place." He tossed his hands in the air. "Yet you expect me to play a game of Reign with half the tiles against loaded dice."

The king glared but offered no answers. "You focus on the Revivalists. Leave AVR to me." Without another word, the king strode away, leaving Laeden in the empty throne room.

Laeden styled a mocking salute to his father's back. *As always, I will have to figure it out for myself.* But as he stood in the vacant hall, he pondered whether or not he could trust Zephyrus—even without his memories.

Later, Laeden joined Markus in the war room. Decorated with paintings and tapestries of Damascus Drake and the leaders of the Great Migration, the war room told the history of New Rheynia. Laeden's efforts against the Revivalists would one day be enshrined in this very hall.

Or so he hoped.

Markus sat at the long table in the center of the room, ledgers, maps, and notes opened before him. "We should have updates from the squadron leaders regarding their reconnaissance. Pirus should be here any moment with—"

A knock at the door heralded Pirus's arrival.

"Enter," Laeden said.

The sandy-haired gatekeeper of Sentigard slipped beyond the precipice of the doorway, a proud smile on his face, and a stack of the reports in his hands.

"Gratitude, Pirus." Laeden took the scrolls. "Dismissed." Pirus saluted and left them to their business. The two dug into the scrolls, praying for good news.

"Wexler's Ravens provided a list of suspicious individuals," Markus said. "Some names of note."

Laeden nodded. *More leads.* "Titus's Riders uncovered a potential Revivalist hideout. More names and places to look into—a good start."

"Blue Bird has a witness to the fires in Marstead, willing to talk," Markus said. "Hmm… that's disturbing."

"What?"

His green eyes traveled across the page again and again before averting to meet Laeden's gaze. "Cavix's Shields have been tracking isolated incidences of escaped slaves in coordination with the Jackals. They started out few and far between, but now with exponential frequency." He handed the scroll to Laeden.

"The Uprising?" Laeden asked as he read. "He believes Celestics may be uniting to defend themselves against the Revivalists. That's the whole point of the Sentinels."

"Clearly, they don't trust us to the task."

Laeden pinched the bridge of his nose with his thumb and forefinger. *Chimera's breath. If the Uprising continues to grow, even if I defeat the Revivalists, the Sentinels will have another opponent to repress… Unless this Uprising has something to do with AVR. Could they be one and the same?* Either way, this only gave the Revivalists' cause more merit. As far as Laeden was concerned, the Revivalists didn't need further justification. Though he disagreed with their tactics, he understood their displeasure.

Laeden pulled at the collar of his doublet. He hadn't had a quiet moment alone with Iylea in what felt like weeks. *How long will my duty separate me from my love?*

Laeden recalled his father's words when asked about letting the mage live in exile.

"There is no need for more unnecessary death." Laeden couldn't understand the king's thoughts. He couldn't read his mind. *But how many will die if I can't stifle these embers before they're stoked to an inferno?*

If it weren't for the progress his men were making with the information they received from Gareth, he didn't know where they would be. Gareth provided them with one of the Revivalists' messengers. If Laeden could get a hold of Aelon again, they would have two solid sources to follow.

For now, Gareth's contact, Banis—the Ratman, they called him—was being tailed by Allaron, a seasoned man long loyal to the Helixuses. Banis had already led them to several others involved in peculiar operations.

An unexpected knock resounded against the door. Laeden and Markus looked at one another, but before they could react, the door creaked open. A boy entered, wearing an apron caked in flour. At perhaps ten years old, he appeared just as confused as Laeden felt.

"Apologies, my prince. I have a message." He strode into the war room and placed a folded letter into Laeden's hand, before sticking out his own palm. "He said you'd pay."

"Who said?" Markus asked.

Laeden opened the note.

Ranger,

Sandy-haired kid, peach-fuzz cheeks—front gate.

Revivalist. Careful who delivers your reports. New lead: High Priest Vellarin. But wait until all other leads are exhausted. The hammer is coming down on noisy rodents. Burn after reading.

Freebird

Laeden curled the scroll in his fist. *My own men? Pirus, that snake.*

Aelon went by the nickname Freebird when he worked as a Hecht delivery boy as a child. Eyeing the nervous boy, Laeden understood where the term *"Don't wreck the runner"* came from. He pulled a silver coin from his pouch.

"He said gold. Not silver."

Laeden smirked, pulling out a gold coin. *Of course Aelon promised gold.* "What's your name?"

"Royce," the boy said. "I make bread."

Laeden knelt down to the boy's level, rubbing the silver and gold coins together. "If one day I wanted to pay you another coin to deliver a message for me, would I find you in the kitchens?"

Royce nodded, eyeing the coins.

"And you'd do that for me, the same way you did this note?"

Royce nodded more vigorously.

Laeden pressed the coins into the small baker's palm. "Good. Run along now."

Royce escaped the room in a hurry as if he were afraid Laeden would think twice about his payment.

"What's going on?" Markus asked. Laeden handed him the crumpled note from Aelon and paced the storied stones of the war room. After a moment, Markus slammed his fist on the table. "Is this true about Pirus? Laeden, who sent this?"

"A trusted source, using a moniker I would recognize." He didn't want to reveal more. If Aelon took such care to avoid detection, Laeden wouldn't expose him now, especially after mentioning the hammer and the rodents. *The Revivalists know they have a mole.*

Markus jumped to his feet. "If this is true, we must arrest Pirus at once."

"No," Laeden said, rubbing his chin. "We will play their games. Let them think we don't know. Perhaps we can give them the same type of subterfuge."

Markus sat back down, and Laeden joined him at the table. With papers, maps, and a thousand questions between them, they had their hands full.

Is this what Father's crown feels like? An anchor confining me to the impossible. The impossible that I chose.

"You have to stop them," Iylea had said. *Six*, he missed her, but the Revivalists needed to be brought to justice first. Iylea would have to wait.

"We have work to do," Laeden said with newfound determination. "Let's get it done."

CHAPTER 20

FEAR AND CONSEQUENCE

Iylea II

Salmantica

"Laeden!"

Iylea bolted upright in bed, her sheets damp with sweat as goose-flesh pimpled her arms. She shuddered, trying to shake away the nightmare's images. Scorpions surrounded her, covering the floor of the queen's study. They snapped at her ankles with their claws and jabbed their stingers at her as she tried to climb a bookshelf in the corner to escape them. The queen and Baron Brusos stood on the tabletop, skewering the scorpions with daggers, killing them one by one. They beckoned for Iylea to come to them for protection. But just as she made it to the long table, Laeden barged through the door, sword drawn.

What could it all mean?

It took all her morning chores to shake herself free from the dream's torment. But the look on Laeden's face didn't leave her. Disappointment, disgust, and rage all blended into one. Despite her every desire, she couldn't tell him about her dreams and visions; it was too dangerous—for both of them.

Though she convinced herself it was noble to withhold the truth from Laeden, deep down she knew it was cowardice that kept her lips sealed.

Would he accept me—a seer? He didn't agree when his father exiled the mage. Why would he make an exception for me?

She'd barely seen Laeden since returning to Salmantica. Her heart ached at the growing distance between them, but perhaps it was better this way.

Cerberynn Brusos had become a frequent visitor of late. *Perhaps that's why I dreamt of her husband. But why the scorpions?*

Even if she wished to discuss her dreams with Laeden, he wasn't home. He left with Prince Damascus that morning to connect with the potential chancellors of Stockhelm. Iylea had the afternoon off from her duties but didn't know what to do with her free time that wouldn't drive her mad. She found herself walking about the castle, alone with her thoughts, until she arrived at the queen's study. The look on Laeden's face in her dream made her shiver.

It's like he knows the truth about me. His disgust at her betrayal deflated her.

But what if he wasn't looking at me?

Staring at the door to the study before her, Iylea rubbed her forehead with her palm, trying to recall the details of her dream. *What if his disgust was aimed at the queen or Brusos? Or maybe Markus. He was a scorpion of House Cassius. Could the Cassiuses be part of the Revivalists?*

She opened the door and walked into the study. She didn't know what she was looking for, or what she would find, but fate or happenstance brought her here. The windows flooded the library with the sun's warmth. Oriented parallel to the windows, a long mahogany table stretched the length of the wall. To her back, rows of bookshelves called to her.

This is the bookshelf I tried to climb.

She approached the back corner of the room and sat at the base of the shelf. A cart with old books stacked high created a tiny alcove for her. *What am I supposed to see here?* It was a riddle with one too many missing clues. Feeling silly, she stood to leave, but the door swung open.

Iylea froze. Her heart *thrummed* within her chest as several footsteps entered the study. She sat back down, sinking into her alcove. The door closed again, and Iylea held her breath.

"Three letters, through the typical channels," a man's gruff voice said. She recognized the voice but couldn't place it. *Markus Cassius?* She heard rummaging on one of the shelves, then a resounding *click.* "Your instructions are inside. Make sure to follow them exactly as written."

"Yes, my lord," a new voice said.

"Is there anything else, my lord?" another added.

"That will be all," the gruff voice answered.

More footfalls, followed by the opening and closing of the door. Iylea still held her breath.

Who are they? What are they doing in the queen's study?

Iylea's head throbbed with the familiar pressure behind her eyes that always accompanied a vision.

No, not now!

"Be still, child," the man with the red eyes said from beside her, but his lips didn't move. His voice resounded in her head.

Iylea nearly jumped out of her skin, backing into the wall with a *thud.*

"What was that?" the lord with the gruff voice said.

Iylea's heart raced, reverberating in her temples. The God with the red eyes and ashen skin held a finger to his lips.

Slow footsteps approached, making their way to her hiding spot behind the cart.

"My lord?" another voice asked.

"Shh."

The footsteps crept closer until he stood beside the cart. She closed her eyes. The God wrapped his arm around her shoulder, holding her close as if to protect her. Despite herself, Iylea shrank into his arms to avoid the lord's detection.

The lord bent down and picked up the book that fell from the cart. He placed it back atop the cart and strode away.

Iylea's held breath released in a slow tremble. The God beside her patted her arm.

The lord with the gruff voice spoke again. "Take this. Make sure it's one of the new messengers. One we can trust."

"A sharp blade. Simple, vicious thing."

"Have it sent to the Cassius guard with these instructions."

Cassius?

Iylea looked into the God's red-eyed stare.

After the lord dismissed his underlings, the door opened, and the footsteps retreated before the door closed again to seal Iylea inside with the God of her visions. Petrified, Iylea's mouth was too dry to speak.

"Do you see?" the God asked aloud.

Iylea shook her head, listening for any sign of the lords' return.

The God stroked her cheek. "Fear clouds your vision, but soon, my child. Soon you will see all. The Reckoning comes." He gave her a sad smile, and as quickly as he'd appeared, he was gone.

Iylea didn't move. She couldn't. After a time, she drew a full breath for the first time since the others entered the room. She put her head in her hands.

Revivalists. This is what he wanted me to see?

She attempted to piece together what she thought she heard in relation to her dreams. *Could it really have been Markus? Shouldn't he have been with Laeden? Why would a knife need to be sent to the Cassius guards?*

Iylea needed to tell Laeden. She didn't see faces or names, but she could tell him what she heard, and perhaps he could make sense of it.

She waited for what could have been hours, alone with her thoughts, fears, and anxieties, before forcing herself to move. Gathering herself, she took her leave, but just as she opened the door, a figure stood, waiting.

Iylea jumped back, raising her hand to her chest, panic surging through her like a tempest.

Ser Daenus held his hands up, palms exposed. "Apologies, my lady. I didn't mean to startle you." The whiskered knight clad in the black-and-red plate of the King's Guard Knights towered over her.

"I'm sorry," Iylea said, with a sigh. "I've been so on edge ever since—"

His voice…

Low, stern… gruff. Her breath caught in her chest. *Him. A King's Guard Knight…*

Unlike the red-eyed God, Ser Daenus wasn't a vision—he was a Revivalist.

If the Revivalists attempted to assassinate the king, what would they do to a girl in the wrong place at the wrong time?

Then it hit her. *Cantella*... Strangled to death and left naked in a heap on the floor. *Wrong place. Wrong time.* Iylea's heart fluttered in her chest.

"Are you well, my lady?"

Iylea cleared her throat, regaining her composure. "Ever since the attack on the king, I've been a bit jumpy, I suppose."

"Precarious times we live in," Ser Daenus said, crossing his arms over his cuirass. "But we are safe here."

She forced a smile, but the muscles of her face quivered. She wasn't safe here. No one was. *Chimera's breath, he could be leading the Revivalists.*

Her dream returned to her, mixing with the information she'd just learned of the knife being sent to the Cassius guard. She had thought Markus, a scorpion of House Cassius, was a Revivalist that the queen and Lord Brusos were trying to stop, but she had it backwards. The queen, Brusos, and Ser Daenus were the Revivalists leading an attack on the Cassiuses.

"What were you doing?" Ser Daenus asked, nodding to the door. "In the study?"

Iylea wiped her sweating palms on the hips of her dress. "Cleaning. Making sure everything is clean."

Ser Daenus's brow twitched as his eyes fell on her empty hands.

"Straightening up, really. I must be going, though. Many rooms in this castle."

Iylea curtsied and scurried off as fast as she could without drawing more attention. She wanted to run into Laeden's arms, but he might as well have been a world away. No longer could she hold him at arm's distance out of her own apprehensions. She needed to speak with him. She needed to tell him the truth.

CHAPTER 21

NIGHTLY RAINS

Zephyrus VIII

Stockhelm

"Drink this." The healer offered Zephyrus a concoction of herbs mixed with water. "It will make you sleep deeper and dream more; you will relive your memories through fragmented dreams."

Zephyrus examined the cup's contents. His nostrils recoiled from the pungency. The healer had half a century of wisdom beneath her gray hair and wrinkles, but drinking this didn't seem like a prudent choice.

"Drink." She lifted the cup to his lips. It tasted like river water downstream from a beaver dam. "You must drink this every day."

He gagged on the thick slog, but his memories would be worth it. He made a fist and downed the cup's contents.

Wiping his mouth with the back of his hand, he returned the cup to the healer. "Why did I lose my memory?"

She didn't meet his eyes as she began packing her vials. "It was not from the ritual at Tharseo's Bastion. To our understanding, the pagan ritual is harmless. Something else was in your system, but the combination could have killed you."

Zephyrus wrinkled his nose. "What do you mean—something else?"

"I mean I would be careful," the healer said. "Someone either tried to kill you and failed or made precisely sure you wouldn't remember anything."

Zephyrus swallowed her words and the bitter tonic. *Patrus was suffering from a headache and memory loss too, but mine was worse.* She continued talking, but Zephyrus wasn't listening.

Who wanted us dead? Or what did they want us to forget? He tried to recall his dream with Threyna. She had said something about him not owing the Arcane Templar.

Threyna asked me to join her. Did I agree? Would the Templar sabotage us if we abandoned them for Threyna's purposes?

The questions swirled in his mind until his head hurt.

"Live." Patrus's last word. As long as Zephyrus lived, there was still hope. Answers would come and, with them, the ability and knowledge to walk out his fate.

Still alive, Patrus… I'm still alive.

The healer vacated the medicus's chambers, leaving Zephyrus alone in the dingy cellar. His head began to swim, and the room twisted and turned as the tonic's effects took hold.

Zephyrus's dream state transported him into a boyish body, gripped by panic. No longer was he in Cassius's ludus, but chains about his wrists, ankles, and throat bound him to the sandstone wall at his back.

Torches lit the surrounding walls and central columns of the room, but the light failed to fend off the darkness. Glowing glyphs emitted a bright green aura from a stone pillar at the center of the room. From the boy's eyes, Zephyrus tried to explore his surroundings, but the boy's fright kept him as trapped as his chains.

The boyish body struggled against the manacles, shouting for his mother, crying for home. Zephyrus didn't understand what was going on, but he felt the child's fear. The dream continued to unfold as a figure stalked from the shadows of the chamber. Clad in a long cloak that dragged in his wake, the concealed figure approached.

His conscious mind attempted to speak, wanting answers, but though he felt the boy's fright, the boy gave no indication he sensed Zephyrus's questions.

The figure drew closer, his outstretched hand leading the way. It glowed orange before erupting into flames. The boy turned away from the sudden brightness, but intrigue captivated his conscious mind. He tried to turn back to see the face behind the fire, but the boy controlled the body.

With a flaming hand raised high, the figure's fingers danced, causing embers to swirl into the air like ascending feathers. The feathers levitated through the shadows until a chandelier burst to light, illuminating the cellar and the figure's face.

Dark wrinkled skin surrounded pale, gray eyes. A trimmed gray beard framed his sly grin.

"Let him go!" a voice called from the shadowed recesses of the room. "You said you'd teach 'em, not torture 'em!"

The man pulled three small throwing knives from his cloak. "If he is what you say he is, Patrus of The Fallen, then we will teach him."

Patrus! Zephyrus's conscious mind sharpened to attention as he pieced the situation together. *This is the Arcane Templar. This isn't some boy… it's me!*

"You don't hafta hurt him!" Patrus roared.

The cloaked man spread the throwing knives like a fan. "We cannot waste the Judges' time on our own people if they have no purpose to bear, let alone a Rheynian. You may forget, but we are at war, and our secrets are not easily given."

The knives levitated before him in a similar fashion to the embers moments before. Instead of traveling upwards, they drifted closer and closer to Zephyrus's boyish body as he struggled within his bindings.

The lazy arcs and gentle circles of the knives suddenly struck like a viper, zipping through the air at impossible speed. Patrus screamed as each one sliced Zephyrus differently, one his arm, the second his leg, and the third nicked the side of his neck. Zephyrus was not immune. The knives' metallic chill, the warmth of the blood trickling down his neck—he felt all of it.

The boy cried out in pain, turning to Patrus in the shadows. "Patrus, help!"

"Use it," the cloaked man said. "Show me what our relatives taught you."

"Stop!" Patrus cried, fighting his way into the light, seemingly restrained by invisible bindings. "He can't heal himself."

"Judges preserve me," the boy said, tears streaking down his cheeks.

The cloaked man inclined his head and lifted his finger to his bearded chin. "The Judges? How does a Rheynian boy find Celestia?"

Zephyrus had wondered the same. He'd figured his connection to the Judges was a product of Patrus. *But even at such a young age, I followed the Judges. This wasn't just Patrus's faith, but my own.*

"Elder Vellarix," said another cloaked figure as he slunk from the darkness behind Patrus. "If he can't heal himself, perhaps he can heal someone else. Someone in need."

Patrus floated in the air in front of Vellarix, contorting to free himself from the invisible bindings.

Zephyrus's conscious mind couldn't believe it. *Could this possibly be real—a memory?*

The cloaked figure stalked toward Vellarix and lowered Patrus from the air. A dozen paces from where Zephyrus was bound, the invisible magic forced Patrus to his knees before the two cloaked mages. Patrus's muscles strained, his veins bulged, and sweat dampened his brow.

Patrus nodded at Zephyrus. "It's gonna be okay, ya hear?"

Zephyrus's boyish dreamself didn't nod, didn't blink—paralyzed by fear. Tears fell from his bleary eyes, and blood trickled from the wounds inflicted by Vellarix's floating knives.

"What a fine idea, Elder Aikous," Vellarix said. "Let us see if this boy possesses the magic you say, Patrus."

Vellarix reached out his hand, summoning the knives that pierced Zephyrus. The blades ripped free from the stone behind Zephyrus and bolted toward Patrus's stomach. All three punched into his flesh at once with a thickening thud. Patrus let out a sharp gasp and fell to the floor in a heap.

With another wave of Vellarix's hand, the chains securing Zephyrus snapped open. Zephyrus's conscious mind was slow, confused, and weighed down with questions, but the boy scampered to Patrus's side. The smell of blood and filth filled his nostrils. Patrus's intestines were eviscerated.

This isn't a memory. Not even a dream—a nightmare.

His dreamself pushed Patrus onto his back and yanked the knives free from his stomach.

Patrus's eyes, wide with fear and pain, bore into Zephyrus's soul. His conscious mind couldn't watch Patrus die again. Zephyrus tried to wake himself from this nightmare, but despite his struggle, he couldn't break free.

The boy hovered his hands over Patrus's stomach, and white mist emanated from his palms. His conscious mind could only watch in awe as Patrus's stomach wounds sealed together.

A tremendous stabbing pain seared through Zephyrus's conscious mind, while his dreamself doubled over in pain. His conscious mind panicked, but the child in the dream was prepared as if he knew this was coming. As quickly as the pain came, it dissipated, leaving Patrus's stomach with only a scar. Patrus pawed at his stomach and let out a relieved chuckle.

Patrus grabbed the boy's hand. Alive and brimming with pride.

Perhaps this was real…

Patrus survived. He had healed him.

The image of Lenox's sword protruding from Patrus's belly impressed upon his dreamscape, threatening to shatter it. *I had the power to heal him. I could have saved him.*

Guilt invaded his conscious mind with a greater grip than Vellarix's hand on his dreamself's shoulder.

"You're a talent, my boy," Vellarix said.

"Told you." Patrus huffed, straightening his ripped and bloody tunic. "This mean you'll train 'em? Help him to fulfill the Acts?"

Aikous exchanged a glance with Vellarix.

Patrus examined them. "The Champion of the Nine… Tharseo born again."

Vellarix snorted, pulling Zephyrus by the shoulder closer toward him. "Despite what your Rheynian masters told you, Patrus, Tharseo will not be born again. Only the Prophets can save us now. But yes, the boy shall be trained."

Patrus grimaced but didn't speak. Zephyrus's conscious mind struggled to make sense of the names and titles, but his dreamself's shoulders slouched at something Vellarix said.

Vellarix squeezed Zephyrus's boyish shoulder and turned him around. He squatted until they were eye level. "Tharseo is gone, but take heart. We are not lost. You shall be reborn to bring honor to the Judges. Whatever name hailed you before, it's no more. You are now Zephyrus, son of the Arcane Templar. And we shall have our vengeance."

What's my real name if not Zephyrus?

He searched his memory, but before he could even process the scene, he woke in a cold sweat with Nallia standing over him, clutching at her ringed finger.

"Zephyrus, thank the Six, I thought you'd never wake." Nallia turned to the others in the room. "He's awake!"

Zephyrus attempted to look around, but chains restricted him.

Cassius's padded feet slapped at the stone floor as he marched over to Zephyrus's cot. "You've enjoyed my hospitality for far too long. I will not suffer a heathen beneath my roof. Renounce the Judges and accept the true Gods of Valencia. Submit to the Facets of Perfection and yield to my authority, or suffer the consequences."

Zephyrus's mind, still foggy from sleep, sharpened to focus. Nallia looked at him with pleading eyes—shining emeralds in the dim light of the medicus's chambers.

Cassius loomed over him, the torchlight bathing him in an orange glow. "My patience will outlast your insolence. If you wish to be beaten in the rains every night, it will not bother me."

Zephyrus grit his teeth, straining against his bindings. He wished to tear free and deliver the Arcane Templar's vengeance right there and then.

Cassius hummed to himself as if enjoying Zephyrus's ire. "Moons may wax and wane, but I will not tire of watching my men abuse you.

Eventually, you will submit, so whether your body or spirit breaks first…" He shrugged. "Makes no difference to me."

Zephyrus's breath came short and sharp.

If my actions dictate my fate, how will the Judges look upon me—a Prophet of Celestia—if I renounce them?

He examined his arm where Vellarix's knife had nicked him in his dream. A remnant of an old scar lined the skin. The healer told the truth; it wasn't just a dream, but a memory. The Arcane Templar sought vengeance. *No wonder why Patrus refused to believe I was an emissary of peace for the king. The Templar couldn't have written that letter… unless the plan was to lie to get close to the king to exact vengeance.*

While there were still too many questions, Zephyrus was confident his past would return to him, and with it, answers would flow like a river. He would learn the meaning of the scroll, who he was, and who he was supposed to be. He would avenge Patrus. Wielder, Harbinger, Herald—all three, or nothing at all—he would not renounce the Judges that gave him the gift of healing.

"*You shall be reborn to bring honor to the Judges,*" Vellarix had said. *"We shall have our vengeance."*

Zephyrus *wanted* vengeance. Vengeance on those who took him captive at sword point. Vengeance on Lenox for murdering Patrus, and Cassius for trying to dictate his beliefs. Vengeance on the king for upholding this injustice, and Laeden for being party to it all.

They all deserve to suffer.

"Father," Nallia said, tugging on the purple silk draped about him. "Allow me to educate him in the ways of Valencianism. Look at him—he's Rheynian."

Cassius swatted her away. "I'll hear none of it. If you're going to lead this ludus, your time can not be wasted teaching barbarians. He accepts, or—"

"He lost his memories," Nallia said, flat and stern. "Give me time and I'm sure I can—"

"You can obey!" Cassius wheeled on her. "He's had his time. Now he must decide: the easy way or the arduous."

Nallia lowered her eyes, but Zephyrus's resolve would not be so easily broken.

"The Judges are with me," Zephyrus said, glaring daggers into the withered owl of a man. "And I am with them."

Cassius smiled. "Have it your way. Lenox, he's all yours. Don't maim him or kill him, but otherwise… have fun."

Lenox stepped into Zephyrus's view, a twisted smile upon his face. "Let's see if your precious Judges can protect you."

⚖

Dragged into the training square. Tied to a palus. Beaten in the pouring rain. Nallia protested Zephyrus's mistreatment, but her efforts bore no fruit.

Punch after punch, Zephyrus endured, but with each strike, his anger grew. The taste for vengeance was teased by Vellarix, but Zephyrus would make it a reality, and he would begin with Lenox.

I should have killed him when I had the chance. But one day, I will claim his life, along with every other slave-owning bastard.

"Break him," Cassius shouted over the rain from the balcony overlooking the training square. "He must be forged into something of worth in the eyes of the Six. If not tonight—tomorrow, or the next night, but he *will* fight for House Cassius, or he'll die in his denial. We will see how long before he begs the Six to save him."

Zephyrus channeled to Vykannis, but none of the Judges offered any response.

A cacophony of curses joined the thunder and rain for hours. Zephyrus's left eye swelled shut, his lip split, and his ribs ached with every labored breath, but he would not renounce the Judges. The Rebels' Rhyme remained in his head, Patrus's voice singing with each blow to Zephyrus's body.

I will persevere. I will overcome.

He would bring honor to the Judges and fulfill his fate as a Prophet of Celestia. But despite the self-talk and positive affirmations, the beatings took their toll.

The guards grew tired from the effort of pummeling him, and eventually, despite Lenox's fervor for beating him, even he needed a break.

Zephyrus welcomed the reprieve. His entire existence pained him, but he would not let them see his weakness. He forced his eyes open to glower at the guards.

Lenox strode away from the others, heading towards the main gate Zephyrus had entered through following the Festival of Stockhelm. Zephyrus couldn't see clearly through the rain and his swollen eyes, but a man cloaked in black waited for Lenox at the gate. The storm and the heavy breathing of the other guards muffled the faraway voices, but this was the type of behavior one might expect from a Revivalist underling.

Who has private conversations in the rain during the dead of night?

The man slipped a small parcel through the barred gate, handing it to Lenox.

"Hey!" Zephyrus shouted. "We're in the middle of something over here."

Lenox scowled at Zephyrus before sending the hooded man away. He marched over to the other guards. "Why don't the rest of you get some shut-eye? I can take care of him from here." The other guards retreated indoors, leaving the two of them alone.

Zephyrus snarled at Lenox, blood bubbling from his mouth. "Why don't we finish what we started? Unchain me. Come on—just me, you, and the Gods we fight for."

Lenox shook his head and opened the parcel. A small unornamented blade caught the torchlight, but carved into the hilt was the balanced scale insignia from Tharseo's Bastion.

Lenox leaned in and grabbed Zephyrus behind the head with one hand and placed the blade against his throat with the other.

Zephyrus sucked in breath. His heart pounded within his breast.

"Still think you're tough?" Lenox's breath, stained with the scent of bitter ale, filled Zephyrus's nostrils.

Zephyrus's fingers curled into fists. *He can't kill me. Cassius said so himself.* Zephyrus furrowed his brow in determination. "Go ahead. Do it. Unless you can't deal with your master's consequences."

Lenox backed away, but another cruel smile crept across his lips. "I don't have to kill you myself."

CHAPTER 22

Clever Lies

Zephyrus IX

Stockhelm

Lenox pushed Zephyrus through the door to the barracks, his knife against the small of his back. Zephyrus wanted to fight back, but his body failed him. He was fortunate Lenox didn't accept his challenge because he wouldn't have had the strength to defeat him.

Before a cell already crowded with men, Lenox lowered the knife to locate his key. If Zephyrus believed he could win, this was his opportunity to initiate, but he could barely stand. The door opened, Lenox shoved him inside, and his opportunity vanished.

Zephyrus fell to the floor, jostling the others from sleep. Lenox shut the barred door. His grin should have been enough to make Zephyrus's blood rise and return the fight to his spirit, but he felt so weak. So tired. He tried to think of the Rebels' Rhyme to give him strength, but in his fatigue, he couldn't harness the words.

"Behold," Lenox said, "the prince's chosen, the Judges' Prophet. Thought himself better than you lot. Said 'No,' to Earl Cassius's face. Take a good look."

Voices muttered as they surveyed Zephyrus's state, sizing him up.

Lenox leaned against the bars. "If he doesn't survive the night, I'll bring Stockhelm's best brothel for the man who ends his miserable life."

He grinned at Zephyrus, as if knowing he were seeing him for the last time. He stalked away, leaving Zephyrus in a cell with eight men.

Time stood still as everyone contemplated their options. The familiar faces of Carsos and Ixion—two men from the slavers' auction—emerged from the shadows.

"Burn me, Carsos, it's the Wielder," Ixion said with a voice like gravel.

"More like the Harbinger for all the trouble he's caused," Carsos said as he and Ixion advanced.

Zephyrus was too tired to fight. His arms hung at his sides, his head spun, and the pain in his ribs made it feel like he had fallen from the sky and landed on a boulder. "I'm not your enemy." He extended a trembling hand to stop them. "They're the enemy. The ones outside the cells."

"Maybe," Carsos said, "but they offer the best brothel in Stockhelm. What do you offer?"

Others in the cell began to snicker.

"Whatever ya do," said a gladiator from a nearby cell, "just get on with it and shut yer burning mouths."

No help. No protection.

Vykannis, if you can hear me—

"I was at the slavers' auction," another man in the cell said. "He tried to free everyone, but he only got them killed, then saved himself by saying he was a gift to the king. All he offers is death. If we kill him—"

"If you *could* kill him, you mean?" A man stepped into the light before Carsos and Ixion. Long black hair fell across pale skin. A scar slashed across the bridge of his nose down to his lip. The letter *T* was burned into the underbelly of his forearm. "Maybe he ain't your prophesied savior, but if he's trying to get me outta irons, he can call himself whatever he likes."

Zephyrus eyed the scarred man. Smaller than Carsos or Ixion, his size didn't seem to even their odds. Still, a fierceness in him slowed their advance.

"He'll get you killed," Carsos said. "You won't see a day of freedom pass before you're worm food, just like the rest of those men at the auction."

An older man with dark skin and graying hair held his hands out. "If we kill the Harbinger, then the Wielder will never rise to defeat him. Maybe we should leave him be. The Age of the End has to happen if the Return is to come."

Zephyrus balked. *Is that right? If I am the Harbinger, does that mean I'm fated only to give rise to another?*

"Burn your Prophets of the Return," Ixion said.

"You willing to risk the best brothel in Stockhelm?" Carsos asked the older man. "I ain't."

Carsos and Ixion advanced on Zephyrus, fists clenched, but Scar blocked their path. Carsos reared back to punch, but Scar grabbed Carsos's punching arm and yanked it behind his back, dragging him to the floor. From his back, Scar swept Ixion's leg out from under him. Another man stepped up to grab Zephyrus, but Scar jumped to his feet to stand between Zephyrus and the rest of the men. Carsos and Ixion regained their footing, ready to come at him again.

"If ya want him, you go through me," Scar hissed.

"Still seven against two," Carsos said with a sinister grin.

"Seven recruits who'll die before they gain the mark of the dominus, against a gladiator of Targarus and a Prophet of Celestia." Scar laughed. "I'll take my chances. Six, I'll wager on it."

His confidence made the others think twice. After some grumbled curses, Carsos and Ixion sat down in the corner opposite Zephyrus.

Zephyrus collapsed. *Still alive, Patrus… barely, but still alive.*

Scar sat down beside him. "The name's Jechtaric. Friends call me Jecht."

Zephyrus nodded. "Gratitude, Jecht, for coming to my aid." He felt broken. Body, mind, and soul. For the first time, he understood why many of the slaves' faces were long with accepted defeat.

"Your aid?" Jecht spoke loud enough for the whole cell to hear. "Six, I thought I was protecting them. Fools can't hold a sword without cutting themselves and they think they could have taken you?" With a chuckle, he leaned closer. "I heard about the slavers' auction and watched you nearly kill Lenox with a cheese knife. You might be as crazy as I am—going to Tharseo's Bastion—Chimera's breath, even crazier."

"I suppose so." Zephyrus sank into the wall, too tired to say much else.

"So what's the plan?" Jecht whispered, all laughter gone from his voice. "How do we escape, join the Uprising?"

Zephyrus had to turn his entire body to look at Jecht due to his swollen eye and aching ribs. "There's no plan."

"What do you mean, no plan?" Jecht asked. "Aren't you the Wielder? Find the Treasures, free the people, and all that?"

Patrus and Nallia thought he could be any one of the three. After hearing each of the prophecies for himself, Zephyrus understood why. "I don't know which Prophet I am."

"So?" Jecht shrugged, his arms hugging his knees.

The question took Zephyrus aback. He didn't know how to explain. Where to even begin. "How long have you been a slave?"

"All my life," Jecht said. "Born a traitor's bastard, I went from womb to cell, but suppose I was lucky to be a Finn and not a Hecht. Ya know, hammers and nails and all that.

"Never stopped looking for a way out. And this place? Don't get me wrong. Targarus's ludus wasn't great, but he looks like Invinius burning Auros compared to Cassius. If there's a way outta this, I'm taking it."

"You must be worse at escaping than I am," Zephyrus said with a laugh. The pain in his ribs made him regret the joke.

Jecht smirked. "Hasn't worked yet, so you ain't wrong. But don't mean I'm not still trying."

"How?" Zephyrus asked, struggling to stay awake.

"Ya gotta keep your head down. Can't take every hit they throw. Sometimes that means bowing, but the best intentions live behind clever lies."

Clever lies…

His eyes drooped as exhaustion seized him, and he fell immediately into dreams.

His conscious mind understood that the longer his eyes remained closed, the more likely someone was to smother him in his sleep, but his fatigue got the best of him. His dreamself—older than before, but still a skinny, scrappy boy—fought against other apprentices under the watchful eyes of Vellarix.

"Very good," Vellarix said after calling an end to combat training. "Go to Master Ronar and resume your study of the elements." Young Zephyrus did as commanded and walked through the sandstone temple with Patrus at his side.

"Yer getting good," Patrus said. "A quick study, like yer mother. I swear, she memorized the Spirit of Divinity in a moon's turn."

Young Zephyrus nodded, but his smile fell at the mention of his mother.

Zephyrus's conscious mind searched for any trace of his mother or father but came away empty.

Patrus cleared his throat. "You been practicin' balancing the scales?"

The torches lit along the way cast eerie shadows of himself along the corridor. His dreamself used the manipulation magic he'd learned from Master Aikous to bend the candlelight around him, eliminating his shadow.

"Alright, Zeph, no one likes a showoff."

His conscious mind was amazed, but a thought struck him.

Aikous, Vellarix, and Ronar. A, V, and R.

He thought they were initials for one person, but what if they were three? Still, it didn't make sense; they spoke of vengeance but offered a letter of peace.

Somewhere between now and arriving at Tharseo's Bastion, something went wrong.

The bending light caused the dream to twist, teleporting him into a different time and place. A woman's auburn hair and blue eyes hung over him. His dreamself reached out for her with little hands.

"Momma," a child's voice called. His conscious mind melted.

Mother?

She picked him up, and the world spun around him. She nestled him into her warm embrace. She danced, spinning him around, bringing him through a doorway to a balcony. His dreamself giggled with glee. Zephyrus couldn't remember a time of such peace.

"One day, son, your daddy's going to come home, and we're going to be the happiest family in New Rheynia." She kissed his forehead and bounced him up and down.

"Domina," a voice called behind them. His mother turned, and Zephyrus saw where the voice came from. A young woman of Stockhelm descent stood before them, holding an open parchment—her mouth aghast. Her mouth continued to move, but the words didn't make any sense. The voice was wrong too.

Zephyrus woke to the sound of Doctore's booming voice. He rubbed his eyes, trying to remember what he saw.

My mother was a slave owner.

She was gone now, probably dead, but more questions arose. *How did Patrus and I end up at the Arcane Templar? How did I end up following the Judges?*

Beside him, Jecht contorted his spine.

"At Targarus's ludus, the gladiators slept on featherbeds," Jecht said, stretching. "Now I can't wait to earn Dominus's mark just so I can getta cell of my own with an itchy straw cot."

Doctore eyed Zephyrus as he let the others out of the cell. He placed an arm out to stop Zephyrus from following the others. "You have until sunset. The dominus will demand you to declare for the Six. Refuse and you will be beaten. It will only get worse. I implore you to think on this. Pray on it. But do not let your life fall forfeit absent meaning." He lowered his arm. "You will work the palus with sword and shield until you are well enough to spar."

Zephyrus limped to the training square, too preoccupied with his dreams to consider Doctore's words. Once upon the sands, Doctore organized them into pairs while his assistant delivered wooden weapons to the gladiators.

Lenox emerged from the barracks, a smug grin upon his squashed face. He strode over to a gaunt-faced gladiator. Discreetly, Lenox pressed something into the man's hand.

Zephyrus narrowed his eyes. *What was that?*

Doctore shoved a wooden sword and buckler into Zephyrus's bandaged hands. "To the palus."

Zephyrus begrudgingly did as commanded. *Clever lies,* he told himself. The combination of rest and Jecht's words restored his vigor. The questions surrounding his mother swirled around him, but answers would come. Son of a slave owner or not, he was set on a path, fated to free people, or give rise to the one who would…

Either way, all was not lost. His personal vendetta against Lenox was still within reach. Lenox's late-night rendezvous coupled with his interaction with the gladiator roused additional suspicion. If Zephyrus could connect Lenox to the other rogue elements within House Cassius, he could trade Laeden information and get some clarification concerning the note addressed to the king.

Zephyrus worked against his wooden opponent. He hacked and chopped, picturing Cassius and Lenox dying beneath his sword.

Nallia emerged from a gold curtain upon the second-story balcony overlooking the training square. Her green eyes seemed to follow Zephyrus's every strike, but he ignored her.

Despite the aches and pains of his beatings, moments turned to hours, and the sun rose into the sky.

"You are of a form despite outward appearances," said a dark-skinned mountain of a man with curly black hair. He approached the neighboring palus holding a heavy wooden mace. "I am Cerik."

Zephyrus hacked at the palus again, not wanting to engage in conversation. "Zephyrus."

Cerik laughed as he clubbed the wooden challenger. "Everyone knows who you are. Word has it you don't remember things."

"I see word travels."

"It always does when speaking of the Judges," Cerik whispered. "Some say you are one of the Three. Is this true?"

Zephyrus only shrugged, unsure of how Cerik would view him. *Last thing I need is another enemy.* "That's what they say."

"Well, any man trusted by the Judges is trusted by me," Cerik said. He smashed his mace into the palus. "If there's anything you need, you can count on Cerik."

Despite being the size of a house, holding a mace that likely weighed as much as Zephyrus himself, Cerik's easy smile comforted him.

Perhaps I am not as alone as I feared?

"Gratitude, Cerik. I appreciate that."

Doctore's whip cracked, and the clack of swords stopped. All eyes inclined to the balcony, where Cassius joined Nallia to rest his hands on the banister. Zephyrus glared at the villain.

"Doctore," Cassius said, "take measure of our wares. Stage a tournament between all who till my sands."

"At your will, Dominus."

Doctore gathered the men into a circle. Zephyrus stood between Jecht and Cerik. For hours, men squared off for the entertainment of the entitled elite upon the balcony. Zephyrus clenched his fists. His palms still hurt from the Seers' scars, but he couldn't help himself.

Every matchup ended the same: one emerged victorious, and the other sulked off in the shame and pain of defeat while the Cassiuses on the balcony applauded.

"Live…" Patrus's last word. *This is no way to live. How many accepted this without a second thought? How many, like Jecht, desire something more?*

"Vossler, Taric—to the sands!" Doctore gestured for each to enter the circle. Taric assumed position with sword and shield in hand. His gaunt face and narrow eyes were set to fire as Vossler stood across from him armed with a spear.

"Begin!"

The two met with vicious grunts. Taric blocked Vossler's spear and kicked its owner to the sands.

"Do you know this man?" Zephyrus asked Jecht and Cerik. Taric was the one Lenox spoke to earlier. Zephyrus hadn't thought much of Taric at first look, solemn and reclusive. During sparring, he went through the motions, but now he fought like a man possessed.

"Taric was a legend in years past," Jecht whispered to Zephyrus. "Have you heard stories of Laytonus?"

Zephyrus shook his head as Taric threw Vossler once again to the sands.

"Laytonus was once Champion here," Cerik said. "Feared, but respected by all."

"Even in Targarus's ludus," Jecht said, "no one spoke ill of Laytonus."

"Taric and Laytonus were closer than brothers," Cerik said. "Lovers, to tell it true. But Stegavax cut Laytonus down in the arena." Cerik nodded across the sands.

Zephyrus followed Cerik's gaze across the circle to Stegavax. Larger than Cerik, Stegavax was monstrous. Layered with muscle, the Champion had long, thick braids of hair that made him look like a feral beast. Jagged teeth filed down to points split through his grin. Dark, narrow eyes cut like daggers at Taric's back. His ham-sized fists clenched as if waiting to join the fight.

"You fight your own in the arena?" Zephyrus asked.

"No," Jecht said. "Never. Stegavax and Laytonus were on the same side. He stabbed Laytonus in the back."

Zephyrus's jaw dropped. He jerked his head in Jecht's direction, but Jecht's gaze remained fixed on Taric and Vossler's bout.

"To some," Cerik said, "the brotherhood of gladiators is sacred. But nothing is sacred to Stegavax. Taric will never forgive, but vengeance eludes him. And now Vossler must endure his wrath for keeping company with Stegavax's shadow."

Vossler jabbed with his spear, but rather than attempting to block it, Taric lifted his arm and pinched the shaft in his armpit. Wrenching around, he snatched it from Vossler's grasp. He followed through with his sword, slamming it into Vossler's chin. Vossler collapsed.

Taric stood over him and spat, throwing the spear to the sands at Stegavax's feet.

“Taric, victor!” Doctore shouted. Vossler stumbled to his feet and exited the circle as Doctore called the next two gladiators.

Nallia and her father clapped as they viewed the spectacle from above. Zephyrus could see how some who only knew a slave’s life could be grateful to be a gladiator, to have a brotherhood. They weren’t alone in their suffering. Yet if they knew of freedom, they would not stand for it.

Perhaps some of the men longed for freedom. They just told their clever lies, hiding behind a disguise of drunken glory.

A stirring turned Zephyrus’s sights back to the circle of gladiators. Taric and Stegavax stood nose to nose on the opposite side of the circle.

“Settle it like men, with sweat and blood.” Doctore pointed with his whip to the center of the circle.

“Your day comes,” Taric said, leveling his finger at Stegavax. “As does Laytonus’s justice.”

Stegavax spat. “You shall leave this world as he did—a relic.”

Before Doctore could raise his whip to signal the start of battle, the two charged at each other. Stegavax hacked with his twin swords in a ferocious attack. Taric backpedaled, then sprang forward, striking Stegavax across the back with his shield. Stegavax turned the momentum into a counterattack and swung his swords. Taric slammed them down and once again struck Stegavax with his shield, this time to the face.

Blood trickled from Stegavax’s nose and lip. He stepped back, but Taric continued his charge. He stabbed, dodged, countered, blocked, hacked, and retreated. Stegavax escaped without further scathing.

“This is how you honor his memory?” Stegavax flashed his pointed teeth.

He charged, chopping high, but was blocked by the shield. Struck low, but Taric’s blade deflected it. Attacked high again, then kicked low. The kick buckled Taric’s knee. Before he could reset, Stegavax slashed both wooden blades across his chest.

Taric stumbled backwards, and Stegavax kicked him to the sands. Taric reclaimed his feet quickly, only to take a vicious slice across the cheekbone. Taric retracted again, raising his shield, but Stegavax’s first blade knocked the shield out of the way. His second came across Taric's face on the other side, dropping him to his knees.

Stegavax circled Taric. "You learn your place before me. On your knees."

Taric struggled to get up, but before he could, a swift kick cast him back down to the sands, this time upon his back.

"Or better yet, on your back!"

"The body will break before the spirit," Cerik whispered.

Zephyrus grunted. Cassius had said something similar the night prior. *How many beatings will I take before Vykannis answers me again?*

Stegavax hacked. Taric blocked and countered, coming down hard on Stegavax's hand, forcing him to relinquish his blade. Stegavax used his now free hand to take Taric by surprise with a hard hooking punch to the face.

Blood flew from Taric's mouth. Stegavax punched him again, then followed through with his left blade arcing from low to high to catch Taric under the chin.

Taric fell, the sands now stained with his blood. He attempted to stand, mounting one last fruitless effort, but Stegavax once again hurled him to the ground.

"You are half the man I am!"

Taric raised his hand as if to signal mercy, but instead pointed at Stegavax. "And you are half the man he was." He attempted to stand but fell.

"Cease!" Doctore shouted. "Stegavax, victory is yours."

Taric laid in a heap upon the sands. Stegavax walked off. None of the men made a sound.

"I will defeat you!" Taric coughed, spitting blood at Stegavax. "You'll fall to judgment for what you did." Stegavax smirked as he walked away.

"Guards, bring him to the medicus." Doctore growled, looking to the sun. "Rest. We'll resume the tournament after the sun's crest."

The guards dragged Taric off, inciting chatter from the other gladiators. Zephyrus couldn't believe his eyes. He frowned, following Jecht and Cerik into the shade.

If Taric sought justice for Laytonus's murder, he would not be able to levy that sentence himself, at least not with brute force. To avenge Laytonus, Taric would need to tell clever lies and become accepted by Stegavax. And once he gained the villain's trust, then, and only then, could he strike Stegavax from this world.

Zephyrus realized the error of his own ways. *Clever lies.* If the Judges could see the intentions of his heart, they would not forsake him if he lied to his masters.

Live.

He needed to stay alive to fulfill his destiny and bring honor to the Judges.

One clever lie, and I shall have my vengeance.

"Doctore," Zephyrus said. "I've made my decision."

CHAPTER 23

A Bloody Demonstration

Laeden VII

Stockhelm

Laeden was relieved to have left Baron Ebron Brusos's ludus. While Damascus inspected Brusos's gladiators for the Kings' Day Games, Laeden took measure of the vying chancellor, but something about him gave Laeden a deep, dark disquiet. Laeden prayed his meeting with Cassius went better. If the Gods were good, Zephyrus would have information that gave him confidence in the Cassiuses.

Their litter followed the road south towards the Head Lanista's home carved into the Hylan Mountains. Due to Stockhelm's vastness and diversity, the need for a chancellor well immersed in the culture was imperative. He couldn't imagine the difficulty of eliminating the Revivalists if they were organized throughout Stockhelm, making this visit with Cassius all the more important.

"We're nearly there," Damascus said beside Laeden, at the head of their caravan.

The setting sun sank behind the peaks of the Hylan Mountains. The nightly rains would soon be upon them.

Beside Damascus rode his sworn sword and knight of the King's Guard—Ser Ellus. Behind them, Damascus's squire, Haedron Allos, and

Damascus's friend, Ser Aemos Horne, sat atop their mounts. A number of guards followed on foot in their wake.

"I wouldn't mind seeing Nallia again," Haedron mused, his head in the clouds.

Damascus smirked over his shoulder. "She's easy on the eyes."

"She's nothing special," Aemos said, with a dismissive wave. "She looks like her brutish brother."

Laeden frowned at the developing conversation. In truth, Aemos was only jealous of Markus because Markus bested him at everything. Atonus Allos appointed Markus his apprentice instead of Aemos, and he had yet to get over it. Aemos also tried to court Markus's sister, years back. Nallia Cassius challenged every one of her suitors to a duel to see if they were worthy. Needless to say, Aemos wasn't.

Damascus huffed. "Don't be petty, Aemos. After all the coin you've spent on sparring lessons, I'm sure, if given another chance, you'd be able to last a round or two against Nallia."

Haedron burst into an obnoxious cackle, chiding Aemos.

Before Aemos's short temper could be set off, Laeden intervened. "Let's remember why we're here. Our nation is on the brink of war. War requires allies. Allies who have the support of the people. People who can either rally to or against our cause."

"Easy, brother," Damascus said. "It is not like tonight is about finding you another senator's daughter to reject."

More snickers.

Laeden ground his teeth, his cheeks flushing. *Firstborn, castle-bred, entitled, patrician snobs.* Crushing his reins between white-knuckled fists, he hissed out his breath.

"We will be on our best behavior," Damascus said. "Cassius's gladiators never disappoint, and I'm sure he will make a fine chancellor when Stegavax wins the omenation. So sit back, relax, and if the Six are merciful, we may get to see Nallia carve up Aemos again."

Aemos stifled a growl as all but he and Laeden laughed. Aemos was always hotheaded, and his training under the eyes of Targarus's Doctore only made him more dangerous once he reached his boiling point.

Still, as they rode, while the others spoke of girls and tourney knights, Laeden's thoughts were with Iylea. The Revivalists. The Uprising. And his father.

The silhouette of the Cassius ludus stood against the orange hues of the setting sun as their retinue ascended the hills to the mountain fortress's front doors where Earl Cassius and his wife waited.

"Prince Damascus, Prince Laeden, it's my great honor to receive you," Cassius said, arms open wide.

Following the Cassiuses through the villa back to the showroom where Zephyrus nearly killed Lenox with a cheese knife, Laeden hoped this night would not be filled with the same type of *excitement.*

"How fares your newest gladiator?" Damascus asked. "The cheese slayer."

"He renounced the Judges and swore allegiance to the Six," Cassius said. "He needed a little convincing, but aside from a few bruises, he will be fine if you wish to see a fresh demonstration tonight."

Laeden bit his lip. He had gotten rid of Zephyrus—the Prophet of Celestia—at his father's orders, but that didn't mean he wanted his asset to be mistreated. His father's warning stuck with Laeden, but as long as Zephyrus remained absent his memories, he was too valuable to be left to waste.

If Cassius was to be chancellor—and chimera's breath, he hoped he would—he needed to make sure the Revivalists had no hooks in him. The chancellor could shift the power within the senate, and his father needed all the allies he could get.

Damascus nodded. "I would like to see him fight again."

"He will need to be summoned from the barracks." With a wave of Cassius's hand, his advisor, Liario, scurried off.

Nallia soon arrived, and the competition for her affections began. Aemos bowed stiffly, Haedron blurted foolishly, but Damascus—as always—drew the attention of the blushing maiden.

The festivities began. They ate as the doctore chose matches, pitting the gladiators against each other either in single combat, free-for-all, or partnered battles so Damascus could select the most entertaining men for the games. The burned gladiator, Fenyx, impressed against the former Targarus spearman, Jechtaric, and Cassius's traditional bruiser, Cerik. Although no clear winner emerged, Damascus was pleased. However, the rest of the gladiators did little to hold Damascus's attention.

"Now that gladiators have been selected," Laeden said, "I would like to speak concerning the chancellorship—"

"I'm not done," Damascus said. "I would see your new man—the cheese slayer."

Nallia fidgeted within her seat. "He has not yet recovered from his—"

"Nonsense, the man can fight," Cassius said. A clap of thunder signaled the beginning of the nightly rains. "Doctore! One more contest." He raised a cup, gesturing to the guards at the entrance to the courtyard.

The gladiators, still stationed within the hall, murmured as four guards escorted Zephyrus into the courtyard.

Laeden held back a wince. Still bandaged from the wounds he suffered during his revolt at the slavers' auction, fresh bruises about his eyes and around his ribs marred his flesh.

Zephyrus's stoic gaze fell upon Laeden.

"Prince Damascus," Cassius said, "against which of my titans would you like to see his skills tested?"

A light rain fell through the sky window, creating ripples in the bath and painting the marble slab within it.

"Who better than the Champion of the house?" Damascus asked.

Another clap of thunder echoed off of the mountains and reverberated through the fortress.

Stegavax took position on the marble slab. The rain came down with greater fervor, drenching the Champion in moments.

Liario leaned down besides Cassius. "My earl, perhaps our guests would like to see an offering of blood. If wood were exchanged for steel, perhaps—"

Damascus raised his goblet. "I second that. Let us see steel."

Laeden examined Liario, then Zephyrus. After Zephyrus's supposed escape attempt that night, and Lenox's volunteering to fight against him in the omenation, this sudden offering of steel seemed suspicious. He looked across his host towards his half-brother.

"That's not necessary, brother," Laeden said. "There will be a time for blood—"

"Our guests desire steel. Steel they shall have." The smell of wine cascaded from Cassius's mouth. The doctore bowed his head, and steel weapons replaced their wooden counterparts.

Thunder roared as rain fell harder.

Stegavax, the greatest Slicer-style gladiator in the history of New Rheynia, twirled his two steel blades. Laeden swallowed. He'd seen Stegavax send dozens of men to the afterlife.

Zephyrus is beyond a competent swordsman, but can he stand against Stegavax?

The rain poured down.

"Now we meet, Harbinger," Stegavax shouted over the rain. He leveled his swords at Zephyrus as the attendant armed him with a sword and buckler.

Zephyrus said nothing. He glanced at Laeden, a serenity in his gaze—a calm before the storm. Bruised and battered as he was, with the world conspiring to kill him, Zephyrus didn't seem in over his head. *Perhaps he is the Wielder*. Laeden never believed in such folktales before, but Zephyrus made him rethink them.

Zephyrus set his sights on Stegavax, but before Cassius gave the signal to begin, Stegavax lunged and stabbed, drawing gasps from the onlookers. Zephyrus blocked with his shield and parried a sweeping slash. He ducked under another chop, stepped over a leg sweep, and sidestepped a front kick. Stegavax continued the onslaught with masterful efficiency, but Zephyrus remained unscathed.

"He is a talent," Damascus said, raising his voice over the falling rain.

One of Stegavax's blows splintered Zephyrus's iron-rimmed shield. He cast the shattered shield at Stegavax and charged. Stegavax slapped the shield away with his blades and recoiled just in time to catch a vicious downward chop between his own two swords. Zephyrus planted a kick to Stegavax's chest, separating the two for a moment before they were nose to nose in another deadlock.

Stegavax headbutted Zephyrus, spewing blood from Zephyrus's nose. Stegavax seized the advantage and swept Zephyrus's leg, toppling him onto the wet marble slab. Stegavax swiped downward but struck nothing but the stone where Zephyrus had been moments ago. Zephyrus sprang to his feet.

Laeden pulled at the fabric of his doublet. *Come on, Zephyrus…*

Stegavax jabbed, but his footwork faltered. Zephyrus caught Stegavax's wrist between his arm and his ribs and torqued, sending one of Stegavax's blades clamoring to the slab and skidding into the pool. Stegavax chopped with his other sword, but Zephyrus caught his pommel and punched with his sword hand, sending Stegavax stumbling back.

Stegavax once again took the offensive and assaulted Zephyrus with a barrage of hacks, cuts, and slashes. A savage slice by Stegavax cleaved through Zephyrus's cheap steel sword. The blade fell from the hilt—a useless defense against Stegavax.

Laeden couldn't believe his eyes. "Cease!"

No one listened.

Nallia gasped, putting her hand to her chest as Stegavax moved in for the kill.

Zephyrus ducked under Stegavax's swipe and punched Stegavax in the gut. Seizing Stegavax's wrist, he wrenched the blade from his grasp. The blade splashed into the pool.

Both unarmed, the two wrestled, thrashing for their lives as Aquarius rained down upon them. Stegavax's advantage in size began to take shape.

Come on, fight…

Nallia whimpered as Stegavax wrapped a large bloody arm around Zephyrus's throat. Zephyrus resisted but couldn't escape Stegavax's chokehold.

Laeden stood. "Stop this!"

No one answered his command.

Zephyrus's face purpled. Stegavax didn't obey. *Stegavax will kill him.*

"Cease!" Damascus shouted, clapping with approval. Cassius gave a signal to his doctore, and with the snap of a whip, Stegavax relinquished Zephyrus from his grasp.

Laeden slumped back in his chair, releasing his breath as if Stegavax had strangled him.

"Well fought," Damascus said. "You have quite the ludus, Earl Cassius. I imagine if your skill as a lanista translates to your role as chancellor, the Revivalists won't stand a chance. I would have Stegavax, Fenyx, and Zephyrus each take position in the Primus on Kings' Day."

Cassius bowed. "You honor me, my prince."

The gladiators were escorted out, the slaves began cleaning, and the guards led the Salmantic guests to their chambers for the evening.

Earl Cassius turned to Laeden. "Shall we discuss your strategy and how I might best serve as chancellor?" His servile grin was a mockery of true respect.

"I would have liked nothing more," Laeden said, matching Cassius's false deference. "Yet I'm afraid I must have words with Zephyrus first."

A twitch of annoyance rippled across Cassius's face. Laeden didn't even pretend to care. At this point, he trusted Zephyrus more than the earl, regardless of his father's warning.

"A slave over an earl?" Cassius's crow's feet deepened.

"I intend no disrespect, my earl," Laeden said. "He led the largest slave outbreak in our country's history, and the increasing number of escaped slaves—this *Uprising*—is putting a strain on the Jackals' resources. I have questions only he can answer, lest the Sentinels be drawn into the Jackals' quarrels. Will you grant me an audience with him?"

Despite his obvious displeasure, Cassius nodded, permitting Laeden to speak with Zephyrus. Dismissed by Cassius, Laeden accompanied the large, bearded guard, Nortus, down the stairs to the barracks.

"I would speak to him outside," Laeden said as they descended.

"As you wish." Nortus stopped before a cell crammed with half a dozen men jostling for space. "Come on, Zephyrus." Nortus unlocked the door.

Zephyrus allowed Nortus to shackle him, his expression as unreadable as the masks worn by the Faceless. Nortus escorted them past the other cells to the door at the end of the corridor. He held the door open, gesturing out into the rain. Stepping outside, they took shelter under an awning.

"Gratitude, Nortus," Laeden said. "You may leave us."

Nortus hesitated but did as Laeden ordered.

Once alone, Laeden examined Zephyrus, wondering if he was the monster his father feared, or the ally he needed. "You've looked better."

Zephyrus shrugged. "Still alive…"

"Praise whatever God responsible. What has happened?"

In previous interactions with Zephyrus, he was enslaved to his passions, his emotions as easy to read as a book, but now Zephyrus's eyes were a cold impasse, betraying none of his inward thoughts.

"Last you were here, one of Cassius's guards by the name of Saulus feigned to free me. After breaking my chains, he tried to kill me, saying I attempted to escape. Didn't work. Lenox tried to finish the job, but you saw how that ended."

Laeden massaged his beard. *Saulus, Lenox—how many more?* "And since my departure?"

Zephyrus frowned. "Lenox received a delivery in the night. A dagger with the balanced scale of Celestia embossed into the hilt. I think he gave the dagger to a gladiator."

Gladiators… with the Revivalists? Laeden shook his head. *Why? To kill Cassius? No. It would be easier for Lenox to do it himself. Why go through all the trouble? And why a dagger with ties to the Judges?*

Regardless, it was too dangerous to permit. "Which gladiator?" Laeden asked. "A gladiator can't have a concealed weapon; it must be confiscated at once."

"I saw Lenox hand him something, the morning after he received the dagger, but—"

Laeden huffed. "But you didn't see him hand the gladiator the dagger…"

"No. I'm not sure *what* he handed him. But what else could it be?"

Laeden nodded. "We need more."

Zephyrus gestured toward the door. "Search him. You'll find it."

"At the risk of letting others know we're on to them, no. If anything, I would bring Lenox in for—"

"Don't," Zephyrus said. The desperation in his tone gave Laeden pause. Zephyrus continued in an attempt to conceal it. "I need him to lead me to the other Revivalists, right?"

Laeden grunted but couldn't disagree. "So be it. Keep up the good work. Markus says we can trust Nortus, so if you must send word, he's your man. Besides the two of you, there's no one under this roof I trust."

Zephyrus nodded, eyes downcast to the puddles beneath his sandals. "Did you ask the king about my letter?" Zephyrus pulled the scroll from his sublingaria.

Laeden valued integrity. He considered his word the equivalent of law. But if the information his father gave him were true, whoever Zephyrus worked for prior to losing his memory was an enemy of the crown.

"He is dangerous," his father had said. *"The men he serves are dangerous."*

Some truths were better left untold. Laeden didn't want to deliver his asset the information that could turn him into an enemy.

"Apologies, Zephyrus," Laeden said, looking Zephyrus in the eyes. "My father had nothing to share concerning the contents of your letter." The breath seemed to seep from Zephyrus's lungs. "But don't lose heart. I've shared it with the brightest minds in New Rheynia. This very moment, they are scouring tomes to connect the dots of this mystery."

Zephyrus nodded and managed a half-smile, but Laeden didn't like how easily the lie came to him.

For the good of the realm…

CHAPTER 24

THE MARIONETTE

Laeden VIII

Salmantica

"Laeden," Iylea pleaded. "I know how it sounds, but I'm positive. It was him!"

Laeden closed the door to his chamber after ushering her inside. He massaged his temples, trying to make sense of the cryptic description she'd provided on their walk up.

Not two minutes after returning to Sentigard, Laeden had been informed that the Prefectus Medicus had received another desiccated corpse from the Vigiles—this one, a Rheynian vagabond. As if the first body wasn't perplexing enough, the second conflicted with his theory that this was some sort of ritualistic sacrifice by the Revivalists. And before he could even take his traveling cloak off, Iylea pulled him aside with the desperate need to speak to him.

Now in his chambers, away from prying eyes and ears, Iylea's gaze darted left and right as if expecting someone lurking in his rooms. Iylea's hysteria made it difficult for Laeden to remain calm, but he couldn't feed into her energy—it would only make things worse.

With a deep breath, he took her by the hand and led her into the sitting room before the hearth. Iylea sat on the edge of a cushioned sofa, so far forward she was practically standing. Her hands fidgeted with the hem of her dress.

"Start over," Laeden said, resting his hand on her knee as he sat down opposite her. "From the beginning."

Fear and paranoia were spreading like a plague through the city already, so it was nothing new for him. It amazed him what people could convince themselves of once an idea entered their minds. People would see ghosts and hear whatever they feared most, but this was Iylea—not people. She needed him to listen, and so he would.

"...After the others left," Iylea said, "he addressed another man, telling him to deliver the package using a new messenger. Then the voice said, 'A sharp blade... simple vicious thing.' And sent it to a guard at House Cassius. At first, I thought perhaps it—"

"Wait, what?" Laeden held his hands up to stop her. "A blade... to House Cassius?" He thought back to what Zephyrus had told him. Lenox received a blade from a messenger in the middle of the night, and the next day, he delivered it to a gladiator.

Six save us...

He returned his attention back to Iylea. "Who? Names, faces?"

Iylea trembled. "I don't know for sure. I hid until they were gone. I waited for..." She looked up to the ceiling as if the Gods held her answers. "I don't know, Laeden. I thought I waited long enough, but I didn't."

A chill washed over Laeden's cheeks as blood drained. "What do you mean—did someone catch you?"

"No, Laeden. Calm down." Iylea took his hand and pulled him back to his seat. "I hid, but when I left, I stumbled into Ser Daenus."

"Ser Daenus, as in Danella's sworn sword?" Laeden asked in disbelief. "You think Ser Daenus is the leader of the Revivalists?" He shook his head.

No. Impossible. Father wanted him to lead *the Sentinels. He can't be with the Revivalists.*

"I swear, Laeden. I know how it sounds, but it was him. I'm sure of it."

"Iylea, this is important..." Laeden gently squeezed her hands. He closed his eyes. *Six, what kind of trouble is she in?* "Does he suspect you might know of his involvement? Has he been following you, watching you?"

Iylea began to tremble. Tears trickled from the corners of her eyes to roll down her cheeks. "I don't know." She stifled soft sobs. "I don't know if it's my imagination, but I feel the weight of lingering eyes."

"Have you seen him following you, though?"

"He doesn't have to, Laeden. We both serve the queen. He clings to her like a shadow, and I must attend her. He is *always* watching me." Iylea put her face in her hands. She dried her eyes and took a deep breath.

A secret gathering of men, the discussion of messengers, and the blade corroborated by Zephyrus's story. Iylea wasn't making this up, *but Ser Daenus?* If it were him, he had plenty of time alone with the king and queen. If he wanted to strike, he could do so himself with little to no resistance. *Why go through all the trouble?*

The marionette had too many strings, too many unknowns that Laeden couldn't presume to understand, but he didn't need all the facts to know Daenus was dangerous.

"Stay here." Laeden lurched to his feet, letting Iylea's hands fall from his own.

"But there's more I must te—"

Laeden bolted out the door.

"Captain Laeden." The Sentinel waiting outside saluted.

"Call a dozen men to the king and queen's chambers," Laeden said, not breaking stride. "An arrest will be made. Now."

Without question, the Sentinel took off down the halls of Sentigard.

It was late afternoon; Danella and his father would be upon their balcony awaiting the setting sun. And so would Ser Daenus. He didn't have a plan, but this wasn't a time for posturing. The threat was too near and too powerful to go unchecked. Laeden couldn't wait for the other Sentinels to arrive.

Already, nightmarish thoughts tore through his mind. He tried to dissuade such notions as irrational. If Daenus wanted to strike, he could have done so at any point. Sensible reasoning aside, the thought of Daenus's sword through his father's back sped Laeden's pace up the west tower stairway. Bounding two at a time, Laeden approached their chambers.

Two sentries stood guard outside of their door.

"I request an audience with the king and queen," Laeden said, through labored breath. "It's urgent." The sentries bowed, then knocked to alert the inner guards. Once the doors opened, Laeden pushed through, advancing towards the balcony.

As expected, the king and queen sat, hand in hand, watching the sunset over the Hylans. His intrusion broke the serenity of the moment, but Laeden didn't care. His father's bodyguard, Ser Ostrey, and Danella's, Ser Daenus, both reached for the pommels of their swords at Laeden's sudden entrance.

"Chimera's breath, Laeden," his father exclaimed. "What are you doing?"

Laeden held a finger towards Ser Daenus. "You dishonor yourself."

"What's the meaning of this?" Daenus asked, his hand still on the hilt of his sword.

Ser Ostrey drew his sword. "My prince, lower your blade."

Laeden examined Ostrey, not realizing he'd drawn steel. He lowered the tip, but kept it drawn. "Ser Daenus is under arrest for conspiracies against the crown. He will come with me on his own accord, or by force, if necessary."

Daenus held out his palms. "My queen, I don't know what he speaks of."

"Laeden, explain yourself," his father said.

"Daenus has conspired with the Revivalists and will be taken in for questioning," Laeden said. The footfalls of Laeden's bustling Sentinels filed onto the balcony. "Ser Daenus, will you comply, or must we take you by force?"

Danella put her hand to her mouth.

"He lies," Daenus said. "I don't know of what he speaks, my queen."

"Then go with them." Danella glared at Laeden. "This will all be set right."

Laeden's men moved in and disarmed Daenus before manacling him.

"Hold him in the dungeons." Laeden sheathed his sword. "I will be down to question him once I've concluded my search."

"Surely this is some mistake," Danella said. "Varros, I warned you of this, didn't I?"

His father gave Danella a silencing stare. "Leave us." He waved off the guards. Laeden stood under the brunt of their harsh glares as the Sentinels and guards fled the balcony.

"On what grounds is Ser Daenus under arrest?" Varros asked once they were alone.

"What proof do you have, to take away my *bodyguard*?" Danella asked, gravitating towards her husband. "Surely, you must have three witnesses who are willing to testify under oath if you can present no evidence."

"One of my informants overheard Ser Daenus assigning messengers to deliver various packages. One such package was confirmed by another informant," Laeden said, looking from Danella to his father. "While I don't yet have proof, I have enough to know you will both be safer with him secured in the dungeons."

"Separating us from our sworn protectors… on whispers and hunches?" Danella asked. "This is our safety we're talking about. Laeden, I appreciate what you are doing, but you are mistaken. I trust Daenus with my life. If he wanted me dead, he could have done so half a hundred times, today alone. Be reasonable. If the Revivalists wanted to expose us to another attack, framing our personal guards would be the easiest way to clear a path for their assassins."

"My men will protect you," Laeden said, but even as he said it, he thought of Pirus, the Revivalist within his ranks. Stifling his doubt, he stood his ground. "Until I'm certain Daenus is not a threat, I must trust my informants and do my due diligence."

"So it only matters if *you* trust the men guarding us?" Danella scoffed, shaking her head—not in anger, but disappointment. "Varros, this experiment has gone on long enough. Deal with this." Danella stormed from the room.

His father put his face in his hands.

"Father, I have just cause for my actions. Once I investigate the study and interrogate him, I will find proof."

His father chuckled. "She said you would do this, you know?"

Thunder rumbled in the distance.

"Do what—my duty?" His father didn't react to Laeden's outburst. He didn't need to. "Apologies, Father, I..."

The king held up a silencing hand. "She said you would make this your personal mage hunt, arresting whoever you wanted without proof." Laeden opened his mouth to object, but the king's glare stopped him. "She's just worried about you."

"I can handle myself," Laeden said.

The king nodded. "Let us hope so. Provide proof, a confession, or three witnesses to corroborate your case against Ser Daenus, and no explanation will be necessary."

Laeden bowed, his fists clenched at his sides. "I will not let you down."

"I expect not, but if you don't have anything by midnight, Ser Daenus will be released and returned to his post. Is that clear?"

Laeden took a sharp inhale. "As clear as the Crystal River, my king."

CHAPTER 25

FINAL WARNING

Danella III

Salmantica

Danella's mind raced her feet as she descended the stairs of the west tower. Twice, she nearly tripped over herself in her hurry; her mind suffered the same consequences attempting to consider what information Laeden had on Daenus.

She thought he was chasing down bad leads after she'd witnessed the Prefectus Medicus performing an exam on an unmarked slave. While she understood why Laeden would pin it on the Revivalists, he couldn't have been further from the truth. Hoping his other leads would run dry, she hadn't concerned herself too much with Laeden playing the part of the Sentinel captain. But Ser Daenus's arrest proved Laeden was far more competent than she'd believed.

He knew about the dagger sent to House Cassius, *but how?* She used different messengers to avoid the mole, but still—not one, but two of his informants confirmed the truth.

How did he know? The Wielder?

Despite numerous attempts on his life, the slave had yet to be put to the funeral pyre.

Could he still be loyal to Laeden?

If so, Laeden was even more resourceful, ruthless, and reckless in his pursuit of the Revivalists than she could allow. She believed Daenus would be protected by the reasonable doubt she wove through Laeden's accusations, but Laeden was becoming a problem she couldn't allow to run unchecked.

There was a reason for the elaborate plots. Overthrowing the king overtly would sow discord throughout the kingdom, disrupting the peace the Gods desired. The threat of the Revivalists couldn't come from within the castle. If Laeden managed to gather evidence against Daenus, the delicate balance of her plans would be destroyed beyond redemption.

She traversed the inner bailey and descended the south tower towards the dungeons. She needed to speak with Daenus. She needed to know what other information Laeden had at his disposal, but as she approached the dungeon guard, she stopped herself.

Her first instinct was to get involved, create a diversion, and interrupt Laeden's investigation, but that would only draw attention to her, her people, or her other plans.

Trust the precautions we've taken. Laeden won't find anything.

She needed to be alone, wait this out, and trust the Six to watch over her. She left the south tower and sought her study, but to her horror, Laeden's men were already in there.

If he found the ledger in her hidden compartment, Daenus was as good as dead. Her mind filtered through every strip of parchment in the ledger—every word she had written held her fate. *Could anything incriminate me? Or would Daenus tell Laeden of my involvement?* The thought of Varros's grief-stricken face at the knowledge of her betrayal haunted her, *but what can I do now?* She felt helpless—nothing to do but worry. Or pray.

She fled the study for the Gods' counsel. The city of Salmantica had six different temples, one erected to pay homage to each of the Valencian Gods. Sentigard, however, had the Royal Basilica. Carved into the Silver Summits along the north side of the castle, the bell tower reigned over Sentigard and the rest of Salmantica. Her father constructed a grand foyer with intricately carved statues of the Six at the altar. Oriented in a row, their visage brought her peace. At this time in the evening, it would be empty, but their presence never left.

Danella knelt down before Phaebia, the Goddess of hope, life, and light. Her youthful face smiled down at her. The Goddess's windswept dress flowed behind her, a basket filled with flowers in the crook of her arm. In her outstretched hand, a single flower reached down for any humble enough to accept it.

Danella lowered her eyes. "My trust is in you, Phaebia. I trust your plans, your provision, and your providence. This present moment is no different than this morning. Only you know the future laid before us mortals, and your guidance through omenations is a gift. Forgive me in my moments of doubt, my desire to control and stoop to self-reliance. Let me be a vessel for your will. If you wish to stop me and my plans, I submit. I only wish to serve you and your siblings. Forgive me if I have transgressed and misinterpreted your will."

Danella raised her eyes to Phaebia's stoney face. Just once she wished to hear an audible reply to her prayers—some validation or confirmation for everything she worked for in honor of the Gods who led her father from the Disasters of Rheynia.

Phaebia didn't reply. Neither did Moterra, Ferrocles, Incinerae, Aquarius, or Hameryn. She stood from the altar, unsure of how much time had passed while she prayed. The nightly rains stormed beyond the walls of Sentigard, but Danella's foundation was restored. She would not blow in the wind of Laeden's accusations. She returned to the inner bailey, secure in her stance; whatever Laeden threw at her, she would overcome.

She walked through the inner bailey and towards her chambers in the west tower, passing her study. Books were strewn about—stacked on the desk or thrown on the floor. The shelves were nearly bare.

Her stomach seized in knots. *Six, what did they find?*

"Keep searching," Markus said. "We'll keep at it all night if we must."

While Danella gaped at the disarray of her study, Varros approached.

"You may continue your search if you wish," the king said, loud enough for the Sentinels in the study to hear. "However, Ser Daenus has been released. Until more reasonable claims are made, witnesses come forward, or evidence is presented, there is no case against Ser Daenus, his honor, or his legacy."

Laeden and his Sentinels escorted Ser Daenus down the corridor. The satisfaction on Daenus's face gave Danella solace, but not nearly as much as Laeden's scowl did.

He found nothing. Praise the Six.

The Sentinel guards released Daenus from his manacles, but Laeden intended to keep him secured with his deadlock stare. Despite the tension in his jaw and the creases lining his face, Laeden could do nothing against the law.

"May I return to my post now, my prince?" Daenus asked Laeden. Laeden mumbled something incoherent beneath his breath. "Apologies, my prince, I could not hear you."

Laeden snapped. "I said…" He took a breath to compose himself before continuing in a much more diplomatic tone. "I said, 'Don't get comfortable.' I'll be watching you, and when you slip up, I'll take you down." He stalked up to Ser Daenus and stabbed his finger into the larger man's chest. "You return to your post, but if anything happens to her on your watch…" Laeden shook his head threateningly.

Varros fixed Laeden with a disapproving stare.

His misconduct will be his undoing.

"I want your mess cleaned up," Varros said, surveying the state of the study. "Next time you make an arrest, is it too much to ask that you have *something*?" He turned on his heel and strode away.

Laeden's clenched fists shook at his sides.

Danella pitied him; she always had. Even as a boy, Laeden hadn't belonged. His parents' annulment allowed Danella and Varros to secure New Rheynian peace through matrimony, but Laeden was pulled from his mother's arms and delivered to Sentigard. At the age of ten, Laeden lost everything he ever knew. The first time she met Laeden as a boy, he looked much the way he did now. Danella never wanted this for him.

Laeden's love for his father, his commitment to his duty, and the fervor for which he sought honor and justice were admirable. But if she had to choose between removing Varros from the kingdom or Laeden, it wouldn't be a difficult decision. His position within the Sentinels made him a problem she had to deal with despite the difficulty of it. She had tried to talk him out of this role with the Sentinels once before; she would have to try again.

Danella placed a hand on Laeden's flexed arm. "Laeden, might I speak with you… alone, just for a moment?" She didn't wait for a reply. Taking him by the arm, she strode down the corridor. Laeden complied, and Daenus followed at a safe distance behind. Once they were out of earshot of the other Sentinels, Danella opened up.

"I know you're frustrated, but misinformation is the Revivalists' greatest strength right now. These diversion tactics are meant to bait you, because once you bite, you're hooked on an idea they can continually use against you. You can't—"

Laeden stopped walking and yanked his arm free of Danella's grasp. "But what if this isn't misinformation? What if I'm not wrong?"

Danella put her hands on her hips. "Laeden, I didn't want you in this role in the first place. It's too dangerous. You're playing with fire and—"

"And I'm gonna get burned?" Laeden shook his head. "Everyone laughed at me when I said the kettle was hot. Everyone mocked me when I tried to warn them. But if not for me and my 'paranoia,' my father would be dead." He let the words hang in the air, echoing off the black stone walls of Sentigard. "I'm the only one who can stop the Revivalists. And I will if it's the last thing I do."

His icy Helixus stare met hers. She hoped it wouldn't come to that, but this was his final warning. If she were willing to sacrifice the love of her life to keep her father's kingdom safe from the Gods' wrath, she could live with herself if all she had to do was sacrifice his son.

"Take this advice," Danella said, imagining herself speaking to her own son. "Squeaking mice attract the cat's claws. You may have saved your father's life, but you put a target on your back in the process. If you continue on like this, attempting to stop the Revivalists may be the last thing you do."

Laeden narrowed his eyes. "What would you have me do—hide like a craven? Run off to Northridge, and wait for the Revivalists to kill my father?"

"No," Danella said, returning to his side to put her hand on his arm. "Fight, assist, serve—but let those with experience lead." Laeden pulled away from her touch. "I just want you to be safe, Laeden."

"And who would you put in charge—him?" Laeden scoffed, gesturing towards Daenus. "I'll take my chances, and you'll take yours." With that, he stormed off, his footsteps fading into the void of silence.

Danella remained unmoved for a time in the darkened corridor. She tried to spare him, but his defiance—his hubris—would be his undoing. *Poor Laeden.* She shook her head. "Come, Daenus. There is much to do."

CHAPTER 26

A Promise Kept, A Debt Paid

Fenyx II

Stockhelm

"Repeat after me." Auron's voice cut through the noise of the rain and thunder. He turned the brand in the fire until it gleamed red-hot. "I stand before Gods and men."

Auron dictated, and Jechtaric and Zephyrus repeated as Fenyx looked on with disgust from the corner of the break area sheltered from the rain.

"...To proclaim my mind, my flesh, and my soul to my dominus, Lentulis Cassius."

Fenyx grew up in this ludus. It took years surviving against other boys in Teluvar's fighting pits and over half a decade of blood and sweat in the training square for him to earn Dominus's mark. Fenyx dedicated his life to becoming a gladiator.

"I swear to give my life for the glory of this house and die in defense of it," the two men repeated after Auron.

Zephyrus had barely been here a week and didn't deserve the honor of being named to the brotherhood. Jechtaric had been branded by another lanista prior to his arrival, but Fenyx felt no swell of pride from the addition. To make matters worse, he'd have to share the glory of the Primus with Zephyrus.

After Jechtaric and Zephyrus recited the last of the words, Auron placed the glowing brand upon the back of their left hands. The skin bubbled to form a raised red *C*—a badge of honor they didn't appreciate or deserve.

"You may rise as new men—gladiators of House Cassius." Auron embraced the newest members of the brotherhood. Fenyx spat on the ground as they clasped each other's forearms.

The other gladiators kept their distance from their newest brothers as well. Normally when a recruit joined the brotherhood, everyone celebrated, but Zephyrus divided the barracks in ways they'd never known. Sure, Taric and Stegavax had their tensions ever since Laytonus's death, but Zephyrus was polarizing in a different way. But this talk of the Prophets of Celestia meant nothing; Zephyrus was a man just like any other, but he stood in Fenyx's way.

All but Stegavax—who didn't care about anyone but himself—and Taric—who spent the last few days in the medicus's quarters—were present. Even with over a score of gladiators, it felt like a hollow affair.

Auron raised his fist. "In celebration of three of our own being selected to the Primus on Kings' Day, Dominus has given us the leftover wine from last night's feast! Observe this moment, take pride in what you have accomplished, and set sights to future accolades."

The men rejoiced as they moved from the sheltered break area to the barracks. Fenyx remained unmoved, leaning against a thick wooden column that supported the shelter.

Auron approached. "Why so glum?"

Fenyx snorted. "Zephyrus barely survives Stegavax, and he is rewarded with the mark of the brotherhood. He didn't win, yet he is treated like Vykannis the Brave."

Auron looked around to make certain no one was within earshot. "Rein in your wagging tongue. Even to me, you must not speak of the Judges. If you were heard, you would pay with your life, and there'd be nothing I could do to save you. There are whispers of war on every lord's lips with this Uprising rabble."

Auron was right, but Fenyx didn't want to admit it. He stared into the black abyss of rain. Every once in a while, the sky would fracture, cleaved in two by giant forks of white lightning illuminating all of Stockhelm. Some bolts lasted long enough for him to see the arena in the shadows of the Stormburn Geyser.

"I shouldn't worry about the successes of others," Fenyx said. "I only wish to honor you when I take to the sands for the first time. I wish for the world to know the name Fenyx, his instructor, Auron, and the ludus of House Cassius."

"I pray the same."

"I will be Champion," Fenyx promised. "One way or another, I will overtake Stegavax."

They returned to the barracks, Auron retreating to his chambers down the hall. On such nights of celebration, casks of wine were left for them to consume. To Fenyx, it just meant his opponents would be slow on the morrow for spending the night in their cups.

Fenyx laid down on his cot listening to the jests of his fellow gladiators. Even Taric returned after spending the last few days with the medicus. He still looked a bloody mess, but Fenyx respected him for standing up for what he believed in, though he lacked the skill to back it up. He closed his eyes and gnawed on his whiteroot.

After the last of the wine, even the rowdiest of the gladiators took to dreams. Fenyx lay motionless in the dim candlelight, but sleep would not come. The drone of snores were interrupted by the occasional clap of thunder. If he listened closely, the rain continued to pour down. But something else disturbed the night.

The candle in the hall winked out. Fenyx sat up in his cot.

A shape moved in the darkness with brisk purpose. A moment passed, but a feeling gripped Fenyx's throat in the silence that followed. An unfamiliar sensation he had not felt in many years returned to him, coiling around him like a strangling snake.

Fear.

He listened to the darkness. *Did I imagine a figure in the shadows?*

A clap of thunder rattled the cell bars, but something else—the tail end of a cry—resounded from down the hall.

Before he could think, Fenyx bolted from his cell, following the screams to the Champion's quarters. Unlike the other cells gated with bars, the Champion's cell had a wooden door with a small, barred window. A struggle from the other side of the door accompanied curses and yelling, but he couldn't see anything in the pitch black. Fenyx tried to force the door open, but it wouldn't budge.

Through the window, the flash of lightning illuminated the Champion's cell. In the brief moment of light, two shapes wrestled in a room painted with scarlet blood. Fenyx shouted and threw himself into the door, blowing the wood into splinters. He didn't see the face of Stegavax's attacker, but he had to be stopped. Stegavax could go to the chain for all Fenyx cared, but he was still a brother who deserved to die a glorious death in the arena. Not a knife in the night.

Fenyx charged into the pitch black and lunged, searching for a body to grab onto. He found one, slick with blood and weak. He shoved the body to the corner.

A shout came and the second body ran into Fenyx. The two grappled, and Fenyx wrestled the shadow to the floor. He grabbed onto what seemed to be wrists, but a sharp sting bit into the side of his arm.

"Laytonus! Laytonus! I must for Laytonus!"

Another bolt of lightning cast a white glow upon Taric's blood-smeared face. He held a small but sharp blade. Darkness returned. Fenyx's eyes widened to let in light, but the shadows reigned.

"I must… For Laytonus!" Taric shouted, spitting blood into Fenyx's face. Taric's wrist, slippery and slick with blood, slid from his grasp. Fenyx headbutted Taric's already-broken nose, sending him rearing back. The knife clattered to the stone floor. Fenyx needed to get it first. He fumbled, searching blindly with his hands.

A glimmer of light shone off the blade. Fenyx reached for it but found Taric's hand grasped around it. The sliver of light darted towards Fenyx's face. He lurched away just in time, but his foot slipped on the bloody stones beneath him. He toppled to the ground as the blade slashed above him. Fenyx kicked at Taric's knee, dropping him to the floor. He grabbed Taric, attempting to seize the blade, but his grip slipped. Taric twisted, rolling Fenyx onto his back.

The glimmering edge stabbed downward. Fenyx seized Taric's hands, the blade's tip less than a hand's span from his face. Taric growled, driving the killing instrument closer and closer.

Fenyx spat into Taric's face and wrenched. The blade sparked as it stabbed into the stone beside him. With a quick jerk, Fenyx turned Taric's wrists and shoved.

The blade slipped into flesh.

Warm blood showered down on Fenyx as Taric let out the soft sound of a fatal wound.

Lightning struck to illuminate Fenyx's blood-soaked hands holding Taric's wrist. The glimmering edge was nowhere to be seen, buried deep in Taric's neck.

Taric sputtered. "For Laytonus…"

His body convulsed as his speech became slurred. His words dissolved into the guttural noises of death. He fell from atop Fenyx to the stone floor.

Fenyx shoved Taric's limp body off him and scooted, hands and feet, away from the fallen form, his stomach in knots.

Burn me… Fenyx had killed before, but the fighting pits weren't like this.

I killed a gladiator of the brotherhood.

The warm glow of torchlight entered the room.

"By the Gods…" Nortus stood with the entire brotherhood at his back, their faces barely recognizable through the flickering torch. But with the light, Fenyx could take in his surroundings.

Taric lay dead—a small blade, embedded to the hilt, protruded from his neck. The balanced scale of Celestia was embossed into the wooden handle. Blood covered the floor. And in the corner, Stegavax heaved labored breaths, clinging to life.

Covered in blood, it was impossible to tell where Stegavax's wounds were, but there were many of them.

"Seize him."

Expecting the guards to go to Stegavax's aid, he was surprised when they grabbed Fenyx and dragged him outside.

"I didn't do anything!" Fenyx shouted. "Taric did it. I defended Stegavax."

His own words returned to him. *"I will be Champion,"* he had said to Auron. *"One way or another, I will overtake Stegavax."*

This was not what Fenyx had in mind.

CHAPTER 27

UNDONE

Nallia II

Stockhelm

"No one can know!" her father said for the thousandth time. "If anyone learns of Stegavax's…"

"He may yet live," Nallia said. "The medicus said the most dangerous time has passed."

They woke to a living nightmare. Stegavax clung to life, nearly murdered in his sleep at the hands of his brother. Had it not been for Fenyx's intervention, he might have succeeded.

Her father paced in furious circles around his tablinum.

"Even if he lives," Auron said, "the Games of Stockhelm are out of the question."

"Chimera's burning breath!" her father shouted.

"My husband, don't worry," her mother said. "The same man who saved our Champion's life might be the one to claim his mantle."

"Fenyx is yet untested upon the sands," her father said. "This isn't Teluvar's pits—this is the omenation for the chancellorship. Just when we're about to climb to heights never imagined…" He growled before wheeling on Nallia. "This is all *your* fault!"

Nallia put her hand to her chest, her eyes wide. *What in Six Hells is he talking about?* "My fault?" She reached for her ring but caught herself and put her hands down at her sides. She had no reason to be nervous. *I did nothing wrong.*

"Yes, *your* fault. You think you can govern these men with kindness—herbs for their pain, healers for their memories—and it's a wonder to you when disaster strikes. You are too soft on them, and they have run amuck!"

Nallia's cheeks flushed. She couldn't believe her ears. "How can you blame this on me? What does a healer have to do with Taric's vengeance? You haven't left for the chancellor's tower yet, but you blame this on me?"

Her mother gasped.

Her father glared. "You dare speak to me in such a manner?"

Nallia twisted the ring about her finger with her thumb. *I did nothing wrong.*

When she didn't beg for her father's forgiveness, he shouted, "Everyone out!"

Her mother, Odetta, Auron, and Liario left in a hurry, but Nallia would not bend beneath his injustice. His bushy eyebrows furled. Like a bird of prey descending on a hare too prideful or too stupid to seek shelter, he advanced on her.

She didn't back down but had to clench her fists to keep herself from spinning her ring.

"What do you think the senators say when I tell them, 'My daughter will govern my ludus,' hmm? They laugh. They say, 'How can she control the beasts of the arena?' I admit you have the eye for identifying talent and bringing out the best of the men, but…" He shook his head. "Perhaps they have been right all along."

The flush in her cheeks rose to her ears. Her toes curled into the soles of her sandals. No words came to mind, but silence would only condemn her. "Beyond a keen eye, and the ability to motivate them, what more could a lanista possess?"

"Discipline!" Her father turned away from her, running his hands through his wispy hair. "Those savages must be forged with firm hands, or they will run wild like the animals they are."

"They are people," Nallia said.

"They are *slaves!* To be beaten, broken, used, and discarded at profit. This is a business."

Nallia glared at her father.

Of course it's a business, but there are other ways to inspire men besides beatings. Maybe I am too soft, but I had nothing to do with what Taric did. Father is just stressed because of the omenation and the pressures of the chancellorship. He will realize he is wrong.

Her father's shoulders slumped, and his face fell into his hands. "Perhaps the fault is mine in placing too much responsibility on your shoulders."

Her anger boiled within, threatening to erupt. "Too much responsibility? Taric attacked Stegavax out of vengeance! Nothing I—"

"With a blade of Celestia!" Her father's face darkened. "How do you think the patricians would view me—the Chancellor of Stockhelm—if Celestics infest my own house? Your tolerance. Your softness." He turned from her, lifting his hands to Valencia to let them fall and slap against his hips. "If Markus were here, none of this would have happened."

Nallia erupted. "That's what this is about?" She stamped her foot, fists coiled at her sides. "I'm a woman, so I'm incapable of levying discipline? I'm soft and weak, and only Markus can lead? What does that say of you, Father?"

His predatory eyes narrowed. He advanced on her, index finger leading the way. "You dare speak to me in such a manner?"

Nallia backed away and dropped her eyes. *Seize hold of yourself, Nallia. You know how to speak with him.* She let out a slow, steadying breath. "Apologies, Father. This is my fault, but let me make this right. Zephyrus has been showing promise since arriving. Let him fight in the omenation, and you—"

"Fenyx will take to the sands." Her father's eyes bore into her, as if daring her to challenge him again.

"But Fenyx has been paraded before Brusos and his wife," Nallia said. "No one outside of the royal family knows of Zephyrus. He stood against Stegavax for the sake of the Six."

"I'll hear no more," her father said. "This is long overdue, but your time in the ludus is over."

Nallia stammered. *What? No! How can you do this?*

"You will join Prince Damascus in Salmantica and attend the Salmantic Games."

Nallia's heart seized in her throat. *But then I'll miss the Games of Stockhelm.*

She'd never missed any of the games, not since she was a little girl. Her defiance withered beneath his shadow.

"Perhaps there, you will serve some good to this house," her father said. "Enough with these duels. This foolish pride. Get married and be someone else's problem."

Nallia's stomach churned, and tears stung her eyes. *He uses me. Offering me—my body—to the prince for his advancement.* "Father, please. I—"

"That is final."

"Father, what about—"

"Question me again and I will remind you that Lentulis, *not Nallia*, is dominus of this house. If you wish to help, send in Doctore and Liario so I might set them to purpose." He waved her away like a horse's tail would a fly.

"Is that all you'd have of me?" She blinked away tears.

He sat down at his desk, shuffling papers about.

He won't even look at me. She bit her lip as the heart and soul she poured into this ludus was stripped away, disregarded. *I'm just a commodity. A trade piece for his gains.* Not knowing what else to do, she dropped her eyes. "As you say, Father."

Cowed, her meek exit from the tablinum became a storm by the time she reached the atrium. *How can he do this to me? My fault?* The skin beneath her amethyst ring was raw from twisting it about her finger. *Perhaps this is my fault. How many times did I speak of the Judges as a means of motivating the men to fight? How many times did I wish someone—anyone—would overtake Stegavax as Champion?*

After sending Liario and Auron back to her father, Nallia's mother came to her.

"Nallia, dear. Come with me." Her mother led her out to the balcony overlooking the training square. Watching the gladiators had always been a comfort, but now Nallia gripped the banister with white knuckles. Mother placed her hand atop Nallia's.

"Calm yourself. I will speak with him. All will be right. Fenyx will prevail in the Primus and secure our position as the Head Ludus. Soon, your father will be chancellor, and he will be begging you to take over the ludus in his name, if you still desire it."

She squeezed the rail tighter. *If I still desire it?* "It's all I've wanted since I was a girl."

Her mother chuckled. "Never have you had the affections of the prince to distract you."

She gave Nallia a kiss on the temple and left her to speak with her father.

Just two nights ago, Damascus asked her to join him in Salmantica in the week leading up to the Salmantic Games. It felt like a dream.

"You will be my honored guest," he said. Damascus was gallant, handsome, and chivalrous—he possessed everything a woman could want. *But could I leave this life behind to be with him? Why do I have to choose?*

It felt like her father took the decision from her. *"Get married and be someone else's problem." How dare he?*

Zephyrus sparred against Jechtaric and Cerik below. A quick study to Auron's tutelage, Zephyrus ascended the ladder within the ludus. Whoever taught him the ways of the sword instructed him well. He hadn't spoken to her or even met her eyes since the beatings, but he trained harder than ever.

Perhaps Father is right.

She turned away from the sands and walked back to her father's tablinum. As she neared, voices teeming with pent-up aggression resounded in the atrium.

"I wish to rise beyond the station of a mere lanista," her father said. "And I will use every advantage to achieve that!"

"You would use our daughter as an *advantage*?"

"Why is everyone questioning my authority? And yes. If all Nallia has to do is spread her legs to secure the position of our family for generations to come, I'd have had her flat on her back, legs spread for the prince's inspection."

Nallia's throat constricted, putting her hand to her mouth. Nausea churned her stomach, but she swallowed the pain and grit her teeth. Betrayed, disgusted, and used, she marched up to the entrance to give her father a piece of her mind, but the sound of an open palm whipping across an old cheek carried from the tablinum to the corridor.

Before she could enter, a grunt accompanied a loud smack. The thud of a body hitting the floor made Nallia's feet turn to stone. Tears streamed down her cheeks.

He hit her…

She couldn't believe this was happening.

"You dishonor yourself, *husband.*" Her mother's tone made the word a curse. She stormed from the room into the atrium, stopping for the briefest moment to eye Nallia. Her mother held her hand to her left cheek, a bruise already forming underneath. Without a word, her mother strode off.

Nallia retreated back to the safety of the balcony, unable to speak to anyone. Her world was falling apart. Her ludus, her family… *my identity.*

The sound of her father's violence and the wounded look on her mother's face haunted her. Auron taught her the basics of swordplay, and although she could have an honest tilt with unpracticed knights, she was no warrior. But she promised herself she would never let a man harm her. She tried to distract herself in the sparring below, to block out her parents' fight, her father's crude remarks, and her failure as a lanista… but never before had she felt so alone, so isolated, or so used.

CHAPTER 28

THE RATMAN

Laeden IX

Salmantica

The game of Reign required both strategy and luck. Laeden's tiles were perfectly positioned to take his father down in a few more turns, but it all depended on the dice. King Varros slid three ivory tiles—his foot soldiers—across the board, just as Laeden expected. As long as his father didn't roll two sixes, he'd be positioned to win in two turns. The first roll toppled and turned before landing.

Six.

Laeden closed his eyes and grabbed his pant leg beneath the table. His father grinned as he tossed the second die.

Six.

Laeden rolled his eyes as his father swiped two onyx tiles from the board. "The dice, forever on your side." He picked up the die to begin his turn. His plan could still work if he positioned his mounted knights to the right side of his father's castle. It would take longer to win, but victory was inevitable. He needed to roll a total of eleven with three rolls.

"Ambitious," his father said as Laeden moved his tiles into place.

"I will not give ground." Laeden rolled the first die.

Five.

"Retreat is always an option. Regroup, refortify, strike again when the enemy least expects it."

The second die landed. Four.

Just one more roll. He smiled at his father. "Why retreat when victory is imminent?" As long as he didn't roll a one, he'd secure victory. He tossed the die. It tumbled and spun on one corner before readjusting.

One.

Laeden dropped his head.

Father plucked Laeden's mounted knight tiles from the board. "My luck has not passed on to you. Your aggression must be tempered if it's to outlast the enemies' defense. You wield a glass sword, swinging it about trying to end the game as quickly as possible."

He wasn't just speaking of the game but of the Sentinels. Laeden had instituted a common uniform—a navy-blue surcoat with a gray sash, a sigil of a silver shield atop a navy-and-crimson backdrop, and the words *Shield The Righteous,* as if the Sentinels were a great house.

"The glass sword is to lull the enemy into comfort," Laeden said. "If they believe they see the threat, they won't suspect the hidden dagger."

His father moved his pikemen forward into the space where Laeden's mounted knights were taken, but Laeden was prepared. Before his father could reach for the die, Laeden scooped them up and rolled for opportunity.

"You didn't see my archers," Laeden said. He only needed a three to once again expose the right side of the castle. The die toppled end over end before spinning to a stop.

Two.

Laeden smacked his forehead with his palm.

"Clever move," his father said. "Unlucky."

Laeden saw the parallels between the game and his own pursuit of the Revivalists. Yes, he made an ostentatious display of the Sentinels. The uniforms were to make his enemies underestimate him while providing a presence on the streets to comfort the people. His hidden daggers were the ones he expected to win him the war. Aelon, Zephyrus, and Gareth all provided leads that would uncover the Revivalists' plans, avert potential disaster with the Cassiuses, or catch the miscreants in the act. If only he had evidence on Ser Daenus, he'd be able to leverage more information toward his cause.

After having the queen's study turned upside down in search of clues, and having Ser Daenus tailed, his men found nothing on him. All his time was spent guarding the queen, as was his duty.

Perhaps Danella was right.

He had no doubt Iylea told him the truth, but perhaps the voice she heard belonged to someone other than Ser Daenus. After Laeden had made a scene of Daenus's arrest, he spooked the true villain away. More information would turn up, but he couldn't be so brash in the future. Still, things had been tense with Iylea ever since. It wasn't her fault, but Laeden needed space from her. She compromised his decision-making process, and he couldn't let that happen. Not anymore.

"Speaking of unlucky," his father said as he moved his tiles to refortify his defenses. "I'm assuming the Prefectus Medicus has no news on these bloodless corpses?"

Laeden cleared his throat. It wasn't a subject he wanted to talk about. He'd hoped something would have come from the autopsy, but in the case of the Klaytonian and the vagabond, the Prefectus Medicus offered only more questions, citing magic more than medicine as to how the subjects were drained. Even though nothing had come of it, Laeden expected the Revivalists would attempt to tamper with his investigation, especially since they had access to the castle, but the men he had spying on the medicus's chambers had nothing to report.

"I no longer believe the Revivalists are the source of our bloodless corpses," Laeden said, regrouping his tiles to prepare for his father's counterattack. "Perhaps they are the result of these 'dangerous men' you refuse to tell me about. Maybe AVR?"

King Varros jostled the dice in his hand, his steel gaze and iron jaw revealing none of his inward thoughts. After a time, he set the dice down on the edge of the table. "You still blame me for the predicament we're in with the Revivalists."

"The Sentinels will triumph. The mages will go into hiding or flee, and the extremists will be eradicated."

His father leaned closer. "Be that as it may, if another mage were to turn up, I would exile them again. And that is not a secret over a game of Reign; I would have that known by the people, the Uprising, and anyone else who opposes my rule."

Laeden shook his head, at a momentary loss for words. *Still you will not admit the error of your ways?* "Don't you see how many are dying at the expense of one mage?"

"A task you've volunteered to handle."

"I have, and I will," Laeden said. "But that's not the point."

A long pause hung between them. They examined one another, each wondering if they could truly trust the other.

"Did I ever tell you what happened to me back in the New Rheynian War?"

Laeden scoffed. "You know you haven't."

His father never spoke of what happened during the war. All he knew was what others told him. His father was believed dead after his ship had been set upon by the Salmantics. Somehow, he survived the shipwreck, wound up on the northern coast of Klaytos, and ferried himself back to Stockhelm just at the end of the war three years later. It was not a heroic story, at least how others told it.

"If you knew, perhaps you would understand the monsters kept at bay by exiling one mage."

Laeden glared at his father. *He always kept his secrets.*

A knock at the door interrupted them, and Markus poked his head in. "Apologies for the intrusion. Urgent news from Stockhelm."

Laeden leveled his gaze at his father. "Whatever needs to be said can be said here. I have no secrets."

Markus nodded, glancing between Laeden and the king. "Word from House Cassius… A gladiator named Taric, armed with a small blade marked with the scales of Celestia, attacked and nearly murdered Stegavax in his cell."

Laeden ran his fingers through his hair. *Six save us. Zephyrus and Iylea were right.* The puzzle fit together. "Someone is trying to sabotage Cassius. The Revivalists are attempting to put their own man in the chancellor's office."

Laeden rubbed the back of his neck, recalling his time at Brusos's ludus. "Tursos, a seasoned and talented gladiator under the tutelage of Targarus, is sent to House Brusos, just in time for the omenation at the Games of Stockhelm. In the same week, the Cassius Champion is attacked by an armed gladiator, with the same weapon seen in the hands of a Revivalist suspect."

If they couldn't kill or control the king, they would secure the other political offices they could. As his father said, *"…regroup, refortify, strike again when the enemy least expects it."*

"We need proof on Brusos," Markus said. "Lenox could be his pawn. We have enough on him now. We can force him to talk."

Another knock at the door—a messenger. "Urgent news from the docks."

Allaron's men were the ones watching Gareth and his leads. Laeden gave instructions that if he needed to alert him, to send him to the docks, although they arranged a specific rendezvous point in advance.

"We shall have to resume the game later, Father."

"Be careful, son."

Laeden and Markus took their leave of Sentigard and went to the predetermined meeting area in the slums along the city's southern wall.

Allaron greeted them, old scars lining his face. "We have a problem." Despite his graying hair and thinning physique, Allaron's time spent fighting under the Helixus banner during the New Rheynian War made him a trustworthy ally.

After ensuring they weren't followed, Allaron led them through the slums to the hideout. "Gareth tried to make contact with the Ratman, but we caught them."

A pit formed in Laeden's gut. *All the tiles in the right places, but no luck.* "Why would Gareth betray us?"

Allaron opened a dilapidated wooden door and gestured inside the shanty house. "Think he thought to protect his friend. Told 'em to leave the Revivalists. Go into hiding. At least that's what he's telling us." Allaron directed them deeper into the hideout. "Through there."

Laeden marched into the poorly lit room. Gareth and the Ratman were gagged and secured to chairs. Laeden stalked over to Gareth, angry enough to strike him.

"A little cooperation and you would have been protected." Laeden yanked the gag from Gareth's mouth. "Why?"

"I told him to get out while he could," Gareth said. "I wanted him to switch to our side."

The Ratman fought against his gag, scowling at Gareth.

"Silence!" Laeden hissed. He turned back to Gareth. "You put your future in jeopardy. Give me one good reason why I shouldn't nail you to a Six Arrowed Star?"

Gareth's eyes grew to the size of dinner plates. "Banis can help. He can tell you more than I can. He's a messenger!"

"So you're telling me you've exhausted your purpose?" He glared at Gareth. "You better hope he talks." Laeden shoved the gag back into his mouth. "Has he said anything of worth yet?"

"Not yet," Allaron said.

Laeden pulled out the throwing knife he'd received at the festival of Stockhelm. It already saved the king's life. *Could it save the lives of these men too?* Laeden flipped the knife around in his hand before aiming it at Banis the Ratman's throat. With his other hand, he tugged the gag from his mouth.

"I will not betray the Gods and speak to the likes of you." He spat at Laeden's boots. "Gareth might be a coward, but I ain't!"

"Ratman has a wife and son," Allaron whispered in Laeden's ear.

The Ratman's mismatched eyes glowered at Laeden. If he was scared, he didn't show it. Laeden twirled the knife in his hand. "You might not be willing to talk to save your own life, but how about the lives of your wife and son?"

The Ratman's face remained placid, but a bead of sweat dampened his brow.

Laeden touched the blade to the Ratman's cheek. "Speak one name, and I will deliver you, Gareth, and your family from this land. Just one name."

Gareth groaned through his gag at the Ratman. The Ratman's yellow-green eyes drifted back and forth as if trying to see every possible future.

"There's only one situation where you make it out of this alive," Laeden said. He didn't want to resort to threats and violence, but he was losing this war. *Come on, you bastard. Just work with me…* "No one needs to get hurt. Just one name."

CHAPTER 29

COURTING

Danella IV

Salmantica

The omenation for the chancellorship was three days away. Danella's plans were in place, leaving no more to do but wait and pray. She ordered Targarus to send one of his best men to Brusos, arranged the assassination attempt on Cassius's Champion, and separated Nallia from her gladiators. Everyone knew the ludus's successes rested upon her shoulders, but Nallia couldn't help the scorpion retain its title of Head Lanista from here.

Encouraging Damascus to invite Nallia to Sentigard was easy. However, she undoubtedly would have only accepted after the omenation. Yet her spy within House Cassius manipulated the earl into blaming his daughter for recent events. With Stegavax out of the picture and Nallia here in Salmantica, the rest was up to Brusos.

If Brusos lost, the Gods didn't want him as the chancellor. She did everything she could to give him the power of the plebs in the senate. Overnight, Brusos could become one of the richest men in Stockhelm. His title of baron would turn to duke, and all he had to do was make sure his man won the rigged contest.

She sat in the throne room beside her husband awaiting Nallia's arrival. She wondered if it were possible, with Brusos in power, to turn the people and the senate against Varros. *If the people called for stricter enforcement of the rebel-rousing Celestics, could Varros oppose?* For now, she canceled every plot against him. If her husband could live and the Gods could be sated, Danella would not complain.

As it was, each morning she woke with guilt, and every night, she suffered a crisis of faith. Chimera's breath, she still loved Varros, but she couldn't disobey the will of the Six.

If only I could keep him and Father's kingdom…

Varros held her hand as Damascus walked arm in arm with Nallia Cassius into the throne room. The expression on Nallia's face was all too familiar: smiles on the outside, panic within. Were it not for the twisting of her ring about her finger, she might have fooled Danella. She did well to conceal her concern for the future of her ludus.

Danella pitied her. She knew what it was like to have the fear of a father's disappointment looming overhead, but more so, she understood how it felt to be used by a father like a form of currency. However, when Brusos won the chancellorship, if Damascus and Nallia were to be wed, the Cassius threat would be nullified. If she were as easy to manipulate as her father, Nallia would be the perfect bride to Damascus.

"Welcome, Lady Nallia," Varros said.

She smiled and curtsied, but her eyes reflected what Danella already knew. *House Cassius is in trouble.*

After exchanging pleasantries, Damascus offered to give Nallia a tour of Sentigard, but Danella interrupted. "My son, where are your manners? It would be unchivalrous of you not to make your intentions known. Nallia is renowned for her abilities as a duelist. Does she not duel any who would court her?"

Nallia stiffened.

Damascus glanced between her and Danella before finding his tongue. "It's true, my lady. I offer challenge, if you choose to accept."

Nallia put her hand to her chest as if she hadn't expected this.

Genuine surprise. My, my, the girl must be preoccupied.

Nallia accepted with a devilish grin.

Damascus offered her a shirt and trousers, but she refused, saying she could fight in anything. Sparring swords were brought to them.

"Fetch some water, Iylea," Danella said. "I have a feeling this will be quite the duel."

"Is there a mercy word you would like to announce?" Damascus asked.

"I will let you choose it, since you will be the one saying it," Nallia said, inspecting the wooden sword.

Varros laughed. "She has more fire than Incinerae."

Damascus grinned. "No mercy then. Shall we begin?"

CHAPTER 30

The Duel

Nallia III
Salmantica

Nallia slid into the combat stance Auron taught her as a girl. She stood side-facing and dropped her center of mass, making her body a smaller target. Damascus stood square to her with both hands upon his sword in a modern knight's stance.

She let her mind go, forgetting her father's cruelty, Stegavax's condition, and Zephyrus's mysteries. Only Damascus's defeat mattered now.

"Begin," the queen said.

Damascus advanced first, as men always did. Auron taught her how best to utilize her speed against larger, stronger opponents with greater reach. She stayed light on her feet, watching his hips and shoulders for the first sign of attack. He reached his sword back toward his right shoulder as he stepped forward. Nallia sidestepped to Damascus's backside and lunged with a stab of her own. Damascus adjusted, switching his stance to block the incoming blow.

He countered. High to the left, low to the right. Nallia met each stroke, deflecting his blade. He moved with practiced grace yet struck with fury.

He's not taking it easy on me. Good.

After an initial approach testing her defenses, Damascus's cuts and hacks came faster. Harder. Nallia could keep up, but she wasn't sure how long she'd be able to continue at this pace.

I will not back down.

She blocked left, right, sidestepped a vertical strike, and countered. Damascus riposted, but retreated as Nallia blocked and continued her advance.

Jab, step, slice, step, jump, sweep, strike.

Her feet led the assault. Damascus spun away from her attack, separating them. They circled each other in ever-tightening arcs. Damascus advanced with even more fury this time.

Thrust, hack, slash!

Nallia dodged, deflected, and blocked again, catching Damascus's sword on her own. They paused then, deadlocked.

"Are you sure you don't want a mercy word?" Damascus asked, his voice low. It wasn't a taunt, but she hated what it implied.

Nallia snarled.

Her father's words entered her mind. "*. . . if all Nallia has to do is spread her legs . . .*"

I'm not a tool to be used. This is my life!

She quickened her step and seized control of her emotions. She cut, hacked, evaded, and slashed until sweat dripped down her face. Damascus only smiled at her. She lunged, but he turned her aside, throwing her out of position. Letting her momentum carry her, she tucked into a tight roll.

He will press, thinking me off balance, but I will turn it against him.

When she sprang up from her roll and stabbed, her sword met nothing but air.

His sword leveled beneath her chin. "Mercy?" he asked from beside her.

No. I can't give up.

She spun away, striking upward to knock his sword away from her. Hoping to catch him off guard, she lunged with a flurry of blows. He blocked the first, dodged the second, and, on the third, his free hand caught her hilt. Nallia attempted to wrench free of his grip, but his own blade pointed at her throat.

"Mercy?" he asked again.

No! She tore free from his grasp and retreated from his reach.

She let out a battle cry and came at him with everything Auron taught her. She fought with all her might, maneuvered with grace, and struck with precision, but he was better than her. He turned her blade aside, exposing her back. He grabbed her and placed his wooden blade across her neck.

His lips were practically against her ear. "Just say the word."

There was no mocking tone in his voice. No bravado or condescending malice one who expected this outcome might have inflected. Even in victory he was gracious. He did not embarrass her. He did not strike her.

How long would he go on like this, waiting for me to surrender? Of all the possible outcomes, is there a better way this can end?

As defeat rested on the tip of her tongue, she thought of her father, the ludus, and the gladiators.

"Would it be such a terrible thing," Damascus said, "if I were to court you?"

She wanted to fight, *but why? What am I proving? Would I spite myself and my desires to make a point to Father? Would it be such a bad thing, to have Damascus's affection?*

Her grip on her sword loosened; the tension in her jaw dissipated.

"Mercy," Nallia whispered.

Damascus relinquished her and spun her around.

Her face felt flushed, sweaty, and tearful. *I must look utterly foolish.*

However, the look Damascus gave her made her stomach flutter as if she'd swallowed a hummingbird. His golden eyes beamed, not with pride or showmanship, but genuine… *respect?*

Have I ever seen that in a man's eyes before?

"You are a magnificent fighter," Damascus whispered. "And a tremendous competitor. It is no wonder your ludus stands in such high regard." He bowed his head.

She tried to thank him but couldn't find the words.

The queen stood, clapping. "Bravo!"

"Well fought," the king said.

Nallia managed a smile at first, but soon it became genuine. "You are most kind."

Damascus wiped the sweat from his brow with the back of his hand. "Now may I show you the rest of the castle?"

Nallia's grin overcame her defeat. She let him lead her away. *Not because Father wants me to, but because I want to.* Thoughts of the ludus fell away in Damascus's presence.

CHAPTER 31

WHITE MIST

Zephyrus X

Stockhelm

"Turn, shield, counter!" Doctore instructed, and Zephyrus executed. In the days following Stegavax's fall, Fenyx was selected to Champion the House in the coming Games of Stockhelm to determine who would be crowned the Head Ludus of the island. The games were foreign to Zephyrus, but to his understanding, the gladiators were able to earn coin based on how they fared in the arena. However, only Head Lanistas secured the popular matches warranting a high purse. Some were motivated by gold and others by glory, but Zephyrus set his sights on a loftier laurel.

Freedom.

He grew closer with Jecht and Cerik with each passing day, but many of the others held him at a distance. To earn the trust of his owners, he needed to fight well. To earn the trust of Laeden, he needed to deliver information on the Revivalists. He did, and he would, but hidden behind clever lies, he wanted vengeance. He wanted his freedom.

He and Patrus led the single largest slave outbreak in history, but they didn't do it alone. If Zephyrus were to achieve his freedom, he needed to earn the respect of the gladiators and have them rally behind him.

But who can I trust?

After Taric's attempt on Stegavax, there was no telling who among the gladiators held ties to the Revivalists. A whisper in the wrong ear could get him killed, but Jecht and Cerik proved not every gladiator enjoyed their chains. Still, he needed something they could rally behind. Being a Prophet of Celestia wasn't enough. If anything, the uncertainty of which prophet made others trust him less and created division within the barracks. If he could unlock the secrets of his past and uncover his mysterious fate, he would become a leader worth following.

Even without him, slaves around Stockhelm were escaping their bondage. As a result, the guards were given extra shifts to ensure none of the Cassius slaves thought to join the rebellion. Though only mentioned in whispers, *the Uprising* was gaining traction. As much as the extra guard duty unnerved the other gladiators, it allowed Zephyrus to keep a closer eye on the guards.

"Step into the blow!" Doctore shouted. "Use his strength against him."

Zephyrus deflected Fenyx's wooden great sword with his gladius and stepped into his opponent, levying a brutal shield bash into Fenyx's ribs. As he recoiled, Zephyrus hacked with his short sword and struck Fenyx's back with the flat of the blade.

Fenyx roared, slamming his great sword into the sand.

"You overreach," Doctore said to Fenyx. "Your strength betrays you. Harness that which makes you formidable."

Fenyx stood and charged at Zephyrus, not heeding Doctore's instruction. Zephyrus parried, exposing Fenyx's back, and attacked with a quick combination of strikes. Fenyx blocked the first, but the second met flesh with a *thwack.*

Fenyx growled. Doctore counseled a calm mind, but his frustration got the better of him. Zephyrus pitied him. After the guards presumed Fenyx was the one who attacked Stegavax, they beat him. Once they stopped hitting him long enough to realize Fenyx saved Stegavax, it was too late to take back the bruises. As much as Fenyx would not admit to his pain or use it as an excuse, it slowed him down.

"Doctore," Dominus said from the balcony. "Have we chosen the wrong Champion?"

"No!" Fenyx charged Zephyrus with reckless abandon. He jumped and reached his great sword overhead, preparing to cleave the earth in two. Zephyrus rolled into the blow to get inside his reach. He lifted his shield to catch Fenyx on the hands. Bones crunched, and Fenyx bellowed, but Zephyrus's vertical slash clipped Fenyx under the chin.

Fenyx fell to his back, groaning. He rose, grasping at his hand and spitting blood. Smashed between the hilt and shield, Fenyx's fingers were already swelling.

Zephyrus reached to aid him, but Fenyx slapped him away with his good hand. Fenyx spat more blood, hobbling towards the barracks. Doctore shouted for him to go to the medicus, but Fenyx ignored him.

Dominus swore before disappearing behind the balcony's curtain.

Doctore glowered at Zephyrus. "Do you think you are helping? Days before the most important match in the history of this house, you injure the Champion?"

Zephyrus blew out his cheeks. He took no pride in it. "Burn me, should I have let him land a blow? Build his confidence?"

Doctore scowled, shaking his head. "You know not the honor of the brotherhood." He stormed off, leaving Zephyrus at the center of the other gladiators muttering curses.

Zephyrus let his wooden weapons fall to the sand. *Really winning their respect.*

If Fenyx couldn't fight, and whoever took his place lost, the blame would rest on Zephyrus's shoulders. Fenyx's fingers were likely broken. The medicus couldn't mend that; it'd be weeks before Fenyx could hold a sword, let alone fight.

Zephyrus remembered his dream at the Arcane Templar. *I healed Patrus. Could I heal Fenyx?* Zephyrus followed Fenyx. Other gladiators mocked him, but they didn't matter right now. Fenyx mattered. *I can help him. What better way to earn the trust and respect of a gladiator than to help one in need?*

Zephyrus approached Fenyx's cell to find him pacing.

"What do you want?" Fenyx snarled, a strip of whiteroot already in his mouth.

Zephyrus did not wait for Fenyx to refuse him. He grabbed Fenyx's hand, unsure how the magic would work. He'd seen it only once, and only in his dream.

"What are you doing?" Fenyx asked.

Zephyrus visualized Fenyx's bones straightening, his joints aligning, and his swelling fading. Tendrils of glowing white mist trickled from Zephyrus's hands and swirled into Fenyx's misaligned fingers. Fenyx's eyes lit up as the bones began to reform, and the swollen knuckles shrunk back to their regular size within Zephyrus's white aura.

Zephyrus couldn't believe his eyes.

"You can't. They'll kill us!" Fenyx tried to pull his hand away, but Zephyrus didn't let go.

Zephyrus felt the pain of his own fingers breaking, though they did not appear to be maimed. "I won't tell if you don't." Zephyrus grimaced. "You are our Champion. You must win for the glory of this house."

For the first time since meeting, Fenyx looked upon him without contempt.

Glory was the only language Fenyx understood. He flexed and extended his fingers, testing their dexterity. Zephyrus attempted to do the same, but his own fingers ached.

"How?" Fenyx whispered. "How do you know the healing magic of Celestia?"

He spoke so quietly Zephyrus had to read Fenyx's lips to understand.

"I don't know." It wasn't a lie. One day, he hoped to learn, but his memories hadn't revealed any new information.

"You should be killed," Fenyx said.

"Not today." Zephyrus smiled, rubbing his own fingers to alleviate the soreness. "They can make us renounce our gods in favor of theirs, but the Judges will return."

To his surprise, Fenyx only scoffed. "There is no *us*. And the Judges aren't returning because they never left. The Valencians are our punishment for losing the elemental magics and the Treasures." He shook his head at Zephyrus.

Zephyrus contorted his brow. "You think the Judges allow us to be cowed as slaves, bowing and scraping instead of living free?"

Fenyx narrowed his eyes. The burned side of his face twitched. "*My* people—not yours, not ours, *mine*—failed the Judges. This is our penance. Here, I have the opportunity to restore honor and receive redemption. But to dream of a life beyond these walls is the path to an early and meaningless death."

Zephyrus wanted to say he'd heard Vykannis's voice. The Judge had saved his life. But Fenyx's exclusion gave him pause before speaking such a dangerous truth. He shook his head. "What meaning can you have here, spilling blood for gold?"

"I am a titan within these walls." Fenyx's burned skin stretched around his smile. "If you want to live free as a beggar, go ahead, but I won't join you. Here, there is glory to be won."

Zephyrus fumbled for words.

"You have my gratitude, but this does not make us friends," Fenyx said.

Zephyrus retracted his chin back.

"There are no friends within these walls and no Gods who wish to see us from this fate."

"You're wrong," Zephyrus said.

Fenyx leaned into Zephyrus, speaking directly into his ear. The eye on the burned side of his face cut through him. "If I see you use magic, or hear you speak of freedom or the Judges again, I'll turn you in. I won't be dragged down by your disobedience."

Zephyrus nearly choked on his disbelief, but before he could formulate a response, Fenyx strode out of the cell and out to the sands. "All for glory."

This society brainwashes their slaves into believing they are responsible for their suffering. How many share that view? And how can I convince them otherwise?

Fenyx would not be an easy ally, but Zephyrus needed more than just Jecht and Cerik to make any significant impact.

He massaged life back into his fingers.

There's still hope. My memory returns and, with it, the power to turn the tide of this war.

He returned to the sands, returned to training, and returned to his clever lies.

CHAPTER 32

THE GAMES OF STOCKHELM

Fenyx III

Stockhelm

The chants of the crowd grew as people from all over New Rheynia flocked to behold the Games of Stockhelm in the newly erected Valencian Arena. Dominus sat upon the pulvinus overlooking the sands with the lesser lanistas of Stockhelm. The exquisite arena held enough rows of inclined benches to accommodate every person in all of Stockhelm. Most of the walls on the inside of the arena were blank, but some were ornately carved depictions of the Valencian Gods. Rumors speculated that each year after crowning a new Champion of Stockhelm, the victory would be enshrined in one of the blank inlays of the wall to be remembered forever.

Today, I will become a Champion of Stockhelm. My likeness will be carved into the wall.

This was the moment he'd been waiting for since being brought to House Cassius as a boy. All the years of training, every match in the fighting pits, it all culminated in this contest.

Fenyx wiped the dampness from his palms onto his britches. The omenation of the chancellorship depended on him. *I must win.*

"This ain't the training square, eh, green boy?" Shagren spat.

Fenyx closed his eyes and released his breath. He hadn't heard Shagren's approach. The sweat of his palms turned to steam as his fingers curled into fists. The Burning wanted to take over. He stepped aside, motioning his hand to the sands to let Shagren pass through the gate.

"After you," Fenyx said. "The veteran takes to the sands before the green boy… to fight against the lesser men. In the contests of inconsequence."

Shagren hissed, stepping forward, but Aelixo and Wardon held him back.

"Shag, no. Save it!" Aelixo said.

"Aelixo's right," Wardon said. "He ain't worth it."

"Listen to your pups," Fenyx said. "Now retreat with your tail between your legs." Ice returned to his veins and the fire to his heart.

Auron strode up to the gate. "Cease quarrelsome tongues and set minds to purpose, or you will all die in disgrace." He set in on Shagren. "Have you no honor? You had best fare well in your contest or die in the trying, because if you fail, I'll make you wish the Judges claimed you!" Auron's face flashed with anger, but then quelled in realization of what he said. "The Gods—burn you!"

"Apologies, Doctore," Shagren said.

"Flee from sight." Auron pointed to where Zephyrus stood with Cerik and Jechtaric.

Shagren and his shadows returned down the ramp into the dimly lit barracks.

"What has you so stirred?" Fenyx asked once they were alone. It was rare for Auron to be quick to anger, and a rarer thing for him to speak of the Judges.

Auron shook his head. "You are not the only one with rivalries." He gestured up to the pulvinus. "Sinion, the lanista, once fought as a gladiator. Never a champion of swords, but a warrior of the mind. His cunning allowed him to never cross blades with one he could not best."

Sinion owned Stockhelm's southern ludus, Arux held the east, and Brusos the north. Aside from Brusos, they were just names, and Fenyx was unsure which face owned which. A rotund dark-skinned man in blue-gray robes sat beside Dominus. At first glance, Fenyx assumed him a server, but adorned in jewels and fine silks, he couldn't be anything short of a patrician.

"I fought against him a lifetime ago," Auron said. "He begged for mercy after I defeated him, but his dominus had the ear of King Damascus II. As the editor of the games, he let him live. I defeated him, yet now he stands above me."

"How did he become a dominus if he was a slave?" Fenyx asked.

"Another tale for another day," Auron said. "You should heed these words instead. You may become Champion, but Stegavax held that mantle too. Now he clings to life for how he behaved as Champion. You will have many enemies, but you do not need to create more beneath the same roof."

The Burning grew within him. *A lecture. Now?* "They mocked me—"

"So you insulted them?" Auron asked. "How one earns respect is just as important as what one does with it."

Fenyx clenched his teeth, biting back his complaints, but before he could reply, horns blared and banners rose as the opening ceremonies began.

The purple-and-gold scorpion of House Cassius hung over the earl's seat. The standards of the gray wolf of Sinion, the orange bull of Arux, and the white-and-black snake of Brusos were erected in a line. The clamor of the crowd bellowed through the acoustics of the arena as the lanistas raised their hands to incite more cheers. The arena shook with the people's stamping feet. Dust descended from the corridor ceiling to rest on Fenyx's pauldrons.

Fenyx's rib cage rattled within his cuirass, but he absorbed the energy, feeding off the crowd's bloodlust. *I will provide them a spectacle, the likes they've never seen. Glory and honor await. I will be Champion. I must not fail.*

Dominus stepped forward, and a hush fell over the crowd. He explained the rules and format of the games and how the omenation would be determined.

Points would be distributed to the victorious house for each match. The house with the most points at the conclusion of the day would select a champion to stand against Fenyx, the Champion of the defending Head Lanista. Though Arux and Sinion had a chance to compete for the chancellorship, everyone speculated that House Brusos was the only realistic challenger.

Most of the morning games contained the lesser lanistas' stock. Steel clashed, and blood spilled, but after each match, only one house celebrated in victory. Arms outstretched, the victors basked in the crowd's cheers. Bathed in the sun's light, and the glorious spray of the fallen's blood, they paraded about the sands to roaring adoration until the next match began.

Soon I will taste victory's sweetness.

Fenyx had won matches before, but only in Teluvar's fighting pits. A fraction`the size of even Cassius's training square, the sands of the pits were only large enough for single combat, and a score of spectators at most. And even then, they were the men waiting to fight, their Dominus, and the gamblers betting on the results. In the pits, it wasn't about the crowd, but survival. Only the strongest survived, and even then, few ever truly became gladiators.

Fenyx would be the exception.

Bout after bout, shouts filled the air, and blood soaked the sand until the sun began to set in the western sky. As expected, Brusos towered over Arux and Sinion in the standings. After the final match before the Primus, Fenyx would face Brusos's Champion.

Fenyx set his jaw. *They will sing songs of my victory.*

In the last match before Fenyx's glorious moment, Zephyrus, Cerik, and Jechtaric entered the arena. Dominus highlighted the implausibility of their ascent within House Cassius and promised they would make mockery of Arux's, Sinion's, and Brusos's men. Each lesser lanista would send a wave of four men at Cassius's three, one after the other.

As they took to the sands, part of Fenyx envied them. The opportunity to face twelve men, twelve potential trophies, twelve offerings to the Judges—it was enticing. But he would have to make do with just one.

And it will be a tale for the ages.

Sinion's four men were up first against the Cassius three. While Sinion's blue-and-gray adorned wolves wore the more modern armor of knights, Cassius's purple-and-gold scorpions favored the trim leather armor of years past.

The horns blared, and the clash began—metal and might against speed and skill.

Zephyrus stepped over the modern Bruiser's spiked flail and countered with an upward swing of his buckler. The shield caught Sinion's gladiator across the helm, sending him sprawling to the earth. Before the Bruiser could find his feet, Cerik's mace came down on the fallen warrior's breastplate. Metal bent, bones crunched, and the heavy armor folded before Cerik's strength.

Zephyrus ducked under a Warden's swinging sword and sliced at the inside of his thigh, dropping him to a kneeling position with a scream. Jechtaric spun and thrust his spear over the Warden's shield and into the space between his helm and gorget. He collapsed to the ground, blood spouting from his neck.

Fenyx had the pleasure of watching Laytonus and Taric fight side by side for years, *may the Judges grant them rest.* But absent their bond or the time spent training together, this trio, led by Zephyrus, was as smooth and polished as any he'd seen fight side by side. Zephyrus's movements flowed from one into the other. No missteps. Nothing wasted. And whenever an opening presented itself, his blade struck deftly.

Somehow, Zephyrus knew the healing magic of Celestia. Fenyx learned the same magic long ago back in Klaytos, when he still believed in the Return of the Judges and had never even held a sword before. So much had changed. Now glory was all that remained. Fenyx was grateful for Zephyrus healing him so he could fight today, but he didn't like feeling indebted to another.

Another adversary fell to Zephyrus. Despite the Slicer's armor, Zephyrus found a gap between the bracer and pauldron and severed the limb clean off at the elbow. The three Cassius titans set in on the remaining Poker, and the spearman quickly yielded, resulting in the loss of another point in the standings. Not that it mattered.

Arux's gladiators posed even less of a threat. Zephyrus continued to expose his opponents' weaknesses while protecting his brothers' flanks, allowing Jechtaric and Cerik to dispatch the lesser lanista's offerings with ease.

When Brusos's gladiators took to the sands, all four charged straight for Zephyrus, ignoring Jechtaric and Cerik. But Zephyrus emerged unscathed in victory. The showing was impressive, but Fenyx would do better. *I must do better…*

The end of the contest dropped Sinion one point for yielding. All of Arux's men fell in defeat, leaving no survivors and no change in their standings. Brusos's men didn't fare much better in their attempt to overwhelm Zephyrus, but at least one of their men was granted life after surviving long enough for the editor to be entertained.

Auron clapped his hand over Fenyx's pauldron. "It is time for the omenation. This is the moment you have been training for. Win and become Champion of Stockhelm. Win and you elevate this House to one of the greatest in New Rheynia. Are you ready?"

Energized by the crowd and intoxicated with the scent of blood, Fenyx's muscles coiled, ready to spring forth. So much hinged on this contest, but Fenyx would not disappoint. The Burning demanded blood, and the debt would be paid.

"Yes," Fenyx said, never averting his eyes from the sands. "Glory awaits."

CHAPTER 33

For the Chancellorship

Zephyrus XI

Stockhelm

S*till alive...*

The crowd roared in approval for the Cassius victory. The Brusos gladiator granted life stared at Zephyrus as if he were evil incarnate. All four of them swarmed him. For some reason, it didn't feel quite so personal with Sinion's or Arux's men, but with Brusos's gladiators, they seemed to *want* him dead.

Jecht grabbed Zephyrus's wrist and punched it up to the heavens. "Victory!"

"We did it!" Cerik shouted, thrusting his mace into the air.

Zephyrus looked at the broken bodies strewn on the ground around him. Ten dead. It was different standing over an enemy, but these men were just slaves. In the eyes of the raucous fanatics in the stands, the only differences between the bodies on the ground were the sigils on their armor. But to Zephyrus they were people forced to fight. He felt no swell of pride, and certainly nothing to celebra—

"Watch out!" Cerik shoved Zephyrus aside. The crowd gasped and booed. Zephyrus whipped around just as Cerik deflected the remaining Brusos gladiator's sword and countered with his mace. The spiked ball crashed into the face of Brusos's last man to the eruption of the arena. He dropped to the ground. Cerik put his foot on the man's shoulder and tore the mace free from his skull.

Eleven dead bodies.

"What in Six Hells?" Jecht asked.

"He attacked Zephyrus while his back was turned," Cerik said.

Zephyrus's breath caught in his throat. *It wasn't just a contest after all—it was personal.* Zephyrus looked to the pulvinus to see Cassius and Brusos standing and shouting at one another with animated gestures.

Doctore shouted from the tunnel gate, but with the crowd's uproar, it was impossible to hear his words. He waved them back to the gate, beckoning their return.

Zephyrus exited the arena alongside Jecht and Cerik before the outraged but still cheering crowd.

Doctore embraced Zephyrus arm in arm once they were through the gate. "Burn me, that was close. Did he get you?"

Zephyrus tried to catch his breath, but his lungs were empty. *Still alive…*

"Brusos doesn't have a shred of honor." Doctore examined him. "You seem fine."

"Thanks to Cerik," Jecht said.

Zephyrus managed a nod, but cold encompassed him. *First Saulus, then Lenox, and now this…* A shiver ran down his spine, as if fear itself slithered down his back. Even before nearly being stabbed in the back, he hadn't felt good about slaughtering slaves for sport, but now the combination was almost too much to bear.

"They're eager for Brusos's blood now," Jecht said to Fenyx, looking out to the crowd. "Best give them what they want."

"Weapons," Nortus said with outstretched arms. They each handed him their weapons, which were passed off to servants to be cleaned, sharpened, and used again to butcher more slaves. Yet absent his sword and shield, Zephyrus's hands trembled at his sides. He felt exposed, vulnerable, and one sharp blade away from being amongst the dead.

Lenox marched up the ramp from the barracks, naked steel in his hands.

Zephyrus stumbled back, trying to hide between the other gladiators.

Lenox drew closer. "Out of the way." He parted the crowd of gladiators gathered around the gate, coming straight for Zephyrus.

Zephyrus swallowed, clenching his fists, ready to defend himself.

Lenox strode past Zephyrus without a passing glance and handed the great sword to Fenyx. "Kill the bastard and we all celebrate under the chancellor's roof."

Zephyrus let go of his held breath. *I'm being paranoid.* But he couldn't calm his broken nerves. His stomach churned, and bile climbed his throat. *I'm going to be sick.*

The herald held his arms up until the crowd quieted. "And now, the moment you've all been waiting for—the Primus!"

Cheers erupted from the stands, forcing the herald to raise his hands for silence again.

"In first place, House Brusos will challenge Head Lanista Cassius in the omenation for the chancellorship of Stockhelm. Representing Baron Ebron Brusos, I give you the savage of Salmantica, the slayer of thousands—Tursos!"

Tursos emerged out of the tunnel opposite the Cassius gate to the roar of the crowd. Wearing a horned helm in the likeness of a bull, he seemed more demon than man. His steel breastplate with matching bracers and greaves reflected the glow of the dying sun.

"Tursos?" Doctore spat. "He is one of Targarus's. How did he end up with Brusos?"

Arena guards dragged the bodies of the dead from the sands to the west gate, leaving crimson streaks in their wake.

Zephyrus gagged. He removed himself from the gate while everyone else watched the omenation for the chancellorship. Hands shaking, knees quivering, and stomach roiling, he strode down the declining slope into the barracks. Once alone, he retched in the corner.

He'd killed men before and hadn't thought twice, but they weren't slaves. He didn't question his sanity when he woke without his memories.

Nor did he doubt his abilities when Laeden purchased him from the slavers. He didn't give up when forced to fight for House Cassius. But now, for the first time, Zephyrus didn't believe he was enough for the tasks his fate demanded of him.

What would Patrus think of me—slaughtering Celestic slaves for Rheynian delight? If I'm supposed to be the Wielder, I need to save these people, not slay them. If I'm the Herald, why does Vykannis remain silent? Perhaps I am the Harbinger…

He retched again. He wiped his mouth with the back of his hand and sat against the wall. Pulling the bloody scroll from his pocket, he rolled it back and forth within his palm.

It would have been easier to just be an emissary of peace. If he never learned of the Arcane Templar or their quest for vengeance, he could have served the king.

I don't know if I can do this, Patrus. I am lost. The Judges chose the wrong person.

The sound of soft voices stole him from his lamentations. *Everyone should be watching the omenation.* Zephyrus pocketed the scroll and crept along the wall, careful not to make a sound or cast any shadows. The voices were just outside the barracks.

"If the broken sword doesn't do the trick, we'll take secondary measures," the voice whispered. "Which one of you will do the honors?"

After a pause, another voice answered, "I'll do it."

"Very well," the first voice said. "Once the deed is done, you will flee. It will be assumed you killed your master and joined the Uprising. I'll arrange for you to be picked up. No longer will your talents be wasted in the arena."

"You picked the right man—"

"Only if this plan doesn't work," the first voice said. "Do not be hasty. You'll have your opportunity to prove your loyalty soon enough. Now return to the gates, or your absence will be noticed."

Zephyrus didn't breathe.

Revivalists. But who?

He couldn't let them get away without knowing who the speakers were. Poking his head out into the corridor, he saw two shapes climbing the slope back toward the gate to the arena.

Carsos and Ixion.

It didn't surprise him they were willing to betray their own people if it benefited them. *But who is the third person? They went the other way, so they must have a key—either a guard or a slaver.* It wasn't Lenox. He would know that voice anywhere.

His nausea gone, Zephyrus returned to the gate to see the rest of the omenation. To his horror, he understood what Carsos and Ixion were talking to the other man about; Fenyx stood against his opponent, armed with only his hilt.

The broken sword…

The same happened to me when I fought Stegavax after Liario had suggested we fight with steel. Zephyrus scanned the pulvinus for Liario, but he wasn't there.

The remainder of Fenyx's blade rested on the sands, glinting in the light of the setting sun. Fenyx backed against the Cassius gate. Tursos advanced, wielding a flaming sword.

"Get inside his reach," Doctore said. "Disarm him. Advance!"

If Fenyx heard, he showed no sign. He trembled before Tursos's flaming sword.

Upon the pulvinus, Dominus tore his hair while Brusos stood in anticipation. Liario appeared behind Dominus, a cold calculative expression on his weathered face. *Carsos and Ixion were speaking with Liario. He and Lenox orchestrated the broken sword. But all this, for the chancellorship?*

They conspired to kill Stegavax, disarmed Fenyx, and made sure, if somehow Fenyx won, Earl Cassius would die and never take the chancellorship. *I must tell Laeden.*

Fenyx held the hilt of the broken sword in front of him. Useless. He rolled to the left to avoid a strike but was unbalanced for the next attack.

Fenyx raised the hilt to block, but Tursos's blow tore it from his grasp. The hilt sailed end over end into the distance.

Fenyx fell to his back.

It was over. Fenyx had accepted it. The other gladiators awaited the final blow. But Zephyrus had a strange feeling as if he'd been here before, watching someone defenseless before impending doom.

He had. He *had* been here before. A memory…

At the Arcane Templar, one of his classmates, Ceres, was losing to Vellarix in his final test. Zephyrus used force magic, just enough to slow Vellarix's strike without anyone knowing, giving Ceres a moment to escape.

Tursos reared his blade back, preparing to plunge it into Fenyx's midsection, but Zephyrus focused all his might into resisting Tursos's arm. Zephyrus's own arm went limp from exertion. Tursos paused mid-swing—just for a moment.

Fenyx rolled to the side just as Zephyrus released Tursos. Tursos's flaming blade pierced the sand, extinguishing the fire.

Fenyx rolled back over the hilt, wrenching it from Tursos's grasp. He sprang to his feet, and, with new vigor, he launched himself at the flameless Tursos. They punched, kicked, and grappled one another.

"Zeph, are you okay?" Jecht asked from beside him. "You don't look too good."

Zephyrus's vision fuzzed, but he stood his ground. "I'm fine." His arm tingled, burning with exhaustion. It wasn't how he remembered it, but this magic—this force—worked.

Tursos punched Fenyx in the jaw. Fenyx spun and fell to the ground, but his hand closed around something. As Tursos advanced, Fenyx flung sand in his attacker's face.

Fenyx picked up a sliver of the broken steel and plunged it into the side of Tursos's neck. Once, twice, again, and again. The crowd roared as Tursos stumbled backwards, grasping at his throat. But Fenyx followed, continuing to thrust the broken blade into Tursos. He fell to his knees, his breastplate now a deep crimson. Fenyx cast the horned helm from Tursos's head to the sands and grabbed him by his black braids.

Poised to strike the killing blow, Fenyx turned toward the pulvinus.

The crowd chanted, "Kill! Kill! Kill!"

Zephyrus didn't watch as Fenyx slit Tursos's throat. Instead, he watched Liario's reaction from the pulvinus. He stroked his beard in observation, not showing his displeasure, but not celebrating with the rest of the Cassiuses.

Another Revivalist.

Zephyrus blinked through his dizziness. *I must keep Cassius alive… for now. One day, he will fall, but not to the Revivalists. To me.*

At least for now, the Revivalists' plans would be delayed. He needed to get word to Laeden and recruit more help within the barracks.

"Fenyx! Fenyx!"

Fenyx basked in the glory of the kill under the crowd's cheers. The gladiators shouted in praise. Zephyrus joined in, despite the aching of his arm, and the dread of what lay ahead.

CHAPTER 34

MASK

Fenyx IV

Stockhelm

The villa and barracks alike were alive with wine, women, and performances, but to Fenyx, such distractions only interrupted his memories of the day. In a moment of silence, he could still hear the crowd chanting his name. When he closed his eyes, he could see blood spouting from Tursos's open throat. The Burning was sated. Glory was his. He didn't even need whiteroot to experience peace. Fenyx couldn't remember a time he ever felt so pleased.

While others were consumed with diversions, Fenyx was to be bathed in the villa. He'd never been offered such before, but it was a concept he could grow used to. *One of the many benefits of being Champion.* On his way out of his cell, Zephyrus barred his path.

Fenyx growled deep within his throat. Unlike the other gladiators, Zephyrus held no cup, no woman.

"What do you want?"

Zephyrus grimaced. "Victory may not have happened if all things went as planned."

"What nonsense are you speaking of?"

"Who gave you the sword?" Zephyrus asked.

Fenyx huffed. Seeing no other way of getting out of this, he played along. *Auron's advice about not making enemies is difficult to heed in moments like this.* "What are you talking about?"

"The sword that broke the moment you stepped onto the sands," Zephyrus whispered, his eyes darting left and right. "Similar to the steel that gave out on me in my match against Stegavax for the princes' pleasure. Who gave it to you?"

The left side of Fenyx's burned cheek twitched. "One of the guards. What of it?"

"Which guard?"

Fenyx crossed his arms over his chest and tapped his foot.

Zephyrus stepped closer. "They gave Taric the knife to kill Stegavax, rigged your sword to break, and why? They're trying to steal the chancellorship."

Fenyx clenched his teeth. "They failed."

"They will try again," Zephyrus said. "I overheard voices beneath the arena. Voices of men in these very barracks. People who conspired to have Stegavax butchered in his sleep, you killed in the arena, and Dominus assassinated."

Fenyx scoffed. "Is this your way of getting me to seek freedom?"

He tried to get past Zephyrus, but Zephyrus sidestepped to block his path.

"Brusos's man tried to kill *you*, not me," Fenyx said. "Perhaps he tried doing us a favor. Stop trying to push your troubles onto me. Can't you just enjoy my victory? Drink, find a woman." Fenyx gestured to one of the masked and silk-clad women prowling the barracks. "Do whatever you must, to be content with the life you have. Quit fretting over conspiracies and do what gladiators do. Kill." Fenyx pushed past Zephyrus without another word.

He climbed the steps leading to the villa, where a guard escorted him to the baths. Typically, Fenyx would be given a linen cloth, a bowl of water, and a strigil to wipe the filth from his body, but standing before a steaming pool of water beneath a sky window surrounded by marble floors and columns, Fenyx knew he was Champion.

His guard left him with two masked women wading towards him through the steaming water. Though there were two, his eyes fixed on one. Despite her mask, Fenyx recognized her—Domina's bodyslave Odetta. With smooth bronze skin and long black curls that hung behind her to skim the water's surface, she slowed, allowing the other masked woman to lead.

"Don't make us come out to get you," said the masked woman. "Water's warm." She cupped the steaming water and poured it down her chest. Beads trickled between her breasts.

Despite her attempts to lure him, his eyes remained fixed on Odetta, cowering behind the other girl. Her pale green eyes stared at the water's rippling surface instead of at him. He'd never taken interest in women before. They were only distractions. But Odetta was different. The maiden bodyslave, to be gifted to the Champion of the House at the age of eighteen.

She was supposed to be Stegavax's, but Fenyx was Champion now. She was his. As if she were thinking the same thing, she inclined her gaze to his. Even beneath her mask, he could see her revulsion as she stared at the burned side of his body. His fleshly desires fled in the presence of shame.

He coiled his fist at his side. "Why are you here?"

"We are to bathe you, Champion," the other woman said.

Fenyx snorted. "Must you wear the masks to hide your disgust?"

"Disgust?" The other woman removed her mask. "The domina has every woman in the villa wearing these. We meant no offense."

Fenyx recognized her but didn't know her name. Nor did he care to learn it. She was nothing. Less than nothing. He was Champion, and he would have all that the Burning desired—all that he was owed for his blood, sweat, and tears. First a bath, then Odetta, and there was nothing Zephyrus could do or say to separate him from his glory.

With a satisfied grunt, he removed his sublingaria and sauntered into the water. Submitting, he allowed them to wash him. Warm and soothing, the water eased the tension from his muscles. The women scrubbed him at first, but then massaged oils into his skin. By the time they were done, Fenyx had never felt so clean.

As the women began to exit the bath, Fenyx grabbed Odetta's wrist. "You, stay."

Odetta attempted to twist free, but Fenyx held her.

"I am Champion now. Soon we will be betrothed."

"You're not Champion yet," Odetta hissed. She splashed water at Fenyx with her free hand and wrenched herself free.

Fenyx scoffed and settled back into the water, leaning his arms on the bath's edge. "True. But soon enough, I will be Champion, and Domina will give you to me. You will be mine. Not Stegavax's. Not Shagren's. Mine."

Odetta scowled, her disdain visible beneath her mask. "You will never have anything in this world. Or the next." She stormed from the bath and wrapped herself in a linen before disappearing from the room. Without so much as a word, the other woman followed in Odetta's footsteps, never looking back.

Free of distractions, Fenyx relaxed, sitting on a ledge within the water. He closed his eyes and relived the final moments of his victory. Enraptured in glory, he didn't hear a new masked woman's approach. Startled, Fenyx splashed about.

"No need for alarm," said a familiar voice from behind a mask identical to Odetta's. She had fairer skin than the slave girls, but by her voice alone, he could tell she wasn't from a brothel.

She disrobed, older than the others, but by no means less beautiful. While the others were girls, she was a woman. Admiring her feminine form, Fenyx reacted to her temptation.

"I don't need your company," Fenyx said in a half-hearted dismissal.

The woman laughed, slipping into the water with deliberate care. "Are you not pleased with my appearance, Champion?"

"I am," Fenyx said, wishing he could disappear into the marble at his back. "But a Champion must not succumb to distractions. I will wait until the domina gifts me my prize."

She snickered. "Did Auron tell you that? Saving yourself, are you?"

Fenyx cowered as she approached from the opposite end of the bath. "I am to be wed to one of the domina's chosen," Fenyx said as she waded nearer. She drew close, inserting her knee between his legs.

She lowered herself deeper, the water coming up to her breasts. "What if the domina didn't choose a slave for you?" The seductress hummed beneath her mask, luring him in with her siren's song. He wanted to back away. He should have made an escape, but he remained, entranced by her beauty.

Fenyx swallowed the knot in his throat as she lifted the mask from her face. Chestnut waves spilled out from the string of her mask, falling past her shoulders. Her green eyes flashed with a hunger he'd never before seen on a woman's face.

Recognizing her, Fenyx coughed. Fear unlike any other coursed through him, and even in the warm bath, cold overtook him. "Domina?" He splashed, trying to slip away, but she seized each of his thighs.

"Not tonight." She climbed on top of his lap, wrapping her arms around his neck. "I'm just a woman, wanting more than a man."

The thunder in his chest did little to stop the reaction of his manhood. Stronger than the Burning and more furious than any flaming sword, the insatiable want—*need*—for her seized him and refused to relent. *What would a Champio—*

She pressed her body against his, whispering in his ear. "Call me Cleotra, Champion."

CHAPTER 35

Elemental Magic

Zephyrus XII

Stockhelm

Zephyrus did his best to protect Jecht and Cerik by disarming or maiming their opponents, but he couldn't slay a single man on the day. Vellarix had given him a gifted curse—a double-edged sword. He possessed incredible ability, but he wielded it against the wrong people. That, paired with the undeniable fact that Brusos's men were assigned to kill him, even in defeat, kept Zephyrus from wanting to partake in the festivities.

"Cheers!" Jecht carried three clay cups towards him. "Drink. You are now a man of the arena." Despite Jecht's contagious smile, Zephyrus couldn't return the sentiment.

If only Fenyx could be so accommodating.

If not for Zephyrus's intervention, delaying Tursos's strike with force magic, none of this would be happening. Fenyx would be dead. No one would be celebrating. Only the Revivalists.

Zephyrus accepted the cup from Jecht despite wanting nothing to do with its contents. "Gratitude. It wouldn't have been successful without you and Cerik."

Jecht looked around, spilling wine as he did. "Where is Cerik?"

Zephyrus shrugged. Women purchased from brothels prowled the barracks, each clad in transparent silks with jewels decorating their necks, ears, and wrists. Aside from the masks obscuring their faces, little else was left to the imagination.

"Perhaps he found better company," Zephyrus said, swirling his cup's contents. The wine was a deep red. *The same shade as the blood-soaked sands.*

"He might have the right of it." Jecht downed the cup he took for himself and then the one reserved for Cerik. "Come on, Zeph, don't make me drink alone…" He trailed off, his eyes following one of the women walking past. "Six Hells..."

Zephyrus grunted.

"Why so glum? You should be celebrat—"

A dark-skinned woman approached Jecht with a seductive touch. Tall and thin with a purple-and-white silk draped around her, she took Jecht by the hand and began to lead him away.

"I'll find you later," Jecht said, disappearing into the chaos of the barracks.

Zephyrus examined his cup again but set it down. *Air will suit me better.* Zephyrus made for the training square, but guards were stationed near every other cell. After Taric's attempt on Stegavax, Dominus took every precaution. Lenox, however, wasn't present, which only made Zephyrus more nervous for Cassius's life, but at least Carsos and Ixion were too indisposed in their cups to carry out any Revivalist order.

Zephyrus exited the barracks into the cool night air. Rain pattered against the awning sheltering the doorway. Drops fell off either side, creating two puddles. Flashes of lightning cracked the black sky to accompany the thunderous shouts of the Gods.

Zephyrus exhaled against the storm.

"Vykannis… if you're listening, I could really use your courage."

No answer.

"The Judges aren't returning because they never left," Fenyx had said. *"The Valencians are our punishment for losing the elemental magics and the Treasures."*

Fenyx couldn't be right. Vykannis had spoken to him. The Rebels' Rhyme said the Judges would return, and Vykannis had. *But why have you abandoned me now?*

After a time of watching the night sky, the sounds from within the barracks died out. Zephyrus eventually became tired enough to ignore his guilt, stifle his curiosity of what his magic was capable of, and give up on his frustration with Fenyx to go to bed.

He reentered the barracks as guards shoved drunken gladiators into their cells. Zephyrus entered his cell on his own volition.

A candle flickered by his cot, alone and forgotten. Beside it rested a vial containing the healer's potion. He was surprised to find it by his bedside, considering Nallia had been away from the ludus, but somehow she'd made arrangements with someone to keep him plied. Most nights, he drank the swill eagerly, hoping to unlock his future by discovering his past. Tonight, he only wanted rest, but he no longer had the luxury of wants. He needed his memories.

Zephyrus tore the stopper from the flask with his teeth and downed the foul-tasting contents. After swallowing the swill, he blew out the candle. Before the wisps of smoke disappeared into the night air, he drifted into dreams.

A kick to the stomach knocked the breath from his lungs. He fell to the ground in the darkness. Attempting to locate his opponent in the pitch black, his vision failed him.

"Again!" Aikous said. Zephyrus used manipulation magic to cancel the sounds of his movement. If he failed, Aikous would hear and strike. He leapt from his back to his feet in one swift jump.

Zephyrus punched where he thought Aikous would be but found only air. He threw a second, but it yielded the same result. A third, a fourth, a fifth, a kick, but none connected with his target. He tried again, but then he was falling, falling endlessly into a sea of black.

Zephyrus woke up covered in a sheen of sweat. The room flickered, bathed orange in the candle's glow. Zephyrus examined the flaming wick.

I could've sworn I blew it out.

He extinguished the flame with his thumb and index finger. By the time he lay back down, he fell immediately back into fitful dreams.

He stood in a dimly lit room before the glyph stone. He placed his hand on the cold black-and-green pillar. Power flowed into him, wrapping its aura around him like a blanket. His dreamself felt a rush of cold, and the room bloomed with light as fire formed in his other hand. He raised it to the ceiling, and a blaze shot forth from his palm; a fiery vortex swirled around the room like a striking viper.

His conscious mind watched in awe, but his dreamself expected this. His other hand became transparent like a clear oasis. A stream of water spouted from it to intertwine with the flame before the two came together, forming a steam cloud. The glow of the room died, and darkness reigned.

Elemental magic…

"You're ready," a voice said from the corner. Zephyrus expected to see one of the cloaked Masters, but Patrus beamed at him. Ceres and Sybex, two of the Templar's most talented mages, stood behind Patrus.

"If you're not the Wielder, you'll make a fine Guardian," Ceres said, brushing his curling black hair out of his dark green eyes.

Sybex slapped Ceres with the back of her hand. "He is the Wielder." She smiled at Zephyrus, her cheeks dimpling. "He must be to receive all this special treatment."

Ronar emerged from behind them, stroking his gray beard. "No one receives special treatment. Prophet or no, Guardian or not, we all have a part to play. The Judges will return. And we will have our vengeance."

Their faces became a blur, and Zephyrus woke again. He sat up, rubbing his eyes. Frustratingly tired, he lay back to stare at the ceiling, but the flickering orange hue of the candle by his bedside made him bolt upright. The flame danced, casting eerie shadows across the wall. Only this time he was sure he had extinguished it.

CHAPTER 36

URGENT NEWS

Laeden X

Salmantica

Celebration filled the feast hall, and for the first time in a while, Laeden allowed himself to enjoy it. With the help of Gareth and Banis, the Sentinels and Vigiles were able to apprehend Elrod Horne for his Revivalist ties. Aemos, Elrod's son, brooded in the corner, but Laeden wouldn't let his sulking bother him now.

For their loyalty, Banis and Gareth were on their way to a safehouse in Valtarcia. Cassius secured the position of chancellor with victory in the omenation, despite the Revivalists' attempts to sway the Gods' favor. Zephyrus supplied the names of three more snakes beneath Cassius's roof. All in all, his Sentinels had accomplished much in the past few days.

Earl Cassius arrived and greeted Nallia, Prince Damascus, and King Varros.

Laeden still didn't understand why the Revivalists wanted Brusos to win. *Is he already within their ranks, or do they believe him easier to bribe?*

Either way, Brusos would be Laeden's next person of interest.

Despite the small successes, Laeden worried for the safety of the soon-to-be chancellor. Zephyrus warned of plans for a gladiator to assassinate Cassius and join the Uprising. The Uprising was another threat, but small, nothing to stop him from taking an evening to himself.

The colors of the royal family decorated the feast hall: blue and gold for House Helixus, and red and black for House Drake. Laeden wore his customary blue, but the darker blue of House Faire—his mother's house. The hall buzzed with excitement as musicians played and patricians danced. The vibrant fabric of the ladies' long dresses reminded him of spring, lively with a breath of hope. To celebrate the inauguration of Cassius as chancellor, purple-and-gold banners lined the dark stone pillars of Sentigard.

With the chancellorship, Earl Cassius would be elevated to the Duke of Stockhelm. The Cassiuses would become a Great House of equal standing to the Helixuses of Valtarcia.

What impact might that have on court politics?

The progressives in the senate pushed for an evolution from the barbarism of gladiatorium to the more modern sport of tourney knights. They thought to repurpose the gladiators to be a part of a standard army across all three islands. Some even sought to use this new army as a mechanism of exploration and conquest to the unknown lands beyond the Hylan mountain range. But now that Cassius, a lanista, would have a major chair within all senate meetings, nothing was certain. Of course, the senate's plans meant little if the Revivalist anarchists got their way.

A cheer reverberated out from where Damascus and Nallia stood. Laeden removed himself from the safety of the balcony overlooking the hall and entered the party. He shook a few hands and engaged in pleasantries on his way to join Damascus and the others. Though the people of the court all smiled at his face, behind his back, they still called him a pseudo-prince.

They can call me whatever they like.

It upset his stepmother more than him. She adamantly and publicly, on several occasions, declared him a true prince and offered to have him legitimized at least twice. But Laeden never wanted her love. He wanted the love of his own mother, but they separated him from her, for *peace.* Part of him pitied Danella. She had always been good to him, yet Laeden seized every opportunity to be a difficult, reclusive youth.

Even in her opposition to Daenus's apprehension, she was only trying to protect me.

As he approached, Danella hugged his father, and people congratulated them. Markus embraced Nallia.

Such a display must not be due to the chancellorship.

"What news?" Laeden asked Damascus's squire, Haedron.

"A royal wedding," Haedron said. "Damascus and Nallia. Can't wait to see the look on Aemos's face when he learns that Damascus beat her in the duel."

Nallia and Damascus. Court politics just got even more interesting.

Laeden pushed past Haedron to congratulate Damascus and the Cassiuses.

Meeting Danella's eyes, he smiled and embraced the queen. "Congratulations, Mother."

"Mother?" she asked, pushing him away and putting her hand to her chest. "Have you ever called me that?"

Laeden blushed. "Consider it a thank you of sorts. For everything."

Danella pulled him back in and wrapped her arms around him again. "You're my son, just as much as he is."

Laeden closed his eyes in his stepmother's embrace.

Damascus gave Laeden a pat on the back. "It's good to see you out from the safety of the corner of the room, brother."

Laeden and Danella separated, allowing him to hug his younger half-brother.

Nallia was a good woman, strong and poised. She'd make a suitable match for Damascus and, eventually, a befitting queen.

"I know the Cassiuses," Laeden said, gesturing to Markus. "If she's anything like him, you've found a fierce companion."

Markus laughed. "Careful, though, she's tougher than a Bruiser in plate mail."

Damascus grinned. "I witnessed the strength of her will… and her sword."

Holding Damascus's arm, Nallia's cheeks reddened.

It was nice to see people smile for a change, a reprieve from blood, death, and fear.

"Congratulations, my lady," Laeden said, bowing to Nallia.

"A day for celebration indeed," the king said, clasping both of his sons on the shoulder. "We must be glad for such opportunities to rejoice considering the current climate."

"Not all are so fortunate," Danella said.

"Aye." Cassius slapped Markus on the shoulder. "Certainly not Brusos!" Cassius's laugh was joined by most, but not the queen.

Danella folded her arms across her chest. "I hope you are referring to your victory in the omenation and not the tragedy that has befallen his house."

Something in her voice gave Laeden pause. *Tragedy?*

"Have you not heard?" she asked Cassius. "Brusos's villa was burned to ash. Scorched corpses lay in its foundation."

Laeden's joy melted. He massaged his temples, trying to sort through the conflicting information between what he thought he knew and what he'd just heard. Laeden wasn't alone in hearing this for the first time.

"What terrible news!"

"The Revivalists?"

"Are Ebron and Cerberynn okay?"

"My sources couldn't confirm or deny their safety," Danella said. "But they suspect the Uprising is responsible."

Damascus looked to Laeden, like he wanted something to be done about it. Cassius and his wife both stood dumbstruck.

"Nothing our new chancellor won't be able to handle," the king said. "For now, let us turn thoughts to celebration, new positions, new love, and future peace and prosperity."

The tension settled, but Laeden's mind wouldn't relent.

The Uprising has yet to strike such an offensive blow. Surely the rebel slaves wouldn't have murdered their own.

Markus rubbed the back of his neck.

"How did we not know?" Laeden asked as he pulled Markus off to a servants' path away from the prying eyes and ears.

His contentment from moments ago vanished. The vibrant colors of the banners and dresses dulled with the disturbing news, and the weight of his badge of office flattened him to the floor.

Markus shook his head, waving his black mane. "I don't know."

"We need answers. Was it the Uprising or the Revivalists? We cannot become divided in our efforts."

Laeden felt someone standing too close behind him. He whirled around, fists clenched.

"We're in the middl—?"

Iylea.

She flinched, stepping backwards. "Apologies, my prince." She stared at her shuffling feet, gripping the hem of her serving dress.

Laeden's fists uncoiled into skyward palms, before running his fingers through his hair. "Apologies, Iylea, I didn't suspect you to be..." He exhaled before whispering to Markus. "Give me a moment." Markus bowed and excused himself.

"I'm sorry, Iylea, I—"

"It doesn't matter." Wrinkles borne of stress furrowed above her brow. "I need to tell you something. And you must listen."

"What is it?" he asked, surveying the feast from the servants' hallway.

"I haven't been completely honest with you."

A knot constricted Laeden's throat. He coughed. *What dishonesty are you capable of?* He returned to scanning the crowd, refusing to meet her eyes, too afraid to listen to whatever came next.

She grabbed his chin, forcing him to look at her, an iron resolve in her yellow-green gaze. "I need you to listen."

Laeden could take on the patricians. He didn't balk before the Revivalists. The king, the queen, nor anyone else had such power over him, but before Iylea, beneath the intensity of her stare, Laeden's composure threatened to crack.

No. I can't put her first.

She'd gotten him in trouble too many times.

Laeden swallowed. "Out with it, then."

Iylea winced at the bite in his tone. "I love you, but what I'm about to tell you is no joke, and it can be the difference between life and death." She leaned in closer. "Nallia is in trouble. The Cassiuses are in trouble. The queen's men—"

"You've told me this," Laeden said, putting his hands on his hips. "I looked into the study and found nothing. I made a fool of myself chasing Ser Daenus and found *nothing*. And what do you mean the Cassiuses are in trouble? Who isn't in trouble? Chimera's breath, the Cassiuses know what's at stake."

"You don't understand! I've seen it. Brusos, Ser Daenus, and… the queen."

Laeden stepped closer and grabbed her by the shoulders. "What have you seen? What are you saying?"

Her mouth moved, but no words came forth.

"Speak." It wasn't a command, but a plea. He wanted a reason to believe he was wrong to have distanced himself—that love held the answers to conquer all things…

"Laeden… I am a seer."

Laeden stepped back, retracting his chin. "A what?"

Iylea seized both of his hands. "I have dreams, and I know the queen, Brusos, and Ser Daenus are up to something."

She isn't joking… Iylea, a seer? The queen a Revivalist? Preposterous.

Laeden didn't believe her. He couldn't believe her. The collar about his neck tightened, strangling him with trepidation. He wrenched free from her grip.

If she's a seer, she's a mage… an outlawed mage. One who, even a few moons ago, would have been nailed to a Six Arrowed Star at the Gilded Gauntlet. But if she's a seer, and she's been right, this entire time…

Laeden eyed Danella.

The queen beamed, her black hair pin-straight beneath her garnet-studded crown.

She is trying to kill the king? Doesn't she have everything she ever wanted?

Danella took his father as a husband to seal the Treaty of 940, breaking up Laeden's family, separating him from his mother.

If this is true, my entire life was built on a lie. My father gave up love for duty to the people of New Rheynia—for peace. Laeden struggled throughout his childhood to accept his father's actions as noble.

Why would she want him dead? Was everything we sacrificed for peace all for nothing?

Laeden tried to piece it together. He paced the servant's hall, his head in his hands. *If Danella and Daenus are both Revivalists, of course she would come to his defense and have a plan in case one of them became a person of interest. But Iylea… a seer?*

He shook his head. "No… this can't be. You're wrong."

Iylea grabbed him by the front of his doublet. "Laeden, you must believe me."

"I believe you," he said, prying her wrists away from him. "I believe you *think* you know something, but these are just dreams. Not prophecies. Not visions."

"Laeden, please. I know what this means."

She extended her hand, waiting for him to take it.

Laeden exhaled, but remained still, leaving Iylea's empty hand hanging between them. Her eyes pleaded for him to take it, to trust her. He wanted to believe her. But he couldn't. He wouldn't. To take her hand, to accept her words—he would lose her forever.

The silence stretched on. Iylea dropped her gaze and her outstretched hand. "I was trying to protect myself, to spare your involvement… I know what will become of me, and you know what you must do. But you must trust me. If you arrest them, the Revivalists' crimes will stop."

"You will not be executed, and you will not be exiled because you're not a…" He shook his head. *Impossible.* "We followed Ser Daenus—he's clean. Brusos is supposedly missing, but he'll be found. And the queen… she's my family."

"Laeden, I know how it seems, but—"

"Captain," a voice said from behind him. Laeden spun to find Markus with a Sentinel messenger beside him. "Apologies for the interruption, but this cannot wait."

Laeden looked back to Iylea. "That's fine. We're finished."

He turned from her before she could react. He didn't want to see her look of rejection. Deep down, he wanted to hold her, to remind her everything would be all right.

I can't look back.

The ground around him threatened to cave in. At least that's how it felt. Leaving her there, alone, felt like a crime.

Nothing the messenger could say would be as disarming as Iylea's words, so by the time they made their way to the war room after Markus insisted they be alone, Laeden's patience had run dry.

"Chimera's breath, what in Six Hells is so important?"

The messenger glanced at Markus before speaking. "Banis and Gareth… they're dead."

CHAPTER 37

SECRET DUNGEON

Danella V

Salmantica

Danella had no need to keep up appearances today. She drank to the celebration of her son's new match, applauded the Targarus gladiators as they were presented to the feast hall, and enjoyed the company of people she'd otherwise have suffered through. Even food tasted sweeter now that the climax of her plans rested on the horizon.

Her seed was planted. Laeden bought it. Somehow, whether by fate, consequence, or desire of the Gods, her plans had suffered. She wanted Brusos to be the chancellor, but that was impossible now. She needed to move forward with the pieces she had, and she would. Binding Nallia to Damascus would allow Danella to have more influence over the Cassiuses and their sway within the senate.

As far as Danella was concerned, she traded pawns with Laeden, but it allowed her to move her tiles to opportune positions. She traded Elrod Horne to discover her mole. The victories Laeden thought he won, she let him have. He'd been a troubled boy, but he had grown into a good man. Varros was a good man too, yet she would sacrifice more than a few good men if it meant quelling the wrath of the Gods and keeping this way of life her father established. Gods willing, it wouldn't come to that. Cassius would be dealt with soon, and the Uprising would take the fall for it.

The formation of the Revivalists gave rise to the Sentinels, but the development of the Uprising couldn't have been more perfect. They didn't trust their Sentinel defenders, so they took it upon themselves. The rebels would reveal themselves for the destructive beacons they were. Everyone would realize how the Celestic disease had corrupted society. The plebs would turn on the rebels, and the Revivalists wouldn't need to push any further. Varros could live, and the Gods would be sated. Everything would work out as the Six intended. They spared Varros thus far—stayed her hand just enough that her plans could take effect without the dire consequences she feared.

The only broken link in her chain of plans was Zephyrus. Lenox, Saulus, Liario, even Brusos's gladiators—they all failed. Like a hydra with nine lives, this gladiator, this Prophet of Celestia, refused to die. One of the Three or not, Zephyrus had stopped nothing, changed nothing, and in a matter of time, he'd be nothing. Perhaps he never was a Prophet of Celestia, or maybe Cassius broke him as he claimed he did.

"More wine?" Varros asked, pouring a goblet for himself. Normally, Varros performing servant tasks would have bothered her, but not today. She nodded, and he filled her cup. "It's wonderful to see you in such spirits, my love. I haven't seen you so lively since the Hechts bled out upon the Six Arrowed Star."

"It's not everyday your son gets engaged to a beauty such as her," Danella returned. "But that was a glorious day, wasn't it?"

Varros chuckled. "Justice was served. I don't know if I'd call it glorious, but it brought us where we are now. I often wonder what life would be like if your brother were still king."

Danella nodded. "You wouldn't be wearing a crown."

Varros hmphed. "Perhaps the realm would be safer." He sighed. "I apologize. At times I get torn between love and duty."

"It's just how you are," Danella said. "The same stubborn naivety true of all Helixuses. But everything will work out as it should, and I will love you all the more."

He smiled at her, a hint of sorrow in his faraway gaze. She examined him, tilting her head to the side. *What darkness clouds your mind?*

"My queen," Daenus said, breaking Danella from her thoughts. "Might I have a word?"

"Is everything well?" Varros asked, concern creasing his crow's feet.

Danella swallowed. *Daenus is never so direct. Something's wrong.*

"Everything is fine, your grace," Daenus said, clearing his throat. "Nothing of import. Just the… I fear one of the queen's handmaidens has been drinking more wine than serving it to others."

Danella didn't need to mask her frustration. *You couldn't have thought of anything better than that?* She gathered her skirts and stood. "Someone just earned themselves Six readings of the Facets and privy duties for the next three moons."

Varros raised his goblet and smiled curtly. "Go easy, my love."

Danella excused herself and followed Daenus out of the hall and into a back entryway.

"You better have good reason for such a disruption," Danella hissed once they were alone.

"Your grace, we have a problem," Daenus said. "One of our spies overheard Iylea speaking to Laeden."

Danella swallowed. *Not another Cantella situation. What did Iylea stumble into? What did she tell Laeden?* She wished someone had only drunk too much wine.

"What words were exchanged?" Danella asked, fearing Daenus's reply.

"She's a seer."

Danella's heart skipped a beat.

A seer? Impossible! Iylea had been in her service since she was a girl. Daenus continued to talk to her, but half a hundred worst-case scenarios flooded her mind.

Danella clutched her Six Arrowed Star pendant in her palm. "How did Laeden respond?"

He rubbed the back of his neck. "It doesn't seem like he believed her, your grace."

She nodded, the gears of her mind turning with frustrating lethargy. *What if he believes her? What else could she tell him? A Celestic seer, a mage—under my nose this entire time.* Heat coursed through her veins. Too much was at stake. *I can't take any chances.*

"Take her," Danella said, the arrows' edges cutting into her palm. "I don't care how, just keep it quiet. The secret dungeon. No one but you and I will know."

CHAPTER 38

Blood Leads to Blood

Laeden XI
Salmantica

B*lood leads to blood. The cycle continues with more malice behind each attack in a vicious circle of anger, vengeance, and death.*

The gladiators fought on the sands of the Six Spear Arena, but Laeden's thoughts were consumed by what he saw on the wall of the isthmus dividing Salmantica and Valtarcia the day before. Gareth, Banis the Ratman, and his family were so close to reaching freedom and protection. The two men Allaron assigned to escort the party also suffered, but perhaps not quite as long.

"The Gods punish traitors," the wall read in the blood of the slain. Two Sentinels were stabbed half a hundred times, their blue-and-gray uniforms painted with the rusty red of dried blood. As gruesome as it was, Laeden forced himself to look upon the four bodies hanging from nooses atop the wall. When he looked at the body of Banis's wife, he saw his own mother's face. Not the queen, but his real mother… what he remembered of her.

How did they know? The Revivalists are always a half-step ahead of me.

A traditional Bruiser slammed a great axe into his opponent's head, splitting his iron half-helm down the middle. The fallen warrior twitched in the sands to the roar of the crowd.

Blood leads to blood.

This all started with one mage. If he received the justice he deserved, if Father ordered his execution as he should have, perhaps Gareth, Banis, and his family would still be alive.

Laeden glared at his father watching the contest below.

No.

This wasn't his father's fault. His father spared the mage. He hadn't spilled his blood. If he had, perhaps the Uprising would have started their assault sooner. The Revivalists would have risen to oppose them, and the Sentinels to deal with both. It seemed inevitable. But the blood was not on his father's, or the mages' hands. The fault rested with the Revivalists.

I need to stop the violence, not perpetuate it. But how?

The next bout of gladiators took to the sands, but Laeden had no doubt of what fate awaited them. Perhaps not today or tomorrow, but eventually, the victors of today would be the deceased of tomorrow, and with their blood, the crowds would cheer.

A handmaiden strode past with a carafe of wine, but it wasn't Iylea. Following her alarming warning and admission of being a seer, Iylea disappeared. Laeden couldn't find her anywhere. No one knew her whereabouts, or if she was safe.

What if I never see her again? I didn't even look back after I dismissed her. How many other awful things did I say? She probably ran away… from me.

"I've seen it," she had said, *"Brusos, Ser Daenus, and the queen."*

He glanced at Danella out of the corner of his eye. The garnets of her crown glimmered in the setting sun. *Could she really be such a monster?* Laeden couldn't believe it. She was always so kind to him. To everyone.

Laeden shook his head, still trying to deny it. He attempted to rationalize any possible motive as to why Iylea would make this up. He couldn't, and that made it worse. *But a seer?* He didn't want to believe her.

How can the woman I love be the monster so many fear? I feared her kind. I wanted the mage executed. How many things did I say to her exclaiming that viewpoint? How could she have ever loved me?

The Primus of the Salmantic Games began. The games Laeden once enjoyed now made him ill. Zephyrus would be fighting in this very arena soon in the Kings' Day Games. There was a purpose to the gladiatorial games, he knew, but now he had difficulty seeing it. He sighed as the games came to their conclusion with no surprises; Targarus's men were left unstained, while the runner-up returned home with more dead men to burn.

The king clapped before standing to silence the crowd. "Another year, Targarus reigns supreme! To conclude a day of spectacular glory, there is good news. My son, Laeden, the captain of the Sentinels, has tidings to share."

The king took his seat as Laeden stood to address the onlookers.

He had no good news to share, but appearances needed to be maintained.

He stared out over the bloodthirsty crowd. The statues of the Six held their spears over the arena, casting a shadow in the sands that appeared like the spokes of a wheel. Patrician and pleb, Valencians and Celestics, free and slave, they all looked to him wanting peace, but there was no peace in this world, only vengeance—and vengeance was a spinning wheel.

The patricians would be on top until the plebs revolted. The Valencians were on top, but the Uprising was proof that the Celestics would fight back. The sweetness of vengeance was ephemeral, but his father set a tone for justice. Laeden would make sure justice reigned.

"Good people of Salmantica," Laeden said, looking out over the grandstands of the arena. "Many strides have been taken in the Sentinels' objective towards freeing New Rheynia from the Revivalists' shadow. These cowards believe they're safe from justice, but their brief revolution of tyranny will not see the Great Houses of New Rheynia fall."

Laeden paused, expecting a cheer, but none greeted his words. *And that was the easy part of my address.* Clearing his throat, he continued.

"We've learned from the Disasters that befell us before the Great Migration. The Six reign in New Rheynia, and that truth must be upheld. Yet the traditions of the Treaty of 940 have lost touch. Let it be known: practicing other faiths is outlawed, but the reprimand for the use of magic will not be death as it has been in years past, but exile from our great society."

The buzz of a few thousand murmurs cluttered the silence over Six Spear. Laeden swallowed. He raised his arms to settle the crowd before they became unruly, but it wasn't until his father stood that silence returned.

"This is the decree of our king, Varros Helixus." Laeden gestured to his father with a trembling hand.

The king met Laeden's gaze and nodded. Laeden took a deep breath, settling his frazzled nerves. The faces of the audience were far enough away that he didn't have to look upon them, but the thought of how many eyes were on him made his stomach flip.

How many of those eyes gaze upon me with cruel intent?

The same anxiety that percolated beads of sweat along his back during the Festival of Stockhelm bubbled up. The thought of how many assassins lurked in the grandstands made the hairs on the back of his neck stand on end.

Laeden clenched his trembling hand into a fist. "To those who defile these laws, or take justice into their own hands, the punishment will be death. One such man has been taken into custody by the brave Sentinels; Count Elrod Horne will be put to trial. Honor and justice will be served as we fight for our families, our faith in the Six, and the future of New Rheynia!"

Laeden punched the air, but the crowd's reaction, expectedly so, was mixed.

Father smiled and clapped. Danella mirrored his sentiment, but Laeden could no longer trust the validity of her outward appearances. He only hoped Iylea heard him, wherever she was. Laeden backed away from the edge of the pulvinus, happy he wouldn't have to answer questions about Brusos, the Uprising, or what happened upon the isthmus wall, but those were problems for a different day.

A glowing ember arced over the arena.

What in Six Hells is that? It streaked straight for them.

A flaming arrow fell onto the pulvinus.

"Move!" Laeden shouted, but too late.

Laeden draped himself over his father as more flaming arrows fell from the sky. Another landed, then another, until the pulvinus burst into flames. The audience panicked, scrambling to safety. Shrieks and cries clashed in calamity.

A wall of fire blocked the doorway to the staircase, but more arrows fell. He covered his father as Markus tore away the burning banners to lead people to safety.

"Protect the king!" Laeden shouted. The stands of the arena were in utter chaos. He scanned the crowd for Revivalist archers, but he saw nothing through the smoke and flame. No more arrows rained down, but that didn't mean the threat was over. As Sentinels and King's Guard Knights spirited the royal family to shelter, Laeden remained on the pulvinus. Vigiles came with buckets of water, extinguishing the flames before they could spread too far, but the damage was done. The statement was made.

Always a step ahead. Like they know my every move.

Brusos, Ser Daenus, and the queen.

They attacked the pulvinus. Ser Daenus and the queen were nearly caught in the crossfire. *Would they be so bold in order to cover their tracks?* So many questions and no answers. *Six save us, Iylea.* He wanted her comfort. He wanted the peace only she'd ever been able to offer him. If only he could speak to her now.

Where are you?

Too many questions. He needed to stop wondering and start finding answers.

CHAPTER 39

THE VOICE

Zephyrus XIII

Stockhelm

The sun scorched hot, even though it had only just risen. Zephyrus stood abreast with the rest of Cassius's gladiators before Doctore, preparing for another day of clever lies. Another day in which Lenox drew breath while Patrus lay dead, and another night absent Laeden's fulfillment of his promises to dispatch the Revivalists beneath Cassius's roof.

"We have but a few days of training before our selected gladiators compete in the Kings' Day Games," Doctore said. "To stand in the Primus against the best in all of New Rheynia, I give you the defier of death, Stegavax!"

The gladiators cheered. Stegavax always had his followers, but since Fenyx claimed his mantle, others were flocking to Stegavax's support in solidarity against Fenyx. Doctore attempted to return Stegavax to form slowly to avoid the plight of setbacks, but Stegavax would have none of it. Despite his vigor, he only appeared to be a shell of his former self.

"To stand beside him, I give you the unproven, but undeniable, talent of Zephyrus."

Other than Jecht and Cerik, no one gave voice towards Zephyrus's standing.

Doctore cleared his throat and hurried onto the next introduction. "And of course, the slayer of Tursos, the broken-blade hero of the Stockhelm Games, your Champion, Fenyx!"

Unenthused applause, more dutiful than celebratory, answered Doctore's introduction. While no one—not even Stegavax—openly crossed Fenyx, there was no debate as to where the brotherhood's loyalties lay.

"Now, to training!"

Just as Doctore reared back his whip, Nallia's voice called from the balcony.

"Doctore, send Zephyrus to the villa."

Zephyrus wiped sweat from his brow. *To the villa—why?* Zephyrus hadn't spoken to Nallia since Lenox and the other guards beat him in the rain.

"Apologies," Doctore said, "but I must incline to the importance of his training."

At least someone has some sense around here…

"Just for a moment. I swear it."

Unrelenting. Such is the nature of the entitled—they get what they want or persist until they do.

Spotting Lenox close by, an idea formed in Zephyrus's head. It was rash, but the man who killed Patrus had lived too long. Zephyrus sent word to Laeden of Lenox and Liario's betrayal to House Cassius, yet nothing had been done. This wasn't out of selfish vengeance. This was his duty to Laeden. *I live to serve…*

"I'll go," Zephyrus said, letting his wooden sword and buckler fall to the sands.

Doctore grunted but gestured for Lenox to escort Zephyrus to the villa. Lenox gripped Zephyrus's arm and shoved him towards the barracks door.

Back inside, Zephyrus's eyes struggled to adjust to the dim light. He'd been led to the villa before—up a flight of stairs, where a locked door waited. *While Lenox unlocks the door, I'll throw him down the stairs.* With no one to witness and Zephyrus's position in the games, he could get away with a mild punishment. But with Lenox dealt with, he'd sleep easier knowing Patrus received justice.

Expecting Lenox to lead the way, Zephyrus stopped at the base of the stairs.

Lenox paused, narrowing his eyes at him. "Get going."

"You have the key," Zephyrus said.

Lenox laughed. "So clever, you are." He reached for the dagger at his belt, but Zephyrus grabbed Lenox by the wrist, forcing the dagger to remain sheathed.

Lenox snickered. He reared his head back to headbutt Zephyrus. Zephyrus's trained instincts took over. He leaned forward and tucked his chin. Instead of Lenox bringing the crown of his head into Zephyrus's nose, he slammed his nose into Zephyrus's head.

Lenox stumbled back, stunned by the blow, but the separation allowed him to draw his dagger. He spat blood. "You're dead."

"You can't beat me," Zephyrus said.

Lenox's black eyes absorbed the darkness of the barracks. With a twisted grin, Lenox drew the dagger across his forearm, slashing through the purple cloth above his golden bracer. A dark stain blossomed on his uniform.

"Guards!" Lenox shouted. "Help. I've been attacked." He tossed the dagger at Zephyrus.

Zephyrus inhaled sharply and instinctively snatched the hilt from the air as Lenox drew his gladius. The clanking of armor and the clamor of voices filled the barracks. Coming from the sands outside and the stairs to the villa above, they swarmed upon him like wasps.

Zephyrus dropped the dagger and put his hands up.

"Seize him," Lenox said, spitting blood and wiping his mouth with the back of his hand. "He stole my dagger!"

"He lies!" Zephyrus yelled. But what good were the words of a slave against those of a guard? Zephyrus had no choice but to submit.

"Tie him to the palus," Lenox said. "He will be whipped for this."

The guards dragged Zephyrus through the barracks and back onto the sands' heat.

Jecht and Cerik advanced, questioning the guards as they tied Zephyrus to the palus.

"Guards," Nallia shouted from the balcony. "What is the meaning of this?"

They didn't answer. Tighter and tighter the ropes dug into Zephyrus's skin, driving his wrists into the splintered wood.

Dominus emerged onto the balcony, Nortus and Liario beside him. "Silence!" Dominus cast a furious glare at the scene before him. Everyone obeyed, other than the ominous squawking of a vulture circling overhead. "Speak, Lenox, explain yourself."

"The slave attacked me in th—"

"Liar!" Zephyrus fought against his bindings but couldn't escape. The familiar cold that accompanied using his elemental fire magic froze the blood in his veins.

No. Not here!

Patrus's words back at Tharseo's Bastion suddenly made sense. *"They'll take us alive, if they don't know what you can do. But if they find out…"*

Zephyrus bit off his protests, and the chill of balancing the scales fled him.

I can't let them know I'm a mage.

"Silence!" Dominus bellowed again. "Lenox, speak."

"The slave seized my weapon and attacked me," Lenox said, displaying his slashed forearm. "He should burn on a Six Arrowed Star for this, but he'll settle for a good lashing."

Nallia scoffed beside her father. "You'd have him whipped… days before the Primus? Father, we can't—"

"Enough!" Dominus bared his teeth, cursing under his breath.

Zephyrus struggled to free himself, but there was no escaping his fate.

Dominus shook his head. "We cannot afford to send injured men to the sands, but he shall be whipped for this. Fifty lashes upon our return from Salmantica!"

Zephyrus closed his eyes and pursed his lips. *Fool. Stupid fool.* He didn't have a plan. He left too much up to chance. *What was I thinking?*

"Henceforth," Dominus continued. "All slaves summoned to the villa must be secured by manacles."

Lenox growled. "My duke, is he to return to the sands, absent punishment?"

Dominus tossed his hands to the scorching sun. "Six save me, see him to the Hill."

Zephyrus didn't know what the Hill was, but he breathed a relieved sigh as the guards removed him from the whipping post.

"You are fortunate that you fight in a few days," Dominus said to Zephyrus, his wispy hair swirling in the wind. "Otherwise, you would have been whipped until my coronation. This punishment is a kindness. Too kind."

His hawkish eyes fell upon the guards from up in his perch. "Feed all slave rations to the horses. Disobedience will not be tolerated beneath my roof." He turned and disappeared into the villa, Nallia quick at his heels in complaint.

Lenox eyed Zephyrus with venomous disdain. He leaned close. "You will die, Prophet. I'll nail your corpse to a Six Arrowed Star, and the Gods will smile."

He underestimated Lenox. Zephyrus had done everything asked of him, by everyone. He played along, told his clever lies, kept his secrets well, and did as he was supposed to. But this time, he was outwitted. He happily would have accepted punishment for Lenox's death if he avenged Patrus, but this sentence was magnified by his own condemnation.

I brought this upon myself. I deserve this.

Two guards began to escort him to the back gate of the training square.

Jecht stepped forward. "If you send him, send me too." He looked at Cerik expectantly.

With a groan, Cerik advanced to Jecht's side. "Aye, and me."

The two guards escorting Zephyrus stopped, looking to Doctore and Lenox for confirmation.

"Honorable fools," Doctore said, shaking his head. He gestured for Lenox to take Jecht and Cerik as well.

A pit yawned within Zephyrus's stomach. *Why would they subject themselves to stand with me in punishment?*

The three were escorted away from the training square through the back gate to the Hill. The Hill wasn't a hill, but the Hylan mountain range

House Cassius was etched into. The yellow slate and dirt ascended in an impossibly steep climb.

Lenox pointed to the crest where the slope of the mountain reached the highest point of the villa. "Get climbing, *slave.* All the way to the top and back down. You go again and again until the nightly rains."

Zephyrus, Jecht, and Cerik went in silence. They made slow progress, the ground eroding with each step. Spiny green-and-red plants with purple flowers grew from the thorny brush littering the hillside.

"Beautiful, but poisonous," Cerik said, breaking the silence as he led the way on all fours. "Lover's Dream. The flower petals have healing properties, but the thorns will make you numb. Too much in your bloodstream, you may even hallucinate."

"This is madness," Jecht said behind Cerik. "At Targarus's ludus, punishment meant half rations or sleep deprivation. Never poisonous hikes up the burning Hylan."

Cerik grunted, hauling his bulk up the mountain. "Not my first time on the Hill. Eventually, we will have to grab the vines to pull ourselves up."

Jecht guffawed. "You just said the thorns are poisonous…"

"Precisely why it is a *punishment*," Cerik said.

The pit that opened within Zephyrus's stomach spouted bile. *They suffer because of me.* "Why did you subject yourselves to this?"

Jecht and Cerik stopped to look back.

"Honestly, I don't know what you were thinking," Cerik said to Jecht.

"That Lenox makes Damascus burning Drake seem like a Faceless saint," Jecht said. "We all know if you got the drop on him, he'd be dead."

Zephyrus snorted. "He cut himself with his dagger and called for the guards."

Cerik raised a brow. "Tip the scales…"

Jecht's scarred face parted in a wide grin. "Six save me, you can't be serious?"

Zephyrus shrugged, and they all shared a much-needed laugh.

"Let's go," Cerik said, "or they'll burden us with packs to carry if we're too slow."

Jecht chortled, but his laughter choked off. "Wait, really?"

Despite Zephyrus's own disappointments and failures, he counted himself lucky to have friends by his side. *What other paths might they walk with me? Perhaps not all of my clever lies need to be told to everyone.*

They spent most of the afternoon climbing up and down the sun-scorched mountain. By the time the sun set, Zephyrus's fingers were numb, his skin burned, and his head ached, yet he was content to have been amongst friends.

Once they were bathed and the medicus cleared them to return to the barracks, Doctore came to check on them. "I respect what you two did today," he said to Jecht and Cerik. "It's honorable to share the burdens of your brothers. However, this walk Zephyrus must do alone."

Zephyrus contorted his brow. *What now?*

Doctore held out a pair of manacles. "You've been summoned by Lady Nallia. I told her you needed rest, but she can be… persistent."

Zephyrus grimaced. "Who will escort me?"

"Nortus."

Nortus led Zephyrus, bound at both wrists and ankles, through the villa. Torches lining the walls fended off the encroaching night, casting dancing shadows along the marble pillars.

"Tell me true, what happened earlier?" Nortus asked.

Zephyrus stopped, his clinking chains coming to rest. "He cut himself and blamed me. I warned you about him."

"Aye, we'll hafta be more careful—"

"I told Laeden about him," Zephyrus hissed. "I told you to tell Laeden about the others, but what's being done?"

"Aye," Nortus said. "Don't wreck the runner. I told 'em."

"And what's being done?" Zephyrus asked. "Laeden sits in his castle while the Revivalists plot murders, and yet I'm the one punished. How many times must I escape death? If Laeden doesn't do something, either I kill Lenox, or he kills me."

"I won't let that happen," Nortus said.

Zephyrus grunted. The two walked in silence until they arrived at Nallia's chambers.

Nortus drummed his knuckles on the door. It swung open after only the second knock.

"Gratitude, Nortus," Nallia said, turning to Zephyrus. "I trust there was no trouble getting you here this time." She wore a pale yellow night silk that hung loosely from her body. She pointed to his chains. "Is all this necessary?"

"Duke's orders, milady."

"Take them off—*my* orders."

After a moment's hesitation, Nortus did as instructed. He stood idly, even after she dismissed him, unsure if he should leave her alone with him. She shoved Nortus out into the corridor, shutting the door and locking it behind him.

"Come now." She took Zephyrus by the hands and pulled him into her chambers.

The room smelled of lavender. Purple drapes and carpets ornamented with gold trim adorned her sleeping chambers. Candles flickered dimly around the room, and a brazier burned in the corner.

"Apologies for today," Nallia said. "After what happened at Brusos's ludus, and the attack at the Salmantic Games… I suppose everyone's on edge."

Zephyrus didn't know what she was talking about. *More attacks?* "The Revivalists?"

"Supposedly, the Uprising attacked Brusos, but the Revivalists are responsible for the attack on the arena. Oh, but I believe congratulations are in order! Word of your heroism upon the sands has spread. I've heard such praise that you might be Vykannis born again… or perhaps the Wielder." She beamed at him.

Zephyrus stared at her, unsure what game she was playing. He bit back a retort. *Whatever game it is, play along—clever lies.* He tried to reason out what this news of the Uprising and Revivalist attacks could mean, but his head still felt fuzzy from the Lover's Dream.

"Many would say I resemble more of the Harbinger," Zephyrus said, contorting his lip.

Nallia shook her head. "Tell me your prophecy and I will put this to rest once and for all."

Zephyrus swallowed, then stifled a cough. He didn't trust her. He couldn't trust her.

She raised her eyebrows and nodded in encouragement.

So persistent. He sighed. "The son of the fallen will rise to prey upon the unworthy. Under cloaks and shadows he hides, to bring light to those hoping. When the rivers and streams run dry, he will summon the unworldly to sever the chains that bind the realm to the holy."

Nallia nodded, her eyes narrow, deep in thought. She sauntered over to a desk beneath a window and pulled several inkwells and parchment from the drawer.

"Again," she said. "And slower this time."

Zephyrus repeated, and she wrote everything down in a flowing cursive. Nallia opened the second drawer of her desk and pulled out a thick tome, earmarked to a certain page.

She pointed. "These are the prophecies of the Three," she said, encouraging Zephyrus to lean over her shoulder. The sweet smell of rosewater filled his nostrils as he looked past her waves of chestnut hair. "Your friend Patrus was right. Your prophecy has elements of all three." She pulled the stopper from a red inkwell and dipped her quill. She painted a red line under certain words of Zephyrus's prophecy.

"Here, here, and here, your prophecy overlaps with the Wielder."

She underlined *under cloaks and shadows,* then *to bring light.* Nallia pointed back to the tome scrawled with the prophecy of the Wielder. "This pertains to the line 'out of the darkness, born into the light,' and here…" She underlined *summon the unworldly,* then pointed to the words in the book: *a wielder of the lost to summon the three.* "The unworldly refers to the Treasures of Stockhelm—the Vykane Blade of Vykannis the Brave, the Orsion Cloak of Orsius the Wise, and the Aeryean Armor of Aeryss the Affectionate." Nallia smiled at him, but meeting his eyes, her face fell. "You don't remember, do you?"

Nallia stood from leaning over her desk, quill still in hand.

Zephyrus exhaled, placing his hands on his hips. Patrus believed people would rally behind the Wielder. Seeing his prophecy side by side with the Wielder's made it feel real, but everything else was lost on him.

"I supposed I must have known it once," Zephyrus said. "But I don't remember."

"Those are the names of the Judges," Nallia said, "and the Treasures they gave to the Celestics to save their tribes from monstrous beasts—if you believe the legends. Tharseo, the first Wielder, defeated the beasts with the three Treasures."

"So what happened to them?" Zephyrus asked, testing her.

Patrus had told him that the Arcane Templar protected the Treasures from those unworthy of wielding such power, but playing coy could give him greater insight as to what Nallia knew, or at the very least reveal her as a liar if she contradicted Patrus.

"Where are the Treasures now?" Zephyrus asked.

Nallia shrugged. "Hidden somewhere, I suppose. Perhaps for the same reasons why the elemental mages were exiled; the elders of Stockhelm feared their powers."

Zephyrus massaged the scruff of his chin. "The elders exiled the mages?"

"The elemental ones," Nallia said. "Prior to the Great Migration. I imagine if the mages remained in Stockhelm, the New Rheynian War would have had a drastically different outcome. That's why most Celestics don't believe in the Return. They believe their enslavement is punishment for losing the Treasures and abandoning the elemental magic."

Zephyrus had witnessed the elemental magic himself in his dreams. *The Arcane Templar must have originated from the exiled elders…*

"How do you know all of this?" Zephyrus asked.

Nallia smiled and pointed at the book. "I'm actually named after the Vykane Blade and Vykannis the Brave. I suppose that always drove my curiosity."

Zephyrus raised an eyebrow. "That's quite the stretch from Nallia…"

Nallia blushed. "It's an abbreviation. No one but my family knows my true name. Just before the treaty of 940, while my father fought in the war, my mother named me. I suppose she found the Judges of great interest too. My father, on the other hand, would not accept having me named after a dead God in an outlawed religion, so Vykinallia became Nallia."

"Vykinallia," Zephyrus said, trying out the name. "What do you believe—about the Judges, the Return, the Treasures?"

Nallia shrugged. "I believe the Judges are real. Although I've never seen their magic, I've heard stories of it. I think the Treasures are real—romanticized by myths and legends, but real."

"And the Return?" Zephyrus asked.

Nallia turned back to the book and Zephyrus's prophecy. "I don't know." She began underlining more lines of text with blue ink and then other phrases with green ink. "The Three, the Prophets—it's definitely scary, but if it's fated to be so, what can I do to stop it?" She turned to Zephyrus. "I don't think I'd want to even if I could."

Zephyrus looked at his own prophecy, painted with mostly blue, a few red, and one green underline. "It seems the blue favors my fate. Which prophecy does this coincide with?"

Nallia pointed to the tome. A black portrait of a cloaked man holding a black sword covered half the page.

The Harbinger.

Zephyrus felt his hopes settle at the pit of his stomach, and his shoulders slumped. *If I'm the Harbinger, I'm fated only to give rise to another.*

The scroll from the Arcane Templar, stained with Threyna's and Patrus's blood, still held secrets—mysteries of his past that might guide his future. Laeden said the brightest minds of New Rheynia were scouring tomes to help him reconnect his past. There was still hope, if not from his Prophecy, from the Arcane Templar. If he just had one more clue, perhaps this would all fit together.

"You're just as likely to be either of the other two," Nallia said.

"Which do you believe I am?" Zephyrus asked, pointing to the blue lines beneath his prophecy. "Seems I'm more suited to the terrible sort."

"I will have to give you my answer after I see you upon the sands with my own eyes," she said, grinning. "Then clouded choices will give way to clarity."

Zephyrus grunted. Crossing his arms over his chest, he turned in a slow circle to admire her chambers. Paintings, carvings, and mosaics dressed the walls, each depicting a gladiator.

"You love the arena, don't you?" Zephyrus asked.

"I do," she said, unabashed. "It's a place where the lowborn can rise, common men can become legends, and it honors the Gods. Whatever Gods you hold dear, they all value the strength of warriors."

Zephyrus fought to keep his face stoic.

"It's a shame I'll be giving it up," Nallia said with a sigh. "I'll miss it."

"You're leaving the ludus?" Zephyrus asked.

"Not yet. My father… he…" She looked at him and swallowed. "I just imagine there will be no role for a queen in a ludus." Her gaze fell to the floor.

Zephyrus nodded. *Queen of the slaves.* Yet even as he condemned her, he couldn't comprehend; if she were leaving the ludus, why concern herself with his memories? His prophecies?

Nallia's cheeks fell sullen. She twisted the amethyst ring about her finger as if she were trying to screw it off.

"Is something wrong?" Zephyrus asked.

Like a dormant volcano that suddenly exploded, Nallia stood and blurted, "I've wanted to be the Head Lanista of Stockhelm since I was a girl." She began pacing about the room. The intensity of her voice continued to grow with every word.

"My brother never wanted it, but I did. My father overlooks me and blames me for his own shortcomings. And now he's found an excuse to marry me off." She shook her head and covered her mouth. "The prince is wonderful, but…" She paused looking at him. "Surely, you don't care about this."

You're being used too. In a way, you're as free as I am.

After a moment of silence and twisting her ring some more, she asked, "Have your memories returned?"

Though he didn't understand her, he found himself wanting to tell her of his dreams. The hooded men, the combat skills, and the magic he learned in the Arcane Templar. The magic that healed Fenyx's fingers, ignited his bedside candle, and restrained Tursos's sword, allowing Fenyx to escape death.

That Lover's Dream is making me a fool. She's one of them—a slave owner.

She cared a little more than the others, but he was just a vessel to earn her family more gold and glory. To share such details would be death.

"No memories," he said.

Looking down at the spinning amethyst ring on her finger, she approached him until their toes touched. Her eyes met his gaze, glowing in the candlelight.

"I'm sorry to hear that, Zephyrus. I will purchase more of the healer's tonics."

There was an innocence in her, a kindness. No one ever looked at him the way she looked at him now. She placed her hand on his shoulder.

Am I hallucinating? Cerik warned him of the effects of Lover's Dream, but this seemed so real. *She uses you,* he reminded himself. Part of him stirred at her touch, but another part of him wanted to fulfill his fate and bring about the Age of the End of New Rheynian power here and now.

"You could do it, you know?" a voice in Zephyrus's head whispered. He froze, his stomach lurching at the familiar voice. *"I can help you."*

This was not a hallucination. This voice was real. The same one that saved him at the slavers' auction. Pain lanced through his stomach, accompanying Vykannis's voice.

Zephyrus swallowed. *"Where have you been?"* he channeled to the Judge.

"I have been waiting for your memories to return so your full potential could be realized," Vykannis said. *"Now you know enough. It could all*

begin tonight. Free yourself, gather the Treasures, free the slaves. Together, we can fulfill your destiny." The voice grew stronger, and so did his stomach pain.

"Kill her and it begins tonight," Vykannis said.

Zephyrus groaned as the stabbing pain in his gut seemed to twist like a knife.

"Zephyrus?" she asked. "Are you okay?"

Zephyrus wanted to hate her. It enraged him that so many lives were cast aside without a second thought. These slave owners placed no value on human life. Patrus died seeking freedom. Threyna killed herself to avoid being enslaved.

"Kill her." Vykannis spoke with the even-keeled and utterly calm voice of reason. *"This is why you were spared—to free yourself, claim the Treasures, and remake the world."*

His stomach roiled, as if resenting Vykannis's words. Sweat bubbled on his brow. The muscles between his shoulder blades tensed. His jaw clamped shut. Heat rose to his cheeks, and anger burned within him.

"Zephyrus?" Nallia took his hand in hers. "What's wrong?"

Vykannis offered Zephyrus everything he wanted: freedom. The ability to fulfill his fate and remake the world. It was tempting, but something felt wrong. He met Nallia's eyes, green as shining emeralds. Her brow wrinkled; her lips hung open and angled downward. She squeezed his hand, calling his name a third time.

This anger isn't mine.

Nallia was far from innocent, but that didn't mean he wanted her dead.

"There must be another path to freedom," Zephyrus channeled.

"All paths require sacrifice," Vykannis said. *"To remake the world, many a flower must fall. Spare none of these Rheynians—they do not deserve it."*

Zephyrus felt like a dagger was carving out his insides. He swallowed bile. *"Not all Rheynians are the same. Those who deserve it will fall. Not her."*

"Who are you to decide?" Vykannis's voice boomed in Zephyrus's mind, no longer the voice of reason, but one of malevolence. *"Kill her!"*

"No!" Zephyrus shouted aloud. Frustration boiled up, and something within him snapped as if the knot in his stomach ruptured. Nallia backed away, raising her hands to defend herself.

He suddenly went cold. The dimly lit candles of the room and the brazier in the corner roared to life, becoming momentary infernos.

Nallia's chin fell, her eyes wide. She inhaled to scream, but Zephyrus seized her and cupped his hand over her mouth. She fought against him, but he held her. The flames died down, and warmth slowly returned to his blood.

A heavy hand thudded on the door to Nallia's chambers. "Milady, I heard a shout."

Burn me. They'll kill me for this. His mind raced, but each avenue remained void of solutions. Vykannis's presence was gone, but so was the pain in his gut.

"I don't want to hurt you," Zephyrus said. "I haven't been forthright."

How will I talk my way out of this?

"Lady Nallia," Nortus said, hammering his meaty fist against the door.

Against Zephyrus's better judgement, he released her. She scrambled away from him, holding herself, but she didn't raise her voice or even speak.

Zephyrus held his hands out in front of him. "My dreams have told me of my training." He did his best to appear relaxed, but prepared to pounce if she cried out to Nortus.

Oh, Patrus, was I always such a fool?

He tried to think of the words to say, the words she would want to hear—the words that wouldn't see him nailed to a Six Arrowed Star—but in the end, only the truth came to mind.

If she calls the guards on me, I will use my gifts and fight for my freedom here and now. I'll give her this one chance.

His heart thundered in his chest, unsure what ramifications might follow.

"I'm a mage of Celestia," Zephyrus said. "But I swear on the Judges, I won't harm you."

Nallia's cheeks flushed, and a slow trickle fell from the corner of her eye. She glanced at the door and opened her mouth but closed it again.

Nortus yanked on the doorknob, jarring the lock. "Open the door!"

Nallia fixed her gaze on Zephyrus. She swallowed and cleared her throat, twisting the ring on her finger.

Zephyrus's blood went cold as heat radiated in his palms. He bit his lip, preparing himself for a fight.

"Everything is fine, Nortus," Nallia said. "I just, uh, stubbed my toe."

A pregnant pause suspended time. Zephyrus balked, allowing the heat in his palms to dissipate. Warmth returned to his blood, and he let out a trembling breath.

"Milady, I heard Zephyrus cry out too."

Nallia never took her eyes off Zephyrus. "Everything is fine, Nortus. Gratitude."

"Unlock the door," Nortus said. "I'm comin' in, and that's fin—"

"Nortus, I said I am fine. Leave us."

They remained still as statues. Nortus's footsteps didn't retreat, but Nallia took a deep breath and straightened her posture.

She closed the distance between them, reaching out with a tentative hand. "I knew you were special from the moment I laid eyes on you," she whispered. "The Gods and the Judges must have seen the same in you to put you on such a perilous path."

She came closer, taking his hand in hers. His breath caught in his throat.

"Your courage to share this with me, the trust you have bestowed upon me… will not be betrayed. I pray one day I'll have the confidence to do the same…" She trailed off.

Zephyrus's pounding heart stopped as silence stretched between them. She sounded as if she weren't finished speaking, but the moment continued absent words. He didn't know if he should respond, what to say. Searching for words, he found none.

"You should go," she whispered, letting her hand fall from his.

Zephyrus nodded, mind as blank as his hand was empty.

"I look forward to seeing you in the Kings' Day Games," she said, "but I think I know my answer."

Zephyrus found his tongue. "What answer?"

She smiled. "I believe you're the Wielder."

Tension fled Zephyrus's corded muscles. *She could have me killed, but instead she offers encouragement, praise—acceptance.*

Zephyrus couldn't help but smile back at her.

"Goodnight, Zephyrus."

"Goodnight, Vykinallia."

As she approached the door to let him out, a sudden realization washed over Zephyrus. Before her hand settled on the knob, he caught her by the wrist. She met his gaze, her smile fracturing beneath his stern expression.

"There's more I must tell you," Zephyrus said. "There's going to be another attack. On your father."

CHAPTER 40

IN THE SHADOWS

Fenyx V

Stockhelm

It was nearly the end of another long day of training, but it wasn't over yet. With only two days remaining before the Primus, Auron drove them harder than ever. Fenyx, Zephyrus, and Stegavax would stand together against the three best gladiators from Kaelus's and Targarus's ludi.

Perhaps once the three of them could have been a fearsome trio. Now however, between Stegavax's rust and Zephyrus's hesitance, Fenyx was prepared to slay all six men who stood against them.

Domina looked down from the balcony. Cleotra—the precious forbidden fruit he never realized he wanted. Part of him wished he never found his way between her thighs. She distracted him from his purpose, but she was so intoxicating.

You can have her in a few hours. For now, focus!

"You must fight as one," Auron said to the three of them. "The men you stand against will be your equals in skill, but stand above you in knowledge of one another. They will protect each other. You must know your strengths and weaknesses—when to attack and when to defend, when to press and when to retreat—not just for yourselves, but for your brothers."

Stegavax glared at Zephyrus. "The Harbinger does not deserve to fight beside me."

"The princes of Salmantica thought otherwise," Auron said.

Stegavax ignored him and pointed his wooden blade at Fenyx. "And you're no Champion. When you fall, all will see that your time in the sun was a lie."

Fenyx bit his lip. The Burning blended with Cleotra's allure, and together, they had enough of Stegavax. Fenyx reared back his two-handed great sword and swung at Stegavax, forcing him to raise his swords to block. Auron yelled something, but the fight had begun.

Stegavax reeled back, conceding ground. He deflected every blow, but not completely. Fenyx's tremendous great sword glanced off Stegavax's shoulder, hip, and thigh. If it were steel in place of wood, he would have painted the sands scarlet with Stegavax's blood.

Stegavax parried a blow and attempted to counter, but before he could, Fenyx swung again, forcing Stegavax to abandon his attack and lurch out of the way. Stegavax fell to the ground. He lifted his wooden swords like a shield to defend himself, but with two quick swipes, Fenyx discarded them from grasp. He stood atop the once fabled Champion and tossed his great sword off to the side.

"This is my house now." Fenyx spat on Stegavax. Whether out of breath, or his pride too wounded to reply, Stegavax made no refute.

"Fenyx," Auron shouted.

Domina applauded from the balcony. "An excellent showing!"

"Did you not hear me?" Auron growled. "You must fight *together*."

Stegavax got to his feet.

"I did hear," Fenyx said, catching Cleotra's seductive gaze. "We must know each other's strengths and weaknesses." He glared at Stegavax. "And now I know the many *weaknesses* of Stegavax."

Auron grunted, rubbing his hand over his scalp. "Focus. Together this time!"

⚖

Fenyx was bathed and escorted to the villa, this time by Odetta. While Dominus attended to whatever tasks a chancellor did, Fenyx would content himself with the comforts of his wife.

Odetta eyed him nervously as she led him through the halls of the villa to the dominus's chambers on the third floor. Just before the door, she turned to face Fenyx, her bronze skin reflecting the torches' glow.

"I was long promised to the Champion of the house," she said. "I was to be his wife, but I know you are Champion now…" Her eyes were downcast, shoulders slumped. "Is it too much to ask you to… protect Stegavax on Kings' Day?"

Fenyx guffawed. *Is this woman serious?*

Her eyes remained fixated on the floor. "He has not yet returned to strength, and I fear his pride will be the death of him. I loved him once, as I'm sure I will love you one day, but if you could keep him safe…"

He needs this timid wisp of a girl to plead for his life. Fenyx couldn't contain himself any longer. He laughed at Odetta. "I fear he won't last the week, regardless of what I do. Besides, I have no use for you. You can have Stegavax."

Without another word, Fenyx pushed past her and opened the door to where his domina awaited him. He closed the door behind him, shutting Odetta out.

"My Champion," she said, her long, bare legs entwined in a sheet on the bed. "You kept me waiting far too long."

Fenyx's desire groaned within him. The Burning was an unquenchable voracity that could only be quelled by the kill, but this new sensation could only be sated by her.

He advanced and lost himself in her rapture. Time was static, concerns were void, and life blossomed. Their euphoria was something only the Gods could understand. He lost himself in her. Moonlight cut through the window, illuminating her body against his. Slick with sweat and desire, they danced upon the pillows as the nightly storms thundered against their own bellows of pleasure. Moments stretched on until the hour grew late.

"You should go," Cleotra whispered, her legs still entwined with his. She traced her index finger down his chest.

He took her hand in his. "It might kill me to leave."

The sound of horses reining up outside shoved them from the moment. Cleotra tugged his face towards her one last time. Her lips met his, as delicate as flower petals, but as fervent as the sun.

"Go," she whispered. "We will meet again soon."

Fenyx gathered himself and fled her chamber. He looked left and right for Odetta but couldn't find her. *Burn me, where is that pathetic girl?* Fenyx flew through the villa as if Jackals were chasing him. *What if I'm caught or questioned? What would I—*

Rough hands grabbed him from behind. Fear stole his enraptured peace. Fenyx attempted to whirl, but the attacker's grip was too strong. He bucked his head back, but his strike found no purchase. He attempted to stomp on his assailant's instep, but, during the strike, he lost his balance and fell into the wall. His attacker pinned his arm behind his back.

Fenyx's breath came in short sharp stabs like Taric's knife in the dark. No time to think, no breath to scream, Fenyx waited for the cold steel to pierce his flesh. *Auron was right—too many enemies. How can this be my end, so far from the glory of the arena?*

"Be still," the voice hissed. "It's Zephyrus."

Fenyx growled. *Zephyrus?* He struggled to free himself, but Zephyrus's hold did not relent. "Let go of me!"

"Silence." Zephyrus released him.

Fenyx wheeled around, ready to clobber him. "You don't belong here."

"Neither do you," Zephyrus said, scanning their surroundings. "What are you doing?"

Fenyx seethed. *The insolence.* "I am Champion. I go where I please."

Zephyrus gave Fenyx a harrowing scowl. "The Revivalists are going to attack Dominus."

Fenyx's nostrils flared. "More conspiracies. What are you really playing at? I know you want your precious freedom."

The creaky door from the stables announced Dominus's return. He climbed the stairs. Zephyrus beckoned Fenyx to a darkened corner of the corridor opposite Dominus's path. Dominus grumbled with each step until he summited the stairway and went to his chambers.

"I warned you of this," Zephyrus said once Dominus left earshot.

"There is no attack. You are delusi—"

Zephyrus held up a silencing finger. The sound of soft footfalls ascending the stairs disturbed the quiet villa. Cloaked in darkness, a figure followed in Dominus's wake.

Zephyrus stalked after him.

Fenyx couldn't believe it. He followed, taking caution to be as quiet as Zephyrus, but Zephyrus's feet barely seemed to contact the floor in his pursuit of the hooded figure.

The gleam of a blade caught the flickering torchlight, and the hooded figure became an assassin. The assassin disappeared into Dominus's chambers.

Fenyx's stomach tightened. *Cleotra!*

Fenyx shoved Zephyrus out of the way. A moment later, a shrill cry erupted into the night. Fenyx charged into the room. The assassin stood over Dominus, the two struggling with a small blade clutched between them. Fenyx launched himself at the assassin and threw him away from the bed. Dominus swore, and Cleotra cried for the Gods.

Zephyrus entered just behind Fenyx and grappled the assassin. Fenyx yanked Cleotra and Dominus from the bed and shoved them to the doorway.

"Guards!" Dominus shouted.

Zephyrus wrestled the assassin. With a jerk of his wrist, the assassin's fingers broke, joints dislocating. The assassin let out a cry, dropping the knife. Zephyrus bent the assassin's wrist backwards and wrenched his shoulder behind him, shoving him to the ground. He groaned but was unable to escape Zephyrus's grasp.

Burn me... he was right!

A stampede of guards stormed into the dimly lit chambers. Fenyx held his hands up while Zephyrus subdued the attacker.

"Stop!" Nallia pushed her way through the guards, Odetta close behind. Nallia balked at the sight of Fenyx before turning to Zephyrus.

"I've got him," Zephyrus said.

"What's the meaning of this?" Dominus shouted, shoving his way back into the room. His glare found Fenyx.

Fenyx's shallow breathing stalled. *What would a Champion say?*

His gaze fell to the floor; his tongue felt foreign between his cheeks. Despite the movement of his mouth, no words came.

Nallia put her hand on Dominus's arm. "Zephyrus warned me of a threat against your life, plotted by the Revivalists. I instructed Nortus to let him out of the barracks to protect you."

"And I summoned Fenyx to watch over you," Cleotra said. "You denied yourself a bodyslave. Is it any wonder we procured your finest fighters to protect you?"

Breath flooded Fenyx's choked lungs. *Thank the Judges for Cleotra.*

Dominus nodded, absorbing the information, but the bloodlust in his eyes failed to subside. "Who is this traitor? I would see his face." He motioned for Zephyrus to pry the assassin from the floor. Zephyrus forced the man into the light and drove him to kneel before Dominus.

Dominus removed the hood covering the attacker's face. Thick, angled eyebrows sat atop a square jaw. Despite the sweat and blood obscuring the assassin's face, Fenyx recognized him immediately. Fenyx's burned cheek twitched.

Carsos! But why?

"One of my own gladiators?" Dominus asked, seizing Carsos by the collar of his cloak. "Who put you up to this?"

Carsos's eyes darted around the room. "If I tell, what will happen to me?"

Dominus picked up the knife meant to kill him and aimed it at Carsos's chest. "If you don't tell, you die!"

The stone in Carsos's throat bobbed.

Cleotra's eyes were wet with tears, but she was safe. *Zephyrus was right.*

"Chimera's breath, who?" Dominus jabbed the blade before Carsos's face. "Say the name! I will spare you, but only if you give me the name."

Trembling overtook Carsos's kneeling form. "Liario. He forced me to!"

Dominus's wily brow contorted above his hawkish eyes. He drove the knife into Carsos's chest.

"You try to murder me?"

The blade retracted and dove back in.

"In my own bed?"

Again. Again.

"You Celestic filth!" Again and again, Dominus stabbed, until the spray of Carsos's blood drenched tattered cloak and silken toga alike. Cleotra and Nallia looked away as Carsos fell from Zephyrus's grasp to the floor.

"Another one, Dominus," Nortus said, dragging Ixion up the stairs and forcing him to his knees. "Zephyrus was right. He was readying horses to make their escape."

"How many horses?" Zephyrus asked.

"Four," Nortus said.

Dominus wheeled on Ixion, the blade, slick with Carsos's blood, leading the way. "Where is Liario?"

"Where's Lenox?" Zephyrus asked.

Fenyx clenched his jaw to still his twitching burns. *Judges preserve me, what is happening?*

The other guards looked around, realizing Lenox and Liario were both missing.

"Find them!" Dominus's roar bellowed louder than the thunder echoing off the Hylan peaks. The guards scattered to do as they were bid, but Fenyx couldn't move. His feet felt like they'd been welded to the floor.

"Is it true?" Dominus asked Nortus. "Liario and Lenox?"

Nortus nodded.

Dominus didn't hesitate. He slashed the knife across Ixion's throat. Ixion dropped to the floor, sputtering his final breaths. Fenyx couldn't believe his eyes.

Promising gladiators, dead—butchered so far from the honor of the arena. What if Dominus found me in his bed?

Ixion croaked on the floor as life flowed from the gash in his throat.

That could have been me…

Fenyx eyed Zephyrus, his eyes more aflame than his red hair. *He was right. What else might he be right about?*

CHAPTER 41

THE TEMPLES

Laeden XII

Salmantica

Three days after the Salmantic Games. Three days—come and gone—and Laeden had nothing. No prisoners, no suspects, no leads—nothing. The attack sent the entire realm into a panicked frenzy, and too much time passed without resolution.

"Surely you must know something," the king asked. "The senate won't keep waiting."

He couldn't meet his father's gaze.

"What about this Uprising business?"

"I don't know." Laeden's heart couldn't sink any deeper.

Three more days and still not a word from Iylea. No one cared that she was gone. Aside from Danella, no one even mentioned her. Their conversation still perplexed him.

"She always had a heart towards the disenfranchised," Danella had said to Laeden. *"Is it any surprise she left for the Uprising?"*

"She said something strange to me, the last time I saw her," Laeden had said. He didn't want to share everything, but he wanted to test Danella to gauge her reaction. *"She told me she was a seer."*

Danella raised her hand to her lips, speechless for a time. *"Perhaps it's better this way. Your father would be faced with a difficult decision if a seer were discovered in our court."*

Was Iylea right about Danella? Was Danella right about Iylea?

"My son," Varros said, putting a hand on his shoulder, dragging Laeden's focus from his self-pity. "You're doing all you can, but you don't have to do this on your own."

Laeden was speechless. *Since when was 'doing all I can' ever enough?*

"You will see this through." His father patted his shoulder. "And the realm will be safe because of your efforts, but there is strength in knowing when to ask for help."

But no one can help. As much as he felt like a failure, he was the only one doing anything to stop the Revivalists. Even Zephyrus had disappointed him. While his plans to bring the Revivalists within House Cassius to justice were still in motion, Zephyrus took matters into his own hands and beat him to it. Now with two dead and two missing, there was no one to interrogate. No one to question. Zephyrus's impatience was a setback—not a victory. He'd exhausted every lead the Sentinels had.

Other than Aelon's lead.

"Thank you, Father," Laeden said, as an idea formed. "I will keep you updated."

With renewed vigor and restored purpose, Laeden left his father. He'd been sitting on Aelon's information for too long, but now his patience would pay off.

He sent for Royce, the kitchen boy Aelon once used to serve as his messenger.

"Deliver this to Markus at the Lion's Academy," Laeden told Royce, handing him a tightly rolled scroll. Royce pocketed the scroll and held his hand out. Laeden placed two gold coins in the boy's hand. With the glint of gold in his eye, Royce nodded and moved to purpose.

Next, Laeden summoned Pirus and went to his chambers. He scribbled a note and dressed himself in his Sentinel cloak in preparation for his night out in the city. It wasn't long before Pirus arrived. Laeden busied himself in his chambers, making it appear like he was rushing.

"Captain." Pirus saluted.

"Pirus, I need you to deliver this to Lieutenant Markus Cassius at once." He handed Pirus a roll of parchment. "No one can know where I'm going but Markus, am I clear?"

"Yes, Captain!"

With his plan in place, Laeden set out into the city to go to the Temples of the Six.

Laeden didn't frequent the temples. He went with his mother as a boy, but ever since his father took the throne in Salmantica, going to the Temples didn't feel right. His father wasn't particularly devout, but he made Laeden go anyway. In Laeden's stubborn youth, not attending was one way of acting out.

The nightly rains fell and thunder rumbled overhead as Laeden made his way through the city streets. While the nightly rains kept some at bay, patrons still crowded the Street of Ale. Although the tavern-lined road was the most direct route to the Temple District, Laeden needed to be alone for his plan to work.

He stopped at the Gilded Gauntlet where the statue of Damascus Drake rose to Valencia. The savior of the Rheynian people, the first king of the new world. His hand extended, he pointed to the future. *He didn't question himself. What great leader would? But how many died to build his empire? How many like Iylea—if her confession were true—suffered on Six Arrowed Stars, praying for death? Did Damascus Drake question himself then?*

Laeden trudged through the puddles of the cobbled streets until arriving in the Temple District. The first temple enshrined Phaebia, Goddess of air, wind, and light. Tall columns ornamented with white banners held up the statue of her likeness; she extended her hand in peace as a symbol of hope and forgiveness.

His mother prayed to her often. While his father fought in the war and before they presumed him dead at sea, Mother prayed incessantly. *Her prayers brought him home, but she lost him either way.* Faith failed, and Laeden never forgave Phaebia.

Wherever Mother is—if she's still alive—does she still pray to Phaebia?

He walked past the second temple erected for Incinerae, Goddess of fire, love, and affection. After his parent's annulment, Laeden wasn't sure if he believed in love anymore, let alone a Goddess of Love. But he met Iylea, and everything changed.

He shoved the feelings aside.

Focus.

Next he passed Moterra, the Goddess of Earth. People prayed to her for a bountiful harvest, but also for wisdom and family affairs. He gave up on Moterra first. Laeden looked away from the statue to avoid reliving the painful memories of unanswered prayers.

The temple of Aquarius, the God of Water, was next. It was the first temple erected in Salmantica after the Great Migration. Deep blue-and-purple banners rippled like waves beneath the statue of the bearded sea God. He recalled his first voyage from Valtarcia to Salmantica after being separated from his mother. He'd been praying to Aquarius for safe travel when his father silenced him. Laeden didn't understand at the time, but the shipwreck his father experienced during the war led to his own disbelief in Aquarius.

Beyond Aquarius, Ferrocles, the God of War, pointed a sword to the sky. Worshiped for his courage in battle and perseverance—if there was a God of War—Laeden needed him now. But if Ferrocles was anything like his siblings, Laeden didn't need another disappointment.

Finally, Laeden stopped before the last of the temples—Hameryn, the God or Goddess of Harmony. No columns or banners adorned the temple, just a statue of the hooded, faceless deity. It was said that Hameryn changed shape, presenting themself to mortals in an acceptable way to change the hearts of the people they touched. Laeden wondered how long Hameryn had been lost to the mortal realm because there was no harmony to be found in any reach of the wide world.

Approaching Hameryn's temple, Laeden didn't need to look behind him to know Pirus was following him.

The Six-damned bastard probably read the scroll the moment I dismissed him.

But that's what Laeden had counted on. If Aelon were right about Vellarin being part of a mole-sting operation, then Laeden's letter to Markus about investigating the temples would have sent Pirus to his Revivalist superiors. However, if Pirus did his job, he never would have found Markus, who had already been sent here, thanks to Royce.

Laeden entered the temple. Simple, peaceful, and unadorned compared to the rest of the temples, Hameryn's was a sanctuary of acceptance. A priest knelt in prayer before the shrine. Laeden didn't disturb him. Instead, he sat down at one of the pews at the front of the temple.

Moments later, the door opened again. Footsteps entered—three or four men, by the sound. Laeden resisted the urge to turn around.

The priest, however, did not. "What is the meaning of this?"

Laeden glimpsed four men wearing Sentinel blue out the corner of his eye. They approached the priest.

"Official Sentinel business," Pirus said.

Laeden's palms moistened. He dried them on his thighs, ready for a fight, but not willing to start it four against one.

Markus, where are you?

"Stand back, priest!" Pirus warned, "Prince Laeden is under arrest for aiding the Uprising and disturbing the king's peace."

Out of time. Laeden stood and drew his sword, assuming a defensive stance. "Traitors." He eyed the faces of men who served him, or at least pretended to. They drew their own swords.

The priest ran to the corner, pleading for them to take the fighting outside, but Pirus and his men ignored him, advancing on Laeden.

They don't need me alive to frame me. He needed to play it safe until Markus arrived, but his fists shook on the hilt of his sword. *These men are the reason why our country is in shambles. Their fear of the Gods' wrath led to the New Rheynian War. That war divided Salmantica and Valtarcia. And the peace treaty that reconciled those kingdoms tore my family apart. I will have my justice.*

The four advanced. Laeden blocked a hack from his left and spun, slamming his elbow into the attacker's jaw. He dodged a vertical strike from another and ducked a horizontal slash from Pirus. He kicked Pirus in the gut, shoving him away. Laeden chopped down at the fourth false Sentinel. The man cried as steel bit into his thigh, his blue trousers drinking the blood.

Laeden blocked, dodged, and vaulted over a pew to give himself space. Unsheathing his throwing knife with the Six Arrowed Star embossed into the hilt, he threw it into the shoulder of one false Sentinel. As the Sentinel stumbled back, Laeden charged forward. With a flurry of blows, he struck the sword free from Pirus's grasp. Thunder boomed outside as Laeden levied his sword at Pirus.

"Stand down," Laeden shouted to the others. They didn't. They attacked, all at once, sending Laeden reeling. Pirus picked up his sword and rejoined the fray. The four backed Laeden against the shrine. He deflected and dodged, but there were too many for him to hope to force their surrender.

The doors to the temple burst inward. Lightning pierced the sky, and light flooded into the dark nave. Markus and six men entered, swords drawn.

"Weapons down!" Markus shouted, as he and his men surrounded Pirus's traitors.

Laeden let out an uneasy breath. "I want them alive! I need answers out of them."

The true Sentinels disarmed and subdued the false.

Markus nodded at Laeden as the prisoners were manacled and forced to their knees before him. "We got them, Captain."

"Perhaps arrive a little sooner next time," Laeden said.

"Perhaps a little more notice," Markus said. "Or don't use yourself as bait."

Laeden grinned, standing over the kneeling men. "Who wants to talk? The first to tell me who shot the flaming arrows at the Salmantic Games won't get sentenced to death."

The men looked at each other, but none spoke.

The priest emerged from the shadow, away from the corner's safety. Old enough to have seen the Disasters of Rheynia, he bowed as he approached. "The Revivalists didn't attack the pulvinus, my prince."

"What do you mean?" Laeden asked.

"I've seen many things." The priest rubbed his gnarled knuckles with his palms. "But I know the elemental magic when I see it. Those arrows were not lit by natural fire."

Laeden narrowed his eyes at the priest. "Magic?"

"Celestic magic, yes."

Breath escaped Laeden's lungs, and his grip on his sword hilt faltered. *Six save me.*

CHAPTER 42

GHOSTS OF THE PAST

Threyna III

Salmantica

"*You're wasting time,*" Paxoran said.

Threyna let her head loll to the side, as if he were lying on the Guardians' table beside her. *Blood and bone, just leave me be.* Threyna had murdered three Guardians of the Arcane Templar—three talented mages, single-handedly. After she'd regained consciousness, she claimed the Vykane Blade, consumed what was left of the Guardians, and, by all the ghosts in Rheynia, all she wanted to do was rest.

"You are not the only one seeking the Treasures," Paxoran continued. *"If you consume more souls, you can continue."*

Bruises faded. Bones mended. Wounds healed. Such were the benefits of being alive.

Back on the cursed island of Rheynia, things weren't so simple. Death inside the curse meant one of three fates. After suffering a death of any kind, a soul could be trapped within its body; the hollowed would live for eternity in a decaying husk unable to heal or regenerate, going mad with pain. Shades had the fortune to leave their bodies, floating like haunted specters left to wander aimlessly, absent sentience. But worst of all were the darklings. Sometimes, when a soul departed its dying flesh, it retained its sentience, longing to live again by invading a host body and assuming control.

After surviving the ghosts of Rheynia, Threyna was content to allow her body's natural healing process run its course. Especially when the alternative was stealing life from others. It was one thing to take from the dead, but it was another to consume the living. After draining the Guardians, she had returned to the surface to consume more souls, hoping to abate the remaining rot and heal her wounds prior to setting off for the second Treasure. She found a vagabond, weak and sick, but still very much alive. Consuming his soul, she barely managed to get the rot to retreat from her wrist to her forearm. There was no equivalency of exchange.

What is a life in comparison to me waiting a few weeks?

Paxoran said she was wasting time, and perhaps he was right, but she was saving it for someone else.

With her bruises lightening to yellows instead of deep purples, and her corrupted veins ebbing back to the scars where the cursed bangle afflicted her, she finally felt well enough to leave the catacombs.

She groaned, sitting upright. *"Ghosts, are you happy now? See, I'm leaving."*

Paxoran grunted. *"The Stormburn Geyser in Stockhelm. The Orsion Cloak."*

Threyna swung her legs over the side of the table and set her feet down on the earthen floor. She knew where she needed to go. She knew who and what would be waiting. More Guardians. More mages doing their duty. More men and women willing to die to defend the Treasures until the Wielder arrived.

As Threyna walked past the desiccated corpses, she wondered if Zephyrus really was the Wielder. She didn't pretend to be a Celestic scholar or study the prophecies of the Return, but there were several instances in his that didn't seem to coincide with the Wielder. While she put little credence into her own prophecy and knew beyond doubt she wasn't the Arcane Templar's version of the Wielder, she was the one with the Vykane Blade at her hip.

The blade possessed a simple elegance to it, but nothing about it seemed extraordinary. She only hoped Paxoran was right that the Treasures were worth killing for. Worth dying for.

Her feet scuffed the sodden ground, squishing as she returned to one of the many ladders she'd discovered throughout the catacombs. Climbing the rungs one by one, she left the death and decay behind to return to the surface.

She ascended into a sealed-off portion of the sewer system and followed the clean, albeit dank, tunnel until she reached the end. A metal case of spiral stairs wound to the surface, adjacent to the Aquarian River. Though it was in the opposite direction of her path to Stockhelm, it put her furthest from the Gilded Gauntlet and anyone who might have been watching it.

The fresh air of the grimy city was a welcomed joy compared to the thin air of the catacombs and the scent of death that drenched it. Dusk had settled on Salmantica, and with it rolling claps of thunder loomed from the east. But that was where she needed to go.

Pulling her hood up, she tucked her braid within her cloak. Head down, she fled the alleyway and entered into the busy street along the channel with others attempting to avoid the rain. She kept to the main roads, hiding in plain sight as she made her way north, bypassing patrols of Vigiles, Sentinels, and Jackals. By the time she reached the rotunda before the moat of Sentigard, a light rain had begun to fall.

She turned off the main road, heading east towards Marstead. The foot traffic thinned, made lighter by the rain's growing urgency. With only a few people on the street, a follower would be easy to spot. Tapping into her Inner Throne, she attuned to the heartbeats of those nearest her and quickened her step. Such a thing against an encroaching storm shouldn't have drawn attention, but a heartbeat began trotting behind her.

Threyna lengthened her stride. If someone was fool enough to follow her, she'd put an end to it in short order.

The heartbeat sped to a canter.

Threyna bristled. *How could the Templars know? How did they follow?*

The rain fell harder. Lightning streaked across the sky, and thunder bellowed in response.

Threyna looked over her shoulder. The street had emptied, and two figures, cloaked in black, strode side by side, keeping pace with her.

Threyna released her grasp on her Inner Throne and turned down a side street. Nestling into the arches of a doorway, Threyna waited to see if they would pass. Not wanting to be wasteful with the use of her Inner Throne, Threyna resisted. She took a deep breath and peeked around the corner.

The figures turned down the same street as her.

She bit her lip. In a few more paces, they would see her.

Patience.

The figures turned to her, their faces dark beneath their cloaks, but they did not stop. They continued down the street, walking past her.

Threyna released her held breath, shoulders sagging.

She exited the cover of the arches and returned the way she had come, but the moment she set foot on the path, four figures emerged from the shadows, blocking her path. The two she thought had passed turned around to box her in.

Gory ghosting dammit.

"Stop there, Threyna," said one of the two hooded figures behind her.

The rain's patter quickened. Gusts swelled between the buildings, whistling against the wooden façades of storefronts and the dark stone stoops of the more elegant living quarters. The hanging oil lamp lights swayed on their hinges, casting the puddling streets in an eerie glow.

Threyna glanced over her shoulder at the woman who spoke.

Sybex.

Slender and fierce as a whip, Sybex strode closer. Her pronounced cheekbones and smooth skin made it appear as if she were etched from onyx. The hard lines of her face paired with the combat-ready stance of her posture to send a chill down Threyna's back.

"I knew Vellarix shouldn't have trusted you," Sybex said. "All Vykannis's courage and none of Orsius's wisdom. He didn't see you for what you were, but I did from the moment I saw you." She drew her gladius with her right as lightning crackled in her left.

"I need the Treasures," Threyna said, reaching for the hilt of the Vykane Blade. "Unless you want to end up like the Warlocks in the City of the Judges, just let me have them. My fight is not with you. It's—"

"Oh, we know," Sybex said.

All six Templars advanced on Threyna.

"The Skeleton King," Sybex said. "Your fight may not be against us, but ours is certainly against you."

Swords, daggers, and Celestic magic encroached. Threyna's feet felt rooted to the cobblestones beneath her—not from fear, but force magic.

"We protect the Treasures," said the man beside Sybex, "from people like you." His black curls spilled out from under his hood to catch the rain.

Threyna recognized him, less from his appearance, and more because of the strength of his force magic, binding her feet to the street: Ceres, the Templar's most talented force-mage.

She recalled Zephyrus telling a story to Patrus how Aikous had assigned them to pick a lock with force magic. While Zephyrus was able to move the pins into place with care, Ceres elected to knock the door from its hinges.

Threyna tapped into her Inner Throne. She couldn't waste time, energy, or her blood magic fighting six mages. She'd barely survived three. If she killed them, the Templar would only send more.

I just need to get out of here.

The time between lightning strikes and subsequent claps of thunder quickened.

"You must think you're brilliant," Sybex said, needing to shout over the pouring rain. "Learning the Treasures' locations, betraying Patrus and Zephyrus." She aimed her sword at Threyna. "I'm assuming Makaryk, Kuhnae, and Brooxus are dead, then." Sybex nodded at the Vykane Blade at Threyna's hip. She shook her head. "Judges preserve them. But their deaths will not be in vain."

The ghosts of the past will always catch up to us, won't they, Laela?

Threyna sank into her Inner Throne. Unwilling to give them the initiative, she conjured a snare of grasping tendrils that rose from under Ceres's feet. In his distraction, the force magic binding her soles to the cobbles relinquished.

As Sybex's crackling fingertips aimed at Threyna, Threyna conjured a spider's web before her. Sybex's bolt of electricity surged into Threyna's net, but never reached her. Lurching out of the way, Threyna hurled the electrified web at the four mages standing between her and her escape. The unsuspecting group convulsed as Sybex's energy rattled through them.

With the other mages ensnared, Sybex lunged for Threyna with her gladius. Drawing the Vykane Blade, Threyna deflected the thrust aside. Thunder blared overhead, and lightning cracked the sky as they traded blows, the rain drowning out the clash of steel.

Conjuring a manacle around Sybex's sword arm, Threyna jousted for Sybex's midsection. Before she could strike, Ceres, now free from her trap, launched Threyna backwards and to her left with a powerful blast of invisible energy.

She thudded into a building. Her left shoulder crunched under the impact and hung limp as she struggled to her feet.

Just as the four mages blocking her way regained themselves from Threyna's electrified web, a pair of Vigiles in their white cloaks stepped onto the street behind Sybex and Ceres.

"Hey!" a Vigile shouted over the rain.

Another raised a horn to his lips. The trumpet pierced through the rain's downfall and the thunder's clamor. The call continued, blaring through the streets and echoing off of the buildings.

Threyna sank deeper into her Inner Throne. The rot sprouted down her arm and up her shoulder like a cursed weed in spring, but she couldn't afford to continue the fight if she was to escape Salmantica and make it to Stockhelm. Threyna conjured a thorny tangle of vines. The bloody tendrils snaked around the four Templars' legs and ripped them from their feet. The vine tugged, dragging them up the street to the approaching Vigiles.

Though they attempted to free themselves, her grip on her blood magic was too strong.

Ceres's force magic fought against her conjuring, but it opened her path.

Threyna ran towards the intersection to continue her way to the northeastern gate.

"Don't let her get away!" Sybex shouted. But the Vigiles were on them.

Ceres flung the horn blower from his feet, lifting him into the air as high as the awnings of the storefronts, but the trumpet's blare was enough. A group of Sentinels in gray and blue stampeded in her direction, coming from the west. Threyna looked over her shoulder before she dipped around the corner. Her conjures would fail, but they bought her the time she needed.

Sheathing the Vykane Blade, Threyna took off to the northeastern gate. She hoped the Sentinels would at least slow down the Templars, but she had no doubt this was not the last time she would see Ceres or Sybex. With her shoulder hanging limp as she ran, and the rot spreading from the scars left by the Skeleton King's cursed bangle, she just wished it wouldn't be soon.

CHAPTER 43

PROPHECY

Danella VI

Salmantica

Danella crumpled up the scroll and tossed it into the hearth. The flames licked at the parchment and scorched the edges before engulfing it in a swell of heat. Two days after losing her foothold within House Cassius, her spies within the Sentinels' ranks were caught by Laeden's cleverness.

Pirus, the fool, walked right into his trap.

"I can take care of them," Daenus said from behind her, speaking of Pirus and the other three Revivalists in the dungeons. "Dead men never speak."

"No." Danella framed her chin with her thumb and forefinger. "Laeden holds them within the castle intentionally. He's trying to bait us into doing just that."

"Do we just let them speak and undermine all we've accomplished?"

"No," Danella said, taking her seat by the fire. "It's time to pray and let the Gods guide our next steps."

She closed her eyes. "Gods, I come as your humble servant. I uphold the Facets of Perfection and honor your strength, determination, and intelligence. Your beauty grants me serenity and faith. Almighty and all powerful, everything I am, everything I have done, and everything I will be is only at your allowance. Gratitude for your guidance.

"I ask you for your infinite wisdom. Help me discern the intentions of my enemies, lead me to do your will, and eradicate these false Judges so your rule over this land can reign supreme." She bowed her head. "Phaebia, grant me hope. Moterra, guide me with wisdom. Incinerae, let my actions be led by love. Ferrocles, grant me the strength to persevere. Aquarius, have compassion for those I have failed to guide to your will. And Hameryn, lead us into a future of peace and harmony."

Danella cleared her mind and waited for the Gods to speak with her. She opened her eyes and watched the tongues of fire dance before her within the hearth. As if directed by Incinerae, the flames split into two sections, mirroring one another before joining back together.

Laeden used Pirus to lead him to other Revivalists within the Sentinels. *Perhaps I can use Iylea to make Laeden appear to be aligned with the Uprising. But I can't risk letting her out.*

Laeden lured her into a trap and took her pawns, but he made one crucial error. Laeden knew Iylea was a seer but did nothing about it. With the fall of House Brusos and the attack at the Salmantic Games, the Uprising had become a more feared villain than the Revivalists.

I can fan that flame.

"We could poison their rations," Daenus said of the Sentinels' prisoners.

"No," Danella said, "they might still prove more use to us alive."

"My queen, Pirus knows my involvement."

"The others?"

Daenus shook his head.

Danella nodded. "See it done then. Just Pirus, though. The others might be our most compelling witnesses." Daenus didn't understand, but he didn't need to; the gears of Danella's mind churned. "Take me to the seer. It is time we make use of her."

They strode from the study and made their way to the secret dungeon. Danella's father had been secretive with the designs of Sentigard, but she grew up in this castle—she knew every stone, hidden corridor, and trapdoor. Not even Varros knew of this dungeon.

Ser Daenus escorted her down the staircase that emptied onto a landing. The staircase continued down and to the left, but Danella kept to the dark stone wall on the right. When the stairwell was clear, she kicked the third stone from the left, and the lever clicked into place. The stones fell away into a steep, narrow stairwell down to the right.

She picked up her skirts and descended with Daenus following close behind. Daenus pulled the lever inside the cramped corridor, and the stairwell above disappeared, reforming the wall. A narrow spiral staircase constructed of black stone glowed in the torchlight, guiding Danella's descent into the dungeon.

Once at the bottom of the spiral stair, Brusos's pale blue eyes and tight-lipped smile greeted her. He sat beside the cell where a filthy Iylea tossed and turned in fitful sleep.

Brusos bowed. "My queen, you have found yourself quite the prize."

"Right under my nose all these years," Danella said. *My best handmaiden.* Other than her trysts with Laeden, she was dutiful, proper, and pleasant. *What will become of her now that I know the monster she truly is?*

"Has she woken?" Daenus asked.

"She has opened her eyes," Brusos said, running his hand through his short black hair. "Muttering, groaning, speaking nonsense—but not awake."

Danella stepped closer to examine Iylea. Haggard and disheveled, she looked more beast than girl. Tangles of hair matted to her forehead. The grime of the dungeon floor stained the serving dress she had worn to the feast. The way her eyes darted back and forth beneath her lids made Danella feel as if she were being watched by the sleeping girl.

"What are your plans for her?" Brusos asked.

Danella averted her gaze from the mage. "That depends. We must wake her and go from there. Before we do that, I trust your accommodations are suitable?"

"Very," Brusos said with another bow. "Your grace is an exquisite host."

After torching his own ludus and villa to lay the foundations for her plans, the least she could do was give the man and his wife a place to stay in her dungeons.

Danella nodded. "Any developments on your end?"

Brusos squinted, and his lips spread into a flat reptilian grin. "Your plan worked magnificently. The Sentinels believe it to be the work of the Uprising. My bodyslave, Falcos, set the fires and led the rest of my slaves to the southern jungles while they wait for orders."

"We will have to provide him with a gift to deliver to the Uprising. Earn their trust."

"And once he is within their ranks, we will dismantle them from within," Brusos said.

"Yes," Danella said, the gears of her mind turning. "I will have to think on that. Unfortunately, our machinations inside House Cassius have fallen to disarray."

"Cassius lives?" Brusos asked, his grin waning.

Danella scoffed. "The weasel lives. Lenox and Liario have taken to the wind as well."

Brusos rubbed his forehead with the back of his hand. His pale eyes provided little emotion, but Danella could sense his displeasure. He couldn't be chancellor until Cassius was dead or framed.

"Don't worry," Danella said. "All will fall into place. For now, you may take your leave. Daenus and I will watch over the seer. We have some questions for her."

Brusos bowed and took his leave to one of the other cells within the dungeon. Danella did her best to make the accommodations welcoming to Brusos and Cerberynn for their sacrifice, but a dungeon was still a dungeon regardless of the finery.

"You place too much trust in him," Daenus said once Brusos left earshot.

"I don't trust people," she said, glaring at her former handmaiden. "I trust the Gods. Now wake her. It's time to see what this seer knows of the Uprising."

Daenus rattled the cell door, trying to jar Iylea awake, but she continued to sleep fretfully. Danella gestured for Daenus to go in and wake her up. He unlocked the cell and went to Iylea, but as he neared, her eyes snapped open. Daenus lurched backwards.

"Too many links on the chain," Iylea said, her eyes rolling to the back of her head, revealing only the whites. "The last rains come. Six will become five. The Harbinger swift to rise. The chain must be undone."

Gooseflesh pimpled Danella's arms. *The Return of the Judges!* "Silence!"

Iylea didn't seem to notice. She continued babbling, repeating the same words like an incantation. Her voice grew louder with each iteration. Daenus advanced to silence her, but she snapped to attention, staring straight at Danella, eyes hauntingly white.

Daenus tried to hold back Iylea's advance, but, as if she bore Ferrocles's strength, she shrugged him off. She came to the cell bars, reaching her arms through for Danella. Daenus, realizing the futility, retreated outside of the cell and locked Iylea within. Her body began to shake as if the Disasters of Rheynia were upon her. Even as she shook, the whites of her eyes stared straight at Danella.

Danella's breath caught. A chill ran down her spine, freezing the breath in her lungs.

Six save us.

The girl spoke in a voice, deeper and raspier than her own. "Brother will fight brother. Father will turn against son. Families bound by blood will tear each other apart, and your pride will be the end of you. Your manipulative rule will crumble, and all you hold dear will be lost in the rolling tides of vengeance, unless you—"

Daenus slashed his sword into the bars of the cell. The loud clang of steel on steel broke Iylea from her terrifying trance.

Danella backed away. Fear opened its arms to her and wrapped her in its cruel embrace. Iylea, opened her eyes, as if seeing them for the first time. Blood drained from her face, and she fell to the ground in a heap. Danella felt like she might collapse, herself.

"My queen," Daenus said, trying to lead her away from the cell. He continued to speak, but Iylea's prophecy repeated in her head, drowning Daenus out. He led her up the spiral staircase. "I will rid her from the castle."

Noise from the stairwell beyond the false wall broke her from her daze. She shushed Daenus and waited for the bustle to pass.

"Do no such thing. I must think." She raised her hands to her temples. *Stay strong. What I do, I do in the name of the Gods.* She nodded for him to pull the lever. They ascended the stairs through the false wall and returned to the stairwell. They continued down the stairs until they met Laeden, Markus, Damascus, Varros, and a host of other guards applauding in the foyer.

Gods, what now? "What news?" she asked her husband.

Varros clapped a hand on Laeden's shoulder. "Laeden caught two of the archers who made the attempt on us at the Salmantic Games."

"The Sentinels brought them to heel," Laeden said. "If not for Markus and my squadron leaders, they may have struck more fires in our city." Laeden looked into her eyes.

Danella's mask splintered. *He knows.*

"The success of an army rests with its leader," Damascus said, breaking Laeden's stare from her. "Do not shroud your achievements in modesty, brother."

"This is great news," Danella said, fighting to keep her voice even-keeled. "Celebrations are in order!" She blocked out Iylea's threats and Laeden's stare. "Where are the villains now?"

"They wait in the dungeons to be executed at the Kings' Day Games," Damascus said, beaming at Laeden.

"Brother will fight brother," Iylea had said.

Will they turn against one another because of my manipulations?

Varros embraced both of his sons with pride.

"*Father will turn against son.*" Iylea's voice echoed in her mind.

But which son? Danella fought away her tears and forced a smile to join in the Sentinels' victory, but Iylea's deeper, raspier voice resounded in her mind. *"…all you hold dear will be lost in the rolling tides of vengeance, unless you—"*

Daenus had interrupted her.

Unless I—what?

No. She was grateful she hadn't heard the rest of Iylea's prophecy. The Judges powered her abilities, not the Gods of Valencia, not the Gods of her father. *It's not true. None of it.* The Uprising would be seen for the violent savages the Treaty of 940 attempted to protect New Rheynia from. When Brusos assumed the role of chancellor, the people would rally for stricter enforcement of the treaty. Varros would see. Laeden would see.

This is the only way. I will not falter.

CHAPTER 44

INTO THE LION'S DEN

Nallia IV

Salmantica

The haze hanging over the Salmantic harbor had yet to burn off despite the arrival of midday. The whole world seemed shrouded in thick fog, obscuring all that lay ahead. *A dark omen.*

Nallia's father made certain all of New Rheynia knew about the Revivalists' failed attempt on his life. He believed it would inspire fear in those who would seek to try again. She feared it would only prompt a more calculative plot against him. He barely lived to tell this tale as it was.

If not for Zephyrus, Father would be dead.

She didn't know how Fenyx fit into the equation, but she was happy her parents escaped unharmed. Still, as long as men like Liario and Lenox were out there, no one was safe.

She witnessed the Revivalists' assassination attempt on the king at the Festival of Stockhelm and survived the pulvinus when they set it ablaze at the Salmantic Games, *but for our own men to conspire against us...*

Liario had tutored her as a girl. He had served as her father's advisor for as long as she could remember. Carsos and Ixion were promising young gladiators. Lenox was rough around the edges, but she hadn't thought him capable of this. If not for Zephyrus, Carsos could have murdered her whole family.

Sailing into the gloom over the Salmantic harbor, Nallia couldn't help but wonder what else Zephyrus's Celestic magic was capable of. It was the most brilliant yet terrifying thing she'd ever seen. She should have told her father about Zephyrus. She was supposed to. Perhaps she would have once she was out of the imminent danger of his abilities, but she showed him grace, and he rewarded her with the information that saw her father's life extended. Now she felt as if she owed him. She couldn't possibly turn him in now. The thought of him nailed to a Six Arrowed Star made her grip the ship's rail with white knuckles.

"Does Laeden know?" she had asked after he explained everything to her. He didn't. She was the only one in all of New Rheynia who knew his capabilities. As a lanista, his potential in the arena titillated her, but as a Valencian who kept to the Facets of the Six, she confronted the same dilemma that started the New Rheynian war: *Did allowing Celestics to practice their faith anger the Valencian Gods to the point of a new wave of Disasters?*

That's what doctrine taught. The Gods destroyed Rheynia because the people worshiped Neutreen, the Goddess of Justice. Damascus Drake, chosen by the Six, led the people away from Rheynia. He forewarned of the impending wrath of the Gods, but it wasn't until the Disasters struck that everyone abandoned Elysianism and Neutreen the Just to follow Damascus Drake to New Rheynia.

Nallia always aligned politically with what her father believed without giving it much thought. Celestics were enslaved, mages who didn't flee were killed by the hundreds, and she never thought twice about it.

Am I on the wrong side?

Zephyrus changed her understanding of everything she'd known in one night.

Nallia felt uneasy as they docked in the Salmantic harbor. They transferred to smaller ferries, where they were escorted up the Aquarian river to the moat of Sentigard. People cheered as the Cassius purple-and-gold banner rippled in the breeze, but she couldn't help but feel that not all the lingering eyes were of adoration.

They arrived at Sentigard to attend the Kings' Day Feast the eve before the games. Twice the size of the Salmantic games, the Kings' Day celebration welcomed every family of note throughout New Rheynia. Every senator, patrician, or well-connected pleb would be at the feast, which only made the prospect of another Revivalist attack more frightening.

Generally, she loved feasts like this, but with everything going on, she couldn't help but feel danger lurking beyond every corner. With so many high profiles in attendance, guards—and not just those of Sentigard, but lords' own household guards—would be stationed throughout the feast hall.

After changing out of her traveling clothes, she saw to her preparations prior to the feast. Presented with a golden dress that Damascus himself had tailored for her, Nallia should have been ecstatic. Despite the gemstones adorning her ears, neck, and wrist, the exquisite silk gown wrapped around her, and her gallant betrothed awaiting her, all she felt was fear.

"You have nothing to worry about," Markus promised as he escorted her to the feast hall. "Well, perhaps not nothing, but one less thing to fear—the Revivalist archers who fired upon the pulvinus at the Salmantic games were apprehended."

"What will become of them?" Nallia asked, her chest still tight despite the news.

"They will be executed to commence the games tomorrow," Markus said.

Nallia chewed her lip as they approached the entryway where Damascus awaited her. Wearing a black doublet with the silhouette of the Drake chimera stitched in red, he struck an imposing figure. The long sword sheathed at his hip, the blade of his grandfather—Damascus Drake—and the garnet-studded obsidian crown atop his short cropped black hair made him look like a man fit to be king of the realm. Beneath the crown, his golden eyes marveled as he spotted her, glowing like she was more precious than the kingdom itself.

Damascus accepted her stiff hand from Markus's arm. "You're as radiant as ever, my lady. I hope you favor the dress as much as it favors you."

Nallia curtsied, her muscles still tangled in knots. "You are too kind, my prince." She smiled curtly, but as he welcomed her into the feast hall, continuing to talk, Nallia had difficulty paying attention. She saw past the tables lined with guests in fancy dresses and exquisite doublets to where Zephyrus stood along with the other gladiators chosen for the Primus and displayed before the court.

With his red hair braided into a tight knot behind his head, and his physique glistening with olive oil between the purple-and-gold accented bracers and spaulders, he appeared a God fit to rule over not just the arena, but the world.

The tension along her spine melted away. Allowing herself to smile, she clutched Damascus's arm.

CHAPTER 45

A BETTER WAY

Zephyrus XIV
Salmantica

Bathed in rosewater, scented with oils, and dressed in the finest linens and armors, they were presented before the New Rheynian elite. Zephyrus had never seen the extravagance of high society. Now being amidst it, he was certain there was no justice in this world. They put no value on human life other than the coin that could be drawn from it.

Zephyrus stood between Stegavax and Fenyx, elevated on a dais off to the side of the feast hall. The Kaelus and Targarus Champions were presented on steps of their own to be gawked at by their betters, but Zephyrus seemed to be the only one bothered by it.

Fenyx spent most of his time sneering at their opposition, concerned only with the competition. Stegavax chose to direct his aggression towards Fenyx for his obvious jealousy. The Targarus gladiators, clad in red, jeered at them, while the Kaelus men in blue assessed their stock.

Zephyrus felt the tightly rolled scroll from the Arcane Templar tucked between his belt and his britches. Patrus told him to abandon it, but it had stuck with him this far, and tonight, Laeden would have answers for him.

The king and the Arcane Templar were connected, but how?

The king had nothing to offer, but Laeden said the brightest minds in New Rheynia would be able to connect the dots. Perhaps, Laeden would arm him with the knowledge he needed to understand his prophecy, to give the gladiators a symbol to rally behind. His time telling clever lies would soon be at an end.

Vykinallia walked into the feast hall, yanking him from the scroll's mysteries. Arm in arm with her brother, she was passed to Prince Damascus. Zephyrus admired her visage as she entered in a flowing gown of gold. Gold jewelry studded with amethysts were wreathed in her hair, hung from her ears, or clung to her neckline.

She's still a slave owner...

She was the enemy, but deep down, she didn't feel like one. When Vykannis encouraged him to kill her, he realized it was the last thing he wanted. At first, he thought his feelings toward her were just a product of the Lover's Dream toxin from climbing the Hill, but he couldn't disregard it as such anymore. After he told her of Lenox and Liario, she trusted him.

She was kind and compassionate. *She could have had me killed... but she didn't.* Instead, she positioned him to protect her father, and he did. He gained her trust that night, but he also gained something even more important; his interaction with Vykannis revealed to him that how he achieved what he set out to accomplish mattered just as much as the end result.

He would have his freedom, but he wouldn't corrupt himself to achieve it. *Maybe that's the only difference between becoming the Wielder or the Harbinger?* There were many questions he didn't have the answers to, but his dreams continued, and his memories would return.

He recalled his latest dream of his mother's smiling face, her auburn hair and light blue eyes singing of love and sorrow. *"I have to leave you,"* she said. *"I must find your father. I will be back. We both will. But in the meantime, you can never forget who you are or where you come from."*

How disappointed she must be, if she's even alive. He wrote her off when he realized she owned slaves, but if Vykinallia deserved better, perhaps his mother did too.

"You look like you're plotting the Age of The End, Harbinger," Stegavax said.

Heat rose to Zephyrus's cheeks, but he didn't avert his gaze. "And you look at Fenyx like a jealous worm."

Stegavax grabbed Zephyrus by the arm and squeezed, his black eyes narrowing atop his pointed teeth. He jammed his finger up under Zephyrus's chin. "You're the worm. Bad enough you wriggling, writhing, and lying to elevate your standing, but now, Carsos and Ixion are dead—because of you."

Zephyrus grit his teeth. Striking with lightning speed, he snatched Stegavax's finger and wrenched it backwards. Stegavax bent to alleviate the tension, but Zephyrus pressed further.

"What are you doing?" Fenyx hissed, pulling Zephyrus off Stegavax. "You dishonor us."

"I stopped Carsos and Ixion from killing the dominus to..." The words died on Zephyrus's tongue. *I killed slaves to save a slaver, to gain information from another slaver.*

"You're the worm. Everyone knows it." Stegavax huffed, crossing his arms over his chest.

Zephyrus pursed his lips. *Is it true?* He was so caught up in his victory over the Revivalists and his own advancement, he hadn't considered how the other gladiators would interpret the deaths of two of their own.

Everyone knows it?

"A word, Zephyrus," Laeden said, yanking him from his thoughts.

He hadn't even noticed Laeden's approach.

Laeden cleared his throat. "A private word."

This war with the Revivalists weighed heavily on the prince. Lines borne of stress streaked his forehead. Frown lines creased around his clean-shaven jaw.

"Wriggle away, little worm," Stegavax whispered.

He ignored Stegavax and followed Laeden out of the feast hall.

"You have gone above and beyond," Laeden said, once they were alone.

"I saw an opportunity, and I struck," Zephyrus said with a bow, despite no longer feeling as good about his success after Stegavax's comment.

"Indeed you did. I wish we could have captured or questioned them, but House Cassius is safe because of your efforts." Laeden's tone indicated he wasn't overly enthusiastic about Zephyrus's results. "The entire realm owes you a debt."

Zephyrus nodded. He gave the prince what he wanted; now he wanted his end of the bargain. "Any luck with the scroll?"

Laeden narrowed his eyes. "Right, yes, of course." He cleared his throat. "Unfortunately, I'm afraid the scholars had little to offer in the way of insight. But, I must say, I owe AVR for sending you; you have served me well." Laeden's eyes searched Zephyrus's, waiting for something, expecting something.

A flicker of his eyes, the subtle change to the rhythm of his breathing. *He's lying…*

After moons of telling his own clever lies, Zephyrus recognized the same in Laeden. He pasted a smile onto his face, giving Laeden the benefit of the doubt. "There must be something you can tell me?"

"Apologies." Laeden shrugged. "It's as I said, but I do have good news on another front."

Muscles along Zephyrus's spine clenched. *He's changing the subject.* He trusted Laeden. Did everything he asked. Laeden saved him from the slavers, in large part due to the mystery of the scroll in his pocket. He hoped it would lead to answers, but here, he finally met the dead end, or at least that was what Laeden wanted him to think.

For a long time, Zephyrus's hope clung to this parchment. The role of a king's servant provided him with safety and security, a tangible truth to hold on to. But he didn't need it anymore. He didn't want it. His prophecy, his faith in the Arcane Templar, the Return, the Judges—each was more real to him than the scroll in his hand.

My fate is still mine to choose. Vykinallia helped me see that. His prophecy, although destined for greatness, even terrible greatness, still left room for choice. Laeden lied, trying to take his choices away. But that lie told Zephyrus all the truth he needed to know.

I am no emissary of peace. We shall have our vengeance.

"In light of your service," Laeden continued, "I will purchase you from Duke Cassius and promote you to a position within the Sentinels—Second Lieutenant. Once the Revivalists are put down, you will be awarded land and titles for your service."

Zephyrus snorted. It was supposed to be an honor. Perhaps it would have been, if Zephyrus didn't realize Laeden was lying to him, attempting to steer him away from his destiny.

No. Zephyrus would not give up on his fate. And if he could choose, as Vykinallia believed he could, he would be the Wielder—to gather the Treasures and free the people, so that never again would any live and die beneath the heel of a master.

Patrus gave his life to save others. Zephyrus might have failed to kill Lenox and avenge Patrus's murder, but this was what Patrus truly wanted: freedom. And not just for himself, but for others. For all.

"Let him free you," Vykannis said.

His presence brought on a new wave of abdominal pain. Zephyrus hadn't heard the voice since he lit the candles of Vykinallia's chambers ablaze.

"You don't need the other slaves to bring about the Return."

Zephyrus considered, meeting Laeden's eyes. *Is Vykannis right?* Laeden offered the position to be the change he wanted to see in the world. *If the barracks won't accept me, why should I fight it?* But as much as Zephyrus was Rheynian, Laeden's people were not *his* people. His parents had abandoned him. The Rheynians would never accept him either. If there was still hope within the barracks, that's where he would make his appeal.

"Accept. Use him as he has used you," Vykannis said.

No, Zephyrus channeled back. *There's a better way.*

CHAPTER 46

FREE THE SLAVES

Laeden XIII

Salmantica

"What do you mean, free all the slaves?" Laeden scoffed. Zephyrus's stoic expression implied no hint of jest, but surely, this was a joke.

"My time in your service has taught me firsthand how your society treats those different from you."

His diplomatic tone could only get him so far. He asked for the impossible. Even if Laeden wanted to, no one man could just snap his fingers and abolish a system that upheld the entire society. It would be anarchy. Destruction.

Laeden bristled. *Free all the slaves?*

A dull ache impressed upon his forehead, beginning to throb.

"Zephyrus, what you ask is impossible. I'm offering *your* freedom. Not the freedom of every Six-damned slave in the country."

Zephyrus shook his head. "We had a deal: information for information. I found your Revivalists, I dispatched them for you, and in return—"

"In return, I offer a high-ranking office within the Sentinels—a position that would catapult you into the heights of the patricians. With such status, you could petition the king for better slave conditions and eventually convince the senate to set them free. If you want change, that's how you do it—not this fairytale idealism in the middle of a war."

"Freedom is not fairytale idealism." Zephyrus shook his head. "All this talk of the Revivalists, but that's not what any of you fear. The Uprising is the real threat..."

Laeden couldn't believe his ears. He raised his hands to the heavens and let them fall to slap against his thighs. "Regardless of what you think you know, the Uprising pales in comparison to the threat of the Revivalists."

"Then why lie to me?" Zephyrus asked.

There was no threat in the question, no malice, but despite Zephyrus's stoic demeanor, Laeden felt like he got punched in the stomach.

Heat rose to Laeden's cheeks. His heart hammered in the veins of his temples, exacerbating his headache. *He remembers his past...*

Laeden took a step back, turning sideways. Behind him, he clenched his twitching fingers into a stilling fist. "I don't know what you're talking about. The scroll? I speak the truth; my father doesn't know you, or AVR."

The lie felt weaker a second time.

Zephyrus's jutting jaw showed no signs of amusement. Whether his memories returned, or someone told him the truth, the seeds were sown. Nothing left to do but collect the harvest.

"We both know you never gave this scroll to the brightest minds of New Rheynia." Zephyrus pulled his hand from his pocket and dropped the bloody, crumpled scroll to the floor between them. "So what did King Varros Helixus actually tell you?"

Laeden swallowed the growing stone in his throat. His headache pounded with each thunderous beat in his chest.

"He is dangerous," his father had said. *"The men he serves are dangerous."*

When Laeden didn't object, Zephyrus continued. "We had a deal. I fulfilled my side of the bargain, so trust I will do so again. Free the slaves, Laeden. Every last one.

"If you don't, I will. And I promise you: blood will rain from the skies if you make me do it. Perhaps not in a day, a week, or even a year. But mark my words. There will come a day of reckoning—a flood of blood through your streets, and you will wish you had set the slaves free."

Laeden inhaled sharply through his nose, gritting his teeth. *This is not a threat, but a promise. Six save us, how has it come to this?* But there was nothing to be said, nothing to be done to make up for Laeden's lies. He couldn't have afforded to tell Zephyrus, a Prophet of the Return, the limited truth he knew, yet he couldn't free the slaves.

The two maintained a deadlocked stare, until too much time passed without resolution.

A shout from the feast hall redirected Laeden's attention. Without sparing another look, Laeden left Zephyrus with haste. *What in Six Hells is going on now?*

Shouting and punching their fists, a crowd surrounded Markus and Aemos Horne. Aemos—his face flushed with wine—stood nose to nose with Markus, hand hovering over his sword pommel.

"You're a traitor!" Aemos shouted.

"You're drunk," Markus said. "Find a brothel and sleep it off."

Aemos seethed, his sword hand twitching beside the dagger at his belt. "I will not stand for this. My father, jailed beneath us, sharing a cell next to the Six-cursed archers from the Salmantic Games. A count in the Salmantic court sits imprisoned, while your Sentinels present no evidence, nor the three witnesses required by law."

Aemos wasn't drunk enough to stumble over his words, but his inhibitions were lowered enough that he might do more than just brandish the steel at his hip.

"All you've done is impose tariffs and taxes while establishments are threatened by fires, murders, and Sentinel inspections," Aemos said. "You've caused as many problems as the Revivalists, and I will not rest until my father is free!"

Things were getting out of hand. People were rallying to Aemos's protests.

I need to stop this before things get worse. Laeden stepped between Aemos and Markus. "What is the meaning of this?"

"That's it, Markus." Aemos stabbed his finger at Markus. "Hide behind your betters."

Laeden held out a restraining hand. "That's enough, Aemos. I don't wish to throw you out of here—"

Aemos shoved Laeden out of the way.

"I challenge you to a duel, Markus! For the honor of my father." Aemos's words ignited the onlookers.

Laeden resituated himself from Aemos's shove, but he did not strike back. He glared at Aemos but knew better than to resort to violence.

Markus strode over to where Nallia and Damascus stood, taking his sister by the arm. "Time to go."

"Go on, run away," Aemos shouted after him.

Laeden summoned guards. Aemos resisted, but they carried him out without issue. However, the damage was done, and the feast was ruined.

The king steepled his fingers together behind the high table. Lines of consternation wrinkled his brow. The queen held herself beside him. Although she appeared unnerved, Laeden couldn't help but wonder: *does she have a role in this?*

Frustrated, betrayed, and angry, Laeden located Zephyrus standing beside his fellow gladiators.

"There will come a day of reckoning—a flood of blood through your streets, and you will wish you had set the slaves free."

Laeden would make certain that never came to pass.

CHAPTER 47

EVIL TOOLS

Zephyrus XV

Salmantica

The walls were cold and slick with condensation as he ran his hand along the stone, waiting for his eyes to adjust to the pitch-black corridor. His feet stalked down the hallway, but he could sense Ronar lurking in the shadows.

Zephyrus's heart drummed rhythmically in his chest. His breath slowed as he tapped into each of his senses. The scent of wax clung to the humid air. *Ronar must have been reading by candlelight.* The beginnings of a smile curled at the corner of Zephyrus's lip.

A throwing knife whooshed by, toppling end over end. Zephyrus sidestepped, letting it sail past and clatter to the floor. A second and third flew through the air, but each met the same fate. Suddenly, warmth licked at his back, and a glow illuminated his own shadow.

Reflexively, Zephyrus canceled his shadow with light-bending manipulation magic. He whipped around, shooting a jet of water from his hands to engulf the flame. A resultant cloud of steam obscured the darkness.

Ronar's silhouette, visible for a moment, disappeared in the smoke. The smoldering flames overcame the scent of wax.

Where did he go?

Another glow of fire, this time closer and to his left. He countered by creating a shield of water, but a crackling bolt of lightning flashed before his eyes. He clenched his fists, and his flesh became stone, nullifying the bolt in his palms.

"Very good," said Ronar's raspy voice. He snapped his fingers, and the training grounds began to glow as a hundred candles ignited overhead. The winding maze and sandstone columns of the training grounds had been his home for how long now? How many years of practice did it take to master the elements? Yet now, absent sight, he defended himself.

"It is time," Ronar said. "You are ready."

Vellarix, Aikous, and Patrus approached from the shadows to join them.

"It would seem the Harbinger has arrived in Perillian," Vellarix said. "It is time for the Seers to determine if the Wielder is among us."

Patrus crossed his arms over his chest. "Elders, I don't like this plan."

"I'm ready, Patrus," Zephyrus said. "How long do you expect me to wait?"

"I'm not talkin' 'bout you," Patrus said.

Another pair of footsteps echoed throughout the training grounds. Stepping into the light, a woman tossed her silver-blonde braid over her shoulder.

Threyna!

His dreamself didn't know her, but Zephyrus's conscious mind would never forget how the life faded from her sapphire eyes.

"This is Threyna," Vellarix said. "A *former* Warlock of Sage." He glared at Patrus until Patrus's defiance was driven to submission. "She has brought news of the Warlocks' demise and perhaps the rise of the Harbinger. She believes she is the Wielder, but there can be only one."

"You will both journey to Tharseo's Bastion and seek the counsel of the Seers," Aikous said, placing his hand on Zephyrus's shoulder.

Patrus cleared his throat.

"The three of you," Aikous corrected. "If she is the Wielder, as she believes she is, you will accompany her to the Treasures' locations."

"And if she's not?" Patrus asked, grimacing in Threyna's direction.

"There can be only one Wielder," Ronar said.

Zephyrus turned his gaze to Ronar, but the face beneath the cloak was wrong. This was not Ronar.

"You've been summoned."

The voice is wrong too.

"Wake up. C'mon now," Nortus said.

Zephyrus sat up in his cot. The dream seemed so real. Questions raced through his mind. *The Warlocks of Sage…* Patrus spoke of them with distrust, Threyna among them. *Could they have betrayed us? Set the slavers on us? Poisoned our minds and stole our memories?*

"You don't owe the Arcane Templar anything…" Threyna had said.

She wanted me to do something else, but what? And what did anything have to do with King Varros?

Nortus unlocked the cell and showed Zephyrus out. Fenyx was awake, as usual, but some others took notice of Nortus's arrival. Many eyed Zephyrus skeptically as Nortus escorted him.

Perhaps Stegavax was right after all.

Following the deaths of Carsos and Ixion, all the gladiators seemed to keep their distance from him. Even Jecht and Cerik. He'd dismissed it at the time, but after Stegavax's words, nothing pertaining to his status in the brotherhood could be thought of as a coincidence.

Nortus tossed Zephyrus a brown rough-spun cloak. "Put this on."

Zephyrus donned the cloak and followed Nortus out of the barracks. Detached from the castle, the barracks were constructed beside the basilica adjacent to Sentigard. The nightly rains fell with a chill seldom found in Stockhelm, for which Zephyrus was glad to have the cloak.

"Bet you're relieved Lenox is gone, eh?" Nortus asked, as he ushered him past the basilica to the castle.

Zephyrus huffed. *I'll be relieved when he's dead.* He wasn't the least bit pleased to have allowed Patrus's murderer to escape retribution, but no good would come of giving it voice. Instead, he gazed upon the grand temple bell tower that stretched higher than the castle. Built of the same dark stone, the ominous shadow loomed over the barracks.

One day I will tear it down, stone by stone.

"Still can't believe it," Nortus said, when Zephyrus failed to reply. "Lenox and Liario? Anyway, Lady Nallia's eager to speak with ya."

Since catching Carsos and Ixion in their assassination attempt, Nallia entered Zephyrus's thoughts more than he cared to admit. After nearly setting her room ablaze with magic, she accepted him, marveled at him, and commended his bravery. She wasn't like the others. He would see Patrus's dream of freeing the Celestics to completion, but he wouldn't burn all of New Rheynia in the process, even if Vykannis was willing to do so. It was easier to believe his purpose was black and white, but that was a lie.

Zephyrus promised himself he would live by his code and no one else's. Not even Vykannis the Brave's. The destination would be achieved, but his journey to get there would not be paved with the same blind violence the Rheynians brought to Stockhelm. Only those who deserved the sword would get it. Nallia did not, but Laeden's last words to him showed which side of the blade he was on.

I was never more than a tool to him, but no longer.

Nortus nodded to the Salmantic guards in black scale armor as they entered the castle. They walked in silence until they stopped before a high arched doorway with the outline of a chimera carved into the cornerstone. Two guards in Sentinel blue crossed their spears from either side of the door, barring Nortus and Zephyrus's path.

"We're here at the lady's request," Nortus said. Both guards straightened their spears. One drummed his knuckles on the thick wooden door. A moment later, Odetta appeared, a disapproving frown upon her face. She beckoned him forward, but once Zephyrus breached the doorway, she slipped out and pulled the door shut behind her.

A fireplace crackled at the opposite end of the chamber. Tapestries emblazoned with the sigils of different houses hung from the wall above the hearth. Vykinallia sat by the fire, wrapped in a red-and-black shawl, staring into the flames. She said nothing. Eyes puffy, cheeks flushed. Zephyrus waited to be addressed, but she failed to acknowledge him, turning the amethyst ring endlessly around her finger.

"Vykinallia?"

She turned to him with a fire in her eyes Zephyrus had never seen from her before. Lines of worry framed her face. She returned her gaze to the fire and pulled the shawl tighter around her, exposing her elbow, bloodied and bruised.

"You're hurt," Zephyrus said, coming closer to her.

She reared back. The reaction stopped Zephyrus in his tracks. *Something is wrong. Never before has she been afraid of me.* "What happened?"

She stood and began to pace, continuing to spin the ring about her finger. His growing affection for her soured with each passing moment. *Did she change her mind about me? Will she turn me in?*

Finally, she stopped pacing. "What are you *not* telling me?"

Zephyrus balked. *Did Laeden tell her of our conversation?* He cleared his throat. "I've told you all I remember."

She shook her head. "I long thought the elemental magic lost to the world, until you…" She turned her palms to the ceiling. "The attack on the pulvinus during the Salmantic Games…" Her voice trembled; fists formed at her sides. "Those responsible were held in this very castle, set to be executed on the morrow, but now, *magically* they've escaped.

"They weren't Revivalists, as everyone seemed to think. They were Celestic mages of the Uprising. Elemental mages who set the pulvinus aflame with magic fire. The same magic that scorched Elrod Horne to ashes in his cell." She pointed her finger at herself. "Am I a fool to have spared you? Are you the Harbinger everyone fears you to be?"

A part of Zephyrus cringed at the mention of the Harbinger. But this was an enemy he'd faced before. He wrestled with doubt, struggled against adversity, questioned his identity, and even though he didn't know who he was before, he knew who he wanted to become. And what he would do. The enslavement Threyna died to escape from, the brutality Patrus suffered in an attempt to free others from it, would end.

Her lower lip quivered beneath watering eyes. Zephyrus advanced, but she retreated.

"Are you involved with them?" she asked.

"No," Zephyrus said, hands presented as if to show his innocence.

"You didn't plot with them or aid their escape?"

"No."

She held Zephyrus's gaze until the tension melted from her face, and she collapsed into the chair before the hearth. "Tell me all magic isn't evil. That it isn't just a force of destruction."

Zephyrus didn't defend himself, or his magic. He felt Vykannis's presence in his mind, as if he were trying to force his way into his head, but another entity resisted him.

"Kill… her…"

Like a door shutting out an intruder, Vykannis vanished, and a serenity came over him.

"Tell me all slave owners aren't evil," Zephyrus said. "That there is more to slavery than just death for coin."

She crept closer, hands twitching as if to strike. "Do you believe me evil?"

"Do you, me?"

She grabbed his hand, her skin silk against his calluses. She opened her mouth, but no words came out. Instead, she stared at their joined hands. "No. You're not evil."

Another pause. The glow of the hearth cast dancing shadows around her chambers.

He took a deep breath, allowing himself to relax. "Magic is a tool," Zephyrus said, admiring her hand within his. "As evil as a sword. It's up to the wielder to decide how it is used." He put his hand on her elbow.

She flinched.

Zephyrus pulled back. *No, she needs to see.* "You're not afraid of me. And you shouldn't fear magic."

Vykinallia swallowed, but when he took her elbow in his hand, she didn't retreat.

Feeling the bruised and swollen tissue, the scrape upon her flesh, Zephyrus focused. White mist emitted from between his fingers and swirled around her elbow.

Vykinallia gasped as the cut sealed. The black and blue of her bruise abated into nothingness, while his own elbow throbbed and stung as if he'd just fallen on it.

"Six save us," Vykinallia said.

"Magic has a balance. Can you say the same of slavery?" His hand fell away from hers. Vykinallia's mouth hung agape. When she didn't reply, he continued. "Am I—like magic, or a sword—a tool to be used?"

She moved her lips, but no words came forth because none would suffice. He proved his point. Slavery tore apart families, sent people to early graves, and forced those too stubborn to die to live in squalor.

"What good can come from slavery?"

She didn't answer. She didn't even look at him. Her eyes fixated on the smooth flesh around her elbow.

Zephyrus strode to the door, elbow stiff and sore, and let himself out.

CHAPTER 48

THE KINGS' DAY GAMES

Zephyrus XVI

Salmantica

Iron bars separated them from the other gladiators, but nothing stopped the threatening words that flowed between them. If their jousts and barbs could locate their true enemies, they might have some worth. Instead they fought one another for the pleasure of patricians.

How many will die for their entertainment today?

The Cassius gladiators were dressed and readied in armor fit for the Gods. Each golden plate, ornamented with purple trim, glowed like the sun. The Cassius scorpion decorated the bracers and greaves—the cuirass, belt, and skirt were as fashionable as they were functional. Holding the purple plumed helm in his hands, Zephyrus began to understand the vanity of glory that went along with fighting for a head ludus in the Primus of the Kings' Day Games. But he would gladly trade golden armor for robes of freedom.

Once dressed, they followed Doctore up the sloped path to the sands of the arena. A gate barred their ascent any further, but onlookers were already filling the stands. It wasn't long before patricians and plebs occupied every seat in the arena, and the sun reached its zenith in its journey across the sky.

Horns blew to the cheers of the raucous crowd, signaling the commencement of the games. The king raised his arms upon the pulvinus to summon silence. His two sons stood beside him.

Zephyrus glared at Laeden. *He will regret the day he denied me.*

"Good people of New Rheynia," the king said once the crowd had quieted. "Today, we celebrate our unity as a nation."

He wore an elegant cape, divided down the middle—on one side the white winged horse of the Helixuses atop a blue backdrop, on the other half, the Drake Chimera, blue atop white. His cape represented New Rheynian society, the strong united to rule the weak.

The king rattled off a history of the kings who came before him to the audience's cheers. Clad in vibrant colors, waving banners of the houses they favored—the plebs and patricians alike shouted their support.

Had I actually been given to the king as an emissary, perhaps I would be out there thirsting for blood with them. My mother owned slaves. Why would I be any different?

The thought of his mother watching from the stands made him sick.

"*You can never forget who you are or where you come from,*" his mother had said.

I'm not one of you, he reminded himself.

"This world we have built has been divided by war—a war that would tear husband from wife, father from son, and brother from brother. Pulling babes at the breast from loving arms, leaving widows and orphans to survive amidst cutthroats and thieves. No, this will not be our fate. I, King Varros, choose peace!"

The king's words moved the crowd, but they only made Zephyrus's blood boil. *Does he not realize his hypocrisy? Slavery has killed more people in the past moon than the Revivalists and the Uprising combined.*

"We have captured the two archers who rained flaming arrows on the pulvinus during the Salmantic Games. They will be shown no mercy for their atrocities. Let this serve as a message to the Uprising and the Revivalists alike; New Rheynia will not bow, bend, or break!"

The crowd roared as the gates opened, and two Helms were paraded around the outskirts of the arena. Clad in chains and escorted by six armed guards adorned in the black and red of House Drake, they dragged their feet as they marched towards their deaths. Boisterous fanatics threw rotten foodstuffs and small stones as they cursed the condemned to the afterlife.

As the guards dragged the prisoners by their chains past Zephyrus's gate, Zephyrus got a closer look. A man and a woman. They stared at the ground as they dragged their feet. Their tear-streaked faces were swollen, cut, and bruised.

Zephyrus strangled the bars that separated him from them. Vykinallia had said the mages escaped, but here they were—broken and defeated. Nothing Zephyrus could do would spare them from their fate.

"Good people of New Rheynia, if this is the Uprising's rebellion, let it die here!" King Varros shouted, and his subjects responded with a droning chant.

"Kill! Kill! Kill!"

The guards' spearpoints drove home, impaling each of the prisoners. Three spears entered each of their backs and protruded through their chests. Their screams were swallowed in the crowd's cheers as their blood stained the sands. Two guards drew swords and simultaneously hacked through the impaled mages' necks, lopping their heads off. They rolled, spewing crimson blood to the audience's roar, teasing the onlookers' appetite for death.

The afternoon went on with match after match, each more bloody and brutal than the preceding fight. Gladiators of lesser houses fought and died. If the Gods were anything like the people of New Rheynia, their hunger for gore was insatiable. The entirety of the sands would be dyed red by the time the nightly rains came.

With each fallen slave, Zephyrus took a personal account. *I will avenge you.*

As the sun began to set in the western sky, Doctore told Zephyrus to see himself readied. Zephyrus returned to the armory where he found Fenyx and Stegavax standing toe to toe.

"You had your time," Fenyx hissed through bared teeth. "This is *my* house now." The burns along the side of his face twitched.

Stegavax held both hands up defensively. "I only wish to make a peace offering." He tossed a pouch to Fenyx. "Whiteroot."

Fenyx glared at Stegavax but accepted the gift. Reaching into the pouch, he inspected Stegavax's offering. He shoved a strip in his mouth before sauntering off with a snort.

Zephyrus released a held breath. As Fenyx left the barracks, Zephyrus donned his armor.

With each piece he put on, the Rebels' Rhyme sang louder in his mind.

Would Patrus still be beside me if we hadn't tried to escape?

He recalled the bodies staining the sands after his last time in the arena. He didn't want a repeat of that. With his newfound purpose to free the slaves, killing them was the last thing he wanted. *Perhaps Stegavax and Fenyx will spare me from having to do the deed myself.*

Regardless of how slowly he put his armor on, eventually, the horns would blow, and he would have to take to the sands. He would have to fight and survive against six of the deadliest slaves in New Rheynia.

"Zephyrus!" Doctore said. "It's time."

Zephyrus gulped. *Clever lies.* Wishing Jecht and Cerik fought alongside him instead of Fenyx and Stegavax, Zephyrus ascended the slope to the gates of the arena, but as he neared, Vykannis's voice filled his head.

"You refused to kill the Rheynian lanista and take your freedom. You refused to accept the freedom offered by the Rheynian prince. Now if you wish to live long enough to fulfill my purpose for you, you must slay the very people I sent you to save."

A shiver rippled down Zephyrus's spine. A cold sweat dampened his brow. He longed for the days when Vykannis left his prayers unanswered. Now the increasing frequency of the Judge's presence haunted him.

"I will not kill other slaves for sport," Zephyrus channeled back.

Doctore spoke to the three of them, but Vykannis's voice drowned him out.

"You are destined for greatness, Zephyrus," Vykannis said. *"But twice, you have denied me. Twice, you have chosen your will over the calling placed*

on your life. Now you must decide: die and free no slaves, or kill, survive, and live to fulfill your destiny."

Zephyrus hated to admit it, but Vykannis was right.

"Live," Patrus had said.

He could free no one if he died, but he didn't trust Vykannis, or the stabbing pains he felt in his stomach whenever the Judge spoke to him.

What are the deaths of a few more slaves in comparison to my fate?

He groaned.

That seems like something the Harbinger would think…

"Zephyrus, listen!" Doctore clapped his hands in Zephyrus's face. "You must fight as one. Show the Gods what you're made of. Are you a leaf to blow in the wind, or are you a tree that plants roots in history and lives on forever?"

"I will honor this ludus," Fenyx said.

"Don't… kill…" Weak and faraway, a new voice filled Zephyrus's mind. *"Patience."*

"Kill, survive, live," Vykannis said, drowning out the weaker voice.

"Who are you?" Zephyrus channeled back to the weak voice.

He'd felt this presence the night before when Vykannis urged him to kill Vykinallia a second time. It had somehow closed the door of his mind to Vykannis's influence.

"You've given the Gods of Valencia a foothold within your mind," Vykannis said. *"They've already killed Orsius and Aeryss. They've tried to kill me as well. Don't listen to them. You must fight. The hope of Celestia rests on you."*

Zephyrus ground his teeth. *Why would the Valencian Gods counsel patience?* He listened for the weak voice's rebuttal, but none came.

The last remnants of the setting sun served as the final grains of sand in an hourglass. Zephyrus was out of time. Attendants ignited torches along the perimeter of the arena, and horns blared, signaling the commencement of the Primus.

The initial wave of cheers subsided, to allow the king to introduce Targarus and Kaelus's gladiators. Arena attendants handed Zephyrus his gladius and buckler, Stegavax his dual blades, and Fenyx his two-handed great sword. For a moment, Zephyrus thought he recognized the attendant who handed him his sword, but the attendant moved on.

Focus.

"To challenge them," the king said, "Duke Chancellor, Lentulis Cassius, offers Zephyrus!" Zephyrus closed his eyes in silent prayer to the warring Gods within his head, but they remained absent as if they had taken their quarrels elsewhere.

He took the first step beyond the precipice of the gate's safety. The crowd roared, but Zephyrus's thoughts drifted to Vykinallia.

"You are more suited towards the hero," she had said.

He looked to the pulvinus as he walked upon the blood-soaked sands. Vykinallia met his gaze, clutching at the elbow he had healed the night prior. A smile touched her lips.

"To stand beside him, the Champion of the Games of Stockhelm—Fenyx!" Fenyx strode out to join Zephyrus, basking in the glory of the crowd's favor.

"Last but not least, I give you the reigning Champion of New Rheynia. The savage, the beast—Stegavax!"

Out of the corner of Zephyrus's eye, Fenyx stiffened, letting out a hoarse croak.

"Everything alright there, Champion?" Stegavax asked, stepping up beside Fenyx.

Fenyx shook his head, gagging.

"Bad whiteroot, eh?" Stegavax smirked.

Zephyrus's jaw unhinged. "You poisoned him?"

The roar of the crowd drowned out the king's voice as the gates closed behind them.

CHAPTER 49

BETRAYED

Fenyx VI
Salmantica

"I will take back my mantle," Stegavax hissed.

The skin tightened on the burned side of Fenyx's face as his lips curled back in a snarl. He ignored the shallowness of his breath, his blurred vision, and the twitch in his fingers.

You can't do this…

But the poison was already running through his veins.

Zephyrus put his hand on Fenyx's shoulder and said something, but Fenyx couldn't make out the words. There were supposed to be nine men on the sands—three Cassius gladiators in gold and purple, three Kaelus men in blue and white, and three Targarus champions in red and black—but his eyes betrayed him. There might as well have been an army before him.

The king's voice continued, but the words were unintelligible.

This was my opportunity to prove to Auron his labors weren't wasted on me, to demonstrate to the dominus that I was worthy of the mantle of Champion, and to earn the love of the people… Stegavax ruined everything.

The Burning took hold of him, radiating through his body like an inferno. It wanted blood more than glory, revenge more than justice.

Stegavax will die.

All eight gladiators on the sands turned south to face the pulvinus, but Fenyx faced Stegavax instead. He was supposed to salute the king, but if Stegavax wasn't going to fight fair, neither would he.

Fenyx reared back his great sword and swung at Stegavax. Stegavax lifted his swords to absorb the attack, but Fenyx's strength threw him off balance. Stegavax rolled across the sands. The crowd gasped and cheered, but Fenyx no longer cared for their desires.

He lifted his great sword overhead and chopped down in a sweeping arc.

Did he expect me to lay down and concede?

He lifted the blade again and slashed down with all his might. Making large, circling arcs with his great sword, he had the advantage of reach. He didn't need to see; he knew how Stegavax would attack. He struck again and felt the vibration through the steel as Stegavax's gladii wilted beneath his blade.

The coward sought to weaken me… fool should have killed me!

But with each strike, his sword became heavier, his arcs slower. He pressed his attack, but it was no use. Stegavax was faster.

Fenyx's head spun. He swung and missed, losing his balance and falling to the sands. Stegavax stabbed down at him, but Zephyrus caught the blow on his shield. As soon as Zephyrus came to Fenyx's aid, he was consumed in a whirlwind of red-and-black and blue-and-white gladiators.

With Zephyrus preoccupied, Stegavax returned. Fenyx scampered away from Stegavax's effortless attack, grinding his teeth. *He's playing me for the crowd's spectacle.*

His sight, his balance, his strength—betrayed him. He needed help.

Where is Zephyrus?

Stegavax kicked Fenyx, sending him sprawling face down to the sands. Fenyx pushed himself up, but steel sank deep into the back of his right shoulder. He cried out and reared back, raising his blade in defense, but there were three Stegavaxes. Fenyx chose the center one and blocked, but Stegavax again shoved him to the ground.

His only reprieve came when Stegavax lifted his swords to the crowd.

In the distance, the blurred shapes of gladiators surrounded the lone figure in gold and purple. *Zephyrus isn't coming to my aid. I'm on my own.*

Fenyx, still on his back, rolled away as Stegavax's steel raked the sands where Fenyx had just been. He stumbled to his feet and stood his ground. *I need to disarm him if I am to survive.*

The Burning wouldn't let him die.

Stegavax leveled both weapons and charged with reckless abandon. Fenyx planted his great sword into the sands and rolled over his maimed shoulder to avoid the fury of body and blade that came his way, his helm flying off in the process.

Stegavax bore down on him again, but Fenyx sidestepped a stab, ducked under a slash, and high-stepped a hack aimed at his shin. With a well-timed shove, Fenyx took advantage of Stegavax's momentum, sending him off balance.

His arm throbbed. Blood trickled down his ribs inside his armor. His right shoulder hung limp, a useless appendage that only served as an easy target for Stegavax.

Stegavax barreled for him again, his braided hair flying behind his plumed helm as he slashed right, left, right, left. Fenyx backpedaled, turning aside the strokes of the assault, but Stegavax relentlessly lunged after him and kicked him in the chest.

Fenyx's great sword slipped from his weakened fingers as he fell onto his back in front of the Cassius gate.

Auron shouted commands, but he could offer no help from behind the steel bars.

Stegavax aimed one blade at Fenyx's chest, the other poised like the venomous tail of a scorpion. Fenyx rolled at the last possible second into one of the false blades of his blurred vision, but the true sword only found sand. Fenyx rolled back the way he'd come, using his body weight to leverage the blade free from Stegavax's grasp. The other blade came for him, but with no other options, Fenyx grabbed the razor-sharp steel with his hands.

He shrieked as blood poured from his palms.

For a moment, they were deadlocked, but Stegavax's persistence and the bite of the sword in his palms overcame Fenyx's will. Blood drenched the blade and flowed onto Fenyx's cuirass, rolling off to trace his outline in the sands.

This is how I die.

The blade inched closer to his golden cuirass, bearing down on him.

It's over.

The Burning within him faded. The point of Stegavax's blade pierced the cuirass below the navel with a shrill cry.

"Judges save me!" Fenyx shouted to the purple sky.

A white bolt of lightning stretched across his field of vision. The crowd screamed, and Stegavax broke focus for the briefest of moments. Fenyx summoned the strength to shove the blade from his armor and rolled. Fenyx forced Stegavax off him and staggered to his feet, grains of sand clinging to his bloody palms. He grabbed the blade he pinned away from Stegavax. The hilt felt strange in his shredded palm, but life pumped through his veins.

"You will die by my blade!" Stegavax screamed. The two clashed as another bolt of lightning flashed. Screams filled the arena, unlike the cheers of the crowd.

Their blades crashed together. Stegavax kneed Fenyx in the groin. Fenyx stumbled back, and the scarlet steel slashed across Fenyx's limp arm and again across the back of his thigh. He fell to a knee and plunged the blade at Stegavax's gut. Stegavax dodged, but too slow. Fenyx's sword pierced the plate and struck flesh. He ripped the blade free and thrust it deep into Stegavax's thigh, forcing him to lose his footing as well. Fenyx slashed but missed just as Stegavax jabbed his sword up and sliced Fenyx in the side of the neck.

The shock came before the pain, but if it were a mortal wound, Fenyx would not die before Stegavax met his end. Fenyx stabbed at Stegavax again, but his blurred vision caused him to miss.

Stegavax punched him in the chin. His sword fell from his grasp. Dazed, he reached to locate the hilt with his bloody palms, but Stegavax climbed atop of him. Stegavax raised his sword high overhead, the point aimed at Fenyx's belly.

One moment, Stegavax was there, and the next, he was gone. Fenyx's head fell to the side, his vision a blurry nightmare. He looked to the pulvinus, searching for Cleotra, but only three shadowy figures graced the pulvinus. His vision narrowed, and unconsciousness seized him.

CHAPTER 50

An Early Storm

Nallia V
Salmantica

"No! What are they doing?" Nallia's father shouted as Fenyx attacked Stegavax.

Nallia gasped, digging her fingernails into the wooden arm of her chair.

"Another Laytonus episode," Targarus scoffed. "You ought to teach your gladiators more discipline."

Kaelus grunted. "Or more respect."

Her father glared daggers at the rival lanistas, but Nallia couldn't look away from the sands. Worse than Fenyx attacking Stegavax, the other six champions surrounded Zephyrus. The Kaelus and Targarus champions joined together to make sport of the lone Cassius contender. She twisted the amethyst ring around her finger like a maelstrom.

No, please! Zephyrus…

"A pity," Laeden said.

"Are you kidding?" Damascus asked. "If every contest were this exciting, I wouldn't miss the tournaments!"

Nallia clasped her hands and prayed. *Ferrocles, grant Zephyrus strength. Phaebia, bestow hope upon his heart. Good Incinerae, be merciful. Moterra, demonstrate your temperance and leave him amongst the living. Hameryn, cease whatever madness has divided Fenyx and Stegavax that they may aid Zephyrus in this fight. Aquarius, I need your compassion. I pray to you!*

Zephyrus rolled away from the onslaught of the opposing champions. He blocked, dodged, and countered, fighting against all six. He looked like Vykannis the Brave born again. She looked down at her elbow. It didn't have the cut and bruise she had suffered last night. Not even a faint reminder of her fall remained after he healed her using Celestic magic.

I am praying to the wrong Gods. She closed her eyes, rubbed her elbow, and whispered to the Judges of Celestia so no one could hear.

"Vykannis, Orsius, and Aeryss, watch over your Prophet. He needs you. I need you. Judges, please deliver him from this carnage."

She returned her gaze back to the arena. Zephyrus fended them off, despite the odds, a speck of gold in a blood-red sea of Targarus gladiators. He ducked under a swiping spear, rolled away from the Trapper's weighted net, deflected a hack of a sword, blocked an axe, and kicked a Targarus Slicer in the chest.

"Fenyx looks drunk," Nallia's mother said as Stegavax cast Fenyx to the ground.

How could this happen?

Zephyrus is going to die.

All of her love for the games evaporated. These weren't games—this was carnage. Brutal, bloodthirsty carnage. No glory. No civic duty.

"Tell me all slave owners aren't evil," Zephyrus said. *"That there is more to slavery than just death for coin."*

I can't. He was right. How did I ever love this?

Zephyrus parried a thrusting trident with a well-timed backhand of his buckler to spill a Kaelus Trapper to the sands. A violent axe swing aimed at his lower leg forced him to lurch out of the way, but he managed to counter, slicing the Bruiser across his inner thigh. The Bruiser cried out, dropping to a knee, but just as Nallia expected Zephyrus to deliver the fatal blow, he didn't. Instead, he drove the hilt of his sword into the back of the man's head.

Targarus's Slicer charged, forcing Zephyrus to retreat to the arena's western wall. While it would protect his flank, there was no escape. His five remaining opponents jostled for position.

He's going to die.

She couldn't watch. She turned away, but she glimpsed an arena attendant standing in the gateway adjacent to Zephyrus. He took off his helmet. Black hair, peppered gray at the temples. A squashed nose over a smug smile.

Lenox!

Nallia stood to her feet and pointed, but everyone's focus remained on the battle.

The gladiators closed in around Zephyrus. With one block of his sword, the blade fell from the hilt to the gasps of the crowd.

Broken.

Horror seized her with grasping hands, threatening to pull her into the deepest depths of the Six Hells. *No. Judges, no!*

"Not again," her father said.

Zephyrus was defenseless. A spear sliced his thigh. A sword chopped down on his pauldron. An axe glanced off of his ribs. Nallia couldn't watch.

Lenox cackled before fading into the shadows beneath the arena.

No, no, no! This can't be happening.

Another slice across his shield arm. A swipe of the spear sent his golden helm toppling to the sands. Zephyrus pushed with his shield, forcing his five attackers to step back.

Defeat weighed heavily on his slumped shoulders.

A tear trickled from the corner of Nallia's eye. *Don't give up. Please, don't give up.*

The Targarus Slicer charged, one blade leveled at Zephyrus's gut. Zephyrus sidestepped the thrust, grabbing the blade with his bare hands. He ducked under the second strike and wrenched the Slicer's sword from grasp. Zephyrus spun, plunging the blade into the belly of his attacker. He kicked his dying opponent away from him and let out a thunderous shout that reverberated throughout the arena. He yanked the fallen Slicer's sword from his stomach and advanced on the others.

Hope reignited in Nallia's chest. She wanted to cheer, to shout. But she couldn't breathe.

The Kaelus Trapper flung his net at Zephyrus, but inexplicably, it never opened, flying harmlessly past. Zephyrus deflected a spear thrust with his buckler and charged the Kaelus Bruiser, kicking him to the sands.

The Bruiser dropped to his knees and fell into Targarus's Warden. Zephyrus blocked the Trapper's incoming trident with his sword and sliced his knee out from under him, severing his lower leg. As the Trapper fell, Zephyrus stabbed downward through his chest. Zephyrus tore the blade free and spun to block an overhand hack from the Warden. The gladiators continued to attack despite their diminishing numbers.

Zephyrus's buckler of painted oak and iron splintered into a pile of tinder before the Targarus attack. Yet he did not falter beneath the impending wrath. With a quick counter and a flick of his wrist, he chopped down, deflecting a Kaelus Poker's spear into the Warden's sword arm. The Warden cried out and raised his shield to defend himself, but Zephyrus vaulted over the Warden's shield and away from the Poker's spear.

Zephyrus abandoned his corner. No longer defending, he pressed his attack against the remaining three gladiators. He dodged, blocked, and countered until his next opportunity revealed itself. The Poker stabbed with his double-edged spear but overextended himself. Zephyrus blocked the thrust down with his splintered shield and jumped over the downed spear to avoid a hack of the Kaelus Slicer's dual blades. When Zephyrus landed, he slammed down hard on the downed spear's shaft, fracturing it in half.

The Poker fell back, and the Warden stepped forward. Zephyrus hacked and slashed with an unmatchable fury. On the fourth cut, the Warden's throat sprayed blood from Zephyrus's gladius. The Poker reared back to throw the broken spearpoint at Zephyrus's blind side.

Nallia shouted in warning, but Zephyrus whirled, deflecting the spear away.

Only the Poker and the Slicer remained. Nallia joined in the crowd's cheers for Zephyrus. He fought like a man possessed, an unstoppable force—a Prophet of Celestia.

Zephyrus, however, turned from his opposition. He didn't continue his onslaught at the remaining champions. Instead, he ran for Stegavax and Fenyx.

Stegavax sat atop Fenyx, his blade raised above his head. Just as he was about to deliver the killing blow, Zephyrus struck the blade from Stegavax's hands and shoved him off of Fenyx.

Suddenly, light flashed and electricity coursed through Nallia's body. She seized and fell from her seat, losing all control. Panic gripped her, but she couldn't think. Couldn't process. She wasn't the only one. Everyone fell from their seats, writhing on the floor of the pulvinus.

Lightning?

Pain sizzled through her helpless body, tingling, and burning. Even once the electricity stopped flowing through her, she found herself numb and unable to move. Her heart thudded in her chest, in her ears, and behind her eyes as she stared at the cloudless sky.

The nightly rains haven't arrived yet.

Nallia attempted to get up, but only managed to roll onto her side.

Footsteps approached, and worn leather boots came into view.

"Grab him," said a woman's voice.

"I've got him," a man said. "Let's go!"

As they marched away, they entered her field of vision. The man and the woman strode to the exit—the true mages of Celestia that had escaped the dungeons to be replaced by runaway slaves for the sake of the execution.

Nallia tried to cry out. She wanted—needed—to stop them, but she was paralyzed.

The mages strode to the exit. Between them, they dragged the helpless body of the King of New Rheynia.

CHAPTER 51

King

Danella VII

Salmantica

Her head spun, her body ached, and her rage was uncontainable. The scent of antiseptic and charred flesh woke her in the medicus's chambers. The electrocuted victims of the mages' attack suffered in varying degrees. Ser Daenus was gravely wounded but would live. A handful of servers, three lower guards, and Ser Ellus of the King's Guard Knights perished during the attack. The Prefectus Medicus's chambers, while large, were filled to capacity.

Danella needed to think, and the groans of the injured weren't helping. She massaged her temples with her palms. The bright white was the last thing she saw before waking up in the medicus's quarters.

She ignored her dizziness as she stood and forced herself out of the medicus's chambers. Her feet wobbled, and the walls seemed to shift with every step, but walking through Sentigard's halls, the gears in her head whirred to piece together the puzzle of all that had happened.

The mages were in her dungeons for the flaming arrows shot at the pulvinus during the Salmantic Games. Had she known they were mages and not just archers of the Uprising, she would have demanded Laeden nail them to the Six Arrowed Star—even if Varros wouldn't have allowed it.

But how did they escape the dungeons? They burned Count Elrod Horne to a crisp within his cell to ensure no witness lived to tell the tale, but the fact that the Uprising had elemental mages—and they abducted Varros—meant that the time for posturing was over.

They had Varros. There was cruel irony in that. She thought perhaps her plans could be achieved without Varros needing to die. All she wanted was to appease the Gods, uphold the Facets of Perfection, and secure her father's kingdom. But now the Uprising had revealed itself, and questions abounded.

Why did the Uprising want Varros? If anything, he defended the Celestics, offering them clemency. If the Uprising wanted him dead, they could have killed everyone on the pulvinus. Why leave everyone and take Varros?

Days had passed, and still they sent no ransom note.

Danella's hand traced the dark stone walls for support. Loneliness and isolation weighed on her. Her mother and father were gone. Her brother, dead. Her husband…

She shoved the pain of her loss down. She could only push forward. If she looked back, she'd be lost. She needed to put Damascus on the throne and unite the New Rheynians against the mages. The Uprising would fight on her terms, not the other way around—not anymore.

Damascus would be king. The strife between the Sentinels and the Revivalists would end, and united, they would destroy the Uprising. Damascus would reinstate the enforcement of the Treaty of 940 and ensure no mage walked the lands of New Rheynia ever again.

I need allies if I am to pull off this plan.

Yet friends would be difficult to come by. Between Ser Daenus needing time to heal and Ser Ellus not surviving the attack, there was only Varros's personal bodyguard Ser Ostrey Wingfoot. With Varros gone, and in light of Ostrey's failure, he would need replacing as well. Protecting Damascus was now her only priority, but the best defense was a unified New Rheynia.

She stepped into the study and closed the doors behind her as her ideas took shape. Retrieving her writing utensils from her hidden stash, she plotted her most daring scheme yet.

Confidence borne of necessity burned within her in ways she never felt before. She loved Varros, but he held her back. She couldn't have lived with herself had she been the one to rob him of life. Yet the mages did her dirty work for her. This was the only way the Six would have allowed it. Now she would finish what she set out to do, unabated, unabashed, and undeterred.

She finished the letter and sealed it with wax. She needed to find Damascus and set him to purpose. A Drake must sit on the throne, and Damascus, regardless of his surname, would lead New Rheynia to safety against the temptations of the false Gods.

Everything I've done, everything I've worked for—it was all for this purpose. And no one, not even Laeden, will ruin it.

She exited the study and descended the west tower. She waved off the handmaidens and guards who attempted to speak with her and made her way through the great hall, past the throne room, and down to the armory, where she expected to find Damascus.

Though Damascus was nowhere to be seen, she found Aelon Ironpine.

He bowed upon seeing her. "Your grace, it's good to see you well."

"And you, Ser Aelon," Danella said.

She needed a new King's Guard Knight. Ser Aelon would serve well. She was relieved to discover he wasn't the mole she suspected.

"It's fortunate you were spared from the carnage. Unfortunately, Ser Ellus and Ser Ostrey were not so lucky."

He tilted his head. "I knew Ser Ellus succumbed, but I hadn't heard of Ser Ostrey's misfortune."

"Oh, well that's because it hasn't happened yet," Danella said. "He is a King's Guard Knight, yet he remains unscathed while the king has been kidnapped. That cannot be tolerated. Wouldn't you agree?"

"I suppose not."

"That leaves two spots open on the King's Guard—three if you exclude Ser Daenus while he recovers—not to mention the additional three swords I hoped to add to protect our new king."

Aelon's tourney-knight smile gave away his interest.

She already had him wrapped around her finger, but there was more she wanted.

Danella approached Aelon and straightened the collar of his doublet. "An esteemed knight of your abilities is required during such perilous times."

He smiled curtly. "I live to serve, your grace."

Danella returned a tight-lipped smile of her own. "That is what I like to hear. In that case, there is something else I would ask of you. It is of the utmost importance and urgency."

Aelon bowed his head. "Anything, my queen."

With Aelon's future in her service secured, she continued her search for Damascus. However, holding her forged scroll in hand, she came across another who could serve a pivotal role in her schemes.

Aemos Horne, the heir—however disappointing he might be—of the late Count Elrod sat on the sill staring out the window overlooking the inner bailey of Sentigard. His pale skin contrasted with his dark hair and flinty gray eyes. Aside from being handsome, he had little else to offer; he had fallen short of every position he attempted to gain. Despite his shortcomings, his quickly ignited passion could be useful if aimed in the appropriate direction.

Aemos's hand supported his cheek as he gazed out into the distance.

Danella cleared her throat. "Apologies, Count Horne, I do not mean to disturb."

"Your grace." Aemos stood, bowing. "Apologies, I did not see you."

"It is I who must apologize," Danella said. "I offer my deepest sympathies for your loss. Your father was a good man." In truth he hadn't been much use since her father was still king, but Aemos didn't need to hear that now.

"Gratitude, your grace. My condolences as well... I can't believe they abducted King Varros."

"The entire realm will grieve if we cannot reclaim him," she said. "I promise you. We will not stand by and let the death of your father or the abduction of my husband go without punishment." She held out her arm, inviting him to walk with her.

She needed to light a spark to make Aemos's pugnacity hers to wield.

"How you respond in these trying times may shape the future of your house and your legacy as Count Horne. I trust you will be up to the challenges ahead."

"Thank you, your grace."

"I've been wondering, though…" She stopped, inspecting the halls conspiratorially.

He surveyed their surroundings before returning his flinty eyes to her.

Tightening her grip on her proverbial mask, she whispered. "Is it possible someone within the castle could have helped the mages escape… and your father witnessed it?" She lifted her hand to her heart. "Why else burn a defenseless man behind bars?"

Aemos tensed.

"Six save me, I hope Laeden didn't have anything to do with this. Gods know he has a soft spot for mages and their sympathizers." She paused to gauge Aemos's reaction, but she didn't need to. The look on his face was easier to understand than the Facets of Perfection.

Damascus wasn't in the armory, the training yard, nor the dining hall. It could only mean the Heart of Sentigard. Damascus always favored the grassy nook enclosed within the castle walls, and he'd become even more infatuated with it after bringing Nallia there. Sure enough, that's where she found him, fighting against the air with his sword in the shadow of the great oak tree the castle was built around. The wind sang with each steel strike.

"I've been looking everywhere for you," she said from the sill overlooking the small courtyard. "There are matters of import we must discuss."

He paused to look up at her. "There are." Rage burned in his golden eyes.

She frowned. "Come, attend me."

Damascus stirred but did not obey. Instead, he jostled the hilt of the sword in his hand.

"Come, my son. There's—"

With a grunt, he flung his sword sidelong. It spun in tight arcs before clattering against the solid oak's trunk and falling to the ground.

She scowled. *Now is not the time for a tantrum.* As king, he couldn't afford to be governed by his impulses. He didn't have the wartime upbringing she and Varros shared. His spring flowers only knew summer's kiss, not winter's bite. She understood that the boy had lost his father and needed time to grieve, but now was the time for action. Not pouting.

Men were so ill-tempered and unruly when it came to managing their emotions. They couldn't separate one from the other, as if the colors on a painter's palette all mixed together. Men seemed incapable of showing their sadness when they grieved. Instead, they resorted to anger as if it would transform their woes into something tangible they could beat into submission.

"Pick up your sword," Danella said with none of a mother's patience.

Damascus mumbled under his breath but collected his blade and resheathed it. Still grumbling, he ascended the rope ladder to the windowsill. Once he summited, he swung his legs around, landing on the floor in full stride.

Danella lurched into motion to keep up with him. "Where are you going?"

Damascus didn't answer. Despite her attempts, he wouldn't speak. Only their footsteps bothered with hurried conversation. He brooded silently as they crossed the bailey, ascended the west tower, and made their way to her study.

But as they approached, panic set in. *Has he discovered my secret?*

He opened the door and ushered her inside. Danella forced a small smile, but once within the study, Damascus slammed the door shut.

Danella shuddered at the crash. "Six save us, must you tear down the entire castle in your wrath? Cease your sulking and—"

"My father is missing," Damascus said, "stolen by mages. My betrothed returned home in fear from their attack. And…" Damascus's shoulders rounded, and his hands tore at his short hair. "I feel helpless."

Danella sighed—in part because her secret was safe, but mostly because her boy needed his mother.

"Consider it a blessing," Danella said, hugging him from behind. "She could have suffered a more grievous injury like Ser Ellus." She came around him and took his hands in hers. "But your father…"

Danella allowed her eyes to water before taking her hands from his to wipe the tears away. They weren't real tears. She didn't have time to process the loss of her husband. She used her tears knowing they would break Damascus's wrath. After three sobs, his arms wrapped around her. She composed herself, pulling her hands away from her face to look up at him.

"Your father isn't just missing…" she whispered. "He's gone, Damascus."

He backed away from her. The shape of the word *"What"* framed his lips, but no sound came forth. She pulled the scroll with the broken seal from a pocket of her dress and handed it to him. He took it slowly, his glossy golden eyes like morning dew in the rising sun.

"They mean to kill him?" he asked. "I don't understand. He protected them. Why would they—"

Danella lowered her gaze to stare at the floor. "Keep reading."

The note said the Rheynian people were foreigners who worshiped false Gods. That they took the Helms' lands and enslaved them. King Varros's attempt to offer exile instead of death was not good enough for the mages. So they killed him.

"He's dead? After all he tried to do for them?" Damascus's expression drooped at first, but then hardened. "They will pay for what they've done."

Those were the exact words she wanted to hear. "They will, my son." She pulled him into an embrace. "You are now the Duke of Salmantica and the King of New Rheynia. You will announce that the mages have demanded we lay down our arms against them. A servile life or exile is not fitting for a superior race such as they," she said, quoting the forged letter. "You will tell the people the mages killed your father and wish to rule New Rheynia in his place."

She stepped back to observe her son. "We cannot let these savages of the Uprising condemn our people to a life of fear. We'll declare war on the mages for what they've done!" A tear streamed down her cheek. Yet these tears were not feigned.

She sacrificed much for the Gods of her father, plotted against her husband, and positioned others against Laeden, but this was her sacrifice—her burden to bear. Now, Damascus would be king.

"All will worship the Six, and you will be the greatest king ever to rule." She stroked his cheek with her hand. The muscles of his jaw clenched, making his pointed chin beard appear like a weapon of vengeance.

"I am so proud of you." The time for sulking was over, and the time for amending Varros's poor decisions had come. Damascus wiped the water from the corners of his eyes and stood to his full height.

"They will die. All of them. On the Star at the Gilded Gauntlet—just as Grandfather did. I swear to the Six, every last mage will die for this!"

The pieces were all in place. She felt the burden fall from her shoulders as Damascus accepted the load. "I'm so proud of you. My king."

CHAPTER 52

DOUBLE-EDGED SWORD

Laeden XIV

Salmantica

"Laeden?"

His head throbbed, and his body felt like it had been taken apart and pieced back together all wrong, like a suit of armor constructed from different-sized men of different armies.

"Laeden?"

He opened one eye, but the world blinded him. The walls echoed with every sound. The beating of his own heart throbbed in his ears and behind his eyes. *Chimera's breath, let me rest.* He didn't want to hear the call of the world. *Six Hells, I never want to move again.*

"Laeden, if you can hear me, wake up!"

Unable to hide from duty any longer, he turned to the familiar voice. Markus's face took shape above him, his long black hair a tangle. Laeden rubbed the sand from his eyes to wake to the world he'd long been absent from. Markus handed him a clay cup.

Laeden drank and wiped his mouth with the back of his hand. "Tell me it was a dream."

Markus shook his head. "A nightmare. What do you remember?"

Laeden rubbed his temples. *The Kings' Day Games. The fight between the Cassius gladiators. The...*

A distant memory of a white bolt sent ice through his veins.

The mages took Father.

Laeden jumped out of bed, not knowing how long he had been incapacitated.

"Any leads, reports, sightings—anything?" Laeden dressed, putting on the first articles of clothing he could find.

"That's the problem," Markus said. "There are too many leads. Some from honest citizens trying to do their part, but others could be the Revivalists trying to distract us. Odds are they have nothing to do with the mages or the Uprising, but their cause is one and the same at the moment. Disarray for the crown and befuddlement for the Sentinels will only serve to strengthen their respective resolutions even if they oppose each other ideologically."

If Iylea told the truth about Danella conspiring with the Revivalists to kill the King, how did the Uprising play into it? Or was Danella right about Iylea being with the Uprising? She knew the ins and outs of the castle, the arena, and where everyone would be positioned.

"There's more." Markus ground his teeth. "According to King Damascus—"

"*King* Damascus?" Laeden shook his head, unable to make sense of it.

Markus drew close. He placed his hand on Laeden's shoulder and pursed his lips.

"Laeden, your father is dead."

Laeden's knees buckled. His breath caught. The ground seemed to fall out from under him. *They killed him?* Laeden let the words sink in. The knowledge squirmed like worms inside a rotten apple, wriggling to get to the core.

They killed him. Father… I've failed you.

"At least that's what the mages say," Markus said. "My deepest condolences, I—"

"Save them," Laeden snapped. "You said it yourself. The Revivalists and the Uprising both have something to gain through spreading lies. I won't accept it till I see proof."

A bustle from the corridor redirected their attention.

A Sentinel barged through the open doorway. "Lieutenant Markus!" With a quick salute, he dropped his hands to his knees, panting. "Captain Laeden, thank the Six you're awake."

"What is it?" Markus asked.

"You must come. Quickly!"

The three of them ran through the castle to the throne room.

"He talks of war," the Sentinel said. "Count Horne's lost his mind. He's gonna kill her!"

After being bedridden, it took all of Laeden's strength to keep up. He couldn't process what the messenger said, but by the time they arrived at the throne room, it all became clear.

Damascus stood before the throne, his arm raised in the air and a crown atop his head. Not the crown prince's circlet, but a thicker, heavier, badge of office—his uncle's crown. Danella stood beside him as they addressed the court packed wall to wall with patrician lords and ladies. Jeers filled the vaulted ceilings, but they were all aimed at a woman bowing on the floor at the center of the throne room.

Damascus held something in his outstretched hand. "They expect us to bow down. To *them.* But they have forgotten what we are capable of."

What's the meaning of this?

"We will remind them that *they* are the savages." Damascus flailed his arms to ignite his audience. "*They* worship false Gods!"

The raucous crowd's approval grew to a crescendo. Laeden had woken to a nightmare in which his father's levelheaded temperance was replaced by Damascus's inflammatory impulses.

"But that's not all," Damascus said. "They claim superiority, demanding we abandon the Six and grovel before them." He scoffed. "I will not bow. Will you?"

The throne room echoed with the patrician's anger. Every voice that would have counseled patience was far from Damascus's side. Those who could have offered prudent advice remained silent. Laeden's eyes focused on Danella.

"We must bind the wounds of our nation's division," Damascus said. "No more will the Sentinels fight the Revivalists because our true enemy has revealed itself. Together, we must rise to bring the Uprising to its knees. We will *not* falter because our cause is just!"

Laeden slunk forward, weaving through the crowd of cheering patricians. Hardly believing his ears, he attempted to devise a plan that could defuse the mob Damascus had incited. He needed to say something. If he didn't, the very war their father attempted to stave off would erupt.

"There will come a day of reckoning," Zephyrus warned. *"A flood of blood..."*

"Now I ask..." Damascus paused to gauge his audience. "Who will help me purge our land of the Celestic rot?" Damascus shouted to the roar of the mob. "Who among you will aid me in converting the barbarians to the Six? Who will scorch the villages of Klaytos so none of your children nor your children's children have to live in fear?"

The patricians shouted with bloodlust. Laeden might as well have been surrounded by Revivalists.

"We will take back our country!" Damascus yelled. "Who is with me?"

Everyone in the throne room erupted to take up Damascus's cry. He basked in the support of the Salmantic patricians. It was worse than Laeden imagined, but more concerning than Damascus's warmongering speech or the full support offered by the patricians was Danella's calm contemplative smile.

Laeden's stomach twisted in knots.

She looks... pleased. Her husband was supposedly dead. *Does she smile believing this is the path to vengeance? Or is this the war she wanted all along?*

"The queen, Brusos, and Ser Daenus are up to something," Iylea had warned.

He hadn't listened.

He couldn't let it come to war. Not like this. Not after he'd lost his mother. Not after all his father risked to maintain the tentative peace between the Uprising and the Revivalists.

Laeden emerged from the crowd and stepped into Damascus's view.

The crowd went silent.

Aemos Horne stood above a girl crumpled in a heap on the floor at the foot of the dais. She was covered in soot and grime, disheveled beyond that of any to have set foot in the throne room before. He only hoped she would not be the scapegoat for his father's abduction like the runaway slaves sacrificed in place of the escaped mages who attacked the pulvinus during the Salmantic Games.

Laeden turned his trembling palms skyward. "Where? Where is our father's body? Where are the hard truths the talk of war should wait on?"

Damascus examined him, his mouth a thin lipless line. The woman bowing on the floor lifted her gaze to Laeden. His heart sank even further. Dirty, thin, and disheveled as she was, Laeden recognized her immediately.

"Iylea!" The euphoria that came with her name on his lips soured at her state of disarray. *Gods, where have you been? What have they done to you?*

She stood to her feet and ran to him, but Aemos grabbed her by the wrist, wearing the black-and-red armor of a knight of the King's Guard.

Laeden gritted his teeth and snarled. "What is the meaning of this? Let her go!"

"All the answers you seek are here," Damascus said, holding up a letter. "Written by their own treacherous hands. Read it for yourself."

"I have no doubt you know your letters." Laeden spoke to the room, but his eyes remained fixed on Iylea.

Stay strong, my love, I'm here.

"My doubt lies in circumstantial evidence, hearsay, and collusion. But this has nothing to do with Iylea. Let her go!"

"This has everything to do with Iylea," Danella said.

The queen's voice pried his focus from Iylea. He met her cold gaze.

"You knew she was a seer," Danella said.

The patricians erupted in murmurs. Laeden cursed himself, darting his eyes back to Iylea. She reached for him. Laeden stepped toward her, but Aemos drew his sword.

"Whose side are you on?" Aemos asked.

Laeden clenched his fists. "The side of truth."

Aemos turned back to the crowd. "Tell the good people the truth then, Laeden. Tell them that my father is dead because you'd rather protect Celestic mages than a Valencian lord!"

The patricians roared in Aemos's support.

"Laeden, this is what it has come to," Damascus said. "They attacked you, *twice*. They abducted and killed Father. We must act now if we are to stop these heretics."

Laeden's fists opened. He splayed his palms before his brother. "Please, Damascus. Look at this." He gestured to the angry mob behind him. "Is this how you will rule?"

"Laeden, Father tried to be civil with these people. Your attempt with the Sentinels was admirable, but they've shown their true intentions. I must protect our people. Can't you see that? The time for peace has ended."

"This war you speak of is exactly what the Revivalists want!" Laeden was grasping at straws. *I must change Damascus's mind. But if Danella is a Revivalist, could Damascus be too? Was he in on it all along, or is he just his mother's puppet?*

"Perhaps you should worry about yourself rather than the Revivalists," Aemos said. "She's a mage. You knew she was a mage, and the only other mages we know have killed my father and the king."

"Iylea is not a—" Laeden's voice cut off.

"A what?" Aemos asked. "Not a mage, you say?" His flinty eyes smoldered like hot coals in a brazier. A smile twisted his lips. "She's already admitted as much. And you—you are worse than her. Your job was to protect. To serve. To 'Shield the Righteous.'"

"I have done every—"

"You've conspired with the mages!" Aemos bellowed, his one hand still grasped around Iylea's wrist, his other brandishing a sword. "The penalty is clear."

Laeden looked to Damascus. "Father's last decree was exile. Not the sword. Please, Brother, don't do this."

"I must defend my people," Damascus said. "She admitted to being a mage. The penalty is death. Let this be a warning to the rest of the Uprising."

The air in the throne room became thin. Laeden's lungs constricted; his heart seized.

"Damascus, this isn't just a war with the mages you're considering; we still fight the Revivalists. Have you even spoken to Grandfather Hallon? What does Northridge say of you going against Father's decree?"

Damascus swallowed.

"You haven't even spoken with him." Laeden shook his head. "This could divide all of New Rheynia. Again. Outright civil war!"

Iylea's eyes were wide with panic.

Stay strong, my love.

Laeden glared at Danella. "Is this not the same war your father worked so hard to end? The marriage between you and Father, was that not intended to mend the wound that divided us? Can't you see—if we fail to learn from the past, we will again fall prey to it."

It became abundantly clear, however, that the old rivalry still lived on. Despite Damascus being half Drake and half Helixus, the Salmantic patricians booed Laeden.

"Pseudo-prince!"

"Craven pleb!"

Blood pumped into his ears. Like a tempest swirling within him, fury and fear moistened his palms and flushed his cheeks. *I must stop this.*

Damascus settled them down. "There will be no civil war. Not between the Sentinels and the Revivalists or Salmantica and Valtarcia. Don't you think Grandfather will want justice for his son?"

Laeden closed his eyes, searching the inside of his eyelids for the words that would make Damascus see reason. "Yes. Justice. Not blind vengeance!"

Damascus shook his head. "It is you who is blind, brother, but you will see. Valtarcia will side with us. The mages will fall. And never again will we make concessions; the treaty will be upheld. We must kill the mage."

Heat flushed Laeden's cheeks. His hands trembled at his sides. *Kill the mage? Kill Iylea?*

"No. No. This isn't how it's supposed to be," Laeden shouted. "Do honor and justice mean nothing to you? What honor is there in killing a helpless woman? This is what Father tried to stop!"

"And he failed!" Damascus shouted. "He died for it, Laeden."

"Why are you so quick to defend the mage but so slow to defend the people?" Aemos spat. His face reddened beneath his black hair. "When did you become the mages' puppet?"

"I never—" Laeden was cut off by the shouting patricians.

"He's a mage!"

"He freed the assassins!"

"That's enough!" Damascus's voice cut through the rest. "Prince Laeden had nothing to do with the mages' escape."

Ser Aelon Ironpine stepped from the crowd. Time seemed to stand still as he examined Laeden. His sullen expression hardened as he set his jaw.

The people will listen to Aelon. He can stop this madness.

Aelon turned his gaze from Laeden to the queen.

"Do it, Aelon," Laeden said. "Tell the people the truth!"

Aelon held up his hands to silence the crowd. He cleared his throat. "My lords and ladies, you've been betrayed." The stone at his throat bobbed. He took a slow deep breath.

"I freed the assassins from the dungeons the night before the Kings' Day Games."

Gasps and shouts filled the throne room, but Laeden's stomach fell to the floor.

What in Six Hells are you saying?

"I replaced them with common criminals," Aelon said.

Laeden felt a stabbing pain between his shoulder blades.

This isn't true.

"I did this at the command of Prince Laeden," Aelon said.

The sting of betrayal seared through Laeden as the angry, bloodthirsty crowd hurled insults at him. Aelon's treachery boiled into anger.

"I did no such thing!" He glared at Aelon, Aemos, Damascus, and Danella.

"Am I to believe his words, or yours?" Aemos growled. "I can only believe what I know. Our fathers are dead, and the one responsible for the mages still has no idea how they escaped. So this mage will die, along with the rest of her kind, and it will be justice!"

"There *will* be justice," Laeden said. "Once we apprehend the true criminals. The ones who tell lies for their own gain." He scowled at Aelon. "The ones who would divide us and prevent us from seeing the true enemy." He snapped his attention to Danella. "This woman didn't kill our fathers…" Laeden looked between Aemos and Damascus.

The crowd silenced for a moment, and Laeden turned to address them.

I can not fail. Not here. Not now.

"The Revivalists believe they're protecting the Six—a noble cause without dispute. Yet they do so by inflicting fear upon the innocent and targeting those with oppositional beliefs." Laeden took a moment to stare at Danella. "There's no honor in that. Magic can be dangerous. And this woman may possess such magic…"

His eyes fell upon Iylea, his heart hammering in his chest. He walked towards her despite Aemos's threatening steel.

"Yet she has not brandished it against us. Caused us no ill will. To blame her for what she is to cast her into the same lot as those who killed Count Elrod Horne, the legendary Ser Ellus, and…" He choked on the words, unable and unwilling to add his father's name to that list.

"It's not fair, and I will not be party to it."

A painstakingly long pause hung over the room as his words settled on the audience, leaving behind the eerie stillness that accompanied the weight of difficult words to hear and hard truths to accept. Defiant eyes and stern jaws softened in the face of humility.

"Have you forgotten the scripture of Valencianism?" Danella asked, breaking the silence. "The Treaty of 940 that our peace was founded upon."

"I once asked Father the same," Laeden said. "I thought he should have killed the mage as the law states. But now, standing before you, I see what King Varros saw. This is not how it has to be. There's been enough blood. There's been enough war. It's time we find another way."

"You speak heresy!" Aemos said.

"If it's heresy to ask for a woman to be judged for her crimes instead of being murdered for someone else's deeds then yes. I speak heresy!"

"Laeden, what are you doing?" Markus attempted to grab his arm, but Laeden's rage couldn't be contained. *I should have seen it sooner.* Danella was at the head of the Revivalists, under his nose the entire time. She wanted war with the mages. She wanted to finish the war her father started.

I should have listened to Iylea from the beginning, but it's not too late.

"Heretic, sympathizer." Aemos jabbed his sword with each barbed word. "They were your prisoners, your responsibility. They killed my father… and our king!"

"Laeden, you are accused of heresy and treason against the crown, but…" Danella paused as the crowd softened to hear her words. "Part the mage's head from her shoulders and I am sure these accusations will be dropped. You must choose which side you're on."

Tremors coursed through his corded muscles. Fear, anger, failure coalesced into a whirlwind that surrounded him and Iylea.

"I love you," Iylea said, her voice shaking. "I always have. Do this. Live." She held out her hand to Laeden and slipped free of Aemos's grasp.

Laeden caught her in his arms and held her. She was so frail. He tried to speak, but his voice died in his throat.

"The flood of blood is coming," she whispered. "You must kill me."

Laeden balked, Zephyrus's promise returning to him. His mind faltered. His mouth worked, unable to form words.

She backed away and knelt before him. "Do it, Laeden. Please."

The crowded throne room yelled, gawking, and threatening, but Laeden heard none of it. He unsheathed his sword. He had no choice. He glared at Damascus.

"Her head!" Aemos spat.

"Do it." Iylea begged from her knees. "Live."

The silver steel gleamed in his hand. "Judge the sword by its actions. Not what it is capable of." Laeden let his sword clatter to the floor. He took Iylea's hand again and pulled her to her feet.

"No," Iylea whispered. She wrapped her arms around him. "Be humble in your sentencing. Survive this, my love." She shoved away from Laeden.

Out of the corner of his eye, Aemos struck. A flash of white steel. A whooshing slash through the air.

Time stood still.

Steel met flesh. Iylea's head parted from her shoulders.

An unnatural ear-piercing screech filled the hall and persisted even after her head thudded to the floor. Her decapitated body crumpled a moment later, spraying blood upon the floor and showering Laeden in the purest extent of his failure.

Her head rolled, leaving a scarlet trail in its wake. A beautiful, horrible comet across the dark stone floor of the throne room.

Laeden fell to his knees. "Six save us."

The head of the woman he loved rolled to a stop before him. Her yellow-green eyes staring sightlessly. Her mouth hung open.

In this moment, Laeden discovered the true meaning of despair. The ear-piercing screech finally subsided, but it continued in Laeden's head as he held Iylea's face in his hands. "Gods, Iylea… I'm sorry. I love you…"

He should have told her more. He should have said it more often. Now he'd never have the chance again.

Danella's heels clapped upon the stone as she came to stand beside Aemos. "Laeden, you will be tried for heresy and treason towards the crown."

CHAPTER 53

At Death's Door

Fenyx VII

Stockhelm

The days and nights following the Kings' Day Games were a blend of waking dreams and living nightmares. He woke and slept and woke and slept so many times that frustration consumed him, but now he was certain he was awake because Stegavax slept on the cot beside him.

In his dreams, Stegavax died beneath his blade. Fenyx walked tall, hoisting Stegavax's long braid like a trophy to display in the Champion's quarters of the ludus, where Cleotra would be awaiting him. But that was the dream, and he'd woken to a nightmare.

"Release me from this damned place!" Fenyx shouted, hoping someone would hear him. Nobody came. *How long have I been here?* The construct of time meant nothing. Moments or hours later, the door to the medicus's chambers swung open.

Auron and the medicus entered.

"He's alive," the medicus squawked.

Auron grunted, arms crossed over his leather cuirass while the medicus examined Fenyx's bandages.

"We thought you for the afterlife," Auron said. "You may yet restore your honor."

Fenyx wilted beneath Auron's stare, a dash of relief in the stew of disappointment.

The medicus peeled back the bandages. "Good, good. No rot. Looks to be mended in no time." He prepared new bandages to re-dress Fenyx's wounds.

"You should be dead," Auron said. "You owe the medicus your life and your gratitude."

"How long have I been here?" Fenyx asked, half afraid to know the answer. *A day? Two days? Certainly it could not have been more than…*

"A week."

Tip the burning scales. "A week!"

"For the first few days, the medicus had you quarantined to prevent risk of infection," Auron said.

Re-dressing his wounds, the medicus examined him over his beaked nose. "The worst should be over. If you were gonna die, you'd have done it by now."

Fenyx grunted, not realizing how dire his circumstances had been. "What of him?"

"Not so fortunate." The medicus shook his head, limping away.

"His wounds weren't as grievous as yours, but where you have recovered, he has dwindled," Auron said. "I must admit he's not one I'd name friend, but he's a gladiator all the same. Your petty quarrels should have brought an end to both of you fools. Nevertheless, he does not deserve to die like this."

Fenyx hung his head. *So far removed from honor and glory. A whole week, lost.* "Auron, when can I be gone from this place and rejoin my brothers?"

"You will not return until you are given leave by the medicus. But to regain standing, you have a long way to go. You have dishonored your name and this house."

Fenyx's shoulders slumped. He'd have coiled his hands into fists if not for the bandages lining his palms. *I didn't choose to be poisoned by my own brother, yet I suffer the punishment all the same.* "Apologies, Doctore. How can I rectify my standing?"

Auron shook his head. "After attacking your own brother before the commencement of the games?" He scoffed. "You have built yourself quite the pyre. I raised you to be better than Stegavax, not become him."

Fenyx ate his tongue. *The truth doesn't matter. What good would come of blaming Stegavax for poisoning me?* His only means of redemption was proving himself more honorable than his previous actions.

"I am nothing if absent my opportunity to become Champion," Fenyx said. "Whatever it takes, I will prove to you I am still worthy."

"Spoken like a true Champion." Auron patted Fenyx's good shoulder. "You'll have your opportunity soon enough. For now, settle for my companionship."

"It would be most welcomed." *Unless I must suffer more lectures.* Fenyx yanked against the manacles binding him to the cot. "But rid me of these irons."

After a bit of hollering and mumbling from the medicus, he unshackled Fenyx. Fenyx hadn't realized how liberating it would be to be out of chains.

Auron brought a chair beside Fenyx's cot. "There's a story I promised I'd tell you. Remember Sinion?"

The gladiator who rose to become a lanista. Fenyx nodded.

"Sinion is a swindler and a thief, yet a clever one. Never fought a match he couldn't win, always bending the rules in his favor. He pitted gladiators against one another, took bets and fixed the games to profit his dominus. His dominus was no fool. He knew what he had in Sinion and made the most of him.

"It's said that every coin he paid for Sinion he made back before he even left the slavers' market. His sticky fingers and silver tongue pulled him from the dredges of the ludus to the villa as a trusted advisor. Over the years his dominus fell ill and succumbed to his ailments. With no wife or trueborn heirs, he left the ludus to Sinion and declared him a lord."

A history instead of a lecture…

"Why tell me this?" Fenyx asked. At one point he cared, but it seemed trivial now.

"Because despite everything you've learned, you're still too thick to understand." Muscles along Auron's jaw tensed. "As Champion you'll have many rivals, but you don't need enemies under your very roof. Yet still, you shun your brothers."

Fenyx bit his lip. *Now the lecture.* "Who have I shunned, other than death this past week?"

Auron shook his head. "He could have let you die. By all means, he *should* have let you die, but he risked all to save you from Stegavax. And it's clear why he's been visiting." He gestured to Fenyx's wounds.

Zephyrus. In fractured moments between his broken dreams, he recalled seeing Zephyrus standing over him. *My wounds were worse than Stegavax's, but I improved, and he floundered. Has he been healing me?*

Auron leaned in and whispered, "His secret is safe with me, but if not for him, you'd have been lost to us."

Fenyx didn't know what to say. He opened his mouth, but words failed him. Auron continued before he could phrase a reply. "I tell you of the rise of Sinion because he couldn't have done it without friends. He made allies with gladiators from other ludi, gained his brothers' trust, and his dominus's favor without inspiring hate from others. He has friends within the barracks of every ludus, at the tables of lords, and, some say, even the ear of the king." Auron paused. "Well, the old king. Point is, should you regain the title of Champion—"

"Regain? Who took my—"

"Who do you think?" Auron asked. "Listen to me, Fenyx. Continue down this path, Champion or not, your life will be fleeting. Without the love of your brothers, who will defend your back?" Auron clapped Fenyx on his left shoulder. "You're not alone, Fenyx. At least, you don't have to be."

Fenyx stewed in silence. *Alone.* Even within a brotherhood, Fenyx had never welcomed anyone but Auron within arm's distance. *Since my village burned, since my enslavement, I've always been alone. But I wasn't when Stegavax tried to kill me.*

"You're right," Fenyx said. "I will become the Champion you believe I can be."

Auron nodded, giving Fenyx's shoulder a squeeze. "I'll speak with the medicus about your release." He strode to the other end of the medicus's chambers, where the stooped old man trifled about.

Though they were in the same room, Fenyx couldn't hear their quiet conversation across the quarters. Sitting on the edge of his cot, Fenyx stared at Stegavax lying on the cot beside him, motionless—at death's door.

I could kill him right now and put an end to one of my enemies.

It'd be as easy as clamping a hand over Stegavax's nose and mouth. There was no fight left in Stegavax, and the medicus would believe he succumbed to his wounds. It would only take a moment. Fenyx glanced to the other side of the chambers where Auron exchanged whispers with the medicus. Obscured in dim candlelight, they wouldn't see.

No one would ever know.

Fenyx lifted his hand towards Stegavax's face.

What would have happened if Stegavax woke first? He wouldn't have hesitated to end my life. If I walk away, Stegavax might die of his injuries. But should he survive, how long before he makes another attempt on my life?

Fenyx's hand hovered over Stegavax's mouth. He could feel the slow warmth of life exhaling from his nostrils. It would be so easy.

"*Do it!*" a voice inside him shouted. "*Kill him.*"

Then Odetta's voice filled his head. *"Keep him safe."*

His hand shook above Stegavax's mouth. Auron and the medicus remained engaged in hushed conversation, oblivious to Fenyx.

"How one earns respect is just as important as what one does with it." Auron's voice joined the conflict in his mind.

Fenyx lowered his hand to his side. *I can't do it.*

Killing Stegavax here would be the furthest thing from honor. If anyone found out, people would spit after saying his name. Auron would never forgive him.

Could I even forgive myself?

A memory of his mother's touch returned to him. After a brawl with another boy in the village, his mother rubbed the tender and swollen rim of his eye, white mist trailing from her fingers. *"We fight a different kind of battle, Fenyx."*

Fenyx took a deep breath. Hovering both hands over Stegavax's wound, he used his body to block Auron and the medicus's line of sight. He envisioned the corruption in Stegavax's blood fading, his torn flesh restitching. Preparing to endure the pain he had inflicted upon Stegavax in the Kings' Day Games, he channeled white mist into the man who tried to kill him.

Curling tendrils flowed from fingertips to bandages and the wounds beneath. Fenyx hadn't used his healing abilities in years. It surprised him he could summon the energy to do so, but the pain he absorbed in balancing the scales blinded him. He bit his lip.

"I long to see your blood upon the sands," Fenyx whispered. "Yet your life is not mine to take." Once he'd done enough to aid without attracting too much attention, he pulled his hands away. He didn't heal every wound, but Stegavax would survive.

The room spun from the exertion of using his healing magic. Fenyx lay back on his own cot. *This will pass,* he told himself. *And I will become the honorable Champion Auron has always wished me to be.* He breathed deeply, closing his eyes and contenting himself that death would not be receiving Fenyx or Stegavax. Not yet at least.

CHAPTER 54

Black and White

Nallia VI

Stockhelm

"Nallia?" Damascus's black brows narrowed over his golden eyes. A gentle breeze swept her hair across her face, giving her an excuse to look away from his stare.

"I'm listening."

She hadn't been, but Damascus continued anyway. Sitting on the balcony watching the sun die in a fiery glow on the horizon, she couldn't help but think of how Zephyrus turned the candlelight into a blaze.

The sun fell beyond the Hylan mountains. The purples of twilight consumed the oranges of day—and likewise, Damascus smothered the light of her hope.

"The mages must be leading the Uprising," Damascus said.

Damascus arrived at the Cassius villa that morning with Markus, the queen, and their retinue for her father's coronation as the Chancellor of Stockhelm. Nallia and her parents were among the first to recover from the aftermath of the electrocution. They were far enough away from the epicenter of the attack to not suffer lasting effects, but in the few days between their return and Damascus's arrival in Stockhelm, much had changed.

The mages murdered King Varros. The court jailed Laeden for conspiring with the Uprising. And Damascus was crowned King of New Rheynia.

"The Sentinels must be repurposed," Damascus said. "Together, your brother and father will lead the Sentinels to root out any other mages and bring them to justice."

"Magic is a tool," Zephyrus had said. *"It's up to the wielder to decide how it is used."*

He was right. She hadn't visited Zephyrus since the attack. After watching him fight to survive against six gladiators, she couldn't stomach her guilt whenever she thought of him. She feared the Revivalists would make another attempt on his life after Lenox gave him the broken sword. She sent Nortus to check in on him, but there was little else she could do.

Damascus wants people like Zephyrus 'brought to justice,' like he did something wrong.

"Nallia, did you hear me?" Damascus asked, his voice tight. "Are you listening?"

Nallia snapped from her reverie. "Apologies, my prince, I—"

"My king. Apologies, my king." Damascus rested his face in his hands. His fingers dragged down his cheeks, stretching the skin. "It is I who should apologize. Surely you care not about such matters."

"Please, my king. You have my undivided attention." She gave him her best smile, but as much as she tried, she couldn't listen to her betrothed. His provincial outlook, specifically as it pertained to faith, grated on her.

He wouldn't demand the murder of children in Klaytos, would he?

"In other news," Damascus said, "we will be wed a week after the New Rheynian Games. Now that I am king, Mother says it's imperative I have an heir. If my Uncle Damascus had fathered an heir, the throne never would have passed to my father or me."

Nallia winced. *He speaks of genocide and children without a breath between.* "Surely you can be more gallant when we speak of making a son?" she teased, hoping he was still the man she thought.

Damascus huffed. "Apologies, my lady. I didn't intend for it to sound so..."

"Duteous?"

"I suppose that would be the word."

A long pause hung between them. She couldn't look at him. Things used to make sense. Everyone played a role in the Facets of Perfection. Nallia's role was simple: take care of those beneath her roof and develop gladiators to inspire the people. But soon she would be queen. The responsibility, although overwhelming, wasn't what bothered her.

Do I still believe in the Facets of Perfection, or even Valencianism?

At the cost of extinguishing magic from the world, she wasn't sure. She rubbed the elbow Zephyrus healed.

Damascus neared, wrapping his arm about her shoulder. "I know you're scared, but I promise you, you're safe."

Nallia contorted her brow. "How can I be safe? Nobody is safe. The streets will be littered with violence. You've all but endorsed the Revivalists!"

Damascus cleared his throat but had the grace to hold his tongue.

"Apologies, I…"

"It's fine," Damascus said, despite the tension in his jaw. "I understand why you're upset. Believe me, going against my father's wishes hasn't been easy, but they killed him. Why should I waste resources protecting the people who ought to be tried for regicide?"

Damascus's embrace sent shivers down her neck.

Like every Celestic in New Rheynia is to blame for your father's death?

She squirmed away from his touch to pace the balcony. "I understand you wanting to find the mages who killed your father, but do you not see a difference between hunting down two murderers and declaring genocide?"

Lips pursed in a tight line, his golden eyes burned like two suns ready to implode.

Nallia refused to shrink beneath his gaze. "Do you believe all magic is evil?" She rubbed her elbow. "Aquarius be patient, Incinerae be kind, and please, Phaebia forgive me, but do you truly believe the world to be so black and white?" Her heart pounded in her chest.

Damascus's pointed chin beard bristled. "The Six are merciful, but they are not without their limits. Our ancestors lost their home." His voice came in tight trembles, as if he couldn't believe he had to explain himself.

"The Six brought destruction down on us for the worship of false Gods, yet they gave us the opportunity to start anew, here in New Rheynia. How would they embrace us if we fell victim to the same mistakes of our ancestors? Would history not be doomed to repeat itself? Nallia, I can't allow that to happen. The mages have tremendous power, I won't deny—but they don't know Valencia's retribution for their use of it."

Damascus wanted Nallia to open her eyes and see the light which must have seemed so clear to him. But she didn't believe in his fears. She saw the magic with her own eyes—the destruction it was capable of, but also the life it could restore.

The Six delivered us here, but were we meant to come as conquerors?

She examined him, cradling his cheek within her palm in search of a soft spot in his heart—an opening through which she could speak to the prince she loved and not the king he'd become. No opening revealed itself.

"I must remove the few to protect the many," Damascus said. "Otherwise, my father will not be the last of their victims."

Nallia took a deep breath. Damascus was committed to the safety of his people. He wasn't good or evil. He did what *he* thought was right. *But he's wrong.*

She nodded in acceptance of his speech despite disagreeing. She conceded, but the time would come again where she would need to be more assertive if she hoped for him to see things differently.

It wasn't until later, during dinner, that she realized she might be too late.

"Tell me, my king," her father said, slicing his roast boar. "How am I to serve you? I imagine the Sentinels have, well…" He placed his fork in his mouth to allow himself a moment to figure out how best to proceed, but Damascus beat him to it.

"I thank you for your hospitality. It's under terrible duress that I must bear my father's responsibilities. I hope you will serve me as well as you would have served him."

"It would be my honor," her father said with his most obsequious grin.

"If I may," the queen said. "We must begin to learn who these practicing Celestics are and see if they have ties to the mages. They may be our best insight towards toppling the Uprising. Perhaps it would be best to start small, say here—in your own ludus."

Nallia's throat constricted, but she kept a placid demeanor.

"Consider it done," her father said. "I will begin first thing in the morning to ensure there is no disruption for the coronation ceremony in the afternoon."

Damascus put down his fork and knife. "Search for false idols, prayers, or anything that could be linked to Celestia, the mages, the Uprising—anything. I am sure many of your slaves have such things stowed away."

Her father began to deny it, but Damascus held up a silencing hand.

"I do not doubt your faith or the rules you have in place, but it wouldn't be fitting if a practicing Celestic were to turn up beneath the chancellor's roof. If anyone is found to be in possession of such blasphemous material, give them the opportunity to swear their allegiance to the merciful Six." Damascus smiled before returning to his meal.

Nallia looked at Markus, hoping he would speak up, but he said nothing, the flesh around his knuckles as white as the Silver Summits.

Damascus continued. "If any provide trouble, see them punished until their Judges answer them."

Nallia shuffled her feet beneath her chair. *Oh, Damascus. What have you become?*

"Wasn't one of your slaves found at that dilapidated Celestic temple?" the queen asked. "The one who once served Laeden?"

Her father swallowed a half-chewed morsel of boar. "Yes, my queen, you speak of Zephyrus. He has since renounced the Judges, sworn allegiance to the Six, and become Champion of this house."

The queen raised an eyebrow. "Perhaps begin with him. We would not want the Champion to be of ill repute."

Nallia's fork slipped from her meat and scraped across her plate. She winced at the metal's screech and offered her apologies to the rest of the table.

Once the attention was off her, her thoughts turned to Zephyrus. Her entire life, she did what was expected, what was best for her family. She did so never questioning what or why, but Zephyrus made her realize the type of bystanding monster she'd become.

Magic wasn't evil. And she would not stand idly by while evil measures were taken to eradicate it. Her heart sank into her stomach.

I don't want to let Zephyrus go, but he is in even more danger now. It's bad enough that the Revivalists are after him, but if he were discovered as a Celestic mage…

She rubbed her elbow.

I must warn Zephyrus.

CHAPTER 55

IDOLS

Fenyx VIII

Stockhelm

Fenyx woke long before dawn. Now that his wounds had healed, he was eager to get back to training. If not for Zephyrus, he would still be in the medicus's chambers—or worse. But he had yet to thank him, and not for a lack of trying; Zephyrus had barely stepped foot beyond the Champion's cell since Fenyx's return. He hoped Zephyrus would stay another day. His sloth would only give Fenyx more opportunities to win back his mantle.

However, as dawn rose, instead of Auron rousing the gladiators from their rest, the Sentinel guards greeted them with the sun.

"Wake up!" shouted a Sentinel, banging the hilt of his sword on his shield. "Step back. Face the wall."

The Sentinel forced Auron to open the cells. Once he opened the first cell, two Sentinels rushed in. Fenyx couldn't see, but he heard Aelixo resisting them.

"Hands on the wall!"

A short whip snapped, unlike Auron's, and Aelixo groaned.

"I won't tell you again!"

They opened the next cell, and two more rushed in. They tore the cell apart, inspecting the cot, the walls, the corners.

Fenyx's heart fell to his stomach.

Auron was right.

Last night, Auron had encouraged all the gladiators to discard any idols, scales of balance, or possessions related to Celestia.

"This is your last chance," a Sentinel shouted. "Cast aside your false Gods or we'll take them from you. If you give them to us, no one'll get hurt. But if we have to find them…"

They forced Zephyrus to exit the Champion's cell as a team of four men entered.

"Is that necessary?" Markus, the son of the dominus, demanded of a Sentinel inspecting Zephyrus's sublingaria with his blade. "I doubt he has anything hidden in there besides what one might expect beneath a man's smallclothes. Blades away."

Fenyx walked over to the wall of his cell, placing his hands on the cool stone. His burns prickled as a chill ran down his back.

Mine are well hidden. They won't find anything. Just do what they say.

The Sentinels approached Fenyx's cell. The door was flung open, and Fenyx closed his eyes. *Be still.* Each moment felt like an eternity as the Sentinels searched Fenyx's quarters. They inspected every crack in the stone walls.

"All clear," one said to the other.

Fenyx released his held breath.

As the Sentinels made their way out, one of their feet scuffed the loose stone in the floor.

"What's this, eh?" the Sentinel said. He knelt to examine the stone.

Dread coiled around Fenyx's chest like a strangling serpent. He turned to face the Sentinels.

"Ay! Hands on the wall!" The other Sentinel pointed his many-tailed whip at Fenyx.

"Found something!" The Sentinel tore the loose stone free of the floor to find the carved idols within the hollowed rock. "Think you're clever, eh?"

The child who first came to the barracks with nothing but his idols and his hopes of glory died within Fenyx.

Judges, why?

More Sentinels rushed into his cell.

The dominus's son, Markus, entered last. "Give up the idols and profess your faith to the Six." He held out his hands to keep the other Sentinels back. "Do this and you won't be harmed."

Fenyx tried to remember the sound of his mother's voice, the embrace of his father—but they slipped away like water through his fingers as he tried to gather the memories. He was four or five years old, sleeping between his parents, when they awoke to screams. His father jumped to his feet and ran outside, his mother close behind.

"Stay here!" she said to Fenyx. "Hide!"

Fenyx hid, but eventually the deer-hide tent began to glow a bright orange. A putrid smell and an unreal heat bore down on him. Fenyx draped the wolfskin blanket over him and peeked outside as a slaver ran by, dragging a screaming child by the hair. Fenyx retreated into the burning tent, tears streaming down his cheeks.

The tent filled with thick black smoke. Heat gripped him in a choke-hold. Boiling oil burned through the deer hide tent—a few drips at first, but then it poured in, sliding down Fenyx's face.

Fenyx cried out in agony and ran, but in his panic, he knocked into one of the support posts. In a rush of pain and flame, the tent caved in, engulfing him in an inferno. He scrambled from the tent's remains and dove into the sand, attempting to smother the flames, but the oil continued to burn. He thrashed about until the flames died and his fatigue overtook his agony.

He awoke to more screams. The smell of his own charred flesh made him throw up, but the sight before him was more sickening; they razed half the village to the ground.

"Mother! Father!" He prayed for them to come embrace him, tell him everything would be fine. That they were safe now and the bad men wouldn't hurt them anymore. But that was just the wishes of a child.

Fenyx found his father lying on the ground, a spear through his belly. His mother, drowned in a pool of her own blood, her throat slit to the bone. Dead. Even if he had been there with them, he couldn't have healed them through such injuries.

Fenyx took the small leather pouch from his mother's hip. Inside were his father's carvings of the three Judges. They hadn't protected them, but they were the last things he had of his parents.

"You won't be needing these anymore," the Sentinel said, examining Fenyx's idols.

"Profess your faith for the Six," Markus said again. "No one needs to get hurt."

Fenyx looked to Auron for aid, but the doctore only nodded.

This can't be the way of things. "No!" Fenyx said, "I will not."

Something struck Fenyx in the side of his head. The world went black halfway through his collapse to the ground.

In and out of consciousness, Fenyx was shackled, dragged, and bound to the palus out in the training square. Too dazed to stand without the support of his chains, he rested his head against the wooden post.

"Embrace the Six," the Sentinel said, unfurling a whip with multiple strips of knotted leather.

Fenyx had endured Auron's discipline before. He would not denounce the Judges nor profess faith in their Gods. "No."

The whip cracked, and pain seared like hot irons across his back. Fenyx screamed, despite himself. He felt as if he'd been whipped half a dozen times in one lash. Fenyx grit his teeth. His bound hands curled into fists.

Crack!

The whip ripped across his back. It burned as if he were ensnared in the oil-soaked tent all over again. Again and again, the whip rose and fell. Each time Fenyx promised himself he wouldn't scream, but he did. He lost count after the twentieth lash, blinded by pain, rage, and every injustice he ever suffered.

When will they stop? When will it end? Judges, what must I do to regain your favor?

He clenched his fists into balls of hopeless hatred.

"Good," a voice said in his head. *"Let your anger temper you into fine steel."*

Fenyx didn't know what he was hearing, but he could no longer stand. He hung limp from where his wrists were shackled to the palus.

"Enough," Dominus said from the balcony. "Leave him there to find his faith in the Six."

Fenyx cried. Perhaps from the pain, the loss of his idols, or even in relief that the lashes were over—but he did not find the Six as he hung from the palus, nor during the coronation ceremony. Even after the sun set behind the Hylan mountains, Fenyx found nothing but fury.

Overhead, the angry orange sky gave way to purple, and night settled over Stockhelm. Fenyx waited for the nightly rains, but for the first time in his life, they did not come.

CHAPTER 56

FAMILY, FAITH, FUTURE

Danella VIII

Stockhelm

Danella hadn't been eager to travel to Stockhelm in light of recent events, but she knew better than most. Now was the time to be bold. She needed Cassius's support against the Uprising, and until Brusos's plans could be made reality, she would have to settle for Cassius. If he could at least threaten the Uprising to be more cautious, it would buy her Revivalists time to find Varros—dead or alive.

Now that her forged letter placed Damascus on the throne, she would have a difficult time explaining if Varros happened to return. Part of her held out hope he still lived. That he might free himself and return to her.

Maybe now he'll understand what I've been saying and do the Gods' will.

But with each passing day, the odds of that possibility diminished.

Despite the commotion, Danella could not rid herself of Iylea's voice in her head. Even after Aemos Horne painted the throne room with her blood, her words still rang in Danella's ears. The way Laeden glared at Damascus made her shudder.

"Brother will fight brother."

Her only path was forward. She plotted with Aemos and Aelon to discredit Laeden's standing within Damascus's eyes. In the eyes of the law, she had the three required witnesses to ensure Laeden would no longer be a problem. With their oathbound testimonies, the trial would be an open-and-shut case, but that didn't please everyone.

Markus accompanied their trip to Stockhelm to see his father's coronation, but he remained quiet, distant, and unreadable. She didn't expect someone like Markus to understand what had happened, or why it needed to happen as it did, but Laeden needed to be taken out of the picture. If Laeden put the idea of diplomacy in Damascus's head, the Uprising would continue to grow, the mages of Celestia would become a greater threat, and the Gods would unleash their wrath upon the lands just as they had back in Rheynia.

Earl Cassius welcomed them, in full support of Damascus's decrees, upon their arrival at the ludus. But the next morning after discovering one of his top gladiators with idols of the Judges, he stopped his whipping as if his punishment was for simple insubordination. Danella wanted the slave hung by the thumbs and whipped until he renounced the Judges and took an oath to Valencianism. But Cassius sent the slave to the medicus after a few lashes and some time chained to a post. For all the fervor he spoke of last night, Chancellor Cassius was soft.

Soft men will not save us from the Gods' wrath.

To her disappointment, Zephyrus, the supposed Prophet of Celestia, had no attachments to the Judges. Danella found it difficult to believe that out of nearly twenty gladiators, only one had ties to Celestia. However, if Zephyrus actually did renounce the Judges and swear an oath to the Six, perhaps she could make an example of him—from the bowels of Tharseo's Bastion to a Champion of Valencia.

At this point, he might be of more use to me alive.

But Zephyrus wasn't her only concern beneath Cassius's roof. Damascus's impressionable mind was susceptible to manipulation, and Nallia needed to be a positive influence, always guiding him back to the Six. Prior to the coronation, Danella went out of her way to speak with Nallia, to give her a nudge in the proper direction.

"You are strong," Danella had said, hoping to create a self-fulfilling prophecy. "I can see it in your eyes. My son needs that strength. Behind every powerful man is a strong woman who got him there."

"Thank you, my queen," Nallia said.

Danella looked down at the floor, letting her mask develop a tear at the corner of her eye. "I am queen no longer… because I did not have the strength or the wisdom to guide my husband. If only I spoke sense to him. If the mage was executed, perhaps my Varros would still be among us."

"King Varros was a good man and a wise king," Nallia said, embracing both of Danella's hands in her own. "He stood up for what he believed in, against terrible adversity. He sought to protect people. He embodied strength and determination in his quest to create more inclusive citizenship. A unified society is a beautiful one."

"Those are five of the six Facets," Danella said. "Yet the absence of faith led to his downfall. We weren't alive during the disasters of Rheynia, but we are not so far removed to have forgotten what the Gods do when their worship is threatened by lesser deities.

"Varros's death is our punishment for our lack of faith. He believed he knew better than the Gods, and we went away from the scripture. 'We must remain favorable in the eyes of the Gods by spreading the Facets of Perfection. It's our duty to guide those in squalor towards the righteous path.' How far we have strayed." Danella shook her head. "I failed my husband."

Danella slipped away from Nallia's grip. "My wish for you is to never know this pain. To stand by your husband, support him in his causes, and guide him back to scripture if he strays from the Gods' path." Her mask began to break, and real tears fell from her eyes. "I have sacrificed much, but that is what it means to rule."

My poor Varros.

Danella wiped her eyes. "Family, faith, and future, those are the Drake words, but the three are difficult to honor, when in supporting one, you may end up failing another. Apologies, I hadn't intended to unburden such sentiments on you, but one day soon, you will be queen, and his yokes will become yours. He will become your family—even more so than your own blood. Your faith will guide you both as you rule. And the future may hinge on every choice you make."

Her words were true and earnest. Danella couldn't remember the last time she spoke with so much candor. She only hoped Nallia would accept, aid Damascus in his responsibilities, and be the queen her father's kingdom needed.

Yet only a few hours later, following the ceremony, Damascus came to Danella in her chambers of the Cassius villa.

"What is it, my king?" Danella asked.

His eyes remained on the floor, looking every bit the boy and not the mighty king she needed him to be. "Nallia suggested having the inquisition end after our wedding. If we spill enough Celestic blood or bring enough to follow the Six, could our matrimony commence a period of peace and stabilization?"

He desired peace—she could see it in his face. Everyone desired peace, but no one was willing to do what it took to secure it. Varros's weakness shone in his eyes.

Nallia's weakness.

Danella's mask smiled, concealing the anger building beneath. "She is a wise woman." *And she'll be the end of us all.* "I suppose your wedding could be as good a time as any, yet we will need to consult the Gods."

Damascus's raised shoulders slackened as he let out a deep breath. With his ease, Danella reaccepted the burden she'd only just shared with him.

I'm not done. It must be me, and me alone. Nallia is no longer a potential ally, but an adversary. There is only one way to spur Damascus to do the Gods' will: Nallia must perish at the hands of the mages.

Thoughts raced through her mind until an idea formed.

"We will have an omenation then," Damascus said, a smile tugging at the corner of his lip. He embraced her. "This week would have been impossible without you."

Danella hugged her son. "I love you."

Yet even as she said the words, she plotted to kill his betrothed. It could be done, and she knew just how to do it. He would never forgive her if he found out, but he would never know.

My country needs me, and I will deliver—regardless of the cost.

"Family, faith, future."

She held him, afraid to let go. But he released her and strode over to the windows. The skies were an ominous black, separated by glowing orbs of light.

Has there ever been such a starry night?

"Mother," Damascus said. "Shouldn't the nightly rains have started by now?"

Danella followed him to the window to inspect the skyline. No thunder rumbled in the distance, no clouds stretched across the horizon—no threat of rain at all.

It's already happening, she thought. *The Gods' wrath is beginning.*

CHAPTER 57

Brothers in Freedom

Zephyrus XVII

Stockhelm

"Attend!" Doctore shouted, interrupting the sparring gladiators. They broke apart and stood in formation. All but Fenyx, of course. "The New Rheynian Games fast approach," Doctore said. "Since the Kings' Day Games finished absent a Champion…" He glared at Stegavax. "We must restore honor to this house.

"Eight will compete upon the pebbles of the Chariot's Arena, each to fight the gladiators of Kaelus and Targarus of equal seed. Our eighth will fight their eighths, our seventh will fight their sevenths, and so on. Those who are victorious in their match earn a point. The victor of the Primus is awarded two points. The house with the most points after all eight have fought wins. If Valencia smiles upon us, perhaps recent disgraces can be redeemed. For now, rest. I will announce the seeding at the conclusion of today's training." Doctore dismissed them for lunch, and so began the competition to get to the bowl of gruel first.

"If Valencia smiles upon us…" Zephyrus scoffed.

With Stegavax finally healthy, and no one clinging to life in the medicus's chambers, the gladiators of House Cassius were the healthiest they'd been since Zephyrus's arrival—*no thanks to the Gods of Valencia.* Yet Fenyx was back there once again. The wounds he suffered weren't fatal, but they would leave worse scars than those he suffered in the Kings' Day Games.

Zephyrus tried to warn everyone after Vykinallia's bodyslave, Odetta, alerted him of the impending search. Zephyrus told Doctore, and he gathered the idols, symbols, and texts from more than half the men. Even Doctore possessed idols, but they were tossed over the cliff along with everyone else's. Everyone but Fenyx relinquished their possessions, and no one would soon forget what happened to him.

If the Gods bore witness to what happened and did nothing, they were more evil than King Damascus.

Amidst such thoughts, food nor rankings offered any reprieve. Zephyrus had run out of time. Hunted by the Revivalists, unwelcomed by the gladiators, and no longer within Laeden's good graces, Zephyrus was on his own. Even with Lenox cast out of House Cassius, he still nearly managed to get Zephyrus killed.

Another broken sword…

Besides Lenox, Zephyrus didn't think he'd be able to lift steel against another slave again. He wanted to be patient. He wanted to spare the lives of the slaves fighting against him. But he couldn't. He killed to survive, as Vykannis had commanded. He told himself it was for the greater good, but he didn't believe it.

Still alive, Patrus… but did I choose the path of the Harbinger to do so? Is there any redemption after what I've done?

His dreams had become nothing but nightmares since the Kings' Day Games. He kept seeing the faces of the slaves he slew and his mother begging him to listen to her. But he wasn't interested in what she had to say. Maybe she could have helped the king's emissary, but Zephyrus let that potential fate go when he dropped the scroll at Laeden's feet. He gave up one possible future to set his foot on the path Patrus left off: freeing the slaves.

One dream, however, gave him inspiration. Master Aikous taught him, Ceres, and Sybex how to pick a lock using force magic. Though Ceres could move mountains with his telekinetic strength, he lacked the control and dexterity to move the pins into position. Sybex, while brilliant with elemental magic, couldn't harness force or manipulation magic. But Zephyrus managed to open every lock Aikous put before him.

Having such an ability was only as useful as the people willing to follow. Right now, he didn't even think Jecht and Cerik would go with him. Things were different within the barracks ever since Carsos and Ixion were killed because of his involvement with Vykinallia. Although Jecht and Cerik didn't say or do anything outright, they seemed to hold him at a distance.

Zephyrus followed the other gladiators to the shaded break area, keeping a respectful distance behind Jecht and Cerik.

At least they still let me sit with them, even if they barely speak to me.

"I hate these exhibition fights," Jecht said, fawning over his wounds from the coronation ceremony. "I don't get a glimpse of steel on skin when it's a matter of life and death, but these exhibition games…" He rolled his eyes. "At Targarus's ludus, we were taught to fight and kill, not play pretend. But here, because we must put on a farce for the crowd, I am to suffer the bumps and bruises of a lesser gladiator."

"I assume I'm of the lesser stock then?" Cerik asked, referencing his bandaged foot.

After sustaining an injury during the Kings' Day Games, Cerik had returned to training, but still walked with a limp.

"You know what I mean," Jecht said, but Cerik shoved Jecht's bruised shoulder.

"Ow!" Jecht grimaced. "No, not you."

"That's what I thought." Cerik sat down beside Jecht and across from Zephyrus, waiting for the gruel line to shorten. Conversation shifted to the impending announcement of the rankings, but Zephyrus had no ear for it.

If they knew a life before their bondage, they would not be so consumed with the trivial glories of their enslavement. I must convince them of the righteous path, but how?

Stegavax and Vossler devoured their gruel a few tables down, but they would sooner step into the Stormburn geyser than join Zephyrus. Shagren,

Aelixo, and Wardon whispered amongst themselves, undoubtedly creating their own rankings. Similarly, they were more likely to listen to a Lover's Dream's thorns than to Zephyrus.

Zephyrus continued to scan the shaded area adjacent to the training square, but he'd done a poor job of making friends since his arrival. His eyes fixed on Doctore standing in the shade beneath the water well's awning.

If I could convince Doctore, the others would follow him. He might be my only hope.

Zephyrus pressed his hands into the wooden table and stood. Jecht and Cerik's eyes followed him, but neither spoke.

He strode over to the water well. "Doctore, might I have a word?"

Doctore didn't look up from the well. "You will find out your ranking with the others." He dipped his cup back into the water and refilled.

"That's not why I've come."

"Why then?" Doctore asked, leaning back against the well, lifting his cup to his lips.

Zephyrus glanced side to side to make sure no surrounding guards or Sentinels could hear. "I don't know what to make of yesterday's events. The search and seizure of our idols, the unjust punishments doled out to the gladiators, the absence of rain. Any and all are more pressing than the seeding of a game."

Doctore smirked, putting his cup down. "That's where you're wrong. Your mind should be set to the coming match. The days will evaporate quickly. Your time will soon be upon you."

Zephyrus wouldn't be dismissed. If he garnered Doctore's support, the other gladiators would follow him, regardless of his past deeds or prophecies. Together, they could rebel from their masters. He needed to appeal to his beliefs.

"You relinquished your own Celestic possessions. You hold the Judges in your heart as well as anyone."

"Shush! Would you have us both whipped?" Doctore scanned the training square to make certain no one heard. He leaned closer and whispered,

"This isn't the first purge of mages, nor the first time Celestics were persecuted. This type of talk, this way of thinking, this *Uprising*—there's only one way for it to end: it'll be the Haunted Hollow all over again."

Zephyrus pursed his lips. *Silence will not serve me. I must convince him.* "How bad must things get before the reward of freedom outweighs the risk of seizing it?"

Doctore set his cup down on the lip of the watering well. "You think this life we have is cruel, but it's a kindness compared to how much worse it can get. Cassius may not be Invinius Auros, but he provides for us and rewards prowess."

Auros. The dominus who freed his slaves, Patrus among them.

"You have the skills to become Champion," Doctore said. "Not only of this house, but all of New Rheynia. Focus on your training. Live in glory with a roof over your head and food in your belly. You could do much worse. Turn from this path, this siren song the Uprising whispers to you. Embrace your fate here and *live*."

Live. Patrus's last word. Surrounded by armed slavers, Patrus's command saved Zephyrus's life, but now Doctore's same advice was a death sentence.

"You have taught me to survive, but what happens when survival isn't enough? Surviving is *not* living. Living is the freedom to worship, the freedom to speak of my beliefs—to make my own choices of *where* I have a roof over my head and *what* I put in my belly. I'm one of the Three. A Prophet of the Return. I will not be another tool, bowing and scraping for the Rheynians while others are fighting for *our* freedom."

Doctore's nostrils flared. His dark eyes narrowed into slivers.

It wasn't enough. Be bolder. Zephyrus leaned closer. "Auron, this life has more for us than enslavement. Join me. Fight with me. Free our peop—"

"You are to be Champion of this house," Doctore growled. "The first seed in the Primus of the New Rheynian Games. Embrace your fate, Zephyrus, not as a Prophet of the Return, but as a Champion. You can accomplish great things. Do not cast your life to the fire."

"But I'll never be free."

"You can earn your freedom," Doctore said. "The absence of rain proves anything is possible. I've lived in Stockhelm my entire life. Never has a night passed without the coming of rain. *Anything* is possible."

"Anything..." Zephyrus agreed. "Anything is possible for those who believe. I believe in a world where you and I embrace as free men who don't have to *earn* our freedom. Where we speak of the Judges we praise openly, without fear. I'm willing to fight for that belief."

Doctore bit his lip and furled his brow, but Zephyrus couldn't back down. If he were to lead a rebellion, it would start here. And if Doctore joined him, the men would follow.

"Auron, I know what you believe in. But are you willing to fight for it?"

Doctore stepped up to Zephyrus, his glare smoldering. Close enough that Zephyrus could feel the heat of his breath, he spoke through bared teeth. "You will walk away, and I will pretend this conversation never happened. But if you speak of freedom, attempt to rouse the others in your mischief, or question my honor again..." He shook his head. "Flee from sight."

Heat rose to Zephyrus's temples as he swallowed his failure. Laeden wanted Zephyrus to become a member of the Sentinels and abandon his people. Doctore wanted Zephyrus to become a dutiful gladiator who accepted undeserved abuse at every turn. Vykinallia wanted her Celestic mage gladiator to conquer the arena.

I am alone. I must forge my own way.

"You disappoint me, Doctore." Zephyrus turned his back and spat in the sand.

Returning to the shade, he collected his bowl of gruel and sat with Jecht and Cerik. Spooning the lukewarm sludge into his mouth, he didn't want to listen to talks of rankings, seedings, and matchups.

I must be free, and I will take as many as I can with me.

With the threat of the Revivalists and the impending New Rheynian Games, he could stay here no longer. He couldn't promise anyone safe passage, especially with the increased number of guards and Sentinels left in the new king's wake, but he needed to try. People would die but they would do so in the quest for freedom, not for entertainment.

Patrus's voice sang the Rebels' Rhyme in his head; Zephyrus began to hum as he twisted his spoon through his bowl of gruel. Those who knew it would approach him or ignore him. Those who didn't would think nothing of it. He wouldn't speak of freedom or rebellion as Doctore warned against. He would just hum and let fate take care of the rest.

Hope…

Zephyrus's throat resonated with the melancholic tones of the Rebels' Rhyme Patrus had taught him—the song of freedom, redemption, and the Return of the Judges. Zephyrus closed his eyes and let the melody consume him.

Faith…

Visions of loss, death, and Rheynian cruelty flashed before him. He couldn't succumb to that. He needed to continue moving forward regardless of the path before him.

Trust…

He finished the song and looked up from his bowl to find Jecht and Cerik staring at him. Zephyrus set his spoon down. Cerik's eyes darted side to side, and Jecht leaned in.

"Did you hear what I heard?" Jecht asked Cerik.

"Aye," Cerik said, his face drawn as if he'd seen a ghost.

Jecht's eyes narrowed, the scar across his face wrinkling. "Is this some game you're playing at?"

"No game," Zephyrus said.

Cerik raised an eyebrow. "Are you a spy or one of us?"

"You owe us the truth," Jecht said.

Zephyrus closed his eyes. "You're right. I haven't been honest. I've been an organization's emissary, a prince's spy, and I still have no idea how to be who I'm supposed to be, but you both have been true friends to me. Friends I never deserved." He leaned closer. "I thought I could tell my clever lies and escape with my freedom, but all my machinations have failed because my aims were too low. However, I can no longer remain here in bondage. I leave to join the Uprising."

Jecht guffawed.

Cerik examined Zephyrus. "What you're considering is madness. We'll be killed if they even hear us speaking of this, and there are more eyes and ears now than ever. You'll never make it out of here."

"The risk is great," Zephyrus said, "but I've run out of time. You two have been brothers to me. I ask nothing of you, but I beg you to consider joining me. I don't know if I'm destined to be the Wielder, the Harbinger, or nothing at all—but I will not remain here."

"Join you?" Jecht laughed. "Now? You crazy bastard." A grin stretched across his face, distorting his scar. "Now, Cerik. Of all times, now."

"Regardless of timing," Cerik said, "how do we know we can trust you? Prophecies aside, we need proof of whose side you're on."

Zephyrus smiled. If Jecht and Cerik came with him, all of this would have been worth it. Although he hoped to free all of Cassius's slaves from bondage, to free two from a life of slavery was worth his sacrifices. He would give them the full truth and let them decide their fate.

"You want proof?" Zephyrus reached under the table and extended his fingertips towards the wrapping of Cerik's wounded foot. He looked around to make sure no one could see beneath the table. Just as he'd done with Patrus in his dream, and Fenyx several times now, Zephyrus visualized the wounded flesh along Cerik's foot. Zephyrus's own foot began to ache as he balanced the scales. He grimaced, but the pain eventually subsided.

"Cerik, your foot seems to be faring better, does it not?"

Cerik screwed up his face. "It continues to heal, but…"

Zephyrus tapped his index finger on the wooden table. "Check your dressings."

Conspiratorially, Cerik did so, undoing the medicus's wrapping. "Burn me," Cerik whispered. As soon as Cerik saw his healed flesh, he rewrapped the bandages twice as fast.

"You're a…" Jecht looked side to side before mouthing the word *mage.* Zephyrus nodded. "You mad bastard."

Cerik's mouth moved, but his tongue remained silent.

"I suppose so," Zephyrus said. "But I have a plan, and I'll be getting out of here. Will you join me?"

CHAPTER 58

THE DIVINE REALM

Iylea III

Unknown

A sea of black threatened to drown her. Not like it had when she'd been thrown in the secret dungeons of Sentigard; this darkness was beyond the lack of sight, but an abyss. An absence of sight. Void of sound. She took in breath, but even her sense of smell failed her.

Where am I?

Iylea's head ached. She put her hands to her face, trying to recall her last memories as if she'd woken from one of her peculiar dreams, but when she did, her hands glowed a cerulean blue. She gasped, not comprehending what she was seeing.

Then it hit her. The flash of steel. Screams, high and shrill. Laeden's broken expression. A turbulence that seemed to rip her apart.

I am dead.

She searched the blackness, but it surrounded her in all directions. She cried into the void, but even her voice was soundless. Panic set her translucent hands trembling. The familiar pressure of a coming vision built behind her eyes, but that was the last of her concerns. Her heart raced within her chest as a cold dread pimpled the back of her neck with gooseflesh.

Even in death I am denied rest.

A white hole appeared in the abyss above her as if she were trapped at the bottom of a well. She reached for the light but found she could actually move upward. Like swimming to the surface of the pool she'd drowned in, she kicked and splashed, fighting for the freedom beyond the darkness. Despite her effort, the bright portal of her escape remained equally as far away. She fought the abyss until her legs were numb and her lungs wheezed, but still, the light was denied her.

Seeing no other option, she closed her eyes and submitted to the pressure from within, only this time she didn't just see into the window of the Gods—she entered it.

Standing in a massive circular foyer with a domed ceiling that stretched impossibly high, Iylea felt as if she had shrunk. Before her, cascading down the wall like a waterfall, a glowing liquid of bright cerulean, viridian, and lilac hues overflowed from one oblong pool to the next. As beautiful as any sight she'd ever seen, and as peaceful as any song she'd ever heard, the display left her in awe.

Beneath her feet, gleaming white tiles with intricately carved glyphs reflected her visage. No longer radiating a cerulean blue light, she was flesh and bone once again, dressed in a gown that would make the patricians of court quake with envy. Iylea didn't believe it.

This is Valencia.

Iylea spun, dwarfed by the grandeur of her surroundings. Behind her and across from the wall of the falls was a circular hole in the floor, wider than she was tall. Adjacent to it, constructed in a gold marbled ivory that matched the columns encircling the outskirts of the atrium, stood a crank. Iylea approached the crank and the glowing chain it held. The links, each as large as her head, were forged of a similar glowing substance as the glimmering liquid descending the wall behind her. Darker hues of purple, green, and blue rippled through the chain, but what caught her eye was what lay beyond.

Iylea neared the outer rim of the circular hole in the floor to follow the links in the chain as they descended to the world below.

Oceans crashed against mountains, winds blew clouds across the sky, and cities stood stark against the green fields of the land. Iylea's breath caught, identifying the Aquarian River that stretched from the Salmantic harbor to wrap around Sentigard.

How am I here? Why am I here?

Feeling a sudden spell of vertigo, Iylea backed away from the hole in the floor.

Voices in the distance drew her attention. Several rooms and hallways branched from the atrium, but Iylea slunk toward the voices. Taking cover behind a column nearest the open doorway the voices came from, she crept closer with a handmaiden's silence.

"Creator's wrath," said a singsong voice beyond the open door. "What do we do?"

Iylea approached the doorway and pressed her back to the edge. Holding her breath, she peeked into the room beyond. Two men and three women stood around a long rectangular table that seemed to be carved from a gargantuan crystal. Furrowed brows and tense shoulders indicated that Iylea arrived in the middle of an argument… *between the Gods of Valencia.*

Iylea felt like a child by comparison to the towering Gods around her, but that made it easier to remain hidden. If they noticed Iylea, they showed no sign of it.

"Thirteen of us," said the woman with the singsong voice. Long and slender, her fingers traced from her brow and down her onyx cheeks. Her long white hair seemed to blow in the breeze, despite the lack of a current. Sparks of electricity seemed to crackle with her every motion. Though the goddess did not appear anything like the depiction of any of the statues in the Royal Basilica, Iylea assumed—if she were one of the Six—she was Phaebia.

"Thirteen of us, gone," Phaebia said. "Only we remain."

"Why did he kill her?" said a large gruff man across from her. His muscled frame, the bracers on his forearms, and untamable black beard could only belong to Ferrocles.

Iylea held her breath. Visions were one thing, but to be in Valencia, to see the Gods face-to-face, was something else entirely. She wanted to run, to hide, but she was unable to move. She swallowed her fear, trying to piece together what she heard.

Thirteen gone…

"I don't believe Aquarius could help himself," said the other man beside Phaebia. Iylea had to adjust her vantage point to see around Ferrocles's bulk, but when she did, she almost staggered into the door.

Ashen skin. Red eyes.

The man from my visions.

"What do you mean, Hameryn?" Phaebia asked.

Hameryn? The red-eyed man is the Valencian God of Harmony?

His skin was cracked, unlike how she'd seen him in visions before. A red glow gleamed through his shattered skin like a candle in an intricate holder.

"Aquarius acquired the taste for divine blood," Hameryn said. "He killed her to absorb the power bestowed on her by the Creator."

Iylea didn't understand. *If Hameryn sent me the visions, then I'm not a seer of Celestia.*

She swallowed, examining the five Gods around the table—youthful Phaebia, matronly Moterra, beautiful Incinerae, burly Ferrocles, and the red-eyed Hameryn.

But who were the thirteen others, and who did Aquarius kill?

"He killed her just for power?" Incinerae stuttered, her voice crackling like a hearth.

"Just?" Hameryn hmphed. "With the addition of *just* Courianne's power, he could have come for you next, and nothing would have been able to stop him."

Incinerae shuddered.

Courianne? I've never heard of any such God before.

"But now—" Hameryn held up his cracked hands as they bled red light. "Aquarius's and Courianne's life-force flows through me. The Creator never intended us to hold such power. This could trigger the reckoning we've long feared."

Moterra leaned forward, pressing her hand into the crystal table. She appeared as if she were carved from a thick tree trunk. Bark formed a carapace armor over her chest and shoulders, and moss and leaves covered her body like clothing, but it was her glare that separated her from how the texts portrayed her.

Moterra spoke, her voice like a falling tree. "How is it Hameryn, our beacon of harmony, managed to defeat such an empowered and wrathful Aquarius?"

Phaebia, Ferrocles, and Incinerae glanced at Hameryn.

Hameryn lowered his chin, peering at Moterra with his browless red eyes. "Perhaps you doubt the lengths I would go to keep the peace among those who still believe in it. I did what I had to."

Only when Moterra averted her challenging gaze and placed her hands on her hips did Hameryn break his stare.

"You did the right thing," Incinerae said, crossing her slender igneous arms over her chest. "He could have picked us off one by one had you not stopped him."

"Perhaps," Hameryn said, "but Aquarius's death will not come without consequence. It will not rain, and the seas will remain treacherous for his passing."

"For how long?" Phaebia asked.

Hameryn shrugged. "Ask the Creator. It seems when one of us is killed, the mortal realm suffers. Remember Arcamedes and what happened to the beasts of the field? It answers some of the questions concerning the undying in Rheynia all these years. Perhaps Aquarius killed Neutreen back then as well?"

Iylea had never heard of Arcamedes before. *But Neutreen? Undead in Rheynia?* Iylea recalled the vision she'd received at Cassius's ludus—the tempest of screaming souls and the crowned man with the ghoulish grin and black veins slithering down his forehead.

The mortal world suffers when a God dies.

Iylea stifled a shiver.

The Disasters. Is it possible they had nothing to do with the Six's jealousy of Neutreen's worship? If that's the case, Celestics are being persecuted out of misguided theology!

Heat rose to her cheeks, and tears stung her eyes. The theological war that saw her father slain and her mother murdered, the treaty that followed—tearing Laeden from his mother—all of it was based on lies.

"I thought Neutreen abdicated her dominion," Ferrocles said as a question.

"That was her intent," Hameryn said, "but I didn't escort her to the Lost Plane myself. He could have killed her on her way and taken the Creator's power from her."

"Poor Neutreen," Incinerae said.

"If that's true, what of the others?" Phaebia asked. "The Corners of Kataan, the Giver and Taker, when they left their seats, they left no ruin in their wake."

Iylea wanted to ask a thousand questions. *How am I here? Why am I here? And what of these other Gods, this Lost Plane, and the Disasters?*

If the Disasters of Rheynia weren't a punishment by the Gods, everything they understood about Valencianism was wrong. *How many mages died? How many still live in fear? How many more will be nailed to Six Arrowed Stars?*

Anger built within her. The Revivalists' reign of terror was borne out of fear of the Gods' wrath. Even in her own circumstance, Damascus gave the order, Aemos swung the sword, and Danella saw to her capture—but all based on the same lie.

"They left for the Lost Plane," Moterra said. "They *willingly* abandoned their positions, taking the Creator's power with them."

"This reeks of Vykannis's mischief," Ferrocles said. "Every moment his soul clings to the mortal realm, he sows discord. He wants the Creator's Reckoning."

Hameryn nodded. The glowing red lightning that illuminated from his cracked flesh pulsed. "Vykannis bound himself to mortal flesh to see us punished."

"As long as he remains in Perillian, there will be no peace," Ferrocles said, making a fist. "We must end him and the Celestic threat."

It was strange for the Gods of Valencia to speak of the Judges of Celestia. All this time, she believed her abilities were the gifted curse of the Judges—*that's why they executed me.* Yet it was always Hameryn she saw. Her mind raced as she struggled to put the pieces together.

"Yes, but what of Courianne?" Phaebia asked. "What trouble has her death brought?"

"She linked us to the mortals," Hameryn said. "Without her, we can offer the mortals nothing but a passing voice through the Whispering Wall. With Invinius and Arkadia refusing to aid in the breaking of the chain, we will need help if we are to stop Vykannis and prevent the coming Age of the End."

Invinius and Arkadia... Auros?

Before Iylea could wrap her mind around what he had said, Hameryn turned to Iylea.

His red eyes burned into her. The light from his cracked skin flared, bathing her in a red glow. His smile made the hair on the back of Iylea's neck stand.

"That is why I have spared Iylea from death and brought her here," Hameryn said. "She can reconnect our realms so that we might guide the mortals to righteousness."

Iylea fell to her knees, gasping. The utterings that had echoed in her mind these last weeks suddenly came together like a puzzle.

"Six will become five. The Harbinger swift to rise. The chain must be undone."

"Too many links on the chain," Iylea said.

"Yes," Hameryn said with a sad smile. "Every incomplete soul becomes a link in the chain. Separating us from the mortals, weakening our ability to influence them. To stop The Age of the End, to prevent the Reckoning, the chain must be undone. We need you, Iylea. Will you help us?"

Hameryn held a glowing hand out to her. The other Gods eyed her, awaiting an answer.

It was all too much—her dreams, her beliefs, why she was killed. But she was positioned for a purpose, to make a difference—to stop the lies that Queen Danella and the Revivalists justified with false doctrine.

She met Hameryn's crimson gaze. "I will."

Hameryn smiled. "We have much work to do."

CHAPTER 59

A Summer Night's Dream

Nallia VII

Valtarcia

Nallia, her parents, and her brother made the trip by sea to the shores of Valtarcia to attend the games. Along with the eight gladiators who would be fighting on the morrow, the household guard and a dozen of the chancellor's newly appointed Sentinels accompanied their party. Although they made the trip several times in years past, this one felt nothing like the others.

The distance between her parents grew—literally and figuratively. They spent more time apart than not, but when they were in forced proximity, if they bothered to speak, they bickered. Markus brooded by himself, unwilling to hold a conversation with anyone longer than a few grunts. And Nallia felt torn between who she was and who others expected her to be.

The only one content was her father. He marveled at the bonfires all over Stockhelm. As the confiscated idols, symbols, and texts of the Judges burned to ash, her country seemed to be falling apart. But the more she thought about it, perhaps it was just her worldview that was unraveling.

Hallon Helixus, the Duke of Valtarcia, had closed the gates of Northridge to guests in light of recent events, so when they arrived in Valtarcia, they were spirited by wagon from the docks to an inn near the Chariot's Arena.

They took up residence in the Winged Helm—the only inn with barracks beneath for lanistas to have convenient lodging close to the arena. Although convenient, the accommodations were by no means extravagant. Her father took one look before deciding he would be sleeping elsewhere. He strode out cursing Hallon for denying him admittance to the castle. Her mother, however, chose to remain at the Winged Helm, further fanning the angry flames between them.

After Odetta helped settle her into her room, Nallia descended the stairs of the inn to the tavern where she found her mother. Surrounded by fools, miscreants, and honest men spending their hard-earned coin, her mother seemed out of place. Her form-fitting wool dress stood out like a bruised thumb next to the Valtarcian women clad in loose layered gowns more suited towards the cold winds. If her mother noticed, she didn't care, throwing back another drink.

Already in her cups.

A bard in the corner plucked a note on his lute, drawing the crowd to gather around, opening a path for Nallia. She approached the bar, her boots sticking to the ale-sodden floorboards with each step.

Nallia took a seat beside her mother. "Mother, may I ask you something?"

"What is it, my sweet?" Her mother examined her with heavy-lidded eyes, a half empty carafe of wine before her.

"Things were once so simple," Nallia said. "I rejoiced to be Damascus's betrothed, but now everything is so complicated."

The left corner of her mother's lip curved upward in a half smirk. "Men are a summer night's dream… when they are present. It's when they get caught up, concerning themselves in their future legacies or the bravado of their past accomplishments, that they become hellish nightmares. But you have yet to ask a question."

Nallia twisted the ring on her finger. "Damascus is like a different person since they put a crown atop his head," Nallia said. "With everything that's happening, I'm questioning everything I know about myself, everything I thought I wanted. I don't know if it's because of Damascus, the chancellorship, you and Father, or…"

She almost said Zephyrus, but she caught herself.

"I don't know," Nallia continued quickly. "There's just so much changing. What if I can't manage it all?"

Her mother swirled her goblet, examining the contents. "Unfortunately, Nallia, I might not be the one to ask about how to 'manage it all.' I doubt drinking is sage advice."

She shrugged and lifted the goblet to her lips. With a grunt, she set it back down.

"You didn't always drink," Nallia said. "What has you so downtrodden?"

Her mother lifted her gaze to the wooden beams of the tavern's ceiling. "The same things all mothers worry about. I never wanted you to marry a king—especially a Drake."

Nallia cowered, glad for the bard's playing to attract the other patrons' attention.

Her mother continued as if she hadn't noticed. "I didn't want Markus to lead the Sentinels, or your father to wrest power beyond our station. We were a happy family. We attended the games together, watched from the grandstands with the plebs. I never wanted jewels and the façade of power. I wanted love! I wanted my children to have love. I gave up on everything I believed in for that love…"

Love. The absence of it in her parents' marriage twisted in her heart like a dagger.

"Mother, I lov—" Nallia cut herself off. She loved Damascus, but the summer night's dream of Damascus, not the hellish nightmare he now represented. *Is it still love, if I only love the good in someone?* She bit her lip, taking her hand from her ring and resting it on her elbow. "I will have love, once peace is restored."

Her mother raised her eyebrow over the brim of her goblet as she drank again. "Peace is a summer night's dream—short and fleeting. The moment you believe it'll last, you'll wake to another hellish nightmare and realize we live in a vengeful realm where war is a long and painful reality. And once it's over, the wounds still linger."

She drank again, her shoulders curling under the weight of her words. "I grew up in Salmantica, through the New Rheynian war. I thought once the war ended, once the treaty was signed, once Helixus and Drake were bound by matrimony, things would be different." She shook her head. "I named you Vykinallia."

Nallia looked around, jaw hanging, to make sure no one heard her full name.

"Your father nearly killed us both when he returned home to find you named, but I always liked the stories of the Vykane Blade. Even if they were just stories, they were stories of hope. Holding you in my arms..." Her mother closed her eyes, smiling, as if she were transported back to those moments of bliss. "Vykinallia—it's a beautiful name, a strong name with character. Nallia doesn't suit you.

"You were named after the Treasure of the Stockhelm people—a symbol of hope. I named you wanting to believe peace could last. Your father poisoned me against those beliefs, and I've become no better than he." She downed the rest of her wine. "Now the Gods see fit to drown our lands in more blood."

Nallia didn't know what to say of her mother's pain. It hurt to see her so, but her pain was greater than just her own. She drank for the woe of the world.

All she wants is hope—something to believe in.

"The Gods can be cruel."

Mother scoffed. "We are cruel to each other. Are we denied rain because of our weak faith in the Six? Or is this a punishment for blaming the Judges for *our* shortcomings? The scales have been disrupted. The world is out of balance."

Once again, Nallia had no reply, but her mother presented ideas she'd never considered before. The tavern-goers erupted in cheers as the bard finished his song.

"And now," the bard said, "has anyone heard 'The Hero of Kings' Day?'"

The crowd cheered, and the bard began to pluck his lute.

"Nallia?" Mother put her hand on Nallia's forearm. "Do you love Damascus?"

Nallia paused. Her stomach didn't flutter at the mention of his name. The sight of him didn't make her swoon. *Do I love Damascus? Did I ever?*

Nallia swallowed the knot in her throat. "I don't know."

Her mother gave her a sad smile. "What does your heart desire?"

"Selfless love," Nallia said. "A man who is trusting, courageous, and honorable. One who sticks to his convictions—who isn't afraid to stand up for himself or others but realizes there's more to life than distinction and glory. I want a love that listens. A love that sacrifices."

Mother shook her head. "There's no love like that, my sweet. Only in the songs."

The bard continued to sing:

Backed to the corner with nowhere to go,
Our hero alone, surrounded by foes
He leapt into action, with sword and fury
Fighting for all but never for glory,
Saved his brothers, one by one
Vict'ry for life, now all have won
Zephyrus the Red. Zephyrus the Red.

Only in the songs… but what if the songs were true?

There were many things Nallia desired that she knew she might never receive. She wanted Damascus to be merciful, her father to be reasonable, her mother to be happy. But the selfless love she desired she had already received, and it wasn't only in a song.

The night before Father's coronation as chancellor, after she warned Zephyrus of the imminent search for items of Celestia, she had considered setting Zephyrus free. Part of her wanted to run away with him, to escape her fears, her problems, and start a simpler life. She told herself she was being childish, but now, she knew in her heart that she loved him.

She wasn't running away from her problems; she was running towards what she believed in. He who did not harm her when she discovered his secret, he who trusted in her at his own peril and healed her to provide comfort. Zephyrus recognized the brokenness in the world and sought to change it. He had the courage to stand up for what was right and not what was accepted. She could never run away with him, but no longer could she hold him against his will.

"I hope you find a love that fulfills the songs, Mother," Nallia said, looking away from the bard to face her. "But I think I've already found mine."

Nallia left the tavern of the Winged Helm, ascending the stairs toward her rooms.

Tonight is the night. I will see him one last time. Then I will let him go.

She recalled one of her first conversations with Zephyrus. All he wanted was equality—freedom—not just for himself, but for everyone. Even though he wasn't able to articulate it, she knew it, yet she did nothing.

If only I saw it sooner.

She called for Nortus to summon Zephyrus up to her rooms and began to ready herself. She longed for him in a way she never did with Damascus, regardless of his crown. Zephyrus was her slave, but she belonged to him.

Her cheeks flushed red as she examined herself in the looking glass. Her heart throbbed in her ears; her stomach fluttered with anticipation. He was the first ray of daybreak. The drop of rain to end the drought. He was the man she would love above all others.

She took a deep breath. *If this is the last time I am going to see him, I must make it count.*

CHAPTER 60

FOR LUCK

Zephyrus XVIII

Valtarcia

Tonight, they would escape from their Rheynian masters. After arriving in Valtarcia, they were delivered straight to their cells in the barracks beneath the inn. Although the chancellor had more than tripled the guard in recent weeks, the inn's sentries stood watch here.

"Valtarcia seems untouched by the chancellor's scourge," Cerik whispered through the bars of his shared cell with Jecht.

"Fewer guards throughout the city too," Jecht said.

"Even so, the Jackals will be our most pressing concern," Cerik said.

Zephyrus's knew little of the Jackals, but in light of recent events, word had it that they brutalized escaped slaves, often sending *less-valuable* slaves back to the house that branded them in pieces to serve as a lesson for others thinking of escape. Even still, the Jackals weren't Zephyrus's biggest concern.

He eyed Fenyx lying on the cot within their shared cell. Fenyx had been distant of late, unusually docile, yet weighed down with something. Zephyrus had never seen him like this. Perhaps the punishment from the chancellor's men had a more profound effect on him than originally thought. Maybe now he would hear reason and join them in their flight from captivity.

Yet the risks couldn't be overlooked. Fenyx had promised Zephyrus he would turn him in if he spoke again of freedom. Doctore, perhaps the only person Fenyx confided in, also threatened the same. If Fenyx denied him again, and word of their plans reached Doctore's ears, they were doomed. However, Fenyx never slept much and was bound to witness their escape. At the very least, Zephyrus needed assurances that Fenyx wouldn't summon guards to impede their path to freedom.

While Jecht and Cerik continued to talk in hushed voices in the cell across from them, Zephyrus took the opportunity to ensure Fenyx would not obstruct.

"How do you fare?" Zephyrus asked, but Fenyx seemed off in another world.

After a moment, Fenyx grunted. "If I open that door, I will be lost." His gaze remained fixed to the ceiling.

"Or you will find what you have been closing your eyes to," Zephyrus said. He knelt at Fenyx's bedside and whispered. "You think the Judges are watching this happen to their people, letting the Gods of New Rheynia exterminate us as punishment? Do you still believe that?"

"It doesn't matter what I believe," Fenyx said. "It changes nothing."

Zephyrus bit his lip. *I too shared that same belief at one point.* Zephyrus put his hand on Fenyx's shoulder. "It changes everything."

"There is nothing to be done."

"You can fight back," Zephyrus whispered. "We don't have to stay here. There is life beyond the ludus, one with purpose, protecting those who still hold the Judges in their hearts."

Fenyx only shook his head.

Frustrated, Zephyrus drew closer. "Fenyx, we leave tonight. Jecht, Cerik, and I. We seek the Uprising."

Fenyx perked up and turned to face Zephyrus for the first time. His upper lip on the burnt side of his face twitched before forming a tight line. His brow narrowed as he rose from his bed to stand over Zephyrus kneeling beside him.

Fenyx held out his hand. "I wish you luck, Zephyrus. Do what you must."

Zephyrus, momentarily baffled, stood to his feet and took Fenyx's forearm in his hand. "If I leave, and you stay…"

"Then it will be easier for me to regain my place as Champion," Fenyx said. "You have your destiny, and I have mine. A few lashes doesn't change that."

Zephyrus wrinkled his nose. *It should change everything.* But Zephyrus was in no position to argue. For now, it was enough that Fenyx wouldn't complicate their escape.

"I hope you find what you seek."

"And I, you," Fenyx said. "You've been a better friend than I have deserved, yet I must stay. Perhaps, one day, our paths will cross again."

Zephyrus nodded. Fenyx released their embrace and returned to his cot to face the wall. There was nothing left for Zephyrus to do but wait.

As the hour grew late, part of him wished he could thank Vykinallia for sending Odetta to warn him of the chancellor's search. To see her one last time. Yet those thoughts were foolish. She would be wed to the king in a matter of days, and he would be joining a rebellion.

Despite her being a slave owner, she was different than the others. She carved a place of her own within his hardened heart. He imagined a different life where people chose to support each other rather than pursuing power, glory, or greed.

In a world like that, maybe she could have loved me too.

"Zephyrus," Jecht said, "it's time." He gestured to the vacant guard post. They only had a few moments while the guards switched shifts.

Zephyrus crept to the door of his cell and placed his hands through the bars to the keyhole in the metal sliding door. He channeled the energy of the force magic as he did in his dreams. Visualizing the pins of the lock, he felt the shape it sought. His fingers began to tingle as he pressed the pins into place.

After a *click*, he slid the iron cell door open, canceling out the soundwaves of the grinding metal with manipulation magic. Jecht and Cerik gaped at one another as Zephyrus knelt before their cell and did the same.

"Praise the Judges," Cerik whispered.

"Time to go," Jecht said. They began to stalk down the corridor, away from the sleeping gladiators, but torchlight flickered around the corner.

"Someone's coming," Zephyrus said. "Back in your cell."

They resituated themselves into their cells as the torches neared. Footsteps approached. After silently closing the doors, Zephyrus climbed into bed and feigned being asleep.

The footsteps stopped in front of his cell.

"Zephyrus," Nortus said. "You've been summoned."

Zephyrus pretended to stir from sleep before facing the burly guard with bleary eyes.

"Now?" Jecht asked. "He's fighting in the Primus tomorrow. Leave us be."

Burn me. Of all times, why now? Seeing no other options, Zephyrus got up to comply, but an uneasy feeling settled in the pit of his stomach.

Nortus put his key into the lock of the cell door. "Hmph, that's odd. Door's unlocked." He shrugged. "C'mon now. We'll have you back in no time." He handed Zephyrus manacles to place on himself.

While Nortus secured the locks, Zephyrus turned to Jecht and Cerik and mouthed, *"Go!"* Jecht nodded, but Cerik shook his head. As Zephyrus followed Nortus from the barracks, he prayed Jecht and Cerik would be able to escape without him.

The timing couldn't have been worse. Anxiety percolated within his gut.

What if I can't get out in time to find them? What if they get caught trying to escape? What if the Jackals find them in the streets?

Nortus led Zephyrus up to the inn before one of the rooms. He began to take Zephyrus's chains off. "Lady Nallia ordered ya be unchained. No funny business, though, ya hear?" Nortus said. "No stubbed toes or whatever." He knocked on the door.

Odetta opened the door and slipped out, passing right before Zephyrus. "Be careful," she whispered.

Zephyrus cocked his brow and opened his mouth to speak, but Nortus nudged him into Vykinallia's chambers. The moment he breached the threshold, the door closed behind him.

Be careful… of what? Zephyrus's swallowed, but standing before the window, Vykinallia, bathed in moonlight, stole the thoughts from his mind. As she gazed out at the rainless night sky, a gentle breeze blew her golden nightgown and tossed her chestnut hair.

She turned to face Zephyrus. Dimples formed in her cheeks, but a growing sadness hid behind her eyes. "Good evening, Zephyrus."

As frustrated as he was with the timing, he was glad to see her one last time. "Hello, Vykinallia."

She smiled, beckoning him closer. "It's not often I hear my true name." She twisted the amethyst ring about her finger a few times, then rubbed the elbow Zephyrus had healed. "You must be curious as to why I've summoned you…"

He needed to speed this along. "To wish me luck in the coming games, I suppose?"

"On the contrary, actually." Vykinallia's gaze fell to her bare feet.

The silent moment stretched on as he waited for her to continue, but his thoughts were consumed with Jecht and Cerik's escape.

"Apologies, but this isn't easy." She closed her eyes and took a deep breath. "Zephyrus, it's difficult to admit when you're wrong. Harder yet to offer restitution once you realize the error of your ways." She sighed. "The treaties, the laws—Six save me—even the games, they're all warped cogs in a broken system."

Her emerald eyes were glossy with tears yet to fall. She took his hands in hers. "I am releasing you. Tonight."

Zephyrus's jaw dropped, and his brow creased. *Did I hear correctly?* The sentiment in her eyes told him all he needed to know. *She's freeing me?*

She released his hands and wrapped her arms around him, burying her face into his chest. Her tears dampened his tunic.

"What will you do?" Vykinallia asked, her words muffled against his flesh. Zephyrus, still in shock, couldn't find his tongue.

"Unite the three," Vykannis said. *"Find the Treasures of Stockhelm and become the Wielder."*

Zephyrus's stomach flared with pain. Grimacing, he stifled any audible form of discomfort. His arms closed around her. He rested his chin atop her chestnut crown.

"I must free the slaves," Zephyrus said. "I planned to flee with Jecht and Cerik tonight… for the Uprising." He pulled away from her so he could look her in the eye. Knowing that this might be the last time he ever saw her, ever spoke to her, he searched for the right words.

"When I was lost, you helped me rediscover who I was. You didn't bend my prophecy against me. You didn't turn me in when you figured out what I am." He shook his head. "You could have denied me the healer who aided my memories, left my scroll upon the training square to blow away with the wind, or kept your knowledge of the Judges and the Return to yourself. Others in your position would have."

Others did.

"But you didn't. And you taught me much." He took her hands in his. "The Uprising forged me into a weapon of vengeance, but I know vengeance is only the easy way out; if we are to be better than the Valencians, we can't do to New Rheynia what they did to Stockhelm. There has to be a better way than blood for blood. You showed me that, and I… I will never forget you."

He wanted to say more. He wanted to tell her the whole truth. It felt right to say so, but the words were trapped within him.

"Don't listen," the other voice strained, faint and weak.

Zephyrus could feel the two presences struggling for the ability to speak within his mind. He tried his best to ignore it, but his stomach pains only worsened.

"Don't listen to him," the weak voice said.

"Ignore the God of Valencia," Vykannis said.

Zephyrus attempted to ignore them both as Vykinallia's hands slid up his arms to frame his cheeks. The stone in his throat tightened as his hands traced her golden dress to her hips.

"You've changed everything," Vykinallia said, tears trickling from the corners of her eyes. "I'm sorry I didn't see it sooner, but you've opened my eyes."

She shook her head, sniffling. "Soon, I will become queen, and I will advocate for change. I will help you free the slaves and bring equality to the people."

Breath escaped his lungs.

Burn me. I love her.

He knew it a while ago, wrestled with it, hated himself for it, but it was true. Yet it didn't change the fact that she was betrothed to the king. As badly as he wanted to ask her to come with him, she had her place in this world, and he had his. It wouldn't be fair for him to tell her he loved her. He could never offer her more than a life on the run. She would be queen, using her power to accomplish Zephyrus's own goal.

He loved her, but he could never have her.

His one hand slid to the small of her back, while his opposite thumb and index finger traced the curve of her jaw as their eyes entangled in one another. Her beauty was unparalleled, her heart true, but even in freedom, he would forever be enslaved to her.

I love you, Vykinallia. Even if I can never tell you… I love you.

He leaned in, and she craned her neck. Their lips met. Hers, soft and warm, did not recoil as he feared they might. Her hands held firm to his face. Silent tears streamed down her cheeks.

Here, with Vykinallia in his arms, Zephyrus was free.

While the voices in his head contended against each other, Zephyrus lost himself in the warmth of Vykinallia's mouth, the taste of her tongue, and the gentle hums that came from deep within her throat. Desire yearned, but the moment could never last.

Eventually, their lips parted, and reality returned.

"You must go," she whispered, her hands falling from his face and her head to his chest. "It's not my wish, but the time has come. To say goodbye."

He didn't want to leave her either. He kissed the top of her head, but her embrace fell away. She strode to her bed and knelt beside it. Reaching underneath, she retrieved a satchel.

"There's a cloak, a dagger, and enough coin to get you by," Vykinallia said, returning to him.

Again, Zephyrus couldn't manage words, but not solely due to her generosity. The war of the Gods within his mind became violent. His stomach lurched with a stab of blinding pain.

"He's mine!" Vykannis boomed, his voice reverberating through his skull.

"Zephyrus?" Vykinallia asked, concern rippling across her face.

Zephyrus tried to ignore the voices, to focus on Vykinallia, but his vision began to blur. He forced himself to remain upright. "I'm fine," he lied as the two presences fought within him.

"He's MINE!"

Vykinallia took the amethyst ring from her finger and held it before him. "I want you to have this. I've had it for as long as I can remember, but I want you to take it… to remember me by."

Fresh tears came to her eyes, but Zephyrus's vision darkened. Her beauty fell away from him as the fight within consumed him.

"Zephyrus?" Her voice began to fade into the distance. "Zephyrus!"

The world went black, and all he heard were the voices.

"He will do my bidding." Vykannis's voice took over the entirety of his consciousness.

"No!" the other voice argued. Weakly at first, but its strength surged. *"You sought to make him your evildoer, but your plots have failed, as all of your schemes will!"*

Zephyrus felt a tearing from deep within him as if his soul were being ripped in two. Vykannis's presence waned as the other God's grew.

"You can't defeat me," Vykannis said, his voice straining. *"Not without destroying yourself."*

Vykinallia shouted to Zephyrus. She might as well have been a world away with how soft her voice was. In the black void of his mind, he reached for her, but she was nowhere to be found.

"Clayvorine found you," the other voice said. *"She showed me your past and your future. You will be defeated, but not by me, Paxoran."*

An explosion tore through Zephyrus's head, thrashing him about as if he were toppled by a tidal wave of fire. But Vykannis's voice, his presence, was banished from his mind.

Vykinallia's rooms in the inn returned to him. The ceiling swirled behind Vykinallia's concerned face, but he felt as if he were at the bottom of a well, looking to the sky. He extended his hand out for her, but he couldn't reach her.

"We have won," the voice said, weak again. *"But your battle is just beginning."*

Too tired to speak, too exhausted to move, he channeled to the victor God. *"Who are you?"*

"I am the last of the Judges," the voice said. *"But you will be our legacy."*

Zephyrus didn't understand, but his fatigue was greater than his ability to formulate the questions he needed to ask to make sense of it.

"I will fade," the Judge said weakly. *"But no longer will Paxoran have access to you. You are free of him. Now the rest is up to you."*

Like clouds being swept away by the wind, the presence of the last Judge waned until no trace remained, leaving Zephyrus drained. He attempted to move. He tried to cry out to Vykinallia, but his voice didn't carry. Exhaustion piled on top of him like a rising tide that sought to drown him.

I can't rest now. Jecht and Cerik are waiting. Freedom is calling.

At the top of the well, far away, Vykinallia's features blurred. His vision narrowed to nothingness, and all went black.

⚖

He awoke to the sound of humming. Lying in a comfortable bed, wrapped in Vykinallia's warm embrace, Zephyrus didn't want to leave. He attempted to move, but he felt so weak.

"What happened?" Zephyrus asked.

Dawn light filtered into the room through the open window.

"I don't know," Vykinallia said. "You just collapsed. I was afraid you—"

"I'm fine," Zephyrus said, despite his body aches and the headache that filled the void left behind by the false Vykannis and the last Judge.

"It's too dangerous for you to flee now," she whispered.

Zephyrus closed his eyes. *Jecht and Cerik…*

Vykinallia stroked his arm with her fingertips. "Win today, and once we are back in Stockhelm, I will set you free. I promise."

"I cannot fight today," Zephyrus whispered. "I can't kill another slave."

Vykinallia turned him toward her. She examined him, her lips a tight line. "Zephyrus, you must. If two more must fall for you to set so many free, won't it be worth it?"

Zephyrus found himself wishing for the Judge's guidance, but he was gone. As was Vykannis, or Paxoran, as the last Judge had called him. Now, he was alone.

He bit his lip. *What I achieve matters, but how I accomplish it is just as important.*

"Come," Vykinallia said, kissing his cheek. She got up from bed and grabbed the satchel she had given him the night before.

Zephyrus forced himself from bed and found Vykinallia's amethyst ring clutched in his palm. He offered it back to her, but she shook her head.

"Keep it," she said, closing his hand around her ring. "For luck."

CHAPTER 61

PUNISH ME

Danella IX

Valtarcia

Danella took a moment upon the docks after stepping off of *The Chimera* to examine the flagship's beauty. It would be the last time she ever saw it.

At the beginning of the Revivalists' gatherings, Elrod Horne pushed his chemical experiments, using the black powder to inspire fear. Yet the explosive nature of the powder had yet to be confined, and without the ability to contain the blasts, Danella wasn't willing to sacrifice the entire city for his experiments. While his studies made progress in the spaciousness of Marstead, she never trusted it enough to include it in any of her plans. But after Elrod's death, he left her with stores of the black powder. Finally, she knew what she'd do with it. She'd set fire to every ship in the Valtarcian Harbor.

Part of her wanted to bring one of her other ships, but she feared it might arouse suspicion if she didn't lose something as well. The explosion she hoped would be misinterpreted as magic fire. She could sway the Valtarcians, who were so quick to defend the Celestics during the last war, and prove to them that they had chosen the wrong side. If she could get Duke Hallon to join Damascus in their opposition of the mages, the war was as good as won.

She took one last look at *The Chimera,* hoping her sacrifice would be enough for the Valtarcians, but feared her father would disapprove of her plan.

No. He would have me sacrifice life itself for the Six.

"Your grace." Ser Daenus approached her on the Valtarcian docks. She was happy to have him back in her service after being bedridden in the wake of the Kings' Day attack but couldn't help but notice the twitch in his fingers.

Curse that Celestic magic. She raised her gaze to meet his eyes. "Yes, Ser Daenus?"

"Duke Hallon closed Northridge… to all."

Damascus, engaged in conversations with the newest members of his King's Guard Knights—Haedron Allos, Aelon Ironpine, and Aemos Horne—snapped to attention at Ser Daenus's news. "What?"

"He's afraid, my son. That's all," Danella said, sensing his anger. "He lost his son, he's disappointed with us for Laeden's imprisonment, and an old man can only handle so much."

"Yes but he's my *grandfather* too. How am I to take this slight?"

"We'll take up residence in the Royal Inn and think nothing of it," Danella said. "Your pride must not be shaken at such posturing."

Damascus nodded, the anger melting from his face.

He was trainable. It would take time, but he could learn.

Once Nallia is dealt with, he'll be more tenable.

Instead of a short lectica ride to the castle, they boarded a covered wagon to escort them to the Royal Inn on the opposite side of the city. Danella and Damascus were seated inside while the knights and guards ushered their caravan. The white stone city, normally alive with commerce, was quiet. Too quiet. Shops were closed, boarded up with signs out front.

"Closed by order of Duke Hallon Helixus."

According to her sources, Duke Hallon had closed much of the pleb's lower city, distributing coin from his own coffers and grain from his stores to support them. Such an act was dangerous. Foolish. Arrogant.

The Gods rewarded the diligent, the courageous, and the strong. Not the fearful. But in closing much of the lower city, Chancellor Cassius's search and seizure of Celestic symbols was slow, if not halted altogether. Hallon should have been wiser after the New Rheynian War.

He must come to reason, lest the Uprising gain a fierce ally. And I a formidable enemy.

The wheels of their carriage kicked up dust from the lower city's dirt roads. Danella waved her hand through the air before her. *Gods, deliver me to the paved upper city.*

"Six, I don't remember these streets ever being so dusty," Damascus said.

"They've never been so," Danella said. "We need rain."

The prolonged absence of rain worried many people, but it would get worse before it got better if the Gods were not sated.

Damascus coughed, flapping a kerchief in front of his face to avert the dust. "The Gods are withholding from us. Perhaps tonight the rains will return."

"Only if we please them," Danella said. "Our interactions with your grandfather cannot descend into disagreement. He must see that the Uprising is a threat greater than we, as a people, have ever faced. We must unite."

As they approached the outskirts of the lower city and the beginnings of the upper city, chatter grew outside the carriage. Their conversation inside the wagon stopped as Danella listened. Though she couldn't make out the crowd's words, the tenor was far from welcoming.

"Clear the way!" Ser Daenus shouted.

Damascus slid open a window and pulled back the curtain. Where the dirt road of the lower city became the cobbled streets of the upper city, Valtarcians barred their access. Holding pickaxes and fishing spears, they stretched from wall to wall.

"Murderer!" one voice cut through the crowd.

"Killer King!"

"Stand down or you're gonna get it!" Aemos shouted, his hand on the hilt of his sword.

"No swords!" Danella cried. "Keep us moving."

"We can't, my queen," Daenus said. "They aren't letting us through."

Damascus furrowed his brow, his face flushing red. "Then make a way through."

Danella grit her teeth. *Six, we can't brawl with civilians in the streets.*

Just then a wave of white horses descended the cobbled streets of the upper city. Clad in blue and gold, the Knights of the Ridge, Duke Hallon's honor guard, reined up behind the gathered crowd.

"Let them pass," a familiar voice said from beneath the plumed helm of the captain of the Ridge Knights.

Danella peered out the window of her wagon. Ser Ostrey Wingfoot, the King's Guard Knight she had dismissed from service following Varros's abduction, waved to the gathered crowd. They stood aside without so much as a second thought.

"Get us out of here," Danella said. "Don't stop until the king's inside the inn."

The wagon accelerated, thrusting Danella back into her seat.

Though the Ridge Knights had broken the blockade, the damage was done. Hallon was showing his strength and making his grievances known. Such a demonstration was no accident.

She placed a trembling hand over her chest, taking hold of the Six Arrowed Star pendant her father had given her before he died.

Danella prayed, and the Six provided. They made it to the inn without further escalation. Once they arrived, Danella and Damascus were spirited into the foyer. The Royal Inn was no standard tavern. Specifically designed for noble guests who didn't wish to stay, or were not welcomed, in Northridge, the Inn was Danella's preferred accommodation when compared to staying with Varros's family.

The high arched ceilings of the foyer were held up by intricately carved white columns. Ornate red carpets ascended the winding twin staircases on either side of the foyer. At the top of the landing, a portrait of her father loomed. From the entryway, the golden eyes of Damascus Drake watched over his Royal Inn. The portrait reflected his later years with his black hair salted gray, but age did nothing to stoop his shoulders. Now he watched over her from Valencia.

The overseer, dressed in a red velvet doublet, stepped from behind his desk and greeted them with a flourishing bow. Two knights in full plate stood sentry behind him.

"My king," the overseer said. "I welcome you to the Royal Inn. Is there anything I can do for you before escorting you to your suite?"

Damascus pointed back to the entrance. "I want guards stationed outside of the Inn and at the door to every room."

"Yes, my king." The overseer bowed again before nodding to his knights.

While Damascus and his new retinue of guards coordinated with the inn's sentries, Danella—accompanied by Daenus—ascended the stairs to the royal chambers.

"Find him and report back his status," Danella said to Daenus. "I want to make certain everything is in order."

Daenus nodded.

Once she was situated in her rooms, Daenus left her. She poured herself a glass of wine and stood by the window overlooking the south side of Valtarcia.

She was displeased by the malcontent of the Valtarcian plebeians, but such was the case when ruling. Not every decision made everyone happy. The plebs didn't know what they needed. They were the equivalent of insolent children complaining of the injustices their parents imposed upon them, not realizing it was for their own good. Once she flattened the Uprising, appeased the Gods, and returned the nightly rains, the common people would have no recollection of ever complaining about the king.

But Hallon will not be held blameless in this ordeal.

She turned away from the streets and placed her goblet down on a table. A portrait of her father's bodyguard—Ser Darrow, the Reaper of Marstead—hung on the wall. She needed a warrior like him now if she were going to stop the Celestics.

This war with the Uprising wasn't personal; it was cosmic. The laws of the world were designed around creating order for the masses, not for all. She hoped Varros would understand that, but he was an idealist. Even now, she knew in her heart that he wouldn't.

"Gods punish me, if I've acted outside of your will," Danella said aloud. "I've given everything for you. My husband is lost to me. Even if he lives, the man I grew to love would never love me if he knew my deeds. I sacrificed my love, for you. Spare me Damascus. Please, Gods, let me have Damascus." She couldn't bear the thought of losing him as well. "Take me now if I have not done your will. Take me, and do as you wish, but do not harm my son."

The burden of these past months seemed at its end just a couple of weeks ago. Damascus was on the throne, enforcing the Gods' will. Yet from Laeden's defiance, seeds of adversity bloomed underground, and her obstacles to overcome only seemed to sprout like weeds.

She put her hand to her face. A knock at the door made her jump.

"Who is it?"

"It's me, your grace," Daenus's gruff voice said through the door.

She stood and straightened her dress. "Come in."

Daenus entered and quickly closed the door.

"Well?" she asked.

"Brusos's thirty slaves, under the direction of Liario and Lenox, loaded every ship in the Valtarcian Harbor with black powder," Daenus said.

Danella nodded. "Very well. Perhaps this will aid Hallon in deciding which side he is on. Liario and Lenox may yet redeem themselves in the process as well."

And soon, Nallia Cassius will be out of the picture, breaking whatever softness remains in Damascus.

Danella plucked her goblet from the table and raised it to her lips. All would be as it was meant to.

CHAPTER 62

THE NEW RHEYNIAN GAMES

Zephyrus XIX

Valtarcia

Standing at the gateway to the arena, Zephyrus wrapped his cloak about himself. Unlike the warm breeze of Stockhelm, these northern winds had a bite to them. Even after the morning frost burned away, the air remained frigid. Since none of the Cassius gladiators were fighting until later in the day, Zephyrus stood alone, craning to see the pulvinus—to see Vykinallia.

The impossible had happened—she set him free. Doctore told him anything was possible just a few days prior, but this wasn't what he was referring to. Vykinallia, a slave-owning Valencian, set him free, knowing exactly who he was and what he would do. Not only would she let him, but she would help. Her words repeated in his head. He replayed their kiss over and over again. His hands upon her face, his lips upon hers. Had all gone to plan, he would have joined Jecht and Cerik and been halfway to finding the Uprising by now. Yet the Gods had interfered.

Now, at sunset, Zephyrus would have to face two Champions—two slaves whom he had vowed *not* to kill.

"If two more must fall for you to set so many free, won't it be worth it?" Vykinallia asked.

His stomach churned at the thought. He retched after the first time he graced the sands. After the second, the faces of the men he'd slain, to save Fenyx from Stegavax, haunted his nightmares. He didn't know if he could do it again.

Can I be the Wielder if I'm slaying the people I'm meant to free?

Paxoran, the deceiving God who had saved his life at the slavers' auction, had wanted to use Zephyrus. *He wanted me to be the Wielder. He wanted what I wanted.*

But the last Judge didn't want Zephyrus to claim the treasures. *But if I'm not meant to be the Wielder, does that make me the Harbinger, the Herald? Or something else altogether?*

Leaning against the bars of the arena, Zephyrus felt more confused than ever before. If he had escaped with Jecht and Cerik, or been able to leave after seeing Vykinallia, he wouldn't have concerned himself with such thoughts. But now, they were better diversions than thinking of the two men he'd have to fight. To kill.

Part of him wished he wasn't alone, but he took comfort in the fact that Jecht and Cerik had made it out.

"How did they escape?" Doctore demanded of the guards when he realized their absence. Zephyrus overheard reports that three Jackals were killed last night. It couldn't have been a coincidence, but Zephyrus accepted it as hope.

Fenyx benefited the most from Jecht and Cerik's departure, vowing to fight and win in their respective places in addition to competing in his own seeding. Fenyx was more than capable of surviving the task. Zephyrus only wished Fenyx could take his place as well.

Vykinallia's amethyst ring, looped through a thread on the inside of his waist, pressed against his flesh.

"For luck."

He peeked beyond the gateway to see if she was on the pulvinus, but she was nowhere to be found. He grimaced and returned his gaze to the arena where three lesser houses fought two on two on two.

Unlike Stockhelm or Salmantica, the arena wasn't filled with sand, but the pebbles that lined the Valtarcian coast. The early matches had less well-known gladiators, but the raucous crowd cared more about the blood on the pebbles than the name of the man it came from. Zephyrus turned away as an axe split through a spearman's shoulder blades to the roar of the onlookers.

The entire day would be filled with the same savagery.

The sun rose high and burned through the shroud of clouds, signaling that the Primus would begin soon. Eight rounds of three gladiators—one from each of the head ludi—would compete for points. To men like Fenyx and Stegavax, this was a prodigious honor.

Zephyrus dressed during the recess. Each of the Cassius gladiators were clad in white padded britches and a matching leather vest. The britches were chased with golden thread and purple ornamentation. Embossed on the vest, the purple-and-gold scorpion of House Cassius raised its stinger high, poised to deliver the killing blow.

"No other armor?" Aelixo asked Doctore.

"No," Shagren said. "Valtarcian tradition. You, your opponent, your weapons."

Once the Games began, the rounds were swift and brutal. Aelixo was first to set foot on the Valtarcian pebbles in the eighth seeding, but also the first to die. Vossler took to the arena next and, although defeated, was granted life for a match well fought. Fenyx fought next in Cerik's seed, easily cutting down his foes, before fighting again in his own seed.

"Four kills and two points!" Fenyx boasted after his second bout.

"At the fifth and sixth seeds," Stegavax said.

Fenyx and Stegavax exchanged a disdainful glare.

Fenyx's burned lip twitched. "Yes, and I have one more at the third seed. A glorious day for House Cassius!"

Shagren fought in the fourth seed and won after a long-fought duel. Then, Fenyx took to the sands for the third time, in place of Jecht. The crowd cheered for him, their mouths still salivating from his last display.

The two men united against Fenyx, but they stood no hope. The blood on Fenyx's great sword from his first bout hadn't even had the chance to dry before it drank more of Kaelus's and Targarus's men.

"Well fought!" Doctore embraced Fenyx as he strode from the arena, the crowd cheering his name. "No one has ever won three contests in this tournament."

"For the honor and glory of Cassius!" Fenyx shouted.

Stegavax fought next. For a time, he looked every bit the gladiator that won him the mantle of Champion, but as the match persisted, he began to wane. His hubris eventually outmatched his endurance, and a trident stabbed him through the belly. Stegavax's lifeless eyes stared at Zephyrus as the arena attendants dragged his corpse from the bloody pebbles. He was no friend to Zephyrus, yet he died an unnecessary death—a slave's death. Despite being a former Champion, there was no ceremony, no celebration of his sacrifices or achievements. Just death, and cheers for the victor who delivered him to the afterlife.

Seven matches came and went.

Doctore put his hand on Zephyrus's shoulder. "It's time." He handed Zephyrus the finest gladius and buckler he'd ever held. The blade was sleek and light, sharpened to a fine edge. He beat the sword against the shield to make sure it was not rigged to break again.

"That is Auros-forged steel," Doctore said. "It shall not fail you, and you shall not fall. Embrace your fate as Champion. Win, and your life begins anew."

Zephyrus swallowed, plagued by thoughts of his prophecy and uncertain fate.

"It's four to three," Shagren said. "Kill the damned Targarus brute first, and we win no matter what." Zephyrus ignored Shagren.

"Kill them and become Champion," Fenyx said. "You deserve it." Fenyx leaned in close so only he could hear. "I don't know why you stayed, but I wish you luck. Even if you stand in my way, you are my true brother from this day forward."

Zephyrus didn't understand the change in Fenyx, but his words were earnest. He nodded, accepting them for what Fenyx meant rather than what they were—encouragement to kill other slaves.

When the horns finished blaring and the crowd settled down, the herald bellowed for all to hear. "To stand in the Primus Maximi, representing House Targarus, the legendary Octus!"

"Zephyrus." Doctore put his hands on each of Zephyrus's shoulders. "This is your moment. Become the man I know you can be and perhaps one day, your longings will be answered. But it all starts now!"

"From House Kaelus, I give you Saurus!" the herald announced.

The Kaelus champion entered to the crowd's applause.

Zephyrus thought of Vykinallia... Jecht and Cerik... the Arcane Templar and their pursuit of vengeance. Patrus's "Rebels' Rhyme" and the Return of the Judges.

"You are where you need to be, exactly when you must," Threyna had said.

I will have my freedom. But first he needed to become the slave, the gladiator everyone wanted him to be. One more clever lie was all it took. He felt Vykinallia's amethyst ring within his belt.

For luck.

"Representing House Cassius, the Chancellor of Stockhelm has chosen one who stares death in the face and defies its embrace. I give you Zephyrus!"

Zephyrus set his jaw. The crowd's noise faded into a dull buzz and then complete silence. The gate opened before him. Men patted his back and wished him luck, but Zephyrus couldn't hear them. His vision narrowed, focusing on the red-and-black spearman and the blue-and-gold axe man standing between him and his freedom. His heartbeat assumed a steady, purposeful rhythm as he faced the pulvinus.

Vykinallia's emerald eyes soaked up the sun and burned with the fire of the torches illuminating the arena. She mouthed something to him, yet he heard her voice as if she whispered in his ear. He could feel the warmth of her breath as the words vibrated into every fiber of his being. *"Freedom."*

Zephyrus closed his eyes. The signal to begin must have sounded because the ground shook as his two opponents sprinted for him.

For Patrus...

The pebbles beneath his feet trembled. He took a deep breath.

For Jecht and Cerik...

The bloodthirsty gladiators charged, their battle cries leading their assault.

For the last of the Judges...

His eyes snapped open just in time to duck under a vicious swing of Octus's spear. He rolled away as Saurus chopped down, smashing his axe head into the pebbles.

Octus possessed long reach and deadly precision with his double-sided spear, while Saurus's great axe had power that neither Zephryus's sword or shield would be able to block. *Block the spear, dodge the axe.*

Another spear thrust stabbed at him like an angry swarm of hornets. He blocked, sidestepping a vicious axe cut. Saurus's breath heaved; his feet dragged.

He's not tired. He's scared.

Zephyrus grunted, shoving the pity and guilt from his mind.

Focus. Fight. Kill.

He waited for his opportunity to present itself. Octus jabbed, spun, and sliced with the other side of his blade. Zephyrus blocked the jab with his gladius, deflected the slice with his buckler, and planted a kick into Octus's chest, sending him backwards. Zephyrus stepped over a sweeping axe cut and took Saurus's leg out from under him with the flat of his blade.

Octus returned with a stab, slice, stab, stab, reverse slice! As Octus turned his back to him, Saurus found his feet and attempted to take Zephyrus from behind. Saurus grunted, reaching the great axe overhead. As he began to hack down, Zephyrus dropped low and swung his buckler into Saurus's knee. Octus's blind spin met Saurus's stumble, and the jagged spearhead slashed into the side of Saurus's neck.

Saurus's eyes went wide, his fingers reaching to stem the tide of blood flowing from the wound. He fell, nearly wrenching the spear from Octus's grasp. Octus attempted to wriggle his spear free of Saurus's neck, but Zephyrus pressed. Zephyrus cleaved down on the spear haft, attempting to separate Octus from his weapon altogether, but just as he connected, Octus released the spear and drew a hooked sickle from his belt.

He slashed upwards.

Zephyrus reared back just as the gleam of the blade passed his nose, so close he could feel the wind of it. He slapped it away with his buckler, blocked a punch, and headbutted Octus on the bridge of his nose. Octus stumbled back in a daze, but by the time he found his footing, Zephyrus stabbed his gladius through the arc of the sickle. He twisted the blade, creating torque, and flung the weapon from Octus's grasp.

Octus scrambled backwards, but there was nowhere to go, no place to hide. He let out a cry and made one last attempt at Zephyrus, but a quick punch with the rounded edge of his buckler stopped Octus in his tracks, dropping him to the pebbles stained with Saurus's blood.

If the crowd cheered, Zephyrus didn't hear it. If the gladiators shouted in victory, they could not raise voice over the pounding in Zephyrus's ears.

Zephyrus picked Octus up and placed his gladius against his throat, looking to the pulvinus. Octus trembled within his grasp.

Vykinallia cheered. Dominus celebrated. The king made an elaborate gesture, pointing his thumb downward. Zephyrus's hearing returned, and his vision widened.

"Kill! Kill! Kill!" the crowd demanded.

"Please, Judges, don't forsake me," Octus said, the apple of his throat quivering.

"Kill! Kill! Kill!"

The barbaric mantra continued, growing louder with each passing moment. Saurus bled out on the pebbles, gasping for breath in the throes of death. Octus quivered within Zephyrus's grasp.

He didn't want to kill Octus. He wanted to kill the crowned man with his thumb turned downward, but he knew what he needed to do. Even still, his hand didn't move.

Just do it. Stick to the plan, gain your freedom.

It would be easy. A quick slip of his arm and Octus's life would spill from his throat in a dark red fountain. *Just end it!*

"Vykannis, spare me," Octus pled. "I fought bravely. Orsius, Aeryss, save me!"

Zephyrus clenched his jaw and tightened his grip on the hilt of his gladius. The "A" of House Auros was imprinted into the pommel of the blade. The same "A" branded on Patrus.

Bile rose within his throat. *I must do this.*

"You will not be forgotten, Octus," Zephyrus said. "Your sacrifice will set Celestics free. The Judges will return."

"Kill! Kill! Kill!"

Octus inclined his gaze, and for a moment, Zephyrus saw Patrus's face.

"Zeph," Patrus said, "don't do this." He blinked away tears. "You were supposed to free us. Not turn on us."

"Patrus," Zephyrus whispered. "I'm sorry…"

Patrus shook his head. "You aren't the Wielder… Everyone who follows you dies." He slackened, eyes staring blankly ahead—dead.

Patrus's scarred face morphed into Threyna's.

"This blood is on your hands," she said. Her throat opened in a crimson line.

Threyna's face turned into Jecht's, but the entire left side of his head was caved in. "You told us to go, and we went. Why didn't you come with us?"

"Where were you?" asked a voice from behind him. Zephyrus found Cerik's face on Saurus's body, a terrible gash through his forehead. "We needed you."

Zephyrus returned his gaze to Octus's body, but this time Vykinallia's face stared back at him. She was pale with a black-and-blue ring around her throat, her neck bent at an odd angle.

"I was wrong…" she said. "You're not the hero. I never should have trusted you."

Zephyrus closed his eyes, unable to look at her. "Forgive me."

"Kill! Kill! Kill!" The unrelenting crowd echoed throughout the arena.

"Don't," Octus said. "Have mercy."

"Go to the Judges," Zephyrus said. "But you will be avenged."

He slid the blade across Octus's throat.

CHAPTER 63

BITTER VICTORY

Nallia VIII

Valtarcia

Nallia clasped her hands over her mouth. *He did it!*

The crowd erupted as Octus fell to the bloodstained pebbles. Zephyrus raised his sword arm to raucous applause, but she knew it to be a bitter victory he never wanted.

Once we are back in Stockhelm, I will free you. She rubbed her elbow.

The crowd praised Zephyrus's name. Her father cheered, before getting up to shake the hands of the other lanistas.

"Well fought," Damascus said. "I suppose once the Uprising is stomped out, we can have our tournaments back," he said to Ser Aelon. "In the meantime, you will have to be the king's justice."

Ser Aelon nodded. "It would be my honor, your grace."

Hallon eyed his grandson. "By *justice*, do you mean sentencing your brother?"

Damascus held up his hands. "Grandfather, we haven't had his trial."

Hallon grumbled to himself, the tension between them thick enough to cut with a knife. While the queen whispered something in Father's ear, Nallia met Zephyrus's gaze.

I will help you. She wanted to hold him and console the broken heart she knew he had. The hours couldn't pass fast enough for her to be reunited with him, even if it would be for the final time.

Her father returned to his seat beside her. "We will be accompanying the king back to Salmantica to attend the trial of the pseudo-prince," her father said. "She wants Zephyrus to Champion the crown during the sentencing in place of Ser Aelon."

Nallia turned back to Zephyrus, her heart sinking to her stomach. *How am I to free him now?* She closed her hand into a fist, cursing herself.

"He will provide solidarity behind the crown's sentence," her father continued. "Laeden was a hero to the plebs. If it should come to a death sentence, Zephyrus swinging the sword would limit any backlash."

Damascus grabbed her by the hand and stood, but her troubled thoughts only grew. He raised his other hand to silence the crowd. "It's my honor to present the people of Valtarcia with the Champion Lanista of the year, Duke Lentulis Cassius, the Chancellor of Stockhelm."

Father stood and bowed.

"Zephyrus of House Cassius shall forever be enshrined in this marvelous victo—"

Far-off eruptions interrupted Damascus. The pulvinus shook, and the grandstands quaked. Nallia had to hold onto Damascus to keep from losing her balance.

Another attack?

Everyone turned to the source of the sound, but the explosions echoed throughout the arena. Dark plumes of smoke billowed into the air in the distance, declaring where they had come from. More explosions, more smoke—coming from the harbor.

Chaos.

Panic.

Damascus attempted to settle the crowd, but his voice was lost in the din of their screams as they ran for exits, trampling each other in the hopes of saving themselves.

"The docks!" Hallon said. "Ridge Knights, to the docks!"

Damascus resituated the crown on his head. "The Six-cursed mages."

The King's Guard Knights ferried the guests on the pulvinus to safety, but Nallia doubted such a place existed. They were rushed through an exit leading back to Northridge.

"Where is the safest place?" Damascus asked.

"The crypts," Hallon said as they hurried along.

"Ser Daenus," the queen said to her bodyguard, "escort the women and I to the crypts."

Hallon waved to the others. "Everyone else with me to the east wall."

The group split as the women were led to safety and the men to the harbor. They turned a corner in the dark torchlit corridors leading to the crypts until they came to a sudden stop.

Ser Daenus drew his sword. "Who goes there!"

A figure, cloaked in shadows, thrust his hand at the King's Guard Knight. Ser Daenus backpedaled as if a tremendous unseeable force shoved him. He crashed into the wall, his sword falling to the ground.

The queen staggered back. "Mage!"

Nallia turned back the way they'd come, pulling her mother along, but the mage pushed past the others and chased them.

"Nallia, go!" Her mother let go of her hand and turned to face the mage.

"Mother, no!"

The mage struck her mother across the face, dropping her to the ground.

The mage didn't stop.

He wants me.

Nallia ran as fast as her feet could carry her, trying to recall the hallways in which they'd come, but in her haste, she made a wrong turn. Damp stone and a locked door greeted her. She yanked on the iron handle, but the door didn't budge.

Dead end.

Her heart raced, blood pumping in her ears with the ominous accompaniment of footsteps growing louder behind her. She couldn't run. She would have to fight. Unarmed, she rubbed her elbow. *Vykannis grant me courage.*

Unsure whether the Judge would answer her prayers, she raised her trembling fists.

The mage approached. He stared at her from beneath his cloak with gray eyes Nallia swore she'd seen before.

Before she could place him, he lurched, shoving a wet rag towards her face. She blocked it away, but he came for her again. She struck him hard in the nose. The mage stumbled backward, creating an opening.

She ran past, but he tripped her. The two fell to the ground in a heap. She swatted at him, but he climbed atop her and pushed the rag into her face. Smelling of something she might have found in the medicus's chambers, the wet rag made her gag. The corridor began to spin.

She punched, but suddenly disoriented, she missed.

No. Her arms flailed, weak and out of control.

No, no, no.

She swung for the mage again, but her limbs disobeyed, and her head lolled to the side.

Not like this… Zephyrus…

Her mind raced, but her body wouldn't respond. Paralysis seized her, harnessing everything but her eyes.

Someone, anyone. Please!

The mage leaned close, examining her face.

Gods, where have I seen him before?

He pressed the rag over her nose and mouth. Unable to fend him off, unable to even scream, he picked her up and threw her over his shoulder. The shouts of her mother attempting to follow chased them through the corridors, but they faded.

Everything dissolved, until all was black.

CHAPTER 64

THE CAVERNS

Threyna IV

Stockhelm

The world was burning.

At least that's what everyone from Marstead to Stockhelm said. The absence of rain and the fire that sank the Valtarcian Harbor spoke to the literal sense of the phrase, but the abduction of King Varros and the prince's betrothed suggested the figurative sense as well.

In Marstead's taverns, many attributed the world's troubles to the lack of patrician leadership. In Stockhelm's town square, the blame lay with the Uprising. Threyna didn't care who was responsible, but if the Uprising the plebs referred to included the Arcane Templar, they were wrong; the Uprising was too busy chasing her to be responsible for New Rheynia's woes.

After spending her entire life growing up in Rheynia's Underground, Threyna was used to lying low—fighting when the odds were in her favor and running when they weren't. Hiding and waiting for the right moment was instinctive at this point. But they had not made it easy. Every plan she hatched, every precaution she took, they all backfired, taking longer than they needed to, all because she had refused to consume unless it was absolutely necessary.

"Consume him," Paxoran said. His voice echoed in her mind as her heartbeat thundered in her ears.

The rot climbed her left shoulder and stretched down to her elbow. It was manageable, all things considered. But she had no idea how many Guardians would be waiting for her within the Stormburn Geyser where the second Treasure waited.

The boy, sickly and frail, clung to a threadbare blanket despite the sun's warmth. Nestled between two barrels beyond the bustle of Nesonia's dock, the boy shivered. He'd been on her overnight voyage from Marstead to Stockhelm days ago, speaking of change for the plebs and liberation for the Celestics. She recalled having similar idealistic fantasies of what would happen in Rheynia when the Underground overthrew the Order and gave the Skeleton King a true death.

Just fantasies.

Maybe it was his starry-eyed optimism and defiant insolence to being told he was wrong, or perhaps it was just because the talk of the boat's voyage centered around Zephyrus's victory at the New Rheynian Games, but when she looked at the boy, she saw Zephyrus. They didn't particularly look alike, but when Paxoran told her to consume him, she saw the man she betrayed and condemned to slavery.

"He is sick," Paxoran said. *"He has not moved in days. Hasn't eaten. He will die whether you consume him or not."*

In the beginning, the more she consumed, the easier it became. But back in Rheynia, those were hollowed and shades. Rarely people. Never children. Somewhere along her journey, the selfish nature of her curse became more and more apparent.

"The Skeleton King will not hesitate," Paxoran said. *"And if you are not strong enough when the time comes—with or without the Treasures—he will defeat you."*

Paxoran was right. She didn't have a choice. *Either I consume this boy, or the Skeleton King will consume the world.*

Threyna sighed.

"Will you do what you must for peace to reign?"

Tapping into her Inner Throne, she told herself that with the balance of the boy's youth, she could make the future he dreamed of possible. As she drew his weakened soul from his body, she convinced herself that without him, she could never defeat the Skeleton King. And once she absorbed the last of his blood to heal her wounded shoulder from when Ceres's force magic hurled her into a building, she promised peace would reign.

As she finished, her connection to her Inner Throne winked out. Crouching down, Threyna surveyed her surroundings, her heart surging in her ears. She attempted to tap back into her Inner Throne, but like trying to put a key in the hole in the dark, she couldn't find the entrance.

Only two people could eject me from my Inner Throne.

Scouring the docks, she saw neither of them. If the Skeleton King were here, he wouldn't have wasted time lurking. But Tyrus was dead.

At least she thought he was.

Regardless, she was not eager to reacquaint with either of them. Seeing Tyrus again after she had fled the City of the Judges to infiltrate the Arcane Templar would yield a similar result to confronting the Skeleton King without all three Treasures.

Threyna tried a third time to tap into her Inner Throne and immediately sank into her seat of power. She sighed.

Hoping it was just a fluke, she left the docks and her anxiety behind, along with the husk of the boy and her memory of him. She set off for the Crystal River and the Stormburn Geyser as the sun crested its zenith on its journey west. Just as no rain would follow the sun, no fear or guilt could accompany her.

Everything will be worth it once he's dead and gone for good.

She repeated the words like a mantra until she arrived at the river. As she entered the cool water to swim upstream into the cenote that emptied into a pool within the Stormburn, her thoughts drifted to her sister, Laela.

What sacrifices have you made on your journey to find a cure?

Threyna swam until she reached the mountainous base. Holding her breath, she submerged, diving underneath the stone, away from the sun's warmth, and toward the fate she'd never chosen but always arrived at—blood.

As she breached the surface on the other side, she found herself in a cavern. Stalactites hung from the ceiling, dripping runoff from the geyser's spray. The droplets fell, rippling upon the water's slow-moving surface.

She swam to the shore where a tunnel, resembling the one within the catacombs, waited.

Threyna's feet squished within her wet boots upon the slick and stony floor. Though there were torches placed on sconces, gloom reigned over the cavern. Threyna took a handful of her Viridite glowstones to light her path, but not three steps onto solid ground, six guardians emerged from the tunnel's mouth.

Blood and bone…

Last to exit the tunnel was Sybex. The lightning mage smirked, shaking her head. "I'm not certain if I'm impressed at your determination or amazed by your foolishness."

Threyna shrugged, tapping into her Inner Throne to see if any more mages lurked deeper within the tunnel. If they did, she couldn't sense them.

Six. Only six.

Threyna dropped her glowstones. "I'm the one who should be impressed," Threyna said, wringing out her braid. "I heard a handful of Sentinels apprehended two mages when last we met. How did you let them catch you?"

Sybex snarled. "Yet here we are. And here, no one will come to save you. Not after what you did to Makaryk, Kuhnae, and Brooxus."

Threyna tossed her wet braid to her opposite shoulder. She drew the Vykane Blade in her right hand and conjured a double-bladed glaive in her left. The other five mages eyed the blood-borne spear she'd summoned into existence, but Sybex's eyes remained fixed on Threyna's—exactly where she wanted them.

"You mean how I drank their blood and feasted upon their souls?" Threyna asked, sinking deeper into her Inner Throne. With their gazes fixed on her, Threyna conjured an orb behind them.

Sybex's left eye twitched. "After we take the Vykane Blade from your lifeless fingers and return it where it belongs, we will free the Wielder from the chains you delivered him into. The Judges will return, and the valor of all who gave their lives to defeat you will be sung about through the ages."

"Is that right?" Threyna said, not allowing her gaze to shift to the growing orb at their backs. "I love a good song. Too bad no one will ever hear it."

From her seat upon the Inner Throne, she curled her fist around the blood orb she'd conjured behind Sybex and the Guardians. It exploded into a thousand shards of broken glass.

CHAPTER 65

RIGGED

Laeden XV

Salmantica

The day had come. Weakened from hunger, soiled from weeks in a dungeon cell, and broken by the betrayal of those he called friends and family, he was manacled and led out of his cell.

Iylea was dead. His father was gone. Damascus was surrounded by the men who condemned Laeden to this fate. And Danella orchestrated all of it. His time spent staring at the walls gave him the opportunity to reason most of it out. He wasn't sure if he was going mad, or seeing clearly for the first time, but there was no escaping this conviction.

A pair of guards escorted Laeden outside. After being locked away for so long, he forgot the warmth of the sun. Its gleam blinded him, forcing him to look at his trembling legs, his joints stiff and muscles weak from inactivity. The guards delivered him to the rotunda beyond the moat of Sentigard for all to witness his trial and sentencing. Several Six Arrowed Stars were erected around the moat.

I hope one of them isn't for me.

Six priests sat on an elevated pavilion before the court. The seventh judge would be Chancellor Cassius, representing the plebeians.

I must convince four of them of my innocence. Hopefully, Markus persuaded his father to vote on my behalf.

The people booed as Laeden drew closer.

The guards delivered him to a box erected before the people on the rotunda. They chained his manacles to an iron ring at the base of his box. As if he had a chance at escaping. Rows of seats angled toward him, all filled with patricians eager to view his trial and see his end.

"The flood of blood is coming," Iylea had said.

She had wanted him to kill her. He couldn't have. Even after these weeks, not once did he question himself. He never could have struck her down, not even to save himself. His only regret was dropping his sword. If he'd held onto it, he could have defended her.

I could've died with her instead of living on only to…

The shadow of the Six Arrowed Star loomed over him.

"Be humble in your sentencing," she said after he refused to slay her. He still saw her dead eyes looking up at him every time he slept.

Humility. Laeden shook his head. *As if that will save me. There's no justice in this world.*

Aemos stepped forward, settling the crowd before addressing the priests. "Merciful Six, please deliver me the justice I seek."

"What are your grievances?" High Priest Vellarin said, following the script of formal trials.

"For aiding and abetting the release of the mages who murdered my father, Count Elrod Horne, I charge the false prince, Laeden of House Helixus," Aemos said.

"And what penance do you seek for such a crime?"

Aemos met Laeden's eyes. "Death."

They read Laeden his rights, the order of the procession, and reminded him he would not be allowed to speak unless someone asked him a direct question.

The morning was filled with several convincing lies, each more incriminating than the last. Aemos built an entire narrative demonstrating Laeden's abuse of power or neglect of responsibilities.

Ser Daenus took the stand first. "Without proof, three witnesses, or any probable cause, Prince Laeden had me arrested at sword point,"

Daenus said. "With little regard for the laws of our country, he sought to establish his rule above the justice system."

Laeden cursed himself. *If I only dug deeper, I could have stopped this before it all started. If only I listened to Iylea.* He had no doubt Aemos's procession would have more than enough lies to convince the priests.

Next to take the stand was Dedrik, one of the traitorous Sentinels who accompanied Pirus when Laeden lured him into a trap at the Temple of Hameryn. Dedrik claimed they learned of Laeden's involvement with the Uprising weeks ago, but Laeden outwitted them and kept them chained in the dungeons as prisoners under the pretense that they were Revivalists.

"He left us there for weeks," Dedrik said. "One of us, Pirus, died in that cell."

The crowd groaned. One of Danella's handmaidens took the stand next, explaining how she overheard Iylea tell Laeden she was a seer. Laeden's eyes fell to his feet.

I failed you, my love.

Once she established Laeden's connection to a known mage, Aelon delivered the killing blow. Laeden glared, but his poisonous gaze did nothing to stop Aelon spewing the same lies he told in the throne room the day Iylea was murdered.

All for the title of a King's Guard Knight…

The betrayal stung. His own men, his brother, his stepmother, and his oldest friend—they had all turned their backs on him. But the shame of his failure hurt worst of all.

Finally, Aemos took to the stand, manipulating the story of the Kings' Day Feast. He blamed the Sentinels for the wrongful imprisonment of his father, Elrod Horne. Aemos's account supported Dedrik's, citing that his father also died in Laeden's care absent evidence of his Revivalist involvement.

"If you need proof in addition to the witnesses I've provided," Aemos said to the priests who sat in judgement, "here is a letter found in Laeden's possession." Aemos began to read Zephyrus's bloody, crumpled scroll signed by AVR.

"The time has come for peace to reign," Aemos recited.

Laeden groaned. *Of course, he neglected to read the part addressed to King Varros.*

"Your policies have pleased us and given us hope under the Six of New Rheynia," Aemos continued. "No longer shall we pursue vengeance or the Judges' Treasures." Aemos rerolled the scroll and cast a venomous glare at Laeden. "Servants of the Six, people of New Rheynia, the false prince Laeden has been appeasing the mages of the Uprising for some time now. Perhaps he didn't know he was being used by them. Perhaps he mistakenly put his faith in their honor instead of the Six of Valencia, but intention aside, his guilt remains."

Laeden's eyelids felt heavy. Fate was cruel. The scroll that led him to purchase Zephyrus to save his father would be the final nail securing him to the Six Arrowed Star. Weighed down by guilt, shame, and failure, he couldn't bear to look any longer. He closed his eyes, wishing they would take his head and be done with it. He would join Iylea and leave this world of lies and deceit to rot.

But he couldn't let them win.

Will anyone come to my defense?

Markus brooded behind him. Grandfather, Hallon Helixus, was also present—his lips in a constant snarl. But the crowd had already condemned Laeden. This trial was rigged. He couldn't prove that everything brought against him was a lie. They had the witnesses, and each had enough truth to make it believable. Nothing Markus or Hallon could say would change that.

"People of New Rheynia," Aemos said, "I seek only justice. These mages have been given too much leash under the Sentinels' governance. It's clear Laeden has worked with them to undermine our peace and prosperity. Attacks like the one on the Valtarcian harbor will not be isolated incidents if those who conspire with mages are still left in positions of power."

Laeden froze. *Attack on the harbor—what is he talking about?*

"Laeden's time as the captain of the Sentinels demonstrated how power corrupted him. His unchecked desire for control spiraled into silencing those who stood against him. Judges of the court, please do not let this villain walk free."

The crowd turned from disappointed to angry. The priests appeared as if they'd already made up their minds. Markus and Hallon watched with long, forlorn faces.

They have no chance at defending me. If they try, what lies would be constructed against them? They would change nothing and join me atop a Six Arrowed Star.

Laeden glowered at Danella. *She* orchestrated all of this. From the beginning, she used her position as the loving stepmother to manipulate him.

"You may have saved your father's life, but you put a target on your back in the process," Danella had warned. *"If you continue on like this, attempting to stop the Revivalists may be the last thing you do."*

She warned him from the beginning, and he played right into her hand. This was never about the truth, honor, or justice; it was about the narrative Danella needed to wipe out the Celestics. The Revivalists were in charge now, and everyone opposed would be swept up in the flood of blood.

"Laeden Helixus, son of Varros," High Priest Vellarin said. "Your defense?"

Laeden's empty stomach roiled.

"Be humble in your sentencing," Iylea had said.

Laeden cleared his throat. "I will not defend myself." Nothing he, Markus, or Hallon could say would change their minds. His only chance was groveling. "I throw myself at the mercy of the throne."

"There will be no mercy," Aemos said. "My father is dead because of you."

Laeden ignored him, focusing on the priests. "Search your hearts. I have conspired with no one. I sought to protect all with honor and justice, but I failed."

The crowd booed.

Each cry against him served as a grating reminder of his failure. He'd been outplayed. In the game of Reign, he'd played his tiles strategically, but the dice—like always—failed him. He'd been outmatched, not because he underestimated the Revivalists' cunning, organization, or their skill at arms. He'd made a graver error.

He underestimated their cruelty. He didn't believe a loving woman could orchestrate an assassination attempt on her husband. *If only I had listened to Iylea.*

Danella held all the tiles. Now Laeden's only choice was to roll the last of his dice.

Laeden glared at Danella. "Nothing I say will sway you from the narrative created. I choose not to defend myself with words but by omenation."

A hush fell over the crowd.

"Laeden, no!" Markus said from behind.

"I request a trial by steel. The Gods will prove my innocence!"

Aemos seethed. His pale cheeks glowed red, but the crowd demanded Laeden's blood.

After the priests called for order upon the rotunda, Vellarin addressed Laeden. "That is your right. Who will fight for your honor?"

"I will be your champion," Markus said to Laeden. "Let me fight for you."

Laeden's tension abated. *Even after all this, he would still die for me.* He grinned at Markus, but he wouldn't let another fall for his failings.

Laeden addressed the dais where the priests and Cassius sat in judgement. The sun felt warm and comforting on his skin. *This is my last chance.* "I will fight for myself."

Declaring his innocence would accomplish nothing, and it was far from true besides. His father tried to protect him from the truth, but now, Laeden finally understood; his father wasn't coerced into exiling the mage. He had wanted to. He chose peace instead of war. Life instead of death. But he had failed too.

Laeden had been so fixated on the word of the Treaty, and following the laws of his people, that he never questioned if they were right in the first place. He was just as guilty as the rest of the blind sheep. King Varros questioned the system, and the Revivalists tried to kill him for it. If the Gods bore witness to this omenation, and there was any wisdom in his father's defiance of the status quo, he would live. And he would attempt to bring about the changes his father risked everything for.

"And who will represent the crown's prosecution?" Vellarin asked.

A hush fell over the crowd as they stared at the dais where Damascus, Danella, and the King's Guard Knights sat.

Danella stood. "We are here today for the people. The Gods will reveal the claims brought forth to be true and just. To defend the crown's claim, Zephyrus, the Champion of the people, will represent our cause in the omenation."

Laeden's heart stopped. *Zephyrus?*

He expected to fight Daenus. He hoped to fight Aelon. He hadn't considered they would choose a gladiator—let alone Zephyrus.

Zephyrus stepped forward from behind Chancellor Cassius, radiating anger, his sword of vengeance already in hand.

"There will come a day of reckoning—a flood of blood through your streets, and you will wish you had set the slaves free," Zephyrus had said.

"The flood of blood is coming," Iylea warned. And now, it was here.

CHAPTER 66

VENGEANCE & JUSTICE

Zephyrus XX & Laeden XVI

Salmantica

Zephyrus

Laeden's time in bondage hadn't favored him, but the irony of the situation did little to please Zephyrus. Zephyrus didn't know or care how true the charges brought against Laeden were, but if Laeden had any knowledge of where Vykinallia was being held, he needed to know.

Two guards released Laeden from his manacles. Laeden had been all scowls during the trial, but now, before Zephyrus, he only stared wide-eyed and mouth agape.

Laeden will meet his just end, but it can wait a moment longer. Zephyrus stepped close so no one else could hear. "Is it true, any of it?"

"Some," Laeden said.

Zephyrus inhaled through his nostrils. *Judges, let him help me.* "Do you know where the Uprising is hiding?"

Laeden narrowed his eyes. "No. I never conspired with them."

Zephyrus's heart plummeted to the depths of despair. *He's telling the truth... How will I ever find her—ever save her—if I don't know where she's being held?*

He didn't even know if she was still alive. If they killed the king, they wouldn't hesitate to kill one not yet named queen.

"It's the truth, Zephyrus," Laeden said. "I've been dishonest with you before, and I'm—"

"Then you're of no use to me," Zephyrus said, turning away.

Laeden grabbed Zephyrus's sword arm at the wrist. Zephyrus wheeled around, teeth clenched. He strangled the hilt of his sword in a death grip.

"I'm sorry," Laeden said, letting go of him, palms raised. "I lied to you. My father feared you. He bent the rules of the treaty to try and appease AVR, but it wasn't enough to stem the tides of vengeance. I see that now. Zephyrus, you were right. About everything."

"It's too late," Zephyrus snarled. "You'll get what you deserve." He strode to the opposite end of the rotunda where their trial by steel would be held.

Laeden failed me. Two guards forced a plain gladius and shield into Laeden's hands, as if there were any defense against Zephyrus's wrath.

The high priest prayed for the Gods to guide the omenation. Laeden's eyes never left his feet. He could sulk all he wanted, but it was too late for him to see the error of his ways now. He used Zephyrus as a tool for his own benefit. Lied about the one thing that could have made the difference for him.

How many others has he used? How many others died believing his lies?

His death would be the first of many in the breaking of this society. Not all needed to fall. Vykinallia had shown him that. But she was the exception. Laeden was the rule.

"We will have our vengeance."

"May the Six condemn those whose testimony is false and leave only the truth left standing," the Valencian priest said.

Zephyrus never enjoyed killing, at least as far as he could remember. He wasn't proud of the slaves who fell beneath his sword, but they were necessary to maintain his clever lies—a sacrifice for the peace he would bring when New Rheynia fell. He would never cease mourning those he couldn't save, but he wouldn't mourn for Laeden.

Laeden would die beneath his blade. Not for the crown's truth, but for the lives of every slave who fell as a tool wielded by their masters. Their deaths would be redeemed in Laeden's death, and that he would enjoy.

"Begin!"

At the priest's signal, Zephyrus charged into striking distance.

Laeden lowered his sword and knelt. "I will not fight you."

Zephyrus reared back his sword and slashed downward.

Laeden

Laeden raised his shield to block Zephyrus's downward strike. The shield buckled beneath the force of the blow, and he fell to his back to the cheers of the onlookers. Zephyrus pressed his advantage. Laeden struggled to regain his footing amidst Zephyrus's onslaught. He could barely withstand the speed and strength of his blows.

Hack, slash, stab!

Zephyrus shoved Laeden with his shield, sending him sprawling to the stones of the rotunda yet again. The jeering crowd cast curses, each reminding him of his many failures.

"Laeden, this is above you," his father said when Laeden convinced him to name him captain of the Sentinels.

Father was right.

The truth pierced deeper than any sword. He was in too deep. He always had been. Ever since he was ripped from his mother's arms and sent to Salmantica with his father, Laeden had lived a lie. He tried to prove himself worthy of attention, affection, and love. Yet he never could admit it when he wasn't enough.

His father had said, *"There is strength in knowing when to ask for help."* But he could never hear it. He became a pawn to his pride.

Wars were never meant to be fought alone.

"I've failed," Laeden said to Zephyrus, standing a few paces away. "I failed you, I failed my father, I failed the only love I've ever known."

Zephyrus ignored Laeden, closing the gap between them with a new storm of attacks.

Sweat dampened his brow, and his deconditioned arms ached from the effort of meeting Zephyrus's steel. His only hope was to survive long enough for his words to break through Zephyrus's armor.

After barely deflecting away another barrage of strikes, Laeden seized advantage of the reprieve. "This all started because the Revivalists were angry that the king exiled a mage instead of executing him. Of those options, both were wrong."

Zephyrus came at him again. He slashed across Laeden's shield, then backhandedly struck with his own shield, tossing Laeden's from his grasp and spilling him to the ground. Zephyrus circled him, not speaking a word, just doing his duty.

He just wants freedom for his people. Now he's a cog in the machine I placed him in.

Laeden stood, keeping his blade down but his other hand up. "You were right, Zephyrus. All along you were right. Men are not tools to be bought and used."

Zephyrus stopped circling.

Laeden continued, this time speaking for all to hear. "I should have fought alongside you to free all the slaves." Laeden turned his back to Zephyrus to face the crowd. "We let fear of the Gods' wrath drive us. We killed in the name of the Gods and called it honor, but we are cowards! We force our faith upon others under threat of exile or punishment. We torture and execute mages, and for what? To appease the Gods?"

Laeden shook his head. "My father, King Varros, chose life. He chose peace, but only in a half-measure. We continually choose war, torture, and death—claiming it in honor of the Gods.

"I am guilty," Laeden said, "of many crimes. But so are you." He stabbed his sword at the dais. "And so are you!" He pivoted, addressing the crowd.

Laeden turned back to Zephyrus and spoke for all to hear. "I deserve to die for being a pawn in the games of kings and queens. I deserve to die for my mistakes." Laeden dropped his blade and knelt before Zephyrus.

"But I pray you all open your eyes and see that we have lost the path to Valencia if we must kill the innocent to walk upon it."

The crowd went silent. Maybe Laeden's words reached their hearts, but Zephyrus stalked closer, like a lion to its prey. If he heard Laeden's words, they had no impact.

The cold steel of Zephyrus's blade touched the side of his throat as he circled behind Laeden, awaiting the king's orders. Damascus's mouth formed a thin line. Danella's golden eyes seemed to glow with eager anticipation.

Laeden closed his eyes and thought of Iylea. *"I love you,"* he whispered to the wind, hoping she could hear him in Valencia. *"I will see you soon."*

Zephyrus

With his blade at Laeden's throat, Zephyrus looked to the dais. Dominus nodded with smug satisfaction from beside the priests. He wouldn't care if Zephyrus spilled Laeden's blood. If Vykinallia were here, she would have protested this. She was nothing like her father.

She was a slave owner, but she saw the light. Before she was taken, she swore to him that once she was queen, she'd seek to end slavery. Zephyrus convinced her of a better way, and she would've changed the world because of it. If he had killed her, as Paxoran wanted, that potential future never would've been possible.

Tied within his garments, her amethyst ring pressed against his skin. *"For luck,"* she said, but it brought him nothing but misfortune.

Zephyrus grabbed Laeden by the hair to expose his throat for the blade.

The bloodthirsty crowd's shouts echoed as they had in the arena. "Kill! Kill! Kill!"

Zephyrus looked down at Laeden, the same way he did Octus. Down on his knees, eyes closed, and palms up—his lips moving in prayer.

"You'll receive the justice you swore to uphold," Zephyrus said.

The Celestic people deserved vengeance for what the Rheynians did to them. Laeden deserved death. But if Vykinallia could change to help his cause, so could Laeden. Zephyrus failed to create an army of gladiators. He wouldn't topple the kingdom with a legion of dead men. But with a handful of changed people...

"You will die, Laeden." Zephyrus adjusted the blade at Laeden's neck. "But not today… not by my hand." He lowered his sword.

Laeden

"What are you doing?" Aemos shouted at Zephyrus. "Kill him!"

Laeden couldn't believe his eyes. Zephyrus stalked around him, coming to a stop between him and his accusers. The jeering crowd fell silent. Cassius commanded Zephyrus to comply, but he remained a statue.

Laeden grabbed his own sword and stood beside Zephyrus.

"Kill them both!" Damascus shouted.

The King's Guard Knights stepped into position, but Markus came to Laeden's side with exposed steel.

"Markus!" Cassius stepped down from his dais. "This is not your fight, son."

Markus ignored his father, glancing at Laeden. "I will not stand idly by while everything I love is taken from me."

A swell of unfamiliar emotions washed over him. He didn't deserve to be spared by Zephyrus. Zephyrus didn't *need to* sacrifice himself for Laeden. Markus didn't *need to* stand beside him. These two men—these good men—would die, choosing to defend Laeden.

Laeden had never before felt so humbled.

Aemos, Daenus, and Aelon unsheathed their swords before Markus, Zephyrus and Laeden. Other Salmantic soldiers surrounded them, pikes aimed. They were outnumbered and poorly equipped, but where Laeden had no fight in his heart against Zephyrus, he had a well of resolve to fight against these traitors. He knew who his enemy was now. They declared themselves to him, and it was time justice was served.

Laeden let out a battle cry and charged at Aelon.

He slashed high to low, then followed across. Aelon met his blade with his own steel as Zephyrus and Markus clashed with Daenus and Aemos. Laeden lunged for the gaps between Aelon's plate mail; the armpits, elbows, behind the knees, and the neck were all vulnerable. He chopped at Aelon's lower leg, but Aelon parried and stepped inside Laeden's reach, shouldering him backwards.

"Give it up, Laeden!" Aelon said over the clang of battle. "You'll never beat me."

Laeden growled. He shoved his shield into Aelon's and chopped downward. Aelon sidestepped the blow, but Zephyrus redirected Daenus in the same direction. Aelon and Daenus collided. Laeden slashed at Aelon, but Haedron Allos and two other King's Guard Knights joined the fray, forcing Laeden to retreat.

"There are too many!" Markus parried Aemos's fury of attacks.

The pikemen encircling them drew closer, forcing them into tighter quarters. Laeden deflected Aelon's thrust and raised his shield just in time to block Haedron's blade.

We're losing ground.

"True Sentinels!" a voice called from the crowd. "Defend your captain!"

Laeden's grandfather, Hallon Helixus, vaulted over a divider that separated the crowd from the rotunda, drawing his long sword. Allaron, one of Laeden's Sentinel Squadron leaders, joined the battle, an axe in his hands. More men in their gray-and-blue Sentinel uniforms abandoned their post to the crown and surrounded the pikemen in black.

The spears aimed at Laeden, Zephyrus, and Markus redirected to the new threats. With the fight rebalanced, Laeden charged with new vigor, pushing Aelon back and hacking at Aemos's knee. Aemos squealed as Laeden's strike took purchase in the gap between the armor. Markus pushed Aemos over and stabbed one of the other guards through the throat. Laeden struck down at Aemos on the ground, but Aelon caught his sword mid-chop.

Engaged with Aelon, Laeden was in a poor position to defend as Haedron approached his back side. Haedron reared his sword. Laeden attempted to dodge, but he saw Haedron too late.

The sword streaked towards Laeden's side, but somehow, an invisible force seemed to stop Haedron's stroke. Zephyrus stood behind Haedron, hand raised.

He did *something* to make Haedron pause.

Aelon surged at Laeden again with a fresh series of strikes. Aemos, hobbled by his wounded knee, continued fighting against Markus, while Zephyrus went blow for blow with Daenus and another one of the King's Guard Knights.

Hallon, Allaron, and the Sentinels who came to Laeden's aid fought the Vigiles and Drake guards. All around them, men fell and died. The coppery smell of blood accompanied the wails of the fallen, sending nearby onlookers fleeing for safety.

"Kill them!" Damascus shouted, directing his reinforcements toward their position. More Drake guards came.

"Ridge Knights!" Hallon Helixus shouted. "Defend Laeden!"

Men in Helixus blue and gold stormed the rotunda to meet the black-and-red Drake guards.

"King's Guard Knights, retreat!" Danella shouted. "Protect your king!"

Daenus stepped back after fending off a flurry of blows from Zephyrus. A Drake guard in black scale stepped in to defend him but fell as Zephyrus drove his sword up under his arm. The guard fell—dead before he hit the ground.

"Let's go!" Daenus ordered the others. Hesitantly, Aelon, Aemos, and Haedron followed.

Blood covered the ground all around them. Allies and enemies, they died the same—screaming in agony. *We must make a way out, or we'll join the dead.* There was no chance of winning this battle, only surviving long enough to fight the next.

"We must escape," Laeden said.

"This way." Grandfather Hallon waved them down an alley away from the rotunda.

"Markus!"

Laeden wheeled around to find Duke Cassius calling out for his son. Cassius staggered before collapsing to his stomach, a dagger protruding from his back.

"Father!" Markus rushed to his side.

"We've gotta g—" Zephyrus cut himself off, wheeling around.

A crossbow bolt zoomed past Zephyrus, but he continued staring into the fray, searching for something. He held up his shield as a bolt punctured through.

Laeden lifted his own shield while searching for cover, but a cry behind him stopped him in his tracks.

Hallon hit the ground—a crossbow bolt lodged in his stomach.

"Gods, no!"

Zephyrus

Lenox.

It was only for a moment, but Zephyrus was sure he saw him. *Where did he go?*

More arrows flew through the air as archers fired down from the priests' dais. Zephyrus growled. Laeden called for his grandfather's aid, but none of the troops would be able to protect them. As long as the archers controlled the high ground, they were doomed.

Lenox would have to wait. Zephyrus charged the dais. Bolts flew by, cutting the air beside him. He channeled his force magic, redirecting incoming arrows to sail past. His arms tingled, already weak from stopping the attack on Laeden.

The archers stepped back to reload as the second row of bowmen took aim. Zephyrus vaulted off one of the viewing benches and dove onto the dais, closing the ground too quickly for them to fire. The panicked bowmen struggled within the close confines.

Zephyrus slammed his shield into the crossbow of the first, throwing him from the dais. He lunged, stabbing the second archer through the belly. Standing, he pivoted, building momentum. With a swing of his gladius, he severed the next archer's head from his shoulders. The remaining bowmen scattered, but Zephyrus was not about to let them get away. He chased down the closest, slashing him across the back, then stabbed another through the ribs.

With the archers disbanded or dead, the Ridge Knights surrounded Laeden's grandfather and spirited him out of harm's way.

Markus rejoined the fight. Cassius lay on the ground in a pool of his own blood—dead. With nothing left to lose, Markus fought like a madman. Bodies fell around him like leaves in autumn. His black-and-yellow tunic, heavy with the weight of the blood of his enemies, might as well have been red. Yet there were still too many enemies.

The King's Guard Knights returned with reinforcements.

Laeden rushed to Markus's position. Within heartbeats, they were surrounded. One of the knights slashed from behind, cutting Markus across his back. Markus staggered into Laeden.

If Zephyrus didn't get to them, they would die. He jumped from the dais and ran towards them, but he felt a presence behind him.

He spun just in time to deflect Lenox's blade away.

Veins throbbed in Zephyrus's neck. A vindictive fury roared within him like a tempest.

Patrus's murderer.

Zephyrus unleashed a reckless onslaught on Lenox. Ignoring his fatigue, Zephyrus abandoned all patience. He hacked and slashed, shoved and stabbed. Lenox met each strike, turning them aside.

His arms were heavy, not yet recovered from the exertion of balancing the scales, but he pressed. Lenox had lived too long. He would not let him escape again.

Lenox jabbed, overextending. Zephyrus saw his opportunity and lunged. Lenox feinted, rearing back in time to block Zephyrus's overeager counter on his shield. Zephyrus pulled back to defend, but too slow.

Lenox's blade pierced Zephyrus's side.

Pain replaced fury. Fear consumed anger.

Zephyrus gasped, dropping to a knee, with Lenox's blade still embedded beneath his ribs.

Lenox twisted his sword. Bile climbed Zephyrus's throat.

Zephyrus roared, but Lenox punched him with the edge of his shield. Glowing orbs swirled in Zephyrus's vision. He fought for focus, but another strike slammed into the bridge of his nose. Pain lanced through his skull, and blood spilled down his face. He tried to stand but couldn't. Tried to lift his sword, but strength fled from him. His vision narrowed on Lenox's smug face as the villain who robbed Patrus of life stood over him.

The same man who killed Patrus would claim his life as well. He closed his eyes.

Patrus… Forgive me.

Within his mind's eye, Patrus fell again beneath Lenox's sword. Zephyrus was supposed to lead him to freedom, but he failed. Not just Patrus, but every Celestic. Blood pooled beneath Patrus's fallen body, his dead eyes staring at Zephyrus.

This is it. I've lost. Lenox, the Revivalists, this society—they've won.

Vellarix, Aikous, Ronar, Threyna… *I've failed them too.*

The dream of Zephyrus's mother returned to him. Her auburn hair swayed in the breeze. *"You can never forget who you are or where you come from,"* she had said. Zephyrus failed her as well. He never found out who he was, nor did he become anyone who could make a difference.

His mother seemed so real before him now, as if he could reach out and touch her. Her cheeks rounded into a gentle smile. She reached out her hand.

Zephyrus took her hand in his. *"I will see you soon, Mother."*

"Soon," she said with a smile. *"But not yet."* She brushed back his hair, tears welling in her eyes.

He shook his head, dropping his eyes in defeat. *"It's over."*

"It's not over," she said. *"You've been afraid to discover who you were, who you are. You've closed me out, but it's time you learned the truth."* She lifted his chin with her index finger until their eyes met.

"The truth?"

His mother shook her head. *"Zephyrus is not the name I gave you. You are Vykanicus Auros. Son of Invinius, the first to free the slaves."*

Zephyrus recalled the *A* branded into Patrus's forearm. *"He freed his slaves,"* one of the slaves from Tharseo's Bastion observed after they were first abducted.

His mother cupped his cheek with her hand. *"You were born to do this, my son. The world can only be freed through you."*

Zephyrus tried to make sense of it all, but his mind swam amidst the flood of memories.

"I'm the only one who can stop the Rheynians?" he channeled.

She smiled, but her eyes were forlorn. *"Not the Rheynians… the Gods. Return home. Claim the sword your father forged for you. Become the man you were born to be, the one you have been all along."* She kissed his forehead. *"For luck."*

She winked and disappeared in a flash.

Lenox stood before him, his blade still embedded in Zephyrus's side.

"Now you die, Zephyrus," Lenox spat.

Zephyrus bared his teeth. "That's not my name."

His arms went numb as he balanced the scales, building a surge of force. The same magic he'd used to save Fenyx from Tursos and Laeden from the King's Guard Knight rattled within him until he couldn't contain it any longer.

With a roar, he released a concussive blast into Lenox's chest. The force hurled Lenox through the air, toppling him onto his back. Still kneeling,

Zephyrus pried the sword from his gut and climbed to his feet. He aimed Lenox's sword at him.

"Mage!" Lenox shouted, but no one was listening amidst the chaos. Unarmed, Lenox turned and ran for the alleyway. Zephyrus began to give chase, but Laeden yelped behind him.

Laeden and Markus were surrounded. Zephyrus could run down Lenox and finish him once and for all, but vengeance left him.

This was never about killing Lenox. This was never about vengeance.

Lenox wasn't his future. Zephyrus lost Threyna before their friendship could have become something. He lost Patrus before he remembered him. Even Vykinallia was lost to him, now. Zephyrus wouldn't let Laeden join them.

Surrounded by a relentless sea of soldiers in red and black, Laeden in his soiled tunic and Markus in his gold surcoat fought back the tide.

Time to balance the scales.

Zephyrus charged the men surrounding Laeden and Markus.

The guards turned to face Zephyrus, but too late. He barreled into them with all his might, staggering a few. One of the soldiers struck at Markus, but Zephyrus used his force magic to stop him mid-swing. His arm went numb from the exertion, but Laeden seized the opportunity and stabbed Markus's attacker in the chest. Zephyrus used more force magic to lower one of the other soldiers' shields and stabbed over the top of it, slicing where the neck met the shoulder.

The soldier fell to the ground, crying the guttural groans of death.

Laeden and Markus fought for their lives as Zephyrus cut his way to their aid, but pain lanced up his arm as steel bit into his skin. It was only superficial, but blood blossomed to trickle down his left arm. Zephyrus recoiled, swinging violently at his attacker. His blade sank deeply into the soldier's ribs. He yanked his blade free as a group peeled away from Laeden and Markus to engage him. Against the wall of shields, Zephyrus sliced and hacked, but was unable to pierce their defenses.

One of the soldiers overextended himself. Zephyrus dodged the blade and hacked down, separating him from his hand. Zephyrus spun around him and drove his blade up the armpit of the handless soldier. He went limp and fell. Zephyrus tried to yank his sword free, but the dead weight of the soldier, combined with his magic-fatigue, wrestled the blade from his grasp.

Zephyrus grabbed the fallen soldier's shield just in time to block an assault from the others. He hid behind the large shield, but one strike glanced off the top of his hip bone. Pain flooded through him as he stumbled backwards.

I need a sword.

A man fell at the edge of Laeden's blade, then another to Markus's, but they were still outnumbered.

"Give up, Laeden!" one of the King's Guard Knights said.

"You're a traitor, Aelon. I'll never surrender to you." Laeden continued to duel, but Aelon was better. Laeden took a slice across the arm, and another along the ribs.

"Surrender now and you'll get a painless death," another knight said to Markus.

"Never, Aemos!" Markus fought, but his fervor weakened as exhaustion took hold.

The largest of the King's Guard Knights advanced on Zephyrus. "All you had to do was kill him and all of these lives would have been spared."

So much death. Death followed him wherever he went. Fatigue weighed on him, his arms heavy, his wounds aching and bleeding. The knight swung at Zephyrus. He tried to defend himself with the fallen soldier's shield, but it wasn't enough.

We're all going to die, Zephyrus realized.

The knight's vicious swing struck the shield from his weak fingers. The knight kicked him to the ground and another one advanced.

"Grab him, Haedron," the large knight said. Zephyrus tried to get to his feet, but he was broken, beaten, and hopeless.

Haedron stalked behind Zephyrus and yanked his hair back. Markus was in a similar posture before Aemos. Laeden was still on his feet, bleeding from a dozen different wounds.

Cold steel pressed against the side of Zephyrus's neck.

This is the end.

The steel grew warm against his flesh.

Incredibly warm, even hot.

Zephyrus must die, so Vykanicus can be reborn.

He raised his hands to the knight before him. A stream of fire erupted from Zephyrus's hands, engulfing the knight.

Haedron released Zephyrus. Zephyrus whipped around, and with a sudden return of warmth to his body, he sent a torrent of water bursting into Haedron's breastplate, sending him flying onto his back.

"He's a mage!" Aemos shouted, but in his distraction, Markus lunged forward and slashed Aemos across the face.

The knight on fire screamed and ran for the moat. Aemos fell to the ground. Laeden still eyed Aelon, but Aelon backed away.

The drawbridge lowered, and more soldiers clad in black and red rushed their way.

Zephyrus was so tired. He couldn't fight any longer.

"Grab him," Laeden said to Markus. "We're leaving."

"He's a mage," Markus said.

"And?" Laeden snapped. "Grab him!"

Zephyrus's eyelids drooped. Markus and Laeden each seized Zephyrus under his arms and dragged him away, a trail of blood following in their wake. Zephyrus's body went limp as he fell into the sweet embrace of unconsciousness.

CHAPTER 67

GOODBYE

Danella X
Salmantica

Danella sat alone by the hearth, a small table with two stools for Reign beside her. Danella never cared for the game; one could make all the proper strategic moves but get shorted with the roll of the dice. She didn't appreciate a game that weighed chance over strategy.

All she did, she did for Damascus, the Gods, and the safety of New Rheynia. She thought if she could turn a Prophet of Celestia into a weapon of her own, no one could stand against her.

How was I to know Zephyrus was a mage? How was I to know he wouldn't kill Laeden?

Laeden escaped with Markus and Zephyrus. Hallon's defiance meant war with Valtarcia. Zephyrus's open use of elemental magic would inspire others within the Uprising, and Laeden's open declaration for freedom and equality would summon the sympathizers to their cause.

How did everything get so out of hand?

Even now, Daenus clung to life in the medicus's chambers suffering from the burns of Zephyrus's magic fire, alongside Aemos, whose face was nearly cleaved in two from Markus's blade. Her tiles were perfectly positioned, but the dice ruined everything.

She walked from the hearth into the bedroom. The bed was modest, unlike many of the others in the castle tower. It possessed no veiled canopy, no exuberant carvings, a common headboard, and no footboard whatsoever—quite fitting for Laeden.

A blue banner with the gold winged horse of House Helixus hung from the right side of his bed. The words *Honor and Justice* were stitched into the banner below the sigil. To the left hung the white-and-blue falcon of House Faire. The words, *Defend the Weak*, were written below. Laeden had done just that. He defended Iylea to her death.

I had no choice but to discredit him. I never would have let them sentence him to death, but he chose a trial by steel.

Laeden was always a petulant child. She couldn't blame him. His father was forced to divorce his mother to marry the daughter of the King of New Rheynia, to make an everlasting peace between Salmantica and Valtarcia. Damascus's reign was meant to be that peace, but now Laeden ruined that.

The irony… and where is Varros now?

She forged the mages' letter to convince Damascus that the time to strike was now. Varros was likely still alive. Her Revivalists had scoured the farmlands of Salmantica to the mountains of Valtarcia, but none found him.

If he's dead, at least he never has to learn what I did to him and his son.

"I had no other choice," Danella whispered. She walked from the bedroom to the balcony. The sun had long since set, but the rains remained absent. A fortnight without rain. The Gods were delivering their disasters even now. War was coming. The drought would slowly starve them if war didn't claim them first. The circumstances would bring out the lowest form of humanity.

She returned to her seat by the hearth and went to drink from her goblet, but it was empty. The carafe she reached for, to pour herself more, was empty too. She cast it into the hearth, shattering the glass and creating a swell of fire.

She took a deep breath. She thought she'd succeeded. Her pride blossomed to think of her father's approval, but it all came crashing down.

A knock came, and the chamber doors creaked open.

"Your grace," Brusos said. "May I join you?"

Danella wanted to be alone, but she waved him in.

Brusos held something in his hands as he entered, closing the door behind him. Danella took a seat before the hearth, gesturing for Brusos to join her. He sat across from her, resting the cloth-wrapped package on his lap.

"How fares our young king?" he asked.

Danella stared at the fire. "His brother's treachery and the disappearance of his betrothed are heavy burdens to bear."

"I imagine the death of his chancellor to be of some consequential load as well."

Danella met his gaze, swallowing to contain her shock. "Cassius is dead?"

"Stabbed in the back during the fray after the trial. I offered Lenox the opportunity to redeem himself, and he has done so splendidly. We can tell the people Laeden and Markus rigged the omenation to make Cassius the chancellor."

Danella was impressed. She didn't want to let him know how impressed. She wouldn't hold back all praise, but she wouldn't give him time to gloat either. "You've done well. So, Duke Chancellor, have you any news on the whereabouts of Markus, Laeden, or Zephyrus?"

"Apologies, your grace, the scouts haven't found them yet. I assure you, they will be caught." Brusos sat up in his chair. "Yet I didn't come to tell of Cassius's demise and my ascent. I come bearing gifts." He handed her the wrapped package.

It was heavier than expected. She unwrapped it to find the tattered cape of Varros Helixus inside. Danella looked to Brusos, tears welling in her eyes.

Divided down the middle, Varros wore the sigils of his father and his wife. On one side the white winged horse of the Helixuses soared across a blue backdrop. On the other, the Drake Chimera roared, blue atop white. Dirt marred the white half, but upon closer examination, it wasn't dirt, but dried blood. She sniffled, holding back her tears, pulling the cloak towards her. As she moved, something heavy fell out of it. Varros's crown dropped from the death-stained cloak to land on her lap. Danella gasped, as air ceased to exist.

My husband…

"His remains were recovered," Brusos said.

Nausea bubbled in her stomach, and a knot rose to her throat. "Remains?"

"One of Liario's men found him in the Salmantic countryside. His cloak and crown hung from a spear lodged into his burning body."

Danella hung her head. It was something she set out to do nearly a year ago. She plotted and schemed to make this happen, to put Damascus on the throne, to appease the Gods. At one point, she thought the Gods would allow her to keep him, but the mages took him. The man she loved. The man she still loved.

He's truly gone.

Danella swallowed her grief. "As the new chancellor, you may take Cassius's ludus as your own."

"Gratitude, your grace." Brusos bowed. "Is there anything else I can do for you?"

She hoped this would be the end of her duties. Her plan succeeded. Damascus was upon the throne, no one was whispering words of blasphemy in his ears, and the Celestics were being put down. But this was only the beginning. So much needed to be done, but she wanted—no, needed—to grieve.

"Bring me word once your bodyslave delivers Nallia to the Uprising," Danella said. "Until then, unless you apprehend Laeden, Markus, or Zephyrus, leave me be."

Brusos bowed before taking his leave. The moment he closed the door, the weight of loneliness settled on Danella's shoulders like never before.

She clung to Varros's cape, wishing he were here to console her. Slowly, she began to crack. Like a bird hatching from its shell, her dam of emotions broke through her mask, fracturing her entire being. The tears seeped through the cracks until the pressure was too much. She shattered into a million brokenhearted sobs, clutching the bloodied cape as if it were the only thing left for her in the world. She wept as if her own tears supplied the nightly rains. She cried until she was breathless, then cried more.

What was it all for? She sacrificed everything for the Gods. Still, she sat in failure. Her husband was gone, yet her father's kingdom was in no less jeopardy than it was the day before. Still so many enemies, so many threats. No peace.

Her husband would still be alive if her father had eradicated the Celestics to begin with. In his old age, he had forced them to sue for peace. He should have wiped them from this world. If he had, his kingdom wouldn't be on the verge of war with Valtarcia, mages, and escaped slaves. No treaty would ensure peace. Only the death of her enemies would allow peace to reign.

There was no more time to cry. She set Varros's crown down on the couch beside her and walked to the fire.

She looked down at her husband's cape one last time. "Goodbye, my love."

The cape fell from her hands into the hearth, and the life she knew before burned to ash.

CHAPTER 68

The Greater Good

Threyna V

Stockhelm

Threyna knelt down beside Sybex's desiccated remains. Her prominent cheekbones, so beautiful in life, were equally unnerving in death. The quiet flow of the cenote and the steady drip from the stalactites were the only disturbances against the Guardians' silent stares. Four bodies littered the slick stones. Two more floated face down in the bloody water.

Threyna examined the black rot along her arm as it abated to the scars left behind by the bangle. The exposed blood she'd gained access to after her shattered glass conjuration carved into the Guardians had sourced most of what she needed to finish them. In the end, there were no defiant last words. No begging. No valiant efforts.

Only death.

Brutal, cold, silent, still, lonely—death.

"The second Treasure waits," Paxoran said.

The flickering torchlight from the sconces, bordering the tunnel into where Threyna assumed the second Treasure waited, danced across the cavern ceiling. Threyna picked up the last of her Viridite glowstones from under Sybex's arm and returned it to her pouch. Sybex's empty eye sockets stared blankly up to the cavern ceiling.

She hadn't wanted to kill the Templars. She hadn't wanted to condemn Zephyrus and Patrus to slavery. All she had wanted was a purpose after the horrors she'd experienced escaping Rheynia. She thought she found that with Tyrus in the City of the Judges, aiding in their pursuit to reclaim their homeland from a foreign tyrant. Her skills, her abilities, even her cursed magic, all served a purpose for bringing good to the world. But the evil she thought she'd vanquished still lived.

She asked the Arcane Templar for help. They could have aided her in defeating the Skeleton King, but they chose their beliefs and traditions over joining her. They chose this death instead of the Skeleton King's.

Now, instead of serving the greater good, she was enslaved to the lesser evil.

I must kill the Skeleton King. Nothing else matters.

Threyna followed the tunnel to its end, where a chest rested in a room much like that in the catacombs beneath the Gilded Gauntlet. She approached the chest. Absent the ornamental stylings of New Rheynia's patricians, the plain chest held power she'd never felt before, even holding the Vykane Blade.

One step closer to her goal, Threyna swallowed and threw the lid of the chest open.

Inside, the Orsion Cloak glowed with power. White with silver trim intricately woven in a floral pattern, the cloak appeared like moonlight given form.

Recalling the first time she'd seen the moon after she and Laela escaped the curse of Rheynia, her thoughts drifted to her parents and the sacrifices they made to keep her and her sister alive. Now her parents were gone, and Laela was...

It didn't matter.

She was the only one left, and only she could make sure the Skeleton King took no more souls to the One True God.

She took the Orsion Cloak in her hands.

"Yes," Paxoran said, wrenching her from her thoughts. *"You have found the second Treasure. Only the Aeryean Armor remains. Then you will bring about the end of the Skeleton King's reign, and we will reforge the world anew."*

Remnants of the black rot tinged her fingertips holding the Judge's artifact.

How can something so corrupt hold something so perfect?

Ignoring her doubts, Threyna cast her own wet cloak aside and placed the Orsion Cloak over her shoulders. The dank cavern tunnel felt warmer and brighter despite the bleakness in her heart. She thought after claiming two of the Treasures, she would feel different.

"You shall find that which you seek, but you possess all you need," the Seers of Celestia had said. But they were wrong. She needed the Treasures.

The elders of the Arcane Templar were wrong too.

Only I can defeat the Skeleton King. And once he is dead and gone, then everything I am, everything I've done—it will all have been worth it.

"One more Treasure," Threyna said.

EPILOGUE

THE FIRST BROTHER

Varros

Stockhelm

Varros stared out the window of Sinion's tower. He squeezed the sill, wishing that if he possessed the strength, he could crush the stone between his fingers. He couldn't. Just like he couldn't stop this war between the Arcane Templar and the Revivalists.

"Is it true?" Varros asked Sinion.

Sinion shuffled his feet behind him. "I'm afraid so, old friend."

A tear trickled from the corner of Varros's eye to roll into the scruff of his bearded cheek. He sniffed, wiping the tear with the back of his hand. "If I wasn't your prisoner, I could have stopped this."

Sinion approached, placing his hand on Varros's shoulder. "You're not a prisoner. And we both know you *tried* to stop this. I'm afraid it has always been fated to come to this. Nothing you could have done would have prevented this war."

Varros hung his head as the last of the sun faded from sight. Dusk crept in, and with it, all the light of the world seemed lost beyond the Hylan Mountains.

His father, Duke Hallon Helixus—dead.

His son Laeden, a fugitive.

Damascus, his heir—a tyrant.

And Danella, his love. His life. She had seen to all of it.

The cannon fire echoed in his head, transporting him back to that fated day on the *Winged Wind*. He, Sinion, and the rest of their crew celebrated a small victory, sinking a Salmantic galley. But their celebrations were cut short as two Salmantic warships swept through the fog on either side of them.

Like a walnut placed between the nutcracker's jaws, cannon fire crushed their ship. Splinters blew through the air, and fires burned as oil-soaked torches devoured the sails. It wasn't a battle, but a massacre. Those who weren't impaled by debris or burned by the flames drowned in the dark waters off the southeastern shores of Stockhelm.

Varros took a deep breath and squeezed the window frame with both hands to reorient himself back in Sinion's ludus. The cannon fire echoing through his mind faded, but the reality of his present situation seemed as doomed as when he had woken up on the shores of Klaytos with Sinion pumping the water from his lungs.

"Sometimes I wish I never would have survived," Varros said. "It would have been better—if you had let me drown, if we would have died of starvation or dehydration upon the Klaytonian sands."

Sinion hummed. "You had said you'd do anything to return to your wife and son. And you did. The Arcane Templar gave you that."

Varros's teeth ground together at the mention of his order.

They 'gave' me nothing but a double-life of looking over my shoulder and fearing my own web of lies.

He pounded his fist against the sandstone wall of Sinion's tower.

"I lost Lenara the moment I returned to New Rheynia," Varros said. "And Laeden never trusted me again. How could he after all the secrets I was forbidden to speak of?"

"Yet you lived," Sinion said. "Better had you died or not, the Judges were not done with you. They gave you a great purpose—the liberation of Stockhelm, the freedom of its people."

"Twenty years," Varros said, turning from the rainless night to face his old friend. "Everything has only gotten worse."

Sinion crossed his arms over his chest, swishing his silken robes in the process. He nodded toward the hearth in the opposite corner of the room and led the way. Before a feather-cushioned sofa patterned with the gray and blue of his house, Sinion plopped down. Varros sat beside him, sinking into the cushions as he sank into his misery.

"Worse, you say?" Sinion said. "For whom?"

Varros's gaze rose to the sigil of the wolf Sinion had adopted as his own above the hearth. It stared down at them, an apt representation of Sinion's role in the Arcane Templar. A lone wolf. A Helm amidst New Rheynia's patricians. A lanista who moonlighted as a liberator for the Arcane Templar. While the display of wealth in his villa and incompetence in his ludus made him the brunt of the patricians' jokes, it allowed him to recruit, train, and hide the Fallen's best fighters beneath New Rheynia's nose.

Being partial to such secrets was one of the many things that kept Varros up at night.

He was part of a rebellion he wanted to stop. He never expected to find love in Danella's arms, but he did. She treated Laeden as her own. They had their own son together, and he was happy again. But playing his two roles as the King of New Rheynia and the First Brother of the Templar put him at constant odds. Their oppositional goals inevitably forced him to choose between his family or his duty. Nothing was enough for the Templar, yet his leniency toward the Celestics in the eyes of the Valencian devout led to the formation of the Revivalists. Love and duty, forever at odds.

"I suppose it's only worse for me," Varros said with a sigh. "I must go speak with Danella and Damascus. If they know I'm alive—"

Sinion sat up, cheeks blubbering. "You told me she attempted to have you assassinated. Why do you still protect her?"

Varros bit his lip. "She doesn't know the full truth."

"She knew you were aiding us," Sinion said. "You believe that if she knew the truth—the whole truth—that she would listen? An assassin—she sent an assassin when she believed you were a sympathizer. What do you think she would do if she knew the truth?"

Varros shook his head. "You don't underst—"

Sinion stood faster than Varros had ever seen him move. "You'd be nailed to a Six Arrowed Star, Varros." His nostrils flared with each heaving breath.

He sat back down, smoothing out his silks. In a much calmer voice, Sinion said, "It is time you chose a side, my friend. This peace you fight for will be won with no half measures."

Varros grunted. "They wanted me to frame innocent people, Sinion. Frame patricians for ties to the 'Uprising' and execute them, until there was no one left to stand against the Templar. What honor is there in—"

"That is your problem." Sinion glared at Varros. "You believe them *innocent*. No one is innocent while people are enslaved."

"You know what I mean," Varros said.

"I'm not sure I do," Sinion snapped. "If you did, you would have done as the Templar ordered. You would have released Zephyrus as you were told. But you were more interested in abiding by the queen's fears than the Judges' prophecies."

Varros blew out his cheeks and ran his fingers through his hair. In truth, he'd hoped Zephyrus, absent his memories and the Templar's brainwashing, would be just another man in the arena. That had backfired.

Sinion scooted closer to Varros on the cushions. "You have been on the inside for far too long. You have lost your way, but I will help you find it again. The Templar won't do anything rash while I vouch for you."

"Tell that to Ceres and Sybex," Varros said. "I freed them from the dungeons, burned Count Elrod Horne alive after seeing me, and still they nearly killed me on half a dozen instances in the time between abducting me and delivering me to you."

Sinion grinned. "Your fight for 'peace' is viewed by many as a betrayal. It is time you fight for the vengeance you vowed to claim for the people of Stockhelm."

Varros shivered.

Vengeance is the worst thing to fight for. Fight for your home, your land, your people, your rights—but not for vengeance.

When the chill didn't abate, Varros balanced the scales. He drew heat into his chest to prepare for the drop in his core temperature. With a flick of his wrist, he ignited the empty hearth in flames, and the scales tipped back to balance.

Sinion smiled. "You may have failed to free the Wielder, resisted being a saboteur, but you are still a weapon of war. Fight for us. We will win this war. And then you shall have the peace you desire."

Varros chewed the inside of his lip, knowing there had to be a better way.

A knock at the door broke them from their conversation.

Sinion beckoned the messenger inside. A Rheynian boy, probably no more than twelve years old, entered in ragged clothes. He wiped his dirty sleeve across his soot-stained forehead.

"What news?" Sinion asked.

The boy bowed. "Ceres has located the Wielder. He will free him, and, together, they will find the Warlock and reclaim the Treasures."

"Very well," Sinion said. "And then we will have our vengeance."

"We will have our vengeance," the boy said.

Sinion and the messenger both turned to Varros expectantly.

Pick a side…

There was a fire in Sinion's eyes. Not a raging wrathful one that would consume all and burn out, but a slow, steady, patient smoldering that would outlast and persist. Unyielding, unrelenting, undying. The Arcane Templar would never rest, never give up on its quest for vengeance. But Varros would find another way, a better way, than blood for blood. Outside the extremes, there was a middle ground that wasn't being considered. He would bridge the gap between the two sides and forge a path to peace. He only hoped he wasn't the last one in the world who had yet to declare for one side or the other.

"That is still what you want, Varros?" Sinion asked. "Isn't it?"

"Yes," Varros said, hiding his true feelings. With love and duty forever at odds, Varros cleared his throat. "We will have our vengeance."

THE END

ACKNOWLEDGEMENTS

After my band broke up, I wanted a creative project that I could do all by myself. I thought that project would be writing. Boy, was I wrong. This trilogy, this story, and this journey never would have come to be what it is without the help of many along the way. A special thank you to my mom, my very first reader and always my biggest fan. To Chersti Nieveen and the team at Writer Therapy who taught me everything I know about story, thank you for your patience, encouragement, and guidance; *A Vengeful Realm* would not have existed in any readable capacity without you! To my fellow writers of the Creators' Conclave, thank you for being my support system, my sounding board, and my think-tank. To my critique partner and friend, L.D. Hudson, thank you for being my most avid cheerleader, my word-count pacer, and my writerly companion; you're the Sam to my Frodo, and I never would have made it to Mordor without you. To the team at Paper Raven Books who shared my creation with the world, Landon Soelberg who brought my characters to life in the audiobook, and Taylor Ash who turned the Rebels' Rhyme into a masterpiece—from the bottom of my heart, thank you! And of course, it takes a tremendous amount of time and energy to create a universe, write a book (let alone a trilogy), and put it out into the world. But it takes a greater degree of patience and love to be the spouse of a writer. Thank you to my wife, Colleen, for believing in me even when I didn't believe in myself.

About the Author

When Tim isn't writing epic fantasy, he can often be found in his garage-gym or in the mountains where he lives. A virtual fitness professional by trade, he integrates his creative passions into movement, training with maces, clubs, staves, and swords to unlock his inner gladiator. To inquire about Gladiator Training, reach out to him at TimFacciolaFit@gmail.com.

More than writing, reading, gaming, playing music, hiking, and paddle-boarding, Tim loves story. If he's not working on his own story, he's helping others develop theirs as an author coach. To inquire about Author Coaching services, visit firsttorchbooks.mykajabi.com.

Living in Arizona with his wife, Colleen, Tim continues writing epic fantasy novels while exploring different storytelling mediums so he can inspire others to hope. To live. And to believe.

Made in the USA
Columbia, SC
11 July 2023